AND PRAISE FOR...

HOTTEST BLOOD

"Editors Jeff Gelb and Michael Garrett haven't run out of hemoglobins or hormones yet.... Check out *Hottest Blood*."
—*Fangoria*

"Every bit *Hot Blood*'s equal... the stories are stronger, more daring... I'd hate to see this series end.... Recommended."
—*Afraid*

"It's a doozy... steamy... If you're looking for something sexy and horrific, an anthology that really goes down to the nitty gritty, get a copy of *Hottest Blood*."
—*The Iguana Informer*

COMING IN 1995...
HOT BLOOD 4

Books Edited by Jeff Gelb

Hot Blood (with Lonn Friend)
Hotter Blood (with Michael Garrett)
Hottest Blood (with Michael Garrett)
Shock Rock
Shock Rock II

Published by POCKET BOOKS

Novels by Jeff Gelb

Specters

Most Pocket Books are available at special quantity discounts for bulk purchases for sales promotions, premiums or fund raising. Special books or book excerpts can also be created to fit specific needs.

For details write the office of the Vice President of Special Markets, Pocket Books, 1230 Avenue of the Americas, New York, New York 10020.

PRAISE FOR
SHOCK ROCK

"Not for the fainthearted . . . a spine-tingling anthology."
—*Playboy*

"A rockin' good read . . ." —*USA Weekend*

"Enough werewolves, vampires, and really sick stuff to keep rock-horror aficionados as happy as the proud owner of a demonically possessed '59 Les Paul." —*Radio & Records*

"One of the best anthologies . . . in a long, long time. Will have you on your feet, raised lighter in hand, screaming for more!" —*Footsteps*

"*Shock Rock* . . . is the bargain of the century. You've got to have this book."
—*Rocky Mountain News*

"Gelb has put together a good collection. . . ."
—*Fangoria*

"Gelb breaks new ground with the variety of talent that turned out new and original pieces of fiction for this collection." —*World of Fandom*

"This book could provide the soundtrack for a mighty strange movie. But the movie would rock. The back beat's solid; the rhythms are steady."
—*Locus*

"There are a bunch of hot licks in this scary stack of stories. You can almost hear the screams."
—*Comic Buyers Guide*

PRAISE FOR . . .

HOT BLOOD

"The best theme anthology since David Schow's *Silver Scream* . . . Rush out and buy *Hot Blood*—but don't say we didn't warn you that you'll be up all night reading it." —*Fangoria*

HOTTER BLOOD

"This collection will be hard to beat."
—*Mystery Scene*

"Acutely readable . . . punctuated with moments of genuine stimulation." —*Locus*

"The best of the best." —*2 A.M.* magazine

"Really smokes . . . every piece of fiction in this anthology is superb." —*Rave Reviews*

"Hotter Blood is an outstanding collection . . . a daring combination of sex and terror . . . mixed with deadly intent by the best writers the horror field has to offer! A must-read for any horror fan!"
—*Cemetery Dance* magazine

SHOCK ROCK II

Edited by Jeff Gelb

POCKET BOOKS
New York   London   Toronto   Sydney   Tokyo   Singapore

The sale of this book without its cover is unauthorized. If you purchased this book without a cover, you should be aware that it was reported to the publisher as "unsold and destroyed." Neither the author nor the publisher has received payment for the sale of this "stripped book."

This book is a work of fiction. Names, characters, places and incidents are either products of the authors' imaginations or are used fictitiously. Any resemblance to actual events or locales or persons, living or dead, is entirely coincidental.

An *Original* Publication of POCKET BOOKS

POCKET BOOKS, a division of Simon & Schuster Inc.
1230 Avenue of the Americas, New York, NY 10020

Copyright © 1994 by Jeff Gelb

All rights reserved, including the right to reproduce
this book or portions thereof in any form whatsoever.
For information address Pocket Books, 1230 Avenue
of the Americas, New York, NY 10020

ISBN: 0-671-87088-2

First Pocket Books printing February 1994

10 9 8 7 6 5 4 3 2 1

POCKET and colophon are registered trademarks of
Simon & Schuster Inc.

Cover art by Gerber Studio

Printed in the U.S.A.

COPYRIGHT NOTICES

Foreword copyright © 1994 by Lonn Friend

Introduction copyright © 1994 by Jeff Gelb

"Favorite Song" copyright © 1994 by Mark Verheiden

"The Last Time" copyright © 1994 by Michael Garrett

"The Sad Story of Billy Psych-Out and the Psyched-Out Encyclopedia of Rock 'n' Roll" copyright © 1994 by Tia Travis

"Elvis Can't Dance" copyright © 1994 by Robert Weinberg and Tina L. Jens

"Better to Burn Out" copyright © 1994 by Scott H. Urban

"Scream String" copyright © 1994 by Edo van Belkom

"Severin Hedz" copyright © 1994 by Th. Metzger

"Mr. Pants" copyright © 1994 by Gary Brandner

"Dead Legends" copyright © 1994 by Rick Hautala

"Rockin' On Home" copyright © 1994 by Nat Gertler

"The Undeadliest Game" copyright © 1994 by Bill Mumy and Peter David

"The Red Sax" copyright © 1994 by Graham Watkins

"He's Hot, He's Sexy, He's . . ." copyright © 1994 by A. R. Morlan

"Oi Boy" copyright © 1994 by Mike Baron

"Track Eight" copyright © 1994 by John F.D. Taff

"Graveyard Shift" copyright © 1994 by Jeff Gelb

Copyright Notices

"Inspiration" copyright © 1994 by Don D'Ammassa

"Shock Rock Jock" copyright © 1994 by Rex Miller

"The Songwriter" copyright © 1994 by Jesse Sublett

"Rock 'n' Roll Will Never Die" copyright © 1994 by Max Allan Collins

"Drumbeats" copyright © 1994 by Kevin J. Anderson and Neil Peart

To Lindsey Gelb. May his life be filled with rock's spirit of independence, excitement, enthusiasm, and creativity.

CONTENTS

Foreword   xiii
Lonn Friend

Introduction   xvii
Jeff Gelb

Favorite Song   1
Mark Verheiden

The Last Time   13
Michael Garrett

The Sad Story of Billy Psych-Out and the Psyched-Out Encyclopedia of Rock 'n' Roll   23
Tia Travis

Elvis Can't Dance   34
Robert Weinberg and Tina L. Jens

Better to Burn Out   50
Scott H. Urban

Scream String   62
Edo van Belkom

Severin Hedz   71
Th. Metzger

Mr. Pants   88
Gary Brandner

Contents

Dead Legends *Rick Hautala*	100
Rockin' On Home *Nat Gertler*	117
The Undeadliest Game *Bill Mumy and Peter David*	128
The Red Sax *Graham Watkins*	160
He's Hot, He's Sexy, He's . . . *A. R. Morlan*	176
Oi Boy *Mike Baron*	197
Track Eight *John F.D. Taff*	212
Graveyard Shift *Jeff Gelb*	227
Inspiration *Don D'Ammassa*	238
Shock Rock Jock *Rex Miller*	254
The Songwriter *Jesse Sublett*	268
Rock 'n' Roll Will Never Die *Max Allan Collins*	287
Drumbeats *Kevin J. Anderson and Neil Peart*	309
The Contributors	329

FOREWORD

Lonn Friend

When Jeff Gelb, my friend for a millennium, asked me to compose the introduction for this excitingly eerie anthology, I was honored. Jeff and I coedited *Hot Blood* nearly ten years ago, and though our careers have taken different paths, our mutual love of rock and horror has kept us joined at the oh-so-hip.

Being the editor of the world's heaviest metal mag has afforded me the company of many a true rocker over the years. I've gotten to know some of the best bangers in the biz, and lemme tell ya, a lot of 'em love the terror of the printed word and the silver screen. Scott Ian from Anthrax, for example, owns every first edition Stephen King has ever published. His king-size King Collection is literally worth a king's ransom! Metallica's Kirk Hammett has an equally priceless array of horror memorabilia, which includes a slew of original six-foot movie posters, latex masks (including an actual Freddy Krueger face), original paintings that were

Foreword

used for the covers of *Famous Monsters of Filmland*, the actual severed head of the doctor from *Re-Animator*, an array of original horror model kits, and props that would make any collector Frankenstein-green with envy.

But where the marriage of rock and horror is especially evident is when the music itself accompanies the deadly image. Can you remember what's happening on the screen in *Return of the Living Dead Part II* when Anthrax's "I'm the Man" is playing? Or when Megadeth's cover of the Alice Cooper classic "No More Mr. Nice Guy" is cranking out of the monitors, who's getting it in Wes Craven's *Shocker*? And has there ever been a more divine melding of carnage and kick-ass riffs than AC/DC's legendary soundtrack to Stephen King's *Maximum Overdrive*?

Concerts are another great place to get shocked musically. While the members of Kiss have taken off their makeup, they still put on a show full of pyrotechnic surprises. Alice Cooper remains a master of threatening theatrics onstage. And there are new bands emerging that have an obvious love of horror, like Gwar, which claims to be from another planet. Gwar's members all have alien names and wear monster makeup and prosthetics onstage. Their shows combine the frightful and the profane in equal doses (watch for that monster member, and wear a raincoat if you're seated in the first ten rows!).

Videos offer the latest arena for shock rock. A recent clip for Billy Idol's "Shock to the System" is reminiscent of *Terminator* territory, with Billy sprouting a robotic headpiece that videotapes unlawful cops in mugging action. He's into the cyberpunk, virtual reality thing. And the bizarre Nine Inch Nails videos, so intense that they can only be shown at clubs, are full of Cronenbergian organic horror imagery. Men being eviscerated, castrated . . . it's a metaphor for how people at certain levels of society are chewed up and spat out by the machine. These rock videos are trying to shock people into realizing how screwed up and frustrating life can be for the common man.

Attempting to hypothesize why rock and horror make

Foreword

such an excellent pairing, one need only analyze the elements that drive each institution. Rock is aggression, anger, blood, sweat, tears, heart, soul, and noise. And doesn't all good horror embody these characteristics? Each has its docile environment as well. Every great rock record has its calmer moments, its ballads, and these "breather" tracks usually fall between two kick-ass smokers. In horror fiction and film, we've all witnessed that suspenseful quiet time when the protagonist is swapping spit with his bodacious babe and suddenly a whining chain saw comes grinding through the living room wall. The elements of shock and surprise—set 'em up for the kill—provide for endless great moments!

Crunching skulls and crushing guitars, a Brian Johnson scream and a Linnea Quigley screech—the music is the murder and the murder is the music. Rock and horror belong together. "For those about to die—we salute you!"

INTRODUCTION

Jeff Gelb

Before you read further, go grab your favorite *loud* rock and roll music, on CD, cassette, or even, if you still remember it, LP.

Got it? Okay. Now, put your favorite song on your stereo system and prepare to crank the volume at least halfway to ear-bleed status.

Now you're ready for *Shock Rock II!* Your enthusiastic response to the first collection proved that the audiences for rock and roll music and horror fiction are intimately intertwined.

My challenge in recreating the excitement of the first book, and hopefully delivering new thrills as well, was in finding new story hooks, and new story contributors, to thrill me . . . and you. Neither proved to be a problem. Rock and roll is a deep ocean and we've just begun to dive below the surface!

I'm very pleased with the band of players I've gathered for your enjoyment in *Shock Rock II*. We have the established

Introduction

masters, including Gary Brandner, Don D'Ammassa, Rick Hautala, Th. Metzger, Rex Miller, and Graham Watkins. There's also a slew of rising stars in this volume, including Michael Garrett, A. R. Morlan, and Bob Weinberg.

I'm proud to introduce *Shock Rock II* readers to horror newcomers like Edo van Belkom, Tina Jens, John F.D. Taff, Tia Travis, and Scott H. Urban. I've also enlisted writers from another great entertainment medium, comics, including Mike Baron, Peter David, Nat Gertler, Bill Mumy, and Mark Verheiden.

These days, there's little difference between modern noir mystery writing and horror fiction. That's why I was especially happy to welcome mystery novelists Max Allan Collins and Jesse Sublett to our ranks.

One goal in planning *Shock Rock II* was to find a rock musician who shared our love of horror on the printed page, and I found him in Neil Peart, drummer for the platinum band *Rush*. Neil cowrote a story with rising star Kevin J. Anderson. And to round out your reading experience, I coerced former *Hot Blood* coeditor and current *RIP*-meister Lonn Friend into penning our foreword.

It's a motley crew (no pun intended!) of talent indeed. It is, if you'll pardon my boasting, a great group of stories, tackling all facets of the rock medium we have grown up with and fallen in love with. To paraphrase, "it's only rock and roll, but we live it!"

So now, drop that needle, push that button, or do whatever you need to do to start your soundtrack to the multimedia experience of *Shock Rock II* . . . 120 decibels of sheer terror!

J.G.
March 1993

FAVORITE SONG

Mark Verheiden

Green spotted the "Help Wanted" sign even across three lanes of interstate traffic. He cranked the wheel of his '66 Chrysler without looking, cutting off a van and a couple of motorcyclists in his rush to make the next exit. The car radio was turned up full volume, a Duane Eddy song blistering the Chrysler's fifty-watt speakers like some twangy jet engine. Knuckles white on the wheel, Green was in sync with Eddy's energy, that pulsing electric grind. For a minute or two, it had a chance of becoming his favorite song.

He was getting good at finding transient work. The sign was a dead giveaway; it wasn't some prefab "Help Wanted" number from the local hardware store, but a big mother, movie poster size, scrawled in red ink like somebody *meant* it. The reader board out front said "Rosman's Rock 'n' Roll Palace—Acres of Free Parking," and most of those acres were dirt and gravel. The tires of Green's car lifted a peacock plume of dust as it pulled to a stop near the front door.

Best bets were the independent theme restaurants. The big chains wanted a half dozen references, social security, driver's license, all that shit. The overextended "little guy" was always looking to shave a buck—cash under the table was just fine.

While he waited for the Eddy song to finish—Green never cut off a favorite song before the fade—he spotted a kid on a stepladder, scrubbing accumulated dust from the restaurant's fake tile walls. The kid turned at the sound of the car radio and smiled, nodding silently, as if tacitly approving of Green's musical taste. Suddenly annoyed, Green abruptly switched off the radio.

Changing into his last good shirt after spritzing with a cheap antiperspirant, Green tried to disguise the three days he'd been white-lining down the interstate. As he cracked the car door, a gust of heat pushed into him like some great, invisible fist. For a moment he thought about turning around, getting the hell out of the dirt and heat, but that "Help Wanted" sign was just too damn easy. The kid smiled again as Green pushed through the double glass doors and stepped inside.

The Palace seemed out of place in the rural community. It was an ersatz fifties luncheonette, modeled after the trendy retro diners that had been springing up in Los Angeles and New York. Red vinyl booths and Formica countertops passed for Eisenhower-era "style" while an incongruous CD jukebox pounded heavy-rotation metal licks. It was the kind of place that scared passing tourists back to the nearest Denny's, but for some reason the tinsel appealed to the small-town locals.

It was just after eleven and the restaurant was still in the process of opening up. Green wandered across the Palace's linoleum dance floor and took a stool at the mirrored bar. A ruddy-faced man in a plaid shirt was kneeling behind the counter, struggling to replace a washer in a broken faucet. "I was looking for the manager," Green said.

Favorite Song

The man wiped his hands on his pants and gave Green a cursory glance. "I'm Jack Rosman."

"I saw your sign," Green said, nodding toward the front window and the backward "Help Wanted" glowing in the glass.

Rosman let out a weary breath, dropping his towel into the bar sink. "Jesus," he said, "you're a sight for sore eyes."

It was a dishwashing job, some busing—about what Green had expected. A buck over minimum wage, no benefits, and straight cash was no problem. Green had pretty much expected that, too. Rosman had been doing double duty since the last kitchen boy quit. He didn't give a shit if Green worked under the table, over the table, or through the goddamn mail slot. Dishes needed to be washed, experience not necessary.

"I can start you in ten minutes," Rosman said, not even pretending to consider the decision.

"Mind if I put a couple quarters in the box first?" Green asked. "I like to hear music while I work."

Rosman pulled some change from his pocket and slapped it on the bar. "Then you'll love it here. Most days that thing's playing nonstop." He made a point of noticing the stain on Green's best shirt. "See me after work and I'll front you a few bucks for a room."

"That's damn generous," Green said, taking the change and playacting like he gave a shit. He leaned into the jukebox and let his eyes wander over the selections. Metal, some hard rock, a few seventies hits for the thirty-something trucker crowd—nothing dangerous, nothing that'd make Rosman's half-drunk cowboy clientele look up and take notice, but adequate.

"You like music?" a new voice said. "I like music, too." Green glanced over his shoulder. It was that kid again, the one from outside. "My dad lets me play anything I want."

Green suddenly realized the "kid" was at least twenty years old. He never would have guessed from the way the boy carried himself, all tentative and cautious, elbows raised like some gawky junior high teenager.

3

Rosman stepped out from behind the bar, giving the boy a mock-serious look. "Did you finish all the walls, Dave? Even the back?"

Dave just smiled, a dumb grin, a baby's grin. "Yeah, Dad," his voice full of childish sarcasm, "all done, okay?" Something about the way he said it pissed Green off. Sweaty fool had spent the entire morning in the goddamn heat, coughing down dirt and dust with every passing car, and yet there he was with that fucking smile, like standing on that stepladder was the greatest piece of fun he'd ever had.

"Better get cleaned up," Rosman said, giving Dave a friendly swat. As the boy walked back toward the kitchen, Rosman noticed Green's look. "That's my son, David," he said, curiously defensive. "He helps me out around the place—cleans up, that sort of thing."

"Yeah, I saw him outside." Green should have stopped there, but he couldn't resist. "He acts kind of funny," he said. "Something wrong with him?"

The older man fidgeted for a moment as Green's blunt question took him by surprise. "Dave's . . . *special.* Doesn't mean I don't love him all the same."

"Never said it did," Green said, struggling to keep the smirk off his face. "Special," my ass, he thought—Mr. High-Pockets-with-a-Fucking-Grin was a damn *retard.* Any other time he would have made something of it, just for the hell of it, pushed it to see the veins pop on Rosman's fat neck. But he needed the job, the old man wasn't asking any questions, and the music box was better than he'd expected.

He punched A-12—"Radar Love" by Golden Earring—and followed Rosman back into the kitchen.

Green had been there two weeks when the old man came up to him. He was surprised it had taken him this long. "Not very friendly, are you?" Rosman said, watching as Green pulled down the grease screens from over the grill. "I'm not bitching about your work, you understand, but I prefer it when my people get along."

Favorite Song

"Did you say something?" Green asked, pretending the noise from the exhaust fans had drowned the old man out. Rosman stared at Green for a moment, then let it pass.

Green had learned never to explain himself, never to open up, not to give a fucking inch until he'd found it. Occasionally one of Rosman's waitresses would try to get friendly, flash her little tits and give him her best blow-job smile, but Green ignored all of them, astonished at their ignorance. None of them understood how little they meant to him, how nothing in his world was going to set right until he found his favorite song.

Green was usually off by seven o'clock; he'd toss his apron, cash out ten dollars' worth of quarters, and study the jukebox like a scientist studying a disease. He fed a dozen quarters into the machine at a time, tying it up half the night, punching in every unfamiliar tune on the board. Nothing even came close. When some townie tried to cut in, Green would back him off—quiet and polite, so Rosman wouldn't notice, but strong enough so the guy wouldn't try again.

It began to work on him, day after day. Even in the wash bay, arms a foot deep in soapy water, Green was always listening. Each new song brought the hope of discovery, but after a few notes the hope would fade, like a sweet candy dissolving in your mouth. He was annoyed by the way everyone took the music for granted, background sop for their feeble conversations and gropings. Was it possible he was the only one who understood?

It was three thirty-five on a Thursday, the lunch rush long gone, when he finally heard it. He was leaning into the gray wash water, picking at a stubborn flake of food with his fingernail, when four hard-on chords churned from the jukebox speakers. Green stopped in midstroke, the filthy dish dripping in his hands. "Christ," he said.

He dropped the dish into the water and pushed through the kitchen toward the dance floor. He was mesmerized, entranced, a smile washing over his face for the first time in weeks. It was a metal song, one he must have heard a thousand times before—but suddenly, for some inexplicable reason, he could hear the *truth* in the music.

The song spoke to him with assaultive clarity, as if it had been written in a code that he was only now deciphering. He stood there on the linoleum, hands dripping soapy water, and listened to mysterious secrets that no one else would ever know. On the surface the lyrics were something about a woman, darkness, pity, but those were just words, *human* words, a ruse to keep the message away from the uninvited.

He stood frozen for five minutes after the song stopped, still tingling from his discovery. Something else was playing in its place, but he didn't hear, didn't care. His search was finally over.

From then on the song was his. Each day he'd fill the jukebox with quarters, careful to disguise his sweet passion among a random selection of pop hits and grinding metal. He would wait for his song in exquisite anticipation, a rising, almost gnawing hunger building inside. And then, suddenly, he would hear the ecstasy of the opening chords.

The music enveloped him, caressed him with the secret understanding that in spite of the bullshit, the two-bit managers and tit-job waitresses, despite every other agony of his life, there was something in the world that belonged just to him. No one else would ever know his private ecstasy; no one else would share in his euphoric, almost sexual delight.

While he was basking in the song's spell, nothing could touch him. The scalding wash water turned clear and cool, his burned hands were soothed. The emptiness of his life was suddenly filled, as if in three minutes and forty-two seconds he had found love, a family, a home, as if the ache of the last thirty years was the dream and the old dreams were now real.

Everyone noticed the change. Suddenly Green was friendly, open, courteous. He took the time to learn the names of the cooks and the counter help. They were reticent at first, but with the song's help Green was able to win them over.

Favorite Song

After a while the song played for him day and night, a blissful ringing deep inside that seemed to carry with it a sense of joyous expectation. He hoped it would never end.

His last day at the Palace had started promisingly enough. Green spent the lunch rush in the kitchen, then worked a brief spell out front while the busboy ate lunch. He hadn't had a chance to get to the jukebox, but it was all right. Everything was all right. One of the waitresses had just walked by, complimenting Green on his smile, and later he remembered thinking that she was nice. "Maybe I'll ask her out one night," he thought, "or maybe we could just talk." He'd like that, a chance to talk.

As if on cue, Green's song suddenly came up on the jukebox. He was surprised and delighted by the coincidence. "Jesus," he whispered to himself, wiping down one of the Formica tabletops with a dirty rag, "it's perfect. It's all perfect."

That's when he heard the voice, bleating and shrill, scraping across the song like fingernails on a blackboard. At first he thought it was some sort of awful mistake, like when an antenna or stray speaker wire picks up a passing radio conversation, or a distant transmitter fades in and out of reception. He waited for it to stop, *begged* for it to stop, prayed for the song to continue in its secret brilliance—

Then he saw him, Rosman's boy Dave, standing at the jukebox with a handful of quarters in his hand, hips swaying awkwardly to the beat. Singing along to the song.

Anger began to rise inside Green's chest, then anger suddenly became horror. The retard had punched up the song, *his* song, but that wasn't the worst of it. The words coming from Dave's mouth weren't the actual lyrics, but the *secrets,* Green's glorious, private mysteries, spewing out so all could hear. That retarded son of a bitch *knew.*

Green felt faint, his legs going wobbly beneath him. He muttered something to Rosman about feeling ill, then stumbled out of the restaurant into the warm afternoon sun. He could still see Dave's face, that empty half-wit smile, mouthing the lyrics but with the real words coming out. Green leaned against the hood of his car, staring into the white dust and gravel, and vomited. The face of the friendly waitress dissolved into a skin-flecked skull, thoughts of any normal life dribbling away like the white-hot retch spilling from his throat.

He drove aimlessly into the night, his body moving automatically and without purpose. Why couldn't it have worked this time, he wondered, why can't it ever work? Time passed without meaning as he tried to reclaim the song, tried to pretend that his awful loss was just some empty nightmare. He was still trying to pretend when he spotted Dave walking home from the restaurant.

Something caught in Green's throat, thick and wet. He pressed his foot against the brake and slowed to a crawl, matching Dave's walking speed. "Want a ride?" Green asked, his voice dry and cracking.

Dave smiled as if they were friends. "Sure. I live right down the road." He slid in on the passenger side, checking out the interior of the Chrysler with the excited look of a kid on his first plane ride.

The area was rural, long stretches of field interrupted by an occasional house. Green had no destination in mind— Christ, he barely knew the area. He only knew that he had to get off the main road, away from people, away from the shrieking pain that filled his head like some horrible, impossibly loud static.

Fascinated by the Chrysler's radio, Dave didn't notice as Green suddenly pulled the car off the main road and turned down a long, desolate irrigation trail. An old barn, long abandoned, loomed at the end of the path, shimmering in the moonlight.

The path was rutted and crude; the sound of the shocks banging against the undercarriage took on its own odd rhythm. As if hearing something familiar in the thumping, monotonous beat, Dave started to hum Green's song.

The sound of Dave's voice was like acid, burning Green with real, palpable pain. He released the steering wheel to clap his hands over his ears and jammed on the brakes, skidding to a wild stop just outside the barn. Reeling and dizzy, he stumbled from the car, the engine and headlights still on.

For the first time Dave realized they were off the main road. Confused, he stepped from the car and tried to get his bearings. "Are we lost?" he asked, turning toward Green.

Snarling like an animal, Green grabbed Dave by the scruff of his shirt and dragged him toward the abandoned barn. Dave didn't struggle; he barely understood that Green was angry. Instead, he looked into the evening sky, a baby-boy smile washing over his face as he spotted the hot, full moon. "Harvest moon," Dave said, parroting something he must have heard years before. "They call that a harvest moon."

The barn hadn't been used in years. Dozens of wooden wall slats had rotted or broken away, allowing hot moonlight to filter through. Green released Dave as soon as they were inside, and the boy knelt in the center of the barn, fascinated by the way the moonlight patterned across the dirt floor. "Hey, look at this," Dave said, spotting an old bottle wedged against the wall of the barn. "I found a bot—"

Green spun the rotted two-by-six like a baseball bat, catching Dave in the stomach. The wood was old and weak; it splintered in a puff of dust and the broken half twirled into the darkness. Caught off guard, Dave folded over like a book, struggling to catch his breath. Green left him there and ran back toward his car.

The barn doors had long since rotted away; even as he opened his trunk Green's eyes were locked on the boy. Gasping for air, picking at the splinters left in his shirt by the rotten timber, Dave struggled to his feet. Woozy and stumbling, he fell against one of the barn's old walls, flattening himself against the beams to keep his balance. "Mr. Green," he called out, "you—you *hurt* me. I want to go home now, Mr. Green—"

Green slammed the car trunk with a thump and came back to the barn dragging a heavy canvas sack. Still gasping for air, Dave tried to move away, tried to understand the clunking metal rattle coming from the bag. Green ignored the boy, untying the knot at the top of the sack so he could reach inside.

"Go ahead," Green said, sliding out a five-pound sledgehammer, "sing it." Dave stared at him, hand clutching his wounded belly, his eyes wide and empty. He still didn't understand the gravity of the charge against him, the magnitude of his crime. He didn't understand a goddamn thing until Green hoisted the hammer shoulder high and started toward him.

"I—I like music," Dave said, tears of pain running down his cheeks. Nervous and afraid, he stumbled over a tree root and fell backward, the slatted, jagged moonlight spotting him like some wild animal.

Dave lifted his hands, an instinctive, defensive motion, like a cow twisting inside a slaughter chute. It didn't matter. Nothing did. Green brought the sledgehammer down on Dave's right ankle, pulverizing the bone and sinking the pant leg a good two inches into the muddy soil. He lifted again and this time went for the knee; the bone and cartilage cracked like dry kindling and a flat pancake of blood oozed into the dirt. Dirty sweat glistening in the moonlight, Green worked his way up to Dave's thigh, hitting it full force once, twice, three times, dodging arterial spray as he worked to sever the limb through sheer brute force.

By now Dave was screaming uncontrollably. For a moment Green was concerned—even out there Dave's howls might be overheard by some nervous farmboy—but his hesitation vanished when he realized what was happening. Even in his agony, the goddamn bastard was *still singing his song*. Dave's screams, hoarse and staccato, were *mimicking* the opening grunge chords.

"You stole it from me!" Green shrieked, driving a glancing blow into Dave's ribs. Even then the boy mocked him. The sound of his bones cracking was the drum riff during the middle eight; the keening howl that rose from Dave's lips was the guitar solo just before the fade. Stamping his foot to the imaginary rhythm, Green brought the hammer down with the bass drum, every second beat, crushing Dave's skull, his face, pounding until the raw white bones jutted out of the ground like shards of broken glass. The screams had stopped, but Green had finally found his groove.

His anger was blunt and hot, just like the song; major chords, no minors, no shading, nothing but pulsing, screaming rage. Bone, blood, and muscle split under his blows, pieces of torn flesh dancing through the air with each pounding beat. Fury building to a crescendo, Green aimed the hammer straight into Dave's crotch. The boy had been dead for several minutes, but the ratcheting blow sent one last, involuntary shudder through the broken corpse.

Breathing hard, Green felt the song begin to fade. It was as if he were suddenly back at the restaurant, the heat coming back into the water, the pain returning to his hands. Dropping the blood-soaked hammer, Green studied what he had done as tears began to stream down his face. Not out of pity for the mangled remains before him, but out of sadness over what he had lost. His song was gone forever.

Picking a pair of bolt cutters and a handsaw from the canvas bag, Green went to work on the body. He peeled the skin away from Dave's battered skull and crushed what was left of the jaws and teeth to prevent dental identification. The bolt cutter took off Dave's fingers and toes; Green would burn these parts separately to make sure the prints were completely destroyed.

He changed his clothes, fetched a box of trash bags from the car and stuffed the dismembered body into a dozen different bags, pillowing out the air and carefully tying the top of each with a red-striped wire band. The load fit easily in his trunk; he waited for the plastic to settle, then closed the lid and drove back into town.

He distributed the bags among a dozen different dumpsters, stopping only once to pick up a six-pack and a pack of cigarettes from the local convenience store. He made a point of leaving what was left of Dave's head in a trash can behind Rosman's Palace, then took his usual parking spot near the employees' entrance and popped the first of his beers. The warm ache in his back and hands felt almost pleasant in the night air.

Rosman arrived for work around ten-thirty the next morning, parking his Charger next to Green's car. "I've got to move on," Green said, following Rosman up the back steps. "Sorry I couldn't give you more warning."

Eyes red and rimmed with fatigue, Rosman barely registered Green's short-notice resignation. "I've been up all night," he said, unlocking the steel security door. "Dave didn't come home last night—he's never done that before."

Green shifted his weight impatiently from one leg to the other, muscles still aching from the night before. "Maybe he got laid."

Rosman gave Green a hard look, then reached for his wallet and counted out six twenty-dollar bills. "That's for the week," he said, nodding toward the rear door. "Close it on the way out."

Green stuffed the bills into his pocket and pulled the door shut behind him, taking the back steps two at a time. He thought he could hear the son of a bitch crying as he slid behind the wheel of his Chrysler and cut a couple of 360s in the hot, dry gravel.

He was calling himself Dave now, working the five-to-closing shift behind the bar at a businessmen's club called Beer and Brisket. This time it had only taken a week to find his favorite song, a New Age tune that was popular with the white wine and cheddar set. Seemed like he was just settling into a routine when he heard the hatcheck girl singing along to his song.

He felt the anger rising again, and he knew what he had to do. And besides, he could always find another job.

THE LAST TIME

Michael Garrett

The Rolling Stones were coming to town for the first time ever, and Jack Holland was prepared to take advantage of the supergroup's visit.

He gazed into the bathroom mirror, shifting his head from side to side, tilting his chin and stretching his lips to reveal as many teeth as possible. Like Mick Jagger, Jack was tall and thin with sunken eyes, square jaw, bulging Adam's apple, and plump, protruding lips. Unlike Mick, however, Jack was still in his early forties and sported a conservative haircut. Still, the resemblance was as strong as ever.

All his life, friends and strangers alike had marveled over Jack's uncanny similarity to the most famous of the Stones, but it had never gotten him more than fleeting recognition as a Jagger impersonator at parties and amateur talent shows. But at long last, Mick and Jack would be in the same town at the same time, and the opportunity for mistaken identity would never be greater.

After putting on the oversize shirt and loose-fitting pants he'd purchased to enhance his likeness to Mick, Jack donned the shaggy wig he'd rented and prepared to strut the sidewalks of the nightclub district. Groupies in search of their idol would do anything to please the man of their dreams, and Jack was anxious to accommodate their wishes.

He belted out a few lines from "Time Is on My Side" and decided that as long as he didn't have to sing, the ladies would never know the difference. His voice was nothing like Jagger's, and Jack's hastily rehearsed British accent was almost laughable, but shit, the local bimbos wouldn't notice. They'd be so absorbed by the opportunity to ball a world-class celebrity that they'd hardly be listening to what he had to say.

Jack winked at himself in the mirror. Women had swooned over Jagger's kisser for thirty years, yet his own identical lips had seldom earned a second glance. As a result, Jack had grown to despise his resemblance to Jagger, because even though the rock star was married, he could still have more women in a week than many men had in a lifetime, while Jack's affections were usually rejected by even the most desperate nymphomaniac. But tonight alone would be worth the years of frustration and jealousy.

How many times would he score? Two? Three? As many times as he could get it up? Jack smiled. And in a flash of delight he realized that the Elvis impersonators didn't know what they were missing. Unless they had practiced their craft before the King had died, they never got a chance to swivel their hips between some unsuspecting young thing's legs in the practice of their deception.

"Tonight, I *will* get satisfaction," Jack said, practicing his awkward British accent with a sneer.

By the time he'd signed six autographs and dodged an expanding mob, Jack had grown disenchanted. The clothes were uncomfortable, the wig itched, and there was a chill in the air. Passing himself off as the real Jagger had been a snap, but he was disappointed that the ladies who'd approached him so far with lust in their eyes looked more like retired Stone Bill Wyman than the sexpots he'd envisioned. He'd expected young women in their early to mid-twenties with blond hair spilling over their shoulders, boobs that hungered to be squeezed, and legs that could wrap around a guy's waist like a pair of boa constrictors.

But just as he was about to resort to an alternate plan, the girl of Jack's dreams exited a restaurant directly in front of him and almost knocked him down. A gleam of instant recognition flashed in her eyes.

"Excuse me?" she said nervously. "Mr. Jagger? I can't believe it's you!"

She appeared to be in her late twenties, with a dynamite figure, a face to kill for, and long, flowing brunette hair that would look even sexier fanned across the pillow in his motel room. Jack cleared his throat and tried not to show his excitement—hell, meeting a broad like this would be nothing unusual for the real Mick. "Don't ask me for directions, love—I'm new in town," he chirped, his accent sounding awful but apparently good enough to convince the girl.

"Oh, wow," she swooned. "Nobody's gonna believe this!"

Her name was Karen, and she claimed that she hadn't really been looking for him, that she'd been stood up at the restaurant where she had planned to break up with her boyfriend. Maybe her story was true, but Jack knew that her reaction to him had been the same as all the others so far that night. The thrill in Karen's eyes sparkled as she shifted her weight from side to side, exposing gorgeous legs through a skirt that was slit practically up to her waist. Jack couldn't help but marvel at the power of celebrity, knowing that such an occurrence was commonplace to rock stars. "Hey, now," he said. "I need someone to show me around town. Interested?"

A joyful expression flashed across Karen's angelic face, and before Jack knew it, he was strolling arm-in-arm with one of the most attractive women he'd ever laid eyes on. Fuck all the record royalties, Jack thought. *This* was the ultimate reason to be a rock star.

But within moments three other women approached Jack for his autograph and he became irritated. "Now, bugger off," he growled after scribbling cryptic signatures on the backs of three crumpled bank deposit slips. Then he leaned over Karen, his height towering over her petite frame, and whispered, "We need some privacy, dear. Would you like to come to my room?" Linked to the magnetic persona of Mick Jagger, Jack felt he could do no wrong.

Karen smiled seductively. "I was hoping you'd ask," she purred. "But can't we go somewhere else, away from your traveling companions? For more privacy?"

"Oh, I've already taken care of that, love," he bragged. "I'm not staying with the rest of them."

His initial inclination had been to check into the most exclusive hotel in town, but then he realized that the *real* Mick Jagger would likely be staying there. Deciding that it wouldn't be advisable to risk a face-to-face confrontation with the man he was impersonating, Jack had instead registered at a modest motel near the airport. He stopped beneath a streetlight and wrapped his arms around Karen. She was starry-eyed as he leaned over to deliver a kiss, and she clung to him like Velcro. Oh, man, he thought as his arousal intensified. I could follow Jagger from town to town and get all the action I've ever wanted. I could write a book about my experiences and become a millionaire. I could—

"Mick!" she interrupted his fantasies. "The concert! You're going to be late!" She was staring at her watch.

Shit! Jack cursed to himself. He'd forgotten about Mick's gig, and couldn't complete the tryst until after midnight. He had no choice but to play along. "You're right," he groaned, momentarily losing his accent. "But you'll meet me afterward in my room, won't you?"

She ran her fingertips inside his shirt and sent an erotic tingle up his spine. "I don't want to leave your side," she whispered as her fingernails traced a path up the side of his face. "Can I go backstage with you, Mick, and watch the show close up? You wouldn't mind, would you?"

"Uh . . ." He had to think quickly. "Security is a problem

tonight, love. In fact, we can't even take the same cab to the concert hall. The guys and I are supposed to ride together in a limo to a special entrance. Sorry."

"Oh, Mick," she moaned in disappointment. "But you'll dedicate a song to me, won't you? Just for me? To prove to all of my friends that you really know me?"

"Uh . . . sure I will, love. If I can remember. I'm not getting any younger, you know."

He slid his hands down her backside and grabbed her ass. The delay in getting her in bed would be unbearable, but what else could he do? The timing was necessary to maintain the charade.

"Can I meet you outside the coliseum afterward?" she begged. "Can we ride to the motel together?"

It was tempting. He could rent a limo and experience the power of celebrity to its fullest, but Jack knew that he dare not place himself in such close proximity to the real Jagger for fear of being exposed. "I'm afraid not, love. There are tight procedures that have to be followed."

An ugly frown spoiled her face, and for a brief instant Karen's beauty was lost. "You'll stand me up, won't you, Mick?" she complained. "You'll find someone else to take back to your room. You're just like all the others. You're—"

"Wait a minute, love," Jack said, grabbing her shoulders and staring deeply into her eyes. "It's you and me tonight, I promise." He reached into his pocket and pulled out his motel key, then wrapped her trembling fingers around it. "You're the one for me tonight, dear," he whispered. "No one else has a chance."

She smiled again. "I told myself that if I was lucky enough to meet you tonight, I'd never let you out of my sight," she whispered as she squeezed him tightly and buried her face in his chest. She rattled the key, then added, "But I feel better now."

Jack squeezed her hand, taking note of her comment. She had been looking for Jagger after all, and now he felt more confident that she would show up.

"I've got to run," he said, his voice filled with genuine

regret. "I'll leave right after the show and I'll be waiting for you. Just remember, it's the Thunderbird Motel. Near the airport."

They kissed again, their passion riveting them together in an embrace that neither wanted to end. Finally Karen pulled away. "I don't want you to be late," she said.

The sight of her ass straining against her skintight skirt drove him crazy as she walked away. Jack was convinced that he would be content to play Mick Jagger for the rest of his life.

"Mick!" a young voice squealed from across the street. "Wait up!"

With a shake of his head, it dawned on Jack that he would have to escape public view or be harassed all night. He scribbled a quick autograph and darted toward his car on an adjacent side street.

He couldn't get her off his mind as he collapsed across the bed, listening to the sound of the shower running in the bathroom and imagining the beads of water streaming down her slender form. Jet engines screamed in the distance, even at this hour of the night. Karen had hurried to the motel after the show, just as she'd promised, and although it was already past one, the excitement of the events to come kept Jack from being tired or sleepy. Hell, he'd be up all night—and what a night it would be. Although the quantity of women he'd experience during the Stones' visit would be less than expected, the quality would surpass even his wildest dreams. Karen was unbelievable. And the irony of it all was that he'd be giving her the thrill of *her* lifetime as well. If he played his cards right, he could arrange for return visits, promising her that she was special and that he would fly into town from points all around the world just to spend an occasional weekend with her. He could stretch this arrangement out endlessly.

Finally the shower stopped. Having readied himself before she arrived, he applied a final blast of breath spray. Jack was only moments away from living every man's fantasy.

The bathroom door opened an inch or so. "Mick?" she whispered. "Will you turn out some of the lights, please? It's like the FBI's interrogation room in there."

"Hey—I've got to see what you look like, love. I'm not into making it in the dark."

"You can leave a light on, Mick. I just don't want it to be so bright."

He complied with her wishes, realizing in an instant that she was right. He'd had every light in the room on, and it would've been like making love under a spotlight. She wanted to seduce him, and Jack didn't want to deprive her of the opportunity.

She stepped from the bathroom with a towel wrapped around her moist body, the ends of her shoulder-length hair wet from the shower. At the edge of the bed she dropped an upper corner of the towel and cupped a breast in her hand, fondling her nipple and driving Jack absolutely wild. Neither said a word. Jack was mesmerized, and Karen seemed intent on providing him with the best show of his life, as if her purpose was to outdo every groupie he'd slept with before.

He started to speak, but Karen shushed him. She crawled onto the bed on her knees and slowly dropped the towel. Jack's eyes were as big as silver dollars. She wore a silver nipple ring on her left breast, and a small tattoo adorned her right breast. He couldn't make out the image in the dim light, but he knew he would investigate it more closely before the night was over. Below her flat stomach, her pubic hair was shaved in the design of a swastika and another silver ring adorned the tender folds of her vagina. The innocence of her face looked odd next to her voluptuous body; while her face was angelic, her body looked like it belonged to a biker's girlfriend deprived of sex. Karen eased closer, pursing her lips, wetting them with her tongue and running a fingertip in circles around her mouth. Jack was so hard he was about to explode.

"I want to fuck you, Mick," she whispered, her fingers busily unbuckling his belt. He reached down to help her, but she pushed his hand away. She seemed intent on doing things her own way. "Wait, Mick," she growled with a sexy purr. "It's *my* turn."

It no longer seemed real. Not only was he about to make love to one of the most beautiful women he'd ever laid eyes on, but she was the aggressor. She was going to fuck *him!* It was almost too good to be true, but here they were in bed together and she was fawning over him as if he were a god—but of course, in her mind, he *was* a god. He reached up to squeeze her breast, but again she pushed his hand away. "Me first," she whispered. "I'll do you, then you can do me."

He closed his eyes and felt the warmth of her lips at his mouth, her tongue probing inside with deep passion. She licked his cheeks, his ears, then paused. "I like it kinky, Mick," she whispered, "in case you haven't noticed."

He cleared his throat to respond, but she covered his lips with her fingertip. "Are you into bondage, Mick?" she purred. Before he could answer, she leaned over and pulled a handful of thick silk strips from her purse on the floor. "The pink ones are for me after I've finished with you," she said. "The blue ones are yours." She slipped a knot around his wrist and secured one arm to the bedpost. As Jack worried about premature ejaculation, she secured the other arm and began working on his feet. Since there were no bedposts at the foot of the bed, she tied his feet to the bed frame. He feared for a moment that, with his hands tied, she might run her fingers through his hair in the heat of passion and dislodge the wig, but he would come up with a good excuse if that happened. Hell, the bitch was so hooked, she'd believe anything.

Karen smiled at him from between his legs, her eyes focused just above his dick, which now pointed skyward. Then she licked his knee and continued all the way up to his balls. Sweet torture, that's what it was, he thought, imagining what might come next. The tip of her tongue traced the length of his dick, then she paused. "Pleasure and pain,

Mick," she growled softly. "Have you ever done a song about pleasure and pain?"

How the fuck should he know? He was no expert on the Stones. He'd never owned more than a couple of their records, and those were among their earlier releases. But before he could answer, she slipped a heavier, padded strip around his face and secured it over his mouth. He couldn't utter a sound.

Jack grew uneasy. His limbs were tied securely. His voice was completely subdued. Could she have an ulterior motive? Robbery? Torture? Certainly not—he was *Mick Jagger,* for Christ's sake.

Pleasure and pain . . .

"I've been waiting for you to come to town, Mick," she drawled, her voice taking on a different, darker tone. Now she was licking the long blade of a knife that had appeared from out of nowhere, its metallic glare dancing across the room. "I'm not rich. I haven't had the money to come to you like Chapman found Lennon. But I've been waiting for you, Mick." The headlights from a car in the parking lot penetrated the thin fabric of the closed draperies and cast a yellowish glow across her face, making her eyes resemble those of a female Charlie Manson. "I knew you'd come to me," she slurred. "They all will, eventually." She took a deep breath and dug her fingernails into the skin of his chest. Jack winced from the pain. "It's fate, that's what it is. And you can't fuck with fate, Mick. No sirree, you can't fuck with fate."

Jack's pulse raced. Suddenly he began to shake; his teeth wanted to chatter, but the gag restrained them. He uttered a muffled moan and tensed against the knotted silk, but she quickly pushed the shiny blade against his neck. Jack felt a stinging sensation, then a thin stream of liquid warmth flowed from the wound at his neck to the pillow beneath his head.

"Shut up and be still, Mick," she growled, her voice now ghastly, like someone possessed. "I've listened to your fuckin' voice all my life. Tonight you're gonna hear *me* for a change."

Jack couldn't speak, but spittle managed to soak through the silk and dampen his chin. Karen's breasts swayed as she positioned herself over him, but Jack no longer found the sight stimulating.

"Chapman was an amateur," she hissed, her voice changing pitch as she spoke. "He didn't stretch it out with Lennon. Just a couple of shots and it was over." She yawned and took a deep breath. "But you and I, Mick, we're gonna get to know each other first. We're gonna make history together. I think you deserve that much before you die."

The madness in her eyes grew more intense by the minute. Tears rolled down Jack's cheeks. "Hey, Mick, don't cry like that," her crazed voice sounded. "Be a *man.*"

Jack thought about his plan, about the fail-safe approach that was to have given him a night of ecstasy. He visualized Karen, the *fantasy* Karen, the one who was supposed to drive him to new heights of pleasure and go down on him with her lips, not with a knife. He struggled again, but she quickly inflicted another wound.

"Pleasure and pain, Mick," she snarled. "We'll fuck, if you can still get it up, and then I'll carve a cute little heart on your chest. Then we'll fuck again and I'll turn your voice into a soprano. You'd be able to sing Beach Boys songs," she said, laughing, *"if I let you live that long."*

Jack struggled against his bonds, but the bitch had apparently known what she was doing when she knotted the silk so tightly. He pleaded with her with his Jagger-like eyes, but her expression remained cold and heartless. "There's no need to rush things, Mick," she purred. "We've got all night." Then she bared her teeth, and as she leaned over to bite his shoulder, she hissed, *"Let's spend some time together."*

THE SAD STORY OF BILLY PSYCH-OUT AND THE PSYCHED-OUT ENCYCLOPEDIA OF ROCK 'N' ROLL

Tia Travis

"I followed the Elvis impersonator into the kitchen. It looked like sale week at the A&P: hamburger buns, cornbread and biscuits, fixin's for the peanut butter and banana sandwiches Elvis liked so much. He turned to me and said, 'Son, some people think I'm crazy, duplicatin' Elvis's pantry. But if you wanna *sing* like the King, you gotta *be* the King. An' everybody knows you *are* what you eat.' He popped a stick of Juicy Fruit—Elvis's gum of choice—into his mouth and grinned. I tell you, those words of his would ring true the rest of my life...."

> p. 824, *The Billy Psych-Out Psyched-Out Encyclopedia of Rock 'n' Roll*

I'll tell you how it started: It was the terminal end of the Billy Psych-Out and the Psychobillies tour. Hardtop down on Interstate 94 outside Two Pines, North Dakota. Me and Billy doin' eighty clicks in a shit-kicked, rust-corroded 1955 Ford Thunderbird. Stereotypical dice swayed from the rearview mirror; tape deck blasted "Love Me Like a Tornado" at 200 decibels. Billy Psych-Out jumped at the wheel like a mental patient on patrol. Anybody'd told him to thumb down the deck a notch, he'd have knocked their butts on the blacktop and they'd better hope to hell they remembered to roll because Billy slowed for no one.

"I'm 'bout done with it," he shouted.

"LOVE ME LIKE A TORNADO! UNNNGGGHHH! TORNADO! YAHHHHH!"

My eardrums broke. "What?"

Billy flashed me a grin that made me wish I was the one in control of the wheel. "The book," he said. "It's done. All I need is one more entry."

"'Bout time."

"You bet your balls it is." He tried to crank the deck but it was already on ten. We'd blown the Radio Shack speakers hours back, or maybe that poppin' sound had been the Thunderbird breaking the sound barrier. We were drivin' damn fast. "Psychedelic Cowboy," a track off one of the *Hoedown in Hell Town* records, came on in a scream of slide guitar and crash cymbals.

"This is my favorite fuckin' song of all time!" he shouted, delighted. He'd said the same thing about the last ten tunes.

"I DON'T WORRY SO DON'T YOU WORRY 'BOUT OFFICER ROY! I'M THE ONE AN' ONLY ESTABLISHED PSYCHEDELIC COWBOY!" Billy could have broken bricks with that sledgehammer voice of his. When he hit you, he hit hard. "GONNA RIDE MY HORSE TO THE COUNTY FAIR! GONNA ACCOUNT TO SOME BUSINESS THERE!"

On the backseat, Billy's coffin-shaped 1962 Vox Phantom thudded on the fake leopard upholstery. The amplifier he'd picked up for ten bucks at a garage sale rattled on the floor. Electrical-taped, the amp shorted out at predictable intervals. Billy didn't give a shit. Just plug him in and let 'er rip. Other rockers could set their hundred-watt amps on five; Billy set his five-watt amp on a hundred. It balanced out.

"IF YOU DON'T HAVE THE MONEY, I DON'T HAVE THE STUFF! THINGS ARE GETTIN' HARDER, TIMES

The Sad Story of Billy Psych-Out

ARE GETTIN' ROUGH!" Billy rolled his eyeballs, lookin' a little too much like a wolfman on LSD for this boy's taste.

I'd had the sinkin' premonition for the last four hundred miles that somehow we'd end up in a blackened, burning wreck of metal and tire tracks en route to Two Pines. You've probably realized by now that Billy wasn't what you'd call a "model driver." Bein' the Psychobillies' manager, I was by definition the only one dumb enough to get into an automobile with a man who, when pulled over by the state patrol for exceeding the speed limit by ten billion miles an hour, would unroll his window and say: "I'll have a Coke and a double burger, please." He pulled that trick on a regular basis, and let me tell you, it went over real well with the state patrol.

Billy's other irritating habit was that of playing a tape over and over, rewinding and rewinding till the listener's auditory channels self-destructed from boredom. There are only so many baby-baby-baby's a man can take before his brain'll crack, if you know what I mean.

To take my mind off it all, I leaned down low in the seat and rolled Billy's book over in my mind.

Billy had been compilin' *The Psyched-Out Encyclopedia of Rock 'n' Roll* for ten years, since before I met him. He had entries on everything from the Trashmen's top-ten TV dinners of all time to Screamin' Jay Hawkins's brand of hair spray to an in-depth exposé of the Chuck Berry toilet tapes, shocking aerial shots of chicks in the bathroom stalls at Berryland.

See, there's one thing you have to understand about Billy Psych-Out. To Billy, the truth of the music was in the details. Not details like how many records a band had or who they played with or what size the audiences were. Any rock zine'll tell you that. No, what stuck in Billy's mind, what made the music real to him, was the little shit.

Elvis was real because Joni Mabe plucked the King's toenail out of the carpet of the Jungle Room in Graceland. Read about it on page 828 of the encyclopedia. Nobody knew if it was really Elvis's toenail, but people came in and stared at it for hours all the same. I think about that toenail sometimes, and damned if it doesn't make E. P. more real to me than *Clambake* ever will. It spooks me how a little clipped half-moon can do that.

Then there's the entry on Jerry Lee Lewis. Billy Psych-Out read about 'im in a *Kicks* article, "I Was a Teenage Rock 'n' Roll Fan." Jerry Lee was playing at the Rocket Room in D.C. It was 1964 and the man who wrote the article asked if Jerry could still cut it with the hot new singers like James Brown and Johnny Rivers. And Jerry Lee blew his stack like he always did, swearin' up a storm and tellin' that poor writer to put those singers on stage, he'd *cut them to pieces* because he was the best rock-'n'-rollin' motherfucker of all time, or something to that effect. You never can tell with the Killer, but take my word: That piece'll tell you more about Jerry Lee's music than any Billboard chart.

You remember Bobby Fuller, page 232 in the encyclopedia. The Bobby Fuller Four put "I Fought the Law" in the books. Bobby was still a kid when his brother Randy discovered his beaten, gasoline-soaked body in his car. Phil Spector and the Standells helped bury him. When you hear a story like that, there's no way you can listen to "Never to Be Forgotten" without a tear in your eye and a pain in your heart. That's how it should be. It's the details, like Billy Psych-Out said, that make the music real.

Now, I'm not trying to depress you. But I want you to understand what made Billy do what he did, what drove him to the brink. That rock 'n' roll encyclopedia was everything to him, and when his belief in that book died . . .

But I'm gettin' ahead of myself.

We reached Two Pines in one piece at six o'clock and pulled the Thunderbird into the parking lot of a little store with a dusty Pepsi Cola sign on the front. That's where we saw him: Buck Nekkid, lead singer and stand-up bass player for Buck Nekkid and the Starkers.

"It's *him.*" Billy's mouth dropped open like a horseshoe. "I don't believe it!"

It was hard to ID the trashabily star without the truck-

The Sad Story of Billy Psych-Out

load of panting, pantyless women he generally had in tow. Still, it *was* Buck Nekkid, soon-to-be page 1,000 in *The Billy Psych-Out Psyched-Out Encyclopedia of Rock 'n' Roll*.

Buck had spent half his life in Two Pines workin' at a truck stop pumpin' gasoline till the Starkers hit pay dirt with their first album, *Hell Rod Rumble*. They followed up with *Teenage Screwup*. Knocked out a couple of hair-raisin' howlers for party-trash comps like *Sleaze Alley, Raunch-a-billy,* and *The Big Strip*. The Starkers were high on sax appeal, low on intellect, and that's how they liked it. The kids lapped it up with a dirty spoon.

Now the Starkers were back in town to do a video of their latest hit, a remake of the Rio Rockers' "Mexicali Baby." Buck wanted the cow plop backdrop of a small town to show the record-buyin' public what a down-home kind of boy he could be. "Down-home" sold records, and nobody wanted to sell records more than Buck Nekkid.

Running into him here in Two Pines was no accident. In fact, Buck was the reason I'd booked the Psychobillies into the Starlite Lounge. We'd be opening not only for the Starkers but also for a ventriloquist's dummy that told pornographic jokes and for a four-hundred-pound table dancer named Miss Temptation. We'd be lucky to earn back the gas money.

The Psychobillies didn't want to detour to Two Pines. They'd been on the road ten weeks, crashin' in the back of the truck. They were tired of breakfasts of Hi-C drink crystals sprinkled on Wonder bread and washed down with lukewarm beer. They wanted to go home.

I did, too, but Billy was hell-bent. He'd tracked the Starkers for years and was determined to wrap up *The Billy Psych-Out Psyched-Out Encyclopedia of Rock 'n' Roll* with an interview with his teen idol. He'd written a billion letters, but Buck (fuckin' surprise) hadn't bothered writing back. Billy figured he was busy making records; me, I didn't think Buck knew how to hold a pencil, let alone operate a mixing board.

Now here he was checkin' out the dark shades rack at the local mom-'n'-pop, and Billy was set to piss his pants with excitement. I was set to piss, too, but it wasn't with excitement. Like I said, it'd been a long haul.

John Ashley in *Hot Rod Girl*—that was Buck Nekkid. He had the juve-delink look nailed down: black leather jacket, motorcycle boots, thick skull ring on his fuck-off finger, sideburns like train tracks.

I could tell the sideburns had set him back a fortune. My barber would have done it for a buck fifty. The man's been buzz-cuttin' since the Japanese attacked Pearl Harbor. He's a bottomless bottle of after-shave so bracing you'd think he was washin' your face in an acid bath. He doesn't take crap from anyone, and you'd better not jump if somebody slams the door or there's a chunk outta the back of your head.

I eyeballed the slicked-up shit-sucker at the door with his expensive *Beverly Hills 90210* haircut. I pictured what he'd look like with a number twenty-five, the $2.99 army special on the hair chart my barber had tacked up beside the oil painting of the bulldogs playin' poker. I grinned.

"Buck Nekkid?" Billy walked up to him, stuck out his hand. "I'm Billy Psych-Out. My band's openin' for you at the Starlite."

Buck pulled a pair of shades off the rack, tried them on. Round two. "Look, can I buy you a drink at the lounge later on? I'd really like to talk to you."

Buck checked himself out in the dusty, rectangular mirror on the rack. "Oh, yeah?"

"I'm writin' a book on rock 'n' roll. I'd like to interview you."

Buck raised a coal-black eyebrow. He took off the shades and I read a cool flicker of interest in his eyes. "What kinda book?"

"The Billy Psych-Out Psyched-Out Encyclopedia of Rock 'n' Roll," Billy said in one explosive breath. "It's just about done. It's a definitive what's what, who's who in rock, and I want a Buck Nekkid interview to top off the trashabilly section. I totally idolize you, man. We cover that Starkers tune off your first album, 'Scratch My Belly, Baby.'" Billy started to hum off-key.

"Uh-huh. Who's that?" Buck said. "Your editor?"

The Sad Story of Billy Psych-Out

Billy looked at me like he'd accidentally deleted me from his memory banks. "Him? Umm, that's our manager. . . ."

"Oh."

Yeah, fuck you, too, I thought.

Buck took out a comb and slicked his hair into place. "So this book of yours, uh—"

"Billy. Billy Psych-Out."

"Yeah. You goin' to publish it?"

"Well, no one's looked at it," he admitted. "I wanted to add the 'Buck Nekkid: Exposed' article first. What do you say? Can I talk to you?"

"All right. But lemme see the book first."

"You bet!" Billy was in ecstasy.

I still had to whiz. I looked at Buck Nekkid's motorcycle helmet on the floor . . .

"I'll bring it to your dressin' room tonight. Are you goin' to be around for the Psychobillies' set?"

Don't fuckin' bet on it, I thought.

Buck smiled a sincere, bonded smile, the same one they'd printed on the front of *Spin* magazine. "I'll try. We have that video to shoot. Later, Willie."

"Billy. Billy Psych-Out."

Buck swiped the helmet off the floor, not knowing how close he'd come to a golden shower. "Don't forget the book. Ten o'clock." The store's door slammed shut, wind chimes knocking tunelessly on the glass. I noticed Buck still had the unpaid-for shades hooked over his thumb.

"You hear that?" Billy said. "Buck's gonna let me interview 'im!"

"C'mon," I said, pissed off for some reason. "Let's see if the truck's here. I told the boys we'd meet 'em at six-thirty, and I'd kill for a drive-thru hamburger."

Billy nodded, but I could tell he hadn't heard a word I'd said. He stared after Buck like Jesus himself had descended from the heavens and was walking down Main Street in a pair of Levi's 501's. Looking back now, I realize the kind of danger Billy was in. He was eyeball to eyeball with his idol, and that was about one eyeball-length too close.

* * *

Picture a sweat-pourin', four-hundred-pound Mamie Van Doren, and that was Miss Temptation. Makeup so thick it looked like she slapped it on with a paintbrush. When she danced, the plaster in the ceiling cracked and ice cubes did the watusi in patrons' drinks. A real good-timey gal.

I was sittin' with the Psychobillies at one of the Starlite's cigarette-holed red vinyl booths. It was ten-thirty. I had one hand in a bowl of salted cocktail nuts and the other wrapped around a cool martini. Miss Temptation rolled offstage to a smatter of handclaps and a thin chorus of "Hey, Baby-Baby." The dummy, a sleazy-looking two-by-four dubbed "Dirty Charlie" by the ventriloquist, had been booed off with threats of conversion into firewood. The audience was jumpy and bored. So were the Psychobillies.

"Where's Billy?" Slim Sapperticker, the stand-up drummer, tapped on the table with a pair of swizzle sticks. "He was s'posed to be here by now."

"I'll check on him," I said, downing the martini. It was my fifth. I still had a not-so-good feeling about Buck Nekkid. "You boys go set up." I wiped my mouth on the back of my sleeve—sharkskin; what the hell'd you expect a manager to wear?—and made for the dressing rooms. I was rounding the corner into the hall when I bumped into Billy.

"Where the hell you been?" I said. "It's showtime."

"I know, I was talkin' to Buck. I let him look at the book," he said. His eyes were too bright.

"You did, huh."

"He was really interested. Said it was the best book on rock 'n' roll he'd ever seen!"

I noticed that Billy's hands were empty. "Where is it now?" I said.

"Huh? Oh, Buck has it. He wanted to read it. He couldn't keep his hands off it. Kept sayin' he'd never seen anythin' like it—"

I had a terrible thought. "Billy, did Buck ask you about anything?"

"Like what?"

"Like maybe how many people know about the book?"

The Sad Story of Billy Psych-Out

Billy looked confused. "I—yeah, I think he did. Come to think of it, I *know* he did. But what's that have to do wi—"

The opening chords to Link Wray's "Run Chicken Run" crackled out of the Starlite's battered PA system. It sounded like the Psychobillies were ready to play, with or without their lead singer.

"I'm on!" Billy yelled. He sped off down the hall before I could ask him anything else.

I started to follow, then had another thought and walked back to Buck's dressing room. I tried the door; it was locked. I knocked loudly.

"What." It was Buck Nekkid.

"I want to talk to you," I shouted.

The door opened. Buck had on a suit identical to the one Elvis Presley wore in *King Creole*. Slick motherfucker.

"What the hell—"

"Billy's book," I said, pushing past him into the room. "Hand it over."

"I don't know what you're talkin' about, Mister Manager." He smiled that same smile he had for Billy, but I wasn't buyin' it.

"The Billy Psych-Out Psyched-Out Encyclopedia of Rock 'n' Roll," I said. I stood squarely in front of him. "Where is it?" I wanted to knock that smile off his face. I remembered that song from *King Creole* about lookin' for trouble. At that moment I was totally prepared to kick the shit out of Buck Nekkid.

He dropped the smile. "Look, *pal*. I don't know what you're talkin' about. The only book I know is *The Buck Nekkid Unbelievable Book of Rock*." He bent over the light-bulbed mirror, smoothed back his patented ducktail. "Now, why don't you just go on out there and enjoy the music."

I couldn't believe it. He must have seen my shocked expression in the mirror. The smile was back, like a barracuda's.

Outside, I heard the Psychobillies rockin' to Joe Clay's "Cracker Jack" at maximum volume.

"You—you think you can steal his *book?*" I said, stunned. Was he really that stupid? I don't know what I'd thought when I knocked on that door, but I doubt it was this. Maybe the public believed the down-home country act, particularly now that there was an MTV video to back it up, but he was a hell of an operator. "You don't think you can actually—"

"I don't think. I *know.* Billy told me there was only one person who knew he wrote it. That's you."

Smart move, Billy.

"You can say what you want, but I have the only copy of Billy's book in existence. And don't bother lookin' for it. It's in the Starlite's safe. I plan to debut *The Buck Nekkid Unbelievable Book of Rock* tonight. Now, if you'll excuse me—" The metal toe caps clinked on his eight-hundred-dollar cowboy boots as he sidestepped me. "I have a show to get ready for."

I let him have it. He went down like a sack of fertilizer. He stared up at me in shock from the floor. Blood poured out of his nose. I felt like kicking it in for him. "When Billy hears about this—" I said between my teeth.

"Billy already heard."

Billy was calm, calmer than I'd ever seen him, and that scared me. I hadn't realized the set had ended. Billy must have come lookin' for one or both of us and stopped when he heard what had happened. He'd been standin' behind the door.

"Billy." I took his arm, tried to back him out the door, but he was immobile. His fists clenched and unclenched at his sides.

"Let's go," I said. "We'll get your book back. This shit stain isn't worth it."

"It was a joke," Buck growled. The blood rolled off his nose and plopped onto the floor. "You can tell your manager friend here I plan to press charges."

Billy stared at him in silence. His eyes were steady, penetrating. Finally he said in a tone that was dead of emotion: "The only thing you'll be pressin' is your ass to the floor, you miserable piece of shit."

Buck looked back and forth between me and Billy, and I

The Sad Story of Billy Psych-Out

don't think he liked what he saw. He backed up on the floor like a caterpillar.

"I'm goin' for a drive," Billy said. "Tell the boys I won't be back for a while."

I nodded. I'd never seen him like this—the lackluster eyes, the dead tone. Billy walked out the door. Just walked out. I never saw him alive again.

People speculate about the Billy Psych-Out Crash-Up, as it came to be known in the months to come. He drove the Thunderbird off a ten-foot embankment and into a tree. He was instantly incinerated; the fireball blasted into the black Dakota night. The police report said it was an accident.

Kids started buying up the Psychobillies' records like never before. Billy's *Psyched-Out Encyclopedia* became a best-seller, and there's even talk of a movie starring Christian Slater as Billy Psych-Out. People lost interest in Buck Nekkid and the Starkers, fuckin' flash in the pan that they were.

But Billy's book, well—it shone on, just like Billy did that night. I took plenty of close-up pictures of the burnt-out Thunderbird. Buddy Holly was on the tape deck when he died—take that any way you like.

Some of you probably think I'm exploiting Billy's death, and maybe I am. But the more people know about Billy, the more they'll understand him, the more they'll realize that when the truth dies, everything else dies with it. I said that on page one of my introduction to Billy's book.

So the next time you play one of Billy's hits—"Itchy Baby," maybe, or "Red-Hot Lovin' to You"—think about him. Think hard, and maybe you'll get a tear in your eye like I do. It's the details that make it real.

Billy would have wanted that.

For Alan Wayne

ELVIS CAN'T DANCE

Robert Weinberg and Tina L. Jens

Gnashing his teeth, Elvis pushed open the lid of his coffin and sat up. Angrily, he reached over and shut off the nearby radio, cutting off the song in midplay. There was a limit even to what the dead could stand. And that crap was two steps over the line.

Eyes that didn't blink surveyed the mausoleum. At least they had followed the instructions of his secret will to the letter. Much as he'd wanted to be buried at Graceland, the thought of grave-robbers digging up his body and holding it for ransom had been too much for him. That was the reason for this special, secret tomb on the other side of Memphis. Here he could rest in peace, undisturbed for all eternity. And, because even in death he wanted to keep an ear on rock and roll, he had specified that a radio tuned to a top-twenty rock station be left playing in the crypt.

He climbed shakily out of the pink, gold-trimmed coffin. It was nicely put together, though there were no racing stripes on the sides as he had requested. It hardly mattered. He had been a pretty easygoing guy in life as well as in death.

Being the King meant putting up with a lot. There had been those incredibly bad covers of some of his greatest hits. Not to mention Presley classics slowed down as ballads, sung by British rockers with Mersey accents, or done as disco soundtracks. None of it had bothered him.

Dimly he remembered laughing at some of them while he was alive. Just dimly, though. He had been dead so long that his brain didn't work that well anymore. His memory wasn't the best anyway, considering all those damned pills he had been taking right before his death. The pills that finally killed him.

Then there had been the impersonators. Hundreds of them, thousands of them now, if the radio could be believed. Young men and old, white and black, even Asian and Latino, dressing like him, acting like him, trying to sing like him. Calling their acts "Tributes to Elvis" and things like that. Personally, he felt that anyone with a decent voice should be trying to make a career on his own instead of living off the King's image. Even though he'd never written any of his own songs, "I always did them My Way," he croaked, testing out his long-dormant vocal cords.

What the impersonators did with their lives was fine by him. They were, after all, his fans, and they had treated his songs with more reverence than he had toward the end.

He could even tolerate the commercials using his songs to sell cars and candy bars and power tools. And the velvet paintings of him that they sold at flea markets. Not to mention the latest indignity, the post office vote on the fat or skinny Elvis stamp.

He blanched at the thought of the week-long movie marathons on TBS, wondering how anyone could sit through some of those turkeys. He accepted it all as part of the legend of the King of rock and roll. Besides, being dead, he didn't care much. Still, he did have a legacy to protect, and this new group had pushed him too far.

According to the disc jockey, the group called itself K.I.D.

Stupid!, which stood for "the King Is Dead, Stupid!" It was a rap group.

Elvis hated rap. Everyone had a right to his own kind of music, but rap wasn't rock and roll. And it didn't belong on top-twenty stations. He was sorry now that he hadn't requested that the radio in his tomb be set to an oldies station. But there hadn't been such outlets when he was alive, and any dial spinning now would surely be noticed by the caretaker.

There were enough stories about him in the tabloids without him providing new material. He trusted the groundskeeper, but big money meant big temptation. Just look at all those miserable biographies by his suck-up friends. He was just glad he'd never revealed to any of them his secret will.

At times it seemed that everyone he'd ever met had written a book about him. There was a virtual library of Elvis books. And they kept on coming. Like that really gruesome account of his death and autopsy published recently. Damned thing had been grisly enough to kill him a second time.

He shook his head, trying to clear the cobwebs. Nobody had any respect for the dead these days. Not like when he was a kid and you showed proper reverence for the dearly departed. If he had been capable of crying, a tear would have trickled down his cheek. But there was no time for crying in the chapel.

New York City was home to K.I.D. Stupid! The disc jockey had mentioned that they were playing a concert in Madison Square Garden a few days from now. Elvis sighed heavily, though his lungs no longer needed air. He remembered playing the Garden on his comeback tour. It seemed *sacrilegious* having rap there, especially rap by K.I.D. Stupid! mocking his music. Elvis knew it was his sacred duty to make sure that didn't happen.

Stiffly, he walked to the door of the tomb. As per his final wishes, the door could be opened from the inside as well as out. He had always worried about being buried alive.

Unfortunately, that had turned out to be the least of his problems.

He usually woke up three or four times a decade. When he did, he'd sneak out of the tomb and head across the street to the Gas and Go Mart.

A quick karate chop got him inside, even though it broke a bone or two. He hit the frozen food cases first, popping a cheeseburger and a chili burrito into the counter microwave. He couldn't eat food anymore—his teeth were too loose and his digestive tract didn't work. But he still liked to smell it.

Next, he cleaned out the cash register. Then he shuffled down the aisle, opening and sniffing candy bars, bags of chips, and cans of Pepsi. His senses satisfied, he cleared out before the police arrived.

Afterward he headed to the Saulmon and Daughter Bookstore. Another karate kick got him in. He stopped first at the magazine rack, grabbing anything with his name or alleged picture on the cover. He was amazed that with all the fake photos the tabloids ran, no one ever caught him on his midnight excursions.

Grabbing a handful of comic books, he moved on to the entertainment and biography section for the new books featuring him. Guarding his legacy required that he stay current with everything written about him. Then he browsed through the nonfiction and history aisles.

His shopping spree always ended in the same place. Over the years, the section had borne the labels "Philosophy," "Religious Studies," "Metaphysics," and, most recently, "New Age." He laughed at the latest label. "New Age" implied that the truths had just been discovered. Many of the books were hundreds of years old.

He'd been into this stuff since the early sixties. In death, it was more relevant to him than ever. For the hundredth time, he wondered why his spirit still remained on earth. No book had an answer to that one.

At the end of each visit, he bagged his selections and paid for them with the money taken from the convenience store.

He could justify taking the cash from the Gas and Go Mart, with what they charged for gas and cheeseburgers, but Mr. Saulmon had been a friend. He'd special-ordered the religion books for Elvis and kept quiet about it when word that the King was into Eastern mysticism would have ruined his career. Heck, it had been a closely guarded secret that Elvis knew how to read. Being a bookworm didn't fit the public image the Colonel had created.

But there was no time for a book run tonight. Carefully, he turned the inner handle of the tomb door and peered out into the darkness. No one was around. The King smiled, his dry, mummified lips crackling like peanut brittle. Tonight he was after that big old pink Cadillac stored in the garage about a mile away. He was the only one who knew of its existence.

Back in his paranoid days, he'd stashed cars with a ready supply of cash all over town. They stayed gassed and ready to go in case he needed to make a quick getaway. Over the years, he had sold or given away most of them, but a few remained. One was all he needed to make it to New York.

At the garage door, he spun the dial on the combination lock, working the rust out of the mechanism. His fingers were creaky from disuse and he fumbled with the lock, trying to hurry. The overhead streetlight made him all too conspicuous to passing traffic. Finally, the lock popped open. His memory wasn't great, but the combination took no thought. It was Priscilla's phone number when she was in Germany.

He pulled the dustcover off the car and climbed in. The keys and cash were undisturbed in the glove compartment. Holding an unneeded breath, he turned the ignition key and held it as the engine turned over, started, and coughed. Nodding with satisfaction, he gunned the motor, checked his mirrors, and backed the pink monster onto the street.

Elvis headed toward North Main. It wasn't the fastest way to get to the interstate, but he was feeling nostalgic. He wanted to cruise past the old Sun Records Studio—"the chicken shack with the Cadillacs out back"—where it had all begun.

Once he hit I-40, he settled in for some serious driving. He had 1,100 miles to cover and sunrise wasn't far off. The King was on his way to New York to take a bite out of the Big Apple.

Percussion and a bass drove the rap beat.

". . . Love me tender and love me true
The Hound Dog's dead so don't be blue
Whiteys can't dance, you know it's so
So they stoled our music and copped our dough.

"The King is dead, make no mistake
Cry no tears for the white, fat fake
He stoled our music, and that's a fact
But we're K.I.D. Stupid! and we're takin' it back."

"You're listening to WRAP radio and that was the title track off K.I.D. Stupid!'s debut album, *Elvis Can't Dance (Cause He's Dead)*. It's just two nights till their big concert in Madison Square Garden. We're here in the studio with two of the members of the band. Say hello to DoJo, the lead rapper, and Reemy, who handles the sampling tapes.

"DoJo, I don't think there's anyone in the country who doesn't know that K.I.D. Stupid! stands for 'the King Is Dead, Stupid!' But can you tell us how you came up with that name?"

"Since the day the slavers put our African brothers in chains and shoved them onto the ships, the white man has hated and feared us. They broke up our families, tried to keep us down by denying us an education—"

"And they're still doin' it now," interrupted Reemy, "with the big-city slums and inner-city schools. And that's a fact!"

DoJo continued, "They tried to strip away our culture.

Look at the music, dance, and fashions of any decade. It's a rip-off from us. Any music you want to listen to—gospel, blues, rock, or rap. . . ."

"Elvis, he was the worst—a white boy who wanted to be tan." This was Reemy again. "He never had an original thought in his life. Just stoled black songs, sang black, danced black, and declared himself King of Rock and Roll."

The DJ protested, "Don't you give him credit for being the first white man brave enough to integrate rock and roll?"

"Brave, shit! He was poor white trash that had nothin' to lose. He—"

With a snarl of disgust, Elvis punched the radio button. He preferred static to the garbage DoJo was spouting. "Son, I never stole nothing in my life," he muttered, "'cept for a few dollars from a certain convenience mart."

He vowed to pay that money back when he returned to Memphis. Assuming he hadn't used up all the funds in the glove box.

It was true that he had listened to and admired the musicians on the black radio stations when he was young. And he had incorporated gospel sounds into his music. He'd been singing that music with his mama and daddy in the church choir when he was two.

But he'd also created a sound never before heard on any radio station or sung by any choir. It was a sound only in his head—the animal in him. It was the animal that made him growl and purr, bump and grind, turn soulful ballads into the hot, sultry music that thrilled the teenagers and frightened the parents. And gave rise to his self-chosen nickname, "Crazy."

Turning the radio on again, he searched for a gospel station. Though he had recorded only four gospel albums during his career, it had been his music of choice when he and his friends gathered around the piano. It seemed to tame the animal in his soul.

He wondered again why he was still on earth. In private, he had turned away from organized Christianity, though he still believed in a supreme being, heaven and hell. However, sixteen years after his death, his spirit hadn't gone anywhere. Unknown, nameless chains held him captive.

The first signs of daylight were streaking across the sky. It was time to hunt for cover. He had always been a night person, traveling after dark and sleeping by day. Even at home he had stuck to his nocturnal schedule.

For a few short months during one of his many dieting and shape-up regimes, Priscilla had lured him out into the sun to ride horses and hold group karate lessons in the yard. But then Priscilla had taken off with the karate instructor. Elvis had banned the sport from his house and returned to his late-night hours.

"We'll have to charge you for a full night, Mister, uh, Crazy. It's house policy. If you're in a band, how come I never heard of the Blue Moon Boys?"

"It's like this, honey. We've been out of circulation for a while, but we're making a comeback."

Quite a while. It had been almost forty years since he'd done the Memphis club circuit with Scotty and Bill, trying to find his sound.

"So I guess you have to stay in your stage makeup whenever you're out in public, huh?"

The King kept quiet. He was glad his appearance didn't scare the girl. He'd sure frightened himself when he first looked in the rearview mirror. The desk clerk was a pretty young thing, the type he'd always liked. She couldn't be any more than eighteen, with long blond hair pulled back in a ponytail. And she hadn't cussed once.

In his better days, he might have made a move on her. Now, five minutes in his room and she'd discover that he wasn't wearing any stage makeup.

"Could you send me up a ham and cheese omelet fried in bacon grease, a peanut butter and banana sandwich with mayo, a bag of chips, a pot of coffee, a chocolate malt, and a hot fudge sundae," he said, figuring he owed himself one sort of treat if denied another. "And a box of aluminum foil."

The clerk looked at him oddly. "Aluminum foil? You planning to wrap up the leftovers?"

"Shoot, darlin'," the King drawled, "the foil is for the windows. I like it dark, real dark, when ah sleep."

Driving all through the night again, Elvis made it to New Jersey in plenty of time to make a necessary stop on one of the back streets of Newark. Even after hearing story after story on the radio, he was amazed at how easy it was to purchase drugs. Not that the hard-core addicts considered Dexedrine—speed—very dangerous. On the road, he had formulated a plan for his encounter with K.I.D. Stupid! Another stop in New York would provide his costume. The only other requirement, an automatic and plenty of ammo, came from beneath the front seat of his car. All his life, he'd believed in being prepared for emergencies.

He spent the daytime in a small motel outside of Newark. The sun was touching the horizon as he steered his car onto the Jersey Turnpike. He'd gotten an early start. The concert was a few hours off, and he had another store to visit.

Cruising through the Lincoln Tunnel, he debated for the last time whether he was doing the right thing. Some folks would say he was doing wrong, practicing censorship of the worst kind. But the King knew he had to stop K.I.D. Stupid!

If they were sampling his songs for some pop dance number, he could overlook it. Instead, they were using his music and his voice on "All Pigs Must Die" and "One Bag of Crack for Sale." Those songs advocated the murder of lawmen and the sale of illegal drugs.

During another radio interview, DoJo stated that "the harassment of blacks by the police and other government agencies made the sale of drugs the only economically *viable* career choice available to people of color."

Tell that to the black lawmen, the King thought angrily. Elvis had been named an honorary deputy by police and sheriff's departments all over the country. President Nixon had even made him an honorary narcotics agent. And President Carter had appointed him as special advisor on the youth of America. The King knew his critics laughed at that, but he took those honors and responsibilities seriously. Very seriously. Even after death.

He knew his critics called him a drug abuser and pill popper. But every one of his pills had been prescribed. He shrugged. He had paid the price for his mistakes. And the members of K.I.D. Stupid! were going to pay the price for theirs.

He cruised through the theater district looking for the right store. Elvis had been avoiding mirrors—his vanity hadn't deteriorated at the same rate as his body—but he knew he looked pretty bad. The clerk at the motel last night had made that clear, especially when a hunk of rotten flesh had dropped off his arm as he was registering. Double the price of the room, in cash, had paid for the man's silence. But bluffing his way into the Garden wouldn't be so easy, looking the way he did.

It didn't take long to find the shop. It was only a few doors wide, but eight stories high. "The Show Must Go On!" read the sign in the window. "Period Costumes: Prehistoric to 25th Century. Flats, Risers, Backdrops, and Props. Everything You Need for Any Show on Earth!"

Elvis had known from his earliest days in Memphis that he was destined to leave his mark on American pop culture, so he was sure the store would have an Elvis costume. He assumed it would be the studded white jumpsuit from his Aloha concert, broadcast live worldwide via satellite. He'd turned to the caped jumpsuits when he could no longer get his weight down for tours. He'd gotten the idea from his comic book hero, Captain Marvel.

He was not prepared to discover that he had an entire section in the store's dead rock star department. It looked like they had a copy of his entire life's wardrobe on the rack. There were white capes and gold lamé, as well as the leathers from his comeback TV special. (Elvis figured he was the only singer in the world who had made more comebacks than Bob Dylan.) There were silk scarves, karate suits, country-western fringed shirts, even the army uniform complete with dog tags and stripes. And all with appropriate wigs to match.

Burrowing in the racks, he came upon an unexpected treasure. His face broke into a childish grin, the skin at the corners of his mouth cracking alarmingly. Pink-striped black pants, pink shirt, and drape-shaped pink sports coat, the outfit dated back to his truck-driving days. Wearing it would put him in the proper mood for tonight's festivities.

His last stop was the makeup counter.

"'Scuse me, missy. Y'all got anything to cover up a skin condition?"

The clerk had her back to him, and started to answer before she turned around. "What's the condition, si-iiir!"

"Well, lack of it, mostly," Elvis told her.

"I think you want," she whispered, avoiding looking at his nearly fleshless face, "a heavy, *heavy* pancake."

Fighting to maintain a professional attitude, she piled together a stack of water-based cake makeup, blush, eyebrow pencil, eyeliner and shadow, and hair dye. "Will there be anything else?"

She gulped as part of his lip peeled away and dropped to the counter. They both stared at it for a moment.

"Sugar," asked Elvis, "you got anything for chapped lips?"

Three hundred-dollar bills had gotten him past a security clearance, plus a glimpse of the evening's schedule. K.I.D. Stupid! should be taking the stage right about now. Which suited the King fine. Heading for the washroom to change, he could hear the rappers launch into their first song.

Stripping off his tattered shirt, he dropped it into the trash. He turned on the water in the sink and ducked his head under the faucet, not waiting for it to warm up. Anxious to finish, he squirted some soap into his hair and worked it in. A whole clump pulled loose when he tugged at a tangle. He reckoned he'd better be a little more careful. Rinsing out the soap, he applied the black dye.

Elvis Can't Dance

Black foam, strands of hair, and bits of skin clogged the drain, causing the water to form an inky cloud in the sink. As Elvis watched, the mixture swirled into the distinct image of a smoking gun. A feeling of relief swept through him. A strong believer in visions, he'd often seen angels and demons in his dreams when he was alive. He felt sure this latest sign came directly from above.

After changing his clothes, he applied his makeup. Ready for action, Elvis bowed his head in prayer. Lifting his folded hands to touch his forehead, he intoned, "Send me some light—I need it bad."

He'd said the same prayer before every concert, as long as he could remember. It was a habit he wouldn't break now.

K.I.D. Stupid! concluded its third number as Elvis walked up the underground ramp behind the stage. In a clear attempt to control the crowd, the stage was raised ten feet off the auditorium floor. The rappers hated police of any type, and this arrangement enabled them to perform without any security guards onstage. There was only one officer patrolling the tunnel. He was leaning on an old photo machine, watching the show. The King strolled up behind him.

"Pardon me, friend," said Elvis, tapping the man on the shoulder. "You got change for a fifty?"

Startled, the guard turned. Catching sight of the King close up, the man's eyes widened to the size of saucers. Silently, he collapsed to the floor in a dead faint.

"Nice," commented Elvis, and ran his fingers through the guard's pockets. Fishing out four quarters, he slipped the man a fifty in exchange.

Depositing the money, the King hurried into the booth and mugged for the camera. A few minutes later he nodded his approval. Not having an envelope, he removed a pen from the unconscious guard's pocket and wrote on the back of the strip, "Please send to the *National Enquirer.*" Then he wrapped the man's hand carefully around the pictures. He wondered what type of story the paper would come up with to explain these.

K.I.D. Stupid! had just finished a song when Elvis climbed onto the rear of the stage. DoJo spouted propaganda after each number, and the King figured the rapper would follow the same routine throughout the night. It was time for him to make his move.

The band was set up in typical formation. DoJo stood front and center, with his drummer slightly behind and to the right. Lead guitar was front far left; bass player, front far right. Reemy was farther back, behind his table full of turntables and tape equipment ready to play recordings of other people's music instead of making some of his own. While DoJo rambled, the other band members crowded around Reemy, passing around a bottle of scotch.

A recording of Elvis singing "Bossa Nova Baby" swelled beneath DoJo's monologue. The King had never been fond of that song, despite the fact that it had been a top-ten hit. In a moment's reflection, Elvis decided he had made the same mistake with managers as with doctors. He'd never sought a second opinion. When the Colonel declared rock and roll dead and ordered Elvis to record more middle-of-the-road stuff, the King had done it. But he often wondered what would have happened if he had told the Colonel to find a different carnival and played the music he wanted.

As the King strode across the stage, "Bossa Nova Baby" faded into "All Shook Up." It wasn't his best, but Elvis liked it better. DoJo spotted him just as he reached the bass player's mike.

"Who the fuck do you think you are?" DoJo screamed.

Elvis grabbed the mike, stand and all, and swung it around. Southern pride welling up inside him, he drawled, "Wel-l-l-l, son, ahm El-vis."

Startled, DoJo looked around for help. But, strictly following the rap star's orders, there wasn't a policeman in sight.

"You boys been pickin' mah music to pieces," Elvis said, grinning the fleshless smile of the long dead. "Now ahm here to do a little sampling of mah own."

Screaming obscenities, the bass player rushed forward,

eager to regain control of his position. Dropping the mike, Elvis bent at his knees and brought his arms up in karate stance. The musician, his instrument still slung around his neck, charged closer. If he managed to get his hands on the King's brittle limbs, it would be all over.

The King waited motionless until his target was in range. Pivoting a quarter turn, Elvis bent at the waist and kicked his heel into the punk's nose. Cartilage slammed into the musician's brain, killing him instantly. Elvis felt a thrill of satisfaction, recalling innumerable karate kicks performed in his stage act during his "middle years." All of that practice had finally paid off.

Not understanding what was happening, the drummer ran to his friend's aid. Elvis saw him coming. Reaching down, he pulled the bass free of the corpse. Holding the guitar like a Louisville Slugger, the King swung for the cheap seats. The bass connected solidly with the drummer's head. The crack of his neck snapping was louder than a home run.

The lead guitarist almost got him, but the King's luck held true. The musician tripped over the bodies of his bandmates. He dropped to his hands and knees. Instantly, Elvis straddled him. With a sureness of movement dating back to his Las Vegas days, he whipped the pink silk scarf from around his neck and looped it over the guitar player's. The King gave it a quick twist and watched the jerk's face turn blue. It only took a few seconds for him to die.

Elvis spotted Reemy cowering behind his table full of equipment. Reaching the tape setup in three strides, the King hauled the rapper across the table. Grabbing him by the hair, Elvis pulled Reemy's head back. Digging into his pocket, Elvis pulled out a handful of pills and forced them down the runt's throat. A second dose, just for good measure, followed.

The first convulsion hit Reemy as he collapsed to the floor. He gurgled once as the speed lit up his system. Remembering the rapper's comments on drug dealing, Elvis considered the boy's death poetic justice.

DoJo had almost made it to the wings, screaming for the police. Elvis stopped a few feet away beside the nearest mike stand. Calmly, the King pulled the microphone out of its clamp.

"Turn around, son. Ah don't like to kill a man when his back's turned."

The rapper stopped screaming and swung around, his face crowned with disbelief. With slow, deliberate movements the King dropped the microphone and picked up the stand, then abruptly rushed his nemesis. Thrusting savagely, he impaled DoJo through the stomach with the pole of the mike stand.

There was no time to savor the moment. Security guards were climbing onto the stage. Reaching into his pocket, Elvis pulled out his automatic. Then hesitated, realizing he was about to fire on policemen.

He had been forced to kill K.I.D. Stupid! They had been corrupting the youth of America—encouraging them to use drugs, sell narcotics, and kill lawmen. And they had been using his songs to do it. Standing there, Elvis wondered if maybe the ones who bought the music, made the rappers famous, weren't equally to blame. Turning, he aimed his gun at the crowd.

It was then that he heard the faint strains of a gospel hymn. For a second, the King thought one of Reemy's tape recorders was playing. But where were those colored lights coming from? Time froze, and he saw his mother.

"Mama?"

She was walking down a golden stairway. His mama, young and beautiful and thin, just like she'd always wanted to be. The one woman he'd worshiped all his life. And with her was a young man in a pure white suit, looking like Elvis had back when he was young and handsome.

"Elvis, it's time to come home, son."

"Who's that with you, Mama?"

"It's Jesse, son," said his mother. The twin who had died at birth. "I've been waiting a long time to introduce you to your twin brother."

Elvis Can't Dance

Elvis looked at his body in shame. The pink suit hid the splintered bones and withered flesh. But he knew they were there.

"I can't come looking like this, Mama," he mumbled. "Besides, I've been stuck here for sixteen years. Heaven don't want me."

"That's 'cause you're stubborn as a mule," said his mother. "You got to stop holding on, son. Forget about that horrible Colonel, and protecting your legend. Let go of the fame. Stop fussing and fuming about how you're going to be remembered and let it go."

"Come on, El," said Jesse. "Pa's waiting."

Elvis suddenly felt himself rising into the air. But there was a weight holding him down. The gun. He dropped it to the stage. And floated up toward the light.

Madison Square Garden was filled with the gentle strains of "How Great Thou Art." And Elvis was singing lead.

A few days later the new issue of the *National Enquirer* hit the stands, headlines screaming.

Massacre at the Garden!
The King Returns!
Elvis Raptured: Ascends Stairway to Heaven!
see photos page 5

But, of course, that version of the story was not reported by any other paper.

BETTER TO BURN OUT

Scott H. Urban

Are you ready? Are you pumped?"

Jack had Barry by the shoulders. The members of both bands encircled them. "You come onstage and do 'Not Coming Home Tonight' with us for the encore. My guys are so excited, they're about to piss their pants. Closing a tour with guitar god Barry McDevitt. I dropped some hints to the press boys, so they'll be expecting something special. It'll be like old times. The Poison Pair, performing together again. Shit, we'll bring down the house."

And for a moment, it really did feel the way it had eleven years ago, when Jack "Hammer" Jenkins and Barry McDevitt had fronted Dynamo, the hardest-rockin' party band in the world.

It almost made Barry forget what he longed to say: *I wanna take my Fender, swing it into your wide fuckin' jaw, and scatter your pearly-whites like marbles across the floor.*

Better to Burn Out

What he said instead was, "Yeah, sure. It'll be great."

Jack had already turned away, cocking his ear toward the stage. Phoenix Rising's recorded musical prologue—an orchestral fanfare that slowly swelled to a crescendo—rumbled through the coliseum, making even the backstage walls shudder. The crowd, realizing the show was only minutes away, roared its approval.

"Listen to 'em!" Jack was grinning like an alky discovering an overlooked bottle of rum. "The closer it gets to showtime, the louder they scream. It's like riding a woman. You start nice and slow and easy. Then it builds up. You get that allover itch. You wanna keep it slow, but you have to go faster. You just can't help it. You're buckin' like a bronco. And then you're there, riding the edge, and man, it's coming, coming . . ." Jack wriggled his eyebrows like a pervert on the prowl, and the musicians howled with laughter. "The show's like that. Two and a half hours of nonstop orgasm. Shit, it's better than screwin'."

"I'm taking a leak," Barry told his band. He slipped into the bathroom and shut the door, thinking, I can't do this, I can't do this without some backup. He dug the vial and the spoon out of his pocket and snorted some Colombian courage. After that, it still wasn't all right, but at least it was something he could handle.

Jack and the rest of Dangerous Curves had gone back to their dressing room. Freez Cochrane, Phoenix Rising's lead singer, took Barry by the arm. He leaned in close, whispering huskily, "Hey, man, are you okay?"

Barry nodded. "I'm cool, I'm cool."

"We were looking for you, right before Jack came in." He couldn't keep the concern out of his voice. "Where were you?"

Barry waved his hand, a signal his friend knew meant, *Later, we'll talk about it later*. "Awright!" Barry shouted. "C'mere!" The four members of the band huddled together, their arms around each other's shoulders. They bobbed their heads once, twice, three times, each time shouting, loud, louder, *louder,* a trio of primal screams that got the blood racing, the adrenaline pumping, and their hands ready to play. . . .

Then the intro reached its climax, a resonating chord that seemed to hold forever, and they were running for the stage, and Barry's guitar was somehow in his hands, and the flashpots exploded, *lights, sound, smoke,* and they were rockin' the coliseum with their opening anthem, "Waking the Dead." The crowd surged to its feet, pumped its fists in the air; a collective animal ready to forget the world outside, ready to be blown out of its seat.

It was the last night of the American leg of their tour, Phoenix Rising and Dangerous Curves on a double bill that had swung them north, through Seattle, Detroit, Cleveland, and Jersey, then south and west, playing Miami, Nashville, Houston, and finally here, California's Midlands Coliseum. It was a sellout. Everyone wanted to see Jack "Hammer" Jenkins and Dangerous Curves perform live the song that had just reached number one on the charts, "Freedom in Your Eyes."

Barry could still remember promoter Randy "The Ringleader" Friedman pitching the tour to him: "Look, it's a natural. You and Jack *were* Dynamo. Tons of people will come just to see you on the same bill. Plus, you both have great new bands. Dangerous Curves has the hottest single in the nation right now. They're even talking about using it in a new Pepsi ad campaign. And the press loves Jack, I tell ya. If we got a shot of him wiping his ass, we could have it plastered on the cover of every magazine in an hour."

"I want top billing," Barry had insisted. "Dangerous Curves opens for us."

Randy had frowned, looked away. "I don't think it's gonna work that way, Mickey-Dee. Right now, Dangerous Curves is getting the airplay. They've got the hot single. Hell, I think your CD is great—it's just not selling like we thought it would." Randy had rapped the top of his desk with his forefinger—a gesture that made Barry want to grab the finger and bend it back toward Randy's wrist until it snapped. "If you open for Jack, you could move a lot of units. We're talking platinum by August."

Barry had tried to talk the boys into saying no, but he had been outvoted.

Now Barry swaggered to the front of the stage as he began his solo. He had studied the techniques of the best. He had borrowed influences from all musical genres, including reggae, funk, jazz, and blues. He had blended them all together in a style that was uniquely his own. He could do much more than play the Fender—he could damn near make it talk.

The audience—"the million-headed monster," Jack had once called it—cheered him on.

God, I hate you. I hate you all. It wasn't until this very moment that I realized how much I hate you. Barry let the fans see none of this. He smiled, high-fived the headbangers in front, and kept playing. *You'll love me for ten minutes, but no longer. Then you'll have to have the star, you'll have to have the hit. Once, my music was all for you. But not tonight. This show is just for* me.

The lights blacked out at the end of the first number. The audience screamed even louder in the darkness. Barry knew guys would be groping their girls—and feeling up females who *weren't* their girls. Floor lights illuminated each musician from underneath as, one by one, they came in on the next number, "Let Me Be Your Grave." Paul Kroger pounded out an ominous, moody beat. Rudy Evans filled it with his bone-crunching bass line. Barry began a wailing intro that was guaranteed to lower the temperature even in the close-packed arena. Finally Freez started singing, his raspy voice growling a song of love and Thanatos. But already Barry could feel the crowd shifting, getting restless.

Damn you, what more do you want? Barry didn't know who or what he was addressing. It might have been the crowd, it might have been the music, it might have been rock and roll itself. *I gave you everything I ever had. And when I had nothing left, I went scrounging for more to offer you.*

He had left home at fourteen. Mom and Dad? They could

offer nothing that would advance him in rock circles, so they might as well never have existed. Dropped out of high school—only now was he beginning to catch up on the reading he had missed. Took any penny-scrimping job he could to save money for that first no-name guitar and amp. It didn't matter what the task was—dishwashing, road construction, building demolition. During the worst times, he had even sold himself to bored middle-management executives, but he didn't think about those days very often. All of it, for what? So that he could spend his spare minutes with the neck in his hands, his callused fingertips against the strings, learning the chords, copying songs off the radio, badgering anyone with the slightest amount of musical talent to teach him whatever they could.

Phoenix Rising was *on*. They were scorching. They were tearing up the stage. Barry knew it, the boys knew it, the roadies knew it. But only four songs into their ten-song set, Barry could already hear whole segments of the crowd shouting, "Dee-Cee! Dee-Cee!" They wanted Jack and the hit single. They didn't care about skill, about proficiency— they didn't care about *music*.

Years ago Barry had been playing with a band called Solar Flexus for five months when the original lead singer returned to Massachusetts (a good move all around, he had always thought) and Jack Jenkins came aboard to man the mike. They were standoffish to each other at first. It took an all-night drinking session, during which they spilled their guts (literally and in the conversational sense) to each other, for them to become friends. But when they did, their ideas, dreams, and goals seemed to mesh so perfectly that they speculated they had been brothers in the womb, separated at birth. Realizing they could never accomplish what they wanted with Solar Flexus, they struck out on their own, auditioned friends, and started Dynamo.

Damn, thought Barry as he soared through one of his showcase solos, how many years ago was all that? Seventeen? Shit, can it be that long?

Dynamo played the club circuit, initially building its

reputation on solid, almost-as-good-as-the-original covers of Aerosmith, Bad Company, and Led Zeppelin. At the same time, Barry and Jack were writing songs they would skillfully weave into their set—almost imperceptibly, so that no one would realize they weren't listening to a forgotten classic by Steppenwolf or Uriah Heep. Almost to their disbelief, audiences liked their originals. A group, small at first but larger with each performance, started following them from club to club just to hear them play. Eventually Dynamo cut a single that received local airplay. After they won a local "Battle of the Bands" competition, an agent caught their act and signed them. Their first single made it into the top twenty and the album went gold.

Barry and Jack became known as the Poison Pair, and if the sobriquet was a rewording of Aerosmith's Toxic Twins, Steve Tyler and Joe Perry, what of it? The local press loved it, and loved them. Soon their outrageous after-dark antics made them partying legends. They tried to see how many groupies they could bring off before they shot their loads. They tried to see who could drink the most nauseating concoctions, sometimes made with liquids not meant to be ingested by humans.

They wrote songs that they were certain would be banned from the airwaves—only to watch those songs become megahits.

Their albums all went to the top. There was a time in the late seventies and early eighties when it seemed that every other song on the radio was a Dynamo tune. Their American tours consistently sold out, and fans loved them in Europe and Japan.

It shouldn't have been that easy.

It never is, Barry thought, it never is.

Barry was swinging his guitar around his head, and then their set was over. He ran toward the wings, saluting the die-hard rockers, the ones who had come to see them instead of Dangerous Curves. Even as they exited, roadies were hustling to tear down their equipment and put up the next stage. Dangerous Curves used elaborate effects in its show. They appeared on stage as if by magic. During the encore, smokepots went off around the arena's ceiling and a laser light show played above everyone's head.

In the dressing room, Barry swung his hair, still wet from the shower, back from his forehead. He held a tumbler of Gatorade in his right hand and picked at the buffet the arena had provided with his left. Paul and Rudy were somewhere, signing autographs, scoping chicks, or talking music. Freez, just out of the shower himself, came up behind the guitarist and slapped him on the back.

"Ah, man! Killer concert! Shit!"

Barry leaned back, smiled weakly. "Yeah, it was great."

A dark look passed over the singer's face. "Man, what the fuck is it?" He straddled a folding chair backward and sat beside Barry. "It's like you been out of it for days. I go looking for you, like right before the show tonight, and I can't find you until we're just about ready to go on. Where the fuck were you?"

Barry shrugged. "Checking the gear. Talking to the crew. Sometimes . . . sometimes I feel I can talk to them more easily than I can to . . . musicians." He looked up quickly, shot a comradely punch at Freez's shoulder. "Present company excluded. Course, you're a screamer, ain't ya? Don't really qualify."

Freez smiled feebly at the joke. "You were great tonight. I never heard you play like that before. Look, I know I'm only an ass-wipe in this business compared to you, but I'd like to think you could talk to me, you know, if you needed. Was it the kids screaming for Jack? Screw 'em. They wouldn't know talent if it came up to 'em in a dark alley and pissed on 'em. So what is it?"

Through the walls, they could hear Dangerous Curves begin its show with the abruptness of a lightning strike. The walls reverberated from the flashpots' concussion. Speakers, piled higher than two men atop each other, throbbed with high-intensity rock for the head-tossing, fist-pumping, hip-shaking crowd.

Barry's fingers turned the plastic cup in front of him,

Better to Burn Out

making wet, sticky circles on the table. "It's . . . it's . . ." He seemed to decide against whatever he'd initially planned to say. Instead he asked, "What do you think of our CD?"

Freez grinned. There was no wrong answer to this question. "Shiiiiit. Best thing to happen to rock since the guitar pick. I never thought I'd be in a band so hot!"

Barry nodded. "You're right; it is good. If it were you and the guys and some other guitarist, you might be looking at a 'forever album'—one of those albums people buy decade after decade, like the Beatles' *Sergeant Pepper* or Pink Floyd's *Dark Side of the Moon*. But with me . . . it's not . . ."

Freez rocked irritably in his seat. "Man, are you thinkin' about *those* days again? When you had to go in the rehab center and Dynamo broke up? You gotta let it go. The past is like shit—you gotta flush it down the toilet."

Barry picked up a slice of gray roast beef, tossed it back on the platter. "I can't help it. It's like a sore tooth—it hurts to touch it, but you can't leave it alone. I keep thinking about my solo record. The critics loved it, the record stores tossed it in the cutout bins. All followed by too much pointless session work, too much coke, too much gin. Then I had to watch Jack's solo album win a Grammy. . . .

"The stuff I'm doing now, with you and Phoenix Rising, is better than anything I've done before. But I'll always be remembered as the guitarist for Dynamo. And I'll always have to watch Jack's songs make number one, while mine . . ." He hung his head. "The day Dynamo broke up . . . should have been the last day of my life."

Freez started to reach out to Barry but pulled back when the guitarist took a piece of paper from his pants pocket. It was a sheet of notebook paper, now more gray than white, tattered from countless foldings and refoldings. Barry spread it open on the table and shoved it over to Freez, who scanned the lines with a frown on his face.

"What the fuck is *this?*" the singer sneered. "Some new song you wrote about an athlete dying young?"

Barry snorted a laugh. "No. It's a poem by A. E. Housman, a British poet. A lot of other people have echoed what he said. The Stones, Neil Young, Def Leppard. But he said it first: It's better to burn out—"

"Than fade like a song on a scratchy forty-five," Freez interposed. "Yeah, I know, I know."

A harsh glint that Freez had never before seen chilled Barry's eyes. "Listen to me. Get Jimmy to drive you back to the hotel. Catch some sleep."

"But I wanted to see you play with Jack—"

Barry's voice dropped to a gravelly snarl. *"Go."*

Freez opened his mouth to protest, then seemed to think better of it. He swung his leg over the back of the chair and left without another word.

Barry went to the edge of the stage, watching Jack from the wings. Although the band was mediocre at best, Jack *did* know how to work a crowd. He not only sang, he pranced, did acrobatics, climbed the equipment, whipped the audience into a frenzy. He made them shred their throats during the obligatory "shout-back": "Does anyone here like to— *PAAAAR-TEEEE?"* If, as he had said, playing to an audience was like fucking, Jack was a consummate lover, stroking the fans into a frenzy, making them skirt the thin line between pleasure and pain, building them up to a climax they would always remember.

"And now," he heard Jack announcing, "I wanna know . . . how many people here tonight . . . remember *Dynamo?*"

The crowd cheered uproariously. Barry knew better than to be impressed. Jack could have told them to kill their mothers and they all would have cheered.

"To close off tonight, I wanna welcome back the world's greatest guitarist—the other half of the Poison Pair—my friend—Barry McDevitt!"

The audience went wild. A spot followed him as he ran onstage, grabbed his Fender from a roadie, and slung the strap across his shoulder. He waved to the crowd.

Evening again, assholes. Back one last time.

Jack put his arm around Barry's shoulders, mugging for

the fans. "Do you think anybody remembers this one?" he shouted into the mike.

"Let's make it come true!" Barry responded, and then he was whirling away, grinding out the raucous opening to Dynamo's biggest hit, "Not Coming Home Tonight." It had defined their image as a good-time, party-hearty band and had spent eight weeks in the top ten. The coliseum vibrated with the force of the crowd's approval.

Gyrating like a hopped-up stripper, Jack launched into the lyrics. For just a second, it felt like the old days, and Barry almost changed his mind. *There's still time to stop it. You don't have to go through with it. Maybe our next CD will do better. . . .* But if he thought he would ever have to open for Jack or anyone else again . . .

No. Let what comes come.

Jack finished the second verse and the bridge, and then Barry was into his solo. He hadn't really practiced, hadn't needed to—playing "Not Coming Home Tonight" was, for him, the musical equivalent of riding a bike. It had been Dynamo's encore for years. He stretched the strings, bent the neck, nearly broke the whammy bar. For once on this tour, the fans were with him all the way, accepting him as part of Jack's entourage, shouting their praise and begging for more.

And that's the problem, isn't it? You'll only ever be second fiddle to Jack "Hammer" Jenkins.

He hit and held the last note. It began to degenerate into feedback. Someone on the control board hit the button that activated the smokepots around the arena's roof. They exploded—

And so did the packets of plastique Barry had added to each one just before the show.

The explosions drowned out even the band. Plaster and chunks of concrete began to rain down on the heads of those closest to the walls. People began to scream, their voices rising above the music and the groan of supporting girders inside the walls and ceiling. Some of the fans, realizing what was happening, began to surge toward the exits. They weren't going to make it: The sheer size of the crowd would keep it crammed in place.

Jack ran up to him, yelling, "What's happening? What the hell is going on?"

"Come on! Sing, damn it!" Barry didn't know if Jack could understand him or not; he could barely make out his own words. "This is the best encore you'll ever have! We're all gonna go together! We're gonna rock to death!"

Massive cracks spiderwebbed across the ceiling. The tortured creak of steel supporting more weight than it could hold echoed in the arena. Larger pieces of the roof began falling into the center sections. Barry saw one cone-shaped wedge crush a girl's skull with the accuracy of a smart bomb. She swayed upright for a second until a panicked bystander sent her toppling.

Jack stood gaping open-jawed at his former partner. Finally he said, "Shit, Barry, people are dying!" He tried to tug Barry offstage. "Come on! We gotta get outta here!"

Barry wouldn't budge, grinned at Jack instead. "We haven't finished the song! You got another verse to go!"

"You're—you're fuckin' . . ." Jack turned to run. Barry swung the Fender off his shoulder and drove its edge into Jack's right knee. The singer collapsed to the stage, howling and clutching at his leg, which now bent the wrong way.

He pulled the Fender back on. Turning to his audience, he watched terrified, scurrying people trample one another, the stronger crushing the weaker against the unyielding floor.

"Listen, Jack!" Barry cried. "Hear those screams? That's the best applause you'll ever hear!"

An overstressed catwalk came loose from its moorings and swung down like a giant's arm. It tore a swath through the crowd, leaving a smear of pulped flesh, blood, and organs that looked like something spilled from a food processor.

Dust and smoke began to obscure the scene. Music— clean, pure rock and roll—was coming to him, coming *through* him. He started playing again, even as jagged shards of masonry fell around him and the wailing, pleading singer.

Better to Burn Out

Jack was trying to pull himself into the wings with a crablike scuttle. Barry did a spinning jig, leaped through the air, and came down on Jack's crooked knee. The rocker arched over onto his back, his mouth going "oh-oh-oh," his eyelids fluttering on the edge of oblivion.

Barry knelt at his side, still strumming the closing notes of "Not Coming Home Tonight."

"We're gonna do it!" he screamed. "Just like you said, Jack! We're gonna bring down the house!"

SCREAM STRING

Edo van Belkom

The mute *twang* of an unamplified electric guitar string echoed softly off the brick walls of the empty stairwell. The sound was followed by two out-of-tune strums, then silence.

World-famous guitarist John Verrill, aka Johnny V, aka Johnny Violent, sat on the edge of a step stringing his burgundy 1969 Stratocaster. The concrete stairwell was cold and barren, the perfect place to spend a few solitary moments before the biggest gig of his life. Sure, plenty of bands had played the L.A. Coliseum before, but this concert was being televised worldwide. If things went according to plan, this one gig would make Johnny Violent and the Throbbing Purploids as popular as U2, the Rolling Stones, maybe even the Beatles.

He'd strung three new strings and was about to set the fourth when he heard the hard scrape of footsteps behind him. His eyes narrowed angrily as he turned around to see who the hell had the balls to bother him before a gig.

Scream String

It was his wife, Jill.

"There you are," she said flatly as she pulled her skirt tight to her knees and eased herself down onto the landing above him. "I've been looking for you for over an hour."

Jill was a slim woman, but not especially attractive. Now in her late thirties, she had been with Johnny from the very beginning. The years had not been kind to her. In the dim light of the stairwell, her eyes looked tired, cupped by large puffy bags and accentuated by crow's-feet that had been scored by time's sharpest knife.

"Well, you found me," John muttered as he stretched the fourth string over the nut and set it into the machine head.

Of course Jill would have to be the one to bother him, she was the only one who could get away with it. Besides being one of the best rock guitarists in the world, Johnny Violent was renowned for having a short fuse and an explosive temper. If it had been anyone other than Jill, they'd have been booking a flight home by now. Still, even though she could, Jill was the last person he'd expect to bother him before a gig. She knew better than anyone that he needed his time alone.

He'd been sneaking off before gigs since the early years when he played downtown dives like El Mocambo and Nag's Head North for beer and pocket change. He'd find some secluded spot and claim it as his temporary inner sanctum. Once there, he'd tune or restring his guitar, write a song, smoke a joint, or just be alone with his thoughts. Now that the band had recorded six double-platinum CDs, it was more important than ever that he have time alone to prepare himself before a concert.

John looked up at Jill but avoided making eye contact. "What do you want?" he said, his voice edged with anger over being disturbed.

"I'm sorry to bother you"—she made a halfhearted attempt at a smile—"but I need to talk."

"Can't it wait?"

"No, Johnny. It can't."

"All right," John said, doing his best to keep himself from

telling her to *fuck off*. He pulled the fifth string from the packet on the step by his knee and let the thin steel wire coil snakelike around his fisted hand. "What's on your mind?"

"Tomorrow night's show in Seattle."

They were flying up the coast after tonight's show to play a cruddy little concert hall just outside of Seattle. The band often did things like that, not only to take a break from the tour but for the publicity it generated as well.

"What about it?" asked John.

"You said it was supposed to be just for the band and a few of the best roadies?"

"It is," John said sharply. "A one-night stand in a five-hundred-seat concert hall. Just like old times, and just for the boys."

Jill closed her eyes and let out a deep, long sigh. "Well, when I called the hotel to see if the case of Heineken had arrived, the concierge told me that *Mrs. Violent* had signed for it late this afternoon."

There was a long, tense silence between them. John was suddenly aware of the warm draft twisting its way up through the stairwell.

"Obviously, there's been a mistake," he said, masking the tremor in his voice by increasing its volume.

"I don't think so, Johnny. You're swinging up to Seattle for a night so you can be with *her.*" The last word echoed once, then died. "Aren't you?"

"Take it easy, babe," John said in a strained voice. "It's not like that at all."

"Don't 'take it easy, babe' me," said Jill through clenched teeth. "I'm your wife, not one of your gum-chewing, bubble-popping bimbos."

"What?"

"God, how much of a fool do you take me for, Johnny? I've been watching you closely on this tour. I *know* you've been cheating on me."

"No, I—"

"Shut up, Johnny! Just shut up and let me finish. . . ."

John was speechless. Nobody told Johnny Violent to shut up. Nobody. Not even Jill.

". . . There's no use denying it. I hired a detective to follow you last month in Toronto. I've got pictures."

The short fuse leading to John's violent temper began to sizzle.

"That's why I'm filing for divorce," Jill said, rising to her feet. "I kept putting it off, thinking you'd get it out of your system, but I can't wait anymore. I've got to do it now, while I'm still young enough to start my life over again on my own."

John set his guitar aside and stood up, the fifth string still in his hand. He was pissed, well past apeshit and halfway to ballistic.

Jill's eyes closed into slits and her lips cracked a blatantly malicious smile. "Don't worry about me, Johnny," she said, her voice wet with contempt. "California divorce law entitles me to half of everything. I'm pretty sure I'll be able to make do with fifteen million."

Outwardly, John was the picture of calm. Inside was another story. The thought of losing half his wealth to Jill in one fell swoop was too much for him to handle. His mind exploded in a white-hot burst of rage; anger flared outward to every part of his body.

He bounded up the steps and stood face to face with her. A vein throbbed in the middle of his forehead as he slowly pulled back his lips and bared his teeth in something that wasn't a smile.

Jill shook her head and let out a condescending little laugh. "You never grew up, did you, Johnny?"

John's open hand arced out, his fingers and palm slapping her right cheek with a loud, fleshy *smack*.

Jill looked surprised, but remained defiant. "Do you know what the roadies call you? Little Johnny Tantrum."

John's hands shot up from his sides in a blur of motion. His strong fingers closed around her throat like a giant steel vise, squeezing off her windpipe and making it hard for her to breathe.

Within seconds he had the guitar string coiled around her neck. As he pulled on the string, it pressed sharply against her flesh, turning the skin there a ghostly shade of white.

"What—are you—" Jill sputtered, her eyes bulging out of their sockets in a look of sheer terror.

"You're not getting a fucking thing," John said in a low, guttural voice he'd never heard himself use before. "It's mine! All of it!"

"Please don't—"

He pulled the string tighter until the thin steel wire cut into her flesh and a line of blood bubbled up from the skin.

"—kill me, Johnny."

Jill's words were little more than wet gurgles as she thrashed about, her hands desperately trying to push John's hands together and relieve the tension on the string.

It was no use. John was too strong . . . too wild . . . too freaked out to be stopped.

The string jerked in his hands as the fine steel strand snapped through the tendons in the meaty part of her neck.

Jill screamed, a keening wail that sliced through the air a moment before dying out in the depths of her throat. The scream lived another second as an echo in the stairwell, then died there as well.

John continued pulling on the string, feeling it grate and scrape against bone, until he was almost holding the string in a straight line in his hands.

Jill's head fell limply to one side. Blood gushed freely from the open rent in her neck and splattered onto the steps like rain. Then her bowels emptied.

John released the tension on the string, his body drenched in sweat and his breath coming in hard, labored gasps. Suddenly, the stink of blood and excrement brought him out of his maniacal haze. He looked at Jill's prone body on the landing, saw the blood pooling out from her ruined neck, and felt his bloody fingers beginning to stick together.

He stopped breathing and for a moment his entire body was racked by raw fear. "What have I done? What have I

Scream String

done?" he moaned softly, twisting and turning against the cold, hard bricks as if trying to hide in the tiny cracks between them.

Just then he heard someone shouting off in the distance: "Johnny.... Five minutes, Johnny...." The voice faded as its source continued searching for him in the stadium's bowels.

For the moment, all his guilt and remorse would have to be pushed aside. He would deal with his emotions later, probably in the hotel room in Seattle. Right now, he had a show to do.

He used Jill's skirt to wipe the blood off the guitar string and his hands. Satisfied that they were both clean, he jumped down a few steps for his guitar. With the quick and sure movements of an expert hand, he set the fifth string, pulled it tight, and wound it into the machine head. A minute later the sixth string was set and he hurriedly began tuning the guitar.

When he was done, he started up the stairs playing a riff from "Flesh Wound," the band's latest hit single. Although he nearly pounded on the Strat, he couldn't drown out the sound of Jill's blood dripping down the steps behind him like water from a leaky faucet.

When he got to the green room backstage, the rest of the band was waiting for him with impatient looks on their faces.

"You cut it a little too close this time, man," said Stuart Green, the band's lanky blond bass player. "This is one show we can't be late for."

"Sorry, guys," said John. "I got carried away and lost track of time."

"Are you all right?" asked Bill "Burnout" Burns, the Purploids' drummer.

From the way they were looking at him, John thought his clothes were stained with blood. He gave himself a quick once-over. If there was any blood on him, it was lost in the deep purple swirls of his outfit. He was about to look up when he realized his right hand was shaking.

"I guess I'm a little nervous," John said, doing his best to crack a smile.

"We all are, man," said Green.

Burnout upended his Heineken, emptied it into his throat and belched. "I'm not," he said.

The deejay stepped onto the stage, walked up to the microphone, and coughed. The crowd impatiently began cheering. Without further hesitation, the deejay said, "Ladies and gentlemen—Johnny Violent and the Throbbing Purploids!"

The entire coliseum broke into a roar that sounded like surf breaking over a pier. The Purploids took to the stage and immediately started into "Brain-Damaged," the band's six-year-old first hit single and signature song.

John stood backstage, feeling the pounding intro to the song beat into his head, chest, and gut like a jackhammer. After just a few bars the throbbing, pulsing music overtook him, masking the deep pangs of remorse, guilt, and fear that were still coursing through his body.

All he could think of now was getting onstage, drinking in the energy emanating from the hundred-thousand-plus crowd and letting the music envelop him like a protective shroud.

Six bars before his solo, John jumped onstage and was immediately captured in the tight, white beam of the spotlight that would be trained on him throughout the show. The crowd roared. Johnny Violent was the one they'd all been waiting for.

John strutted around the stage for a few beats to show off his long mane of obsidian black hair, and then it was solo time.

He started with an A and ran a quick scale up to a high E. Even though he'd rushed the tuning of the guitar, it sounded good, real good. After a few runs down the neck, John climaxed the solo by scaling up to an A on the fifth string and holding it there. After a few beats he bent it. As the note curled over the packed coliseum, it changed . . . slowly turning into a mind-numbing, bloodcurdling scream.

Under the lights, John could see people in the first few rows cupping their hands over their ears to try to block out the horrifying cry. For a moment he wondered if the same thing was happening all around the world.

John spun away from the crowd and began twisting the volume and tone controls on his guitar, but they had no effect on the awful sound. He tried the toggle switch. Nothing. In fact, the scream seemed to be getting louder, like some wild pulse of feedback that had to be allowed to run its course.

John looked up. The other members of the band were still playing, but they were looking left and right for someone who knew what the fuck was going on.

Nobody knew a thing.

Except for John.

The scream had a familiar sound to it. It was the same sound Jill had made when he'd killed her. Her death scream had been captured on the thin steel guitar string as clearly as if it had been recorded on tape.

He ran downstage to his wa-wa pedal and pushed back on it. Nothing happened. He kicked it, but the terrible scream would not die.

One by one the band stopped playing until all that could be heard was the scream.

Then that died as well.

And the coliseum was silent, as if it were empty.

Johnny killed me!

The words cut through the air like a knife. John stood erect in the center of the stage as if the knife had been buried deep into the small of his back.

Johnny did it!

The voice was that of a woman, but sounded only vaguely like Jill's. It was as if the words had been stretched and compressed a dozen times before being sent through the amps.

Johnny, killer!

John pulled the guitar from his shoulder and held it at arm's length as if it were diseased. As he watched in horror, the fifth string—the scream string—vibrated like a displaced vocal cord.

Johnny—

Before the voice could say another word, John grabbed the Strat's neck firmly in his hands and swung the guitar over his head like an axe . . .

And in one swift motion brought it crashing down onto the stage.

Seeing Johnny Violent smash his priceless 1969 burgundy Stratocaster in the opening minutes of the concert left the crowd dumbfounded.

Again John brought the Strat down onto the stage. Pieces of wood and metal broke away from the guitar, sending a terrible black noise through the wall of speakers at each end of the stage.

When the cops stepped onto the stage, the crowd must have thought it was all part of the show, because the coliseum suddenly erupted into a standing ovation.

John kept swinging the guitar, pounding it into the stage until it was little more than junk in his hands. Then he got down on all fours and searched the debris for the fifth string.

When he picked it up, he could feel it trembling in his hand. He held it close to his ear, and felt his heart fall deep into the pit of his stomach.

Why, Johnny? Why? Jill's voice cried faintly through the string. It asked the question once more, then faded into silence.

Rough hands took hold of John and lifted him up off the stage. He looked around. There were cops everywhere.

One of them pried open his fisted right hand and slid the guitar string into a small plastic bag. Then they pulled his arms behind his back and clamped cold steel rings to his wrists.

"Mr. Violent, you have the right to remain silent . . ."

The words were picked up by a nearby microphone.

And the crowd went wild.

SEVERIN HEDZ

Th. Metzger

Things were going well for the first time in years. The tour was half over and nobody in the band had threatened to kill anyone yet. The crowds were small but enthusiastic, and the two roadies had finally figured out how to set up the PA and board without electrocuting themselves.

Not only that, but Rudi had a fine piece of sweet-meat lying crossways on the front seat of his car. Her name was Marlena and she definitely had talent. Eighty miles an hour on the interstate. His radar detector beeping happily and Marlena slurping away. It was beautiful music.

The night before, Marlena had almost wet herself with delight as she slid in beside him and got a whiff of the brand-new vinyl seats. The car was old—a behemoth, midnight blue Continental—but he'd had all the upholstery replaced. And the smell of the sweet vinyl fumes had made her drunker than the banana daiquiris she'd sucked down while she'd waited backstage for Rudi to change into his street clothes.

Marlena was humming now and the vibrations worked their way up through his guts. He tried to concentrate on the road, the cars ahead. But it was no use. He could hear her now, not just feel her voice. He slowed down. He closed his eyes and hoped for the best. Her head bobbed up and down. He felt himself losing control.

An eighteen-wheeler blared its horn at him and he opened his eyes. His car was halfway onto the shoulder. He jerked the wheel back and Marlena came up for air. The truck zoomed by and she waved.

That night, the band was bad. Terry, the bass player, had drunk too much Colt 45 for supper. Vince, the drummer, played as if he had Liquid Wrench in his veins. And the guitarist, a scrawny kid named Scratch, seemed to be purposely missing his cues. But Rudi gave it his all. A couple hundred people had come out to get the Severin Hedz experience, and he wasn't going to shortchange them. There were even a few not-bad-looking girls up front, following his every move.

The band roared through the set like a locomotive with one driver wheel about to fly off. They were sloppy, the PA kept feeding back, the acoustics in the club were horrible. But Rudi didn't mind one bit. He bellowed and screeched, thrashed and wailed. And as he'd said many times before: As long as it's loud and it looks good, it's okay.

He came off the stage to be greeted by a pair of bottle blondies who had been hanging by the stage all night. He was ready for them, pumped up, drunk on his own adrenaline. He felt he could even go for a three-way that night.

Away from the beer-and-smoke atmosphere of the club, the girls would have looked like a couple of college kids who'd spent a lot of money trying to look like hookers. Rudi had no voice left and his legs felt weak, but when they took hold of him and started to tell him how great he was, the old surge returned.

Before he could get them out to his car, however, there was Marlena. He hadn't seen her for a couple of hours. Once he'd hit the stage, heard the first chords of "Thick and Juicy," he'd forgotten all about her.

Now she stood with her arms crossed over her chest, shaking her head at him as though he'd been a bad little boy.

"Let's go," she said, taking him by the sleeve.

"Hey, Jeeziz, wait a—"

Marlena shoved the protesting girl against the wall. The other backed down, getting a good look at the expression on Marlena's face.

"Get lost," she said. "He's taken." Still clutching Rudi's arm, she shoved past the girls, through the back corridor, and out to the parking lot. She got in the car and handed him the keys. He didn't remember giving them to her before. "You think you can drive?" she said. The wild, angry look was gone. Alone with him again, she seemed almost ecstatic.

"Yeah, I guess so."

She took the keys back, leaned over, and started the engine. "Good." Her hand ran up the inside of his thigh, over the sweat-glued denim. She tugged at the brass tab on his zipper.

The motel was only a few blocks away. They took the long way to get there.

The first night—it felt like months ago—he'd found Marlena slightly repulsive. But he'd sort of grown to like that; he had a soft spot for soiled goods. She wasn't a small girl. She had haunches you could cut some impressive steaks from, thighs and calves that would provide generous portions.

Face down, she wasn't bad-looking. "You ready?" he'd said, stroking her great curve.

"Willing and able," she'd murmured, wiggling excitedly.

Even then, diving into her deep end, things weren't quite right. And now, that nagging feeling had almost coalesced into something he could name. Not doom exactly, not dread, but somewhere in the neighborhood.

"I can drop you off at the bus station in Erie," Rudi said, on the road again the next day. Youngstown was about thirty miles behind them.

"What's the matter? Don't you like me anymore?" Marlena purred.

"Yeah, of course, sure. But you know . . . I just figured . . . I mean, the way it usually goes . . ."

"But we've only been together a few days."

That was exactly his point. Three days was two more than he'd ever taken a girl on tour. He'd always dropped them, shunted them off to the roadies, told them flat out, "It's been nice, but it's over."

"I *need* you, Rudi. I need you bad."

He was going to ask her again exactly where she was from (she'd mentioned Altoona, King of Prussia, Intercourse, Lititz) when she started nibbling at his earlobe. "I *need* you, Rudi. Everybody always treated me like a piece of trash. But you're a star, you're famous, and you make me feel wanted."

The feeling—like she'd put tiny hooks in his stomach and was pulling them with invisible wires—grew as they headed north on the thruway. Ten miles outside of Niagara Falls, he felt truly sick, but told himself it was just the cloud of industrial stench hanging over the city. A few miles closer, he actually saw it: a green-blue-black haze. And passing within the city limits, he got his first absolute hit, an acrid reek like a dull razor scraped over his olfactory nerve.

Marlena, however, seemed to enjoy this crude petrochemical nectar, the result of a hundred years of electroplating, hydrolysis, fractioning, and ester conversion. She had the same eager look on her face as when she'd first gotten a whiff of Rudi's car.

The city itself was unremarkable: dull frame houses clad in peeling asbestos, blighted urban streets. Burger Shack, Fish-a-rama, Wings and Things, Amazing Taco, Kieshka

Kastle (this was western New York after all), and Frozen Whip.

"I want ice cream," Marlena cooed.

"Not now."

"Please?"

He hated the whine in her voice, the look of near desperation in her eyes. "We don't have time," he said, knowing full well that they didn't need to be at the club for the sound check until five.

"Puh-leeze?" She snaked her arm around his shoulders and took his earlobe between her teeth.

"All right, all right." He yanked hard on the wheel, U-turned, and pulled into Frozen Whip. He wasn't surprised when she opted for the Mega-Swirly: a triple portion of double fudge that looked like something that had leaked out a culvert behind a nuclear power plant. Her tongue went to work, shaping and reshaping the mound of soft serve.

A pair of locals in matching acne sat nearby, eyeing Marlena. One of them grabbed his crotch and grinned.

"Can you believe that?" Marlena said.

"What?"

"He just called me a slut."

"Forget about it." Rudi tried to steer her out the door.

"No! He called me a slut." She went toward the kid. "You want to say that again loud enough for my boyfriend to hear it?"

The kid hesitated. But this was already an affair of honor. He spat out a silver sprinkle. "What are you supposed to be?" he said, poking Rudi in the chest.

Marlena came between them. "He's not supposed to be anything. He *is* the lead singer with Severin Hedz. You ever heard of them?"

"Come on, let's go," Rudi said. But she'd planted her feet and wouldn't budge.

"So you're a big star, huh?"

Rudi tried to smile. "Look, we gotta get moving. You want some free tickets to the show tonight? Give me your names and I'll get you in. We're playing the Donjohn, over on Cataract Street."

The kid didn't know if any of this was for real. Part of him was sure he was being made a fool of, but the possibility of free tickets was too tempting to turn down.

"He called me a slut! Do something about it!" Getting no response from Rudi, she turned her attention to the kid. "This is the real thing, you little shit. Rudi and me forever. I'm not a slut."

"I didn't call you anything," the kid said at last. He'd decided. He wanted the free tickets.

"Make him apologize, Rudi."

"Look, I didn't say anything."

"Make him—"

"Shut up a second!" Rudi could have walked out right then, gotten in the car, and been done with her. Let her find her own way back home to Shickshinny or Zelienople or wherever the hell she was from.

But he didn't. He took the kids' names, told them they'd be on the guest list, and coaxed Marlena out to the car.

By the time they made it to the motel, she'd thawed a little. But it took a stop at the 7-Eleven to stock up on cheese balls and gummy bears to make her drop the pout.

"I need to get some sleep," Rudi said, dumping his bag on the bed. "Why don't you go for a walk or something? Go see the falls."

"No, I wanna stay with you. I can't stand being apart."

He lay down on the bed and she sat beside him with a stack of black-and-white promo pictures. They were all the same, Rudi and the others posed in their best leather and spandex, but Marlena shuffled through them as if looking for something.

The photos were embarrassing to Rudi, the kind of thing he'd thought was cool when he was nineteen. Teased hair, pouty look, lots of flashy jewelry. In one of the pictures he had a mike cord wrapped pythonlike around his thigh.

He thought about chucking it all—the band, the road, the

endless loading and unloading of equipment, the girls with no names.

Marlena, however, was near rapture; this was a wet dream come true for her. She'd caught a live one. She'd found the thing she'd been looking for so long.

It took Rudi a long time to get to sleep. He listened to the traffic on the highway, the thump of the TV next door. He had the feeling—though he didn't open his eyes to check—that Marlena was watching him the whole time, like a guard watching a prisoner.

They were really on that night. It felt good to shout and shake, spew and shimmy. The words—or what passed for words—blew out of his mouth like shrapnel from a cannon. He was all over the stage, humping the stacks, making the lizard tongue for the girls, thrashing on the floor like a baby in an ecstatic tantrum.

They roared through "Devolver" faster than they'd ever done it, and Rudi felt an amazing sense of freedom. He clung to the mike stand as if it were the only stable object in the middle of a hurricane and belted out the lyrics:

> "Squeeze your baby till she whines,
> rub the monkey till it shines,
> buff that skull and sniff your fingers
> I love that smell that always lingers."

Up front there were a good hundred fans throwing themselves against each other. It had been a long time since there'd been this kind of crowd. Rudi rode the wave of pure adrenaline. There was power, there was sex, there was unadulterated frenzy. And if he'd ever forgotten the reason he put up with lousy gigs and endless road food, this was a solid reminder.

He felt like a king, ruling over his tiny but perfect kingdom. The club was long and narrow, with the bar along one side. He could just make out the plate glass windows at the far end, beer signs throbbing with their letters all backward.

There was a break scheduled between sets, but the band was so tanked up that they got halfway through the second set before they realized it. After "Jerk the Cross," Rudi finally signaled for them to stop, and they headed backstage to the tiny dressing room.

It wasn't long before the girls were there, too. Rudi was still riding the buzz from the concert. The other guys, too, were cranked. Everything seemed bigger, better, stronger, more intense. And the girls: Rudi couldn't have imagined a more perfect finish to the set.

"God, you were so great," one of them cooed in his ear. Another was in his lap, and a third stroked his hands like a trainer massaging a victorious boxer. "I've never seen anything like it."

Severin Hedz was scheduled to play Niagara Falls two nights in a row. If tomorrow was anything like this, there was no question that this would be the best gig they'd ever done. Maybe it was just luck, maybe they really were good, or maybe it was just the weird chemicals in the air. Rudi didn't know and he didn't care. He just wanted to enjoy it.

Another girl was kneeling between his legs now, stroking her hands over his thighs. He looked down into the most gorgeous face he'd ever seen. The buzz, the surge, started to take on a purely physical form. Her hands slid farther upward.

"Not here, not now, baby," he said, shaking himself out of the daze. "We've got another set to do. But stick around. Just be here afterward. . . ." He held her head in both hands. Pale blue eyes, honey blond hair. She was flawless, like a porcelain doll. "What's your name?"

"Leah."

"Well, Leah, you just stick around, all right?"

He felt a cold tendril of air circling around him. He looked up, and there was Marlena.

"We were great," Rudi said. "Did you like it? Weren't we great?"

She didn't answer. Terry and Scratch and Vince left the room. One of the girls unwrapped herself from around Rudi and took off with them.

"Beat it," Marlena said to the others.

They waited for Rudi's command.

"Get rid of them," she said, her voice hard and cold and flat.

Another pulled away and scurried out of the dressing room. Still Leah was at his feet.

Marlena came at her, grabbed her by the hair, and yanked her upright. "Go," she hissed. "Get out. You're not wanted here."

Now Rudi stood, trying to knock Marlena's hand away. "Who the hell do you think you are? I say who comes and goes." He put his arm around Leah's shoulders. "And I think it's about time I told you to take off. It's over, bitch. It was nice, but now it's over."

She looked at him as though he were speaking some foreign tongue.

"Out! Over! You understand? I've got a date with Leah and her friends tonight, all right? So just take off. It's all over."

"You said you loved me. You wrote that song about us."

"What the hell are you talking about?"

"That song, 'Love Chain.' You played it that first night I saw you. You said you wrote it for me." The look on her face was awful. Pain, confusion, humiliation. And something more: flat-out craziness. "Remember? 'If I can't have you, then nobody can.' You wrote it for me, for us. It's true. You and me forever."

"It's over," Rudi said. "Understand?" He called one of the roadies in from the hallway. "Give Marlena some money to get home. Is a hundred enough?"

"No! I want you!" she snarled. "You and me forever and ever. If I can't have you, then nobody—" The roadie pulled her off and Rudi fled, Marlena's abject wails following him all the way to the stage.

The second set was good, but nowhere near as good as the

first. Everything was right, and still it seemed something was wrong. They trimmed a few songs off the set and didn't come back for an encore.

Rudi hurried back to the dressing room and found Leah still there. "That girl," she said. "The one you . . ."

"Marlena? What about her?"

"The bouncers threw her out. But before they did, she told me to give you this." She handed him one of the band's promo pictures. Rudi's face had been obliterated by cigarette burns. The words "Tru Luv lives 4-ever" were scrawled on the photo in scarlet lipstick.

He took Leah and two of her friends back to the motel with him. They went through a few quarts of Colt 45 and a handful of pills. They were up and at it until four-thirty, but the moment—that timeless moment when he had her perfect face cradled between his legs looking up at him as though he were a god—was impossible to recapture.

He woke about noon. The girls had taken off. The cigarette butts, bottles, and strewn clothes might have been their mess. Or it might have been just the wreckage of a drunken night by himself. The TV was on, with the sound off. The picture throbbed like a toothache. He found the promo photo, his face burned to nothing, stuck on the bathroom mirror with a piece of gum. He didn't remember putting it there, though given the state he'd been in the night before, that wasn't surprising.

The band started with "Dragon Bone" that night. The chords and breaks and solos were all in the right places, but something was definitely wrong.

> "I been draggin' this bone all around town,
> turn you inside out and upside down."

Rudi bellowed the words, strangling the mike stand with both hands. With the lights in his eyes he could make out none of the faces in the crowd, but still he searched. Distracted by a feeling of complete vulnerability, he missed one of his cues and the band had to run through the opening of "Venus Sharp" again.

Though the smoke and stale beer stench was heavy in the air, Rudi thought he noticed another scent growing stronger as he soldiered through the set. It was probably just the toxic city air, but it had a strangely sweet tang to it. Spent acid dregs and artificial orange. Peppermint and sulfur dioxide. Chocolate and charred bone.

Rudi signaled to Scratch to drop the last song of the first set. The crowd didn't care, the management didn't notice. The last chords and bass drum thunder died out, and Rudi fled backstage to the dressing room. He stood a moment outside the door, almost afraid to go in. Then Vince and Terry went by and he felt bolder. He pushed back the door and found, to his surprise, that the room was empty. A cigarette butt, however, was still burning in the tinfoil ashtray.

Rudi flopped down on the tattered sofa and closed his eyes. Scratch came in and Rudi heard him relieve himself into the sink. Vince wandered in, grabbed a bottle of beer, asked a few questions Rudi didn't reply to, and wandered out. The lone trail of cigarette smoke continued to unfurl from the butt. He grabbed it, crushed it out, and again got a powerful whiff of noxious fumes. Something burning that wasn't meant to burn.

The club owner came back and asked when they were going to start the second set. Rudi shrugged, saying, "Let's get it over with," and went back to the stage.

The soundman said over the PA, "Ladies and gentlemen, put your hands together again for Severin Hedz!" Scratch meandered onto the stage and plugged in. Vince hunkered down behind his set and began pounding a martial four/four. Rudi grabbed the mike. He looked out at the crowd, and a tide of black emptiness swept over him. He was all alone, stranded on some storm-battered shore. "No Fun!" he shouted to Scratch, and they blasted into the old Stooges tune.

He pounded his foot on the rickety stage, belting out the

few words he remembered, garbling in his own. "No fun! I want my fun. When I run, when I drive, too much fun being alive."

Coming to the place where Scratch usually took his solo, Rudi fell to his knees and banged his fist on the stage, shouting incoherently. He was in a trance now, swept up in his own black mood and the grinding roar of the band. He heard a crash and a low throbbing, and felt brilliant lights kicking him like iron-shod boots. He looked up and there were two white-hot spots trained on him. But they were too low to the ground and were coming at him. The roaring grew louder, and he realized that it wasn't the band. He struggled to his feet, shielding his eyes against the light.

"Turn off the . . ." But the words died in his mouth. He saw now what had happened. Those weren't spots, those were headlights. Someone had driven a car through the front windows of the club and was plowing headlong toward the stage. It was as if time had slowed down, though. The car was definitely moving: He could feel the momentum as the lights grew bigger and bigger. It seemed to take forever for the car to get there, crushing the tables and chairs in its path. The screams of the crowd were low and drawn-out and seemed to come from very far away. The air was soon choked with unbreathable fumes, as if by crashing through the exterior wall, the car had let in a tidal wave of all the foul air outside.

Then Rudi knew whose car it was and who was driving. He saw Marlena behind the wheel, a big, ugly, soulless grin on her face. She swerved the car from side to side, like a little kid on the bumper cars. Behind, in the wreckage, Rudi saw mangled bodies, people trying to crawl to safety.

Terry, the bass player, was still thumping away, oblivious as always to anything but his own little world. Scratch, however, had already fled the stage, and Vince was trying desperately to get his equipment off to the side. The screams of the wounded, the crunch of furniture, the labored throbbing of the car engine combined to make a strange ambient music. And even more strange, Rudi stood his ground, still clutching the mike as if waiting for his cue.

The car came to a halt a few feet from the stage. By pure force of habit, Rudi said into the mike, "Test, one two," and finding the PA still working, shouted the first thing that came to mind: "That's my car!" The words echoed dimly in the smoky din.

The window rolled down. Marlena stuck her head out and shouted back, "That's right, and this is yours, too." Something flew through the air and thumped onto the stage. Rudi didn't look at first. He was still staring in disbelief at Marlena. If she slammed her foot on the gas pedal, the car could probably buck right over the low stage lip and flatten him like the others. But the total unreality of the situation gave him a fool's courage.

"That's my car. Get out of my car!" It was a mess: windows broken, fenders mangled, the leather roof torn and flayed.

"You liked her so much, you can have her," Marlena shouted, pointing to the thing she'd tossed at him. He looked down. It was Leah's head. The perfect doll-like features were still intact. But the scalp had been shaved clean and something protruded from the mouth. Rudi pulled it out, as if removing some parasitical worm: a long braid of honey blond hair.

Marlena blared the horn, blew Rudi a kiss, and dropping the car into reverse, roared out of the club. As she careened through the wreckage, one of the bartenders popped from his hiding place and aimed a shotgun at the car. The vehicle blew out through the hole in the windows as the shotgun fired.

A few more screams erupted. Plaster fell from the ceiling and Rudi heard a siren, far away.

The next couple of gigs on the tour were cancelled, but the band picked up again a week later in Scranton. There'd been a sputter of interest in the media. MTV's *News in Rock* had devoted an entire segment to the "tragedy" and there was some talk of a major label sending a scout to check them out. But nothing really changed. Nothing except Rudi.

The crowd in Scranton wasn't enthusiastic, but not hostile either. A few girls were waiting outside the dressing room when Rudi came off the stage. In the smoke-and-beer light, they looked like pasty reptiles. Rudi told them he wasn't interested.

They got a late start the next day. By the time they were on the road, they only had a few hours of daylight left.

Rudi drove the van now. The others kidded him about buying another car to replace the Continental, which had yet to be found. But he didn't joke back. He set his jaw like a boxer waiting for the killer blow, kept his hands tight on the wheel, and watched the miles of frozen Pennsylvania landscape roll by.

Vince was asleep, Scratch was drunk, and Terry was deep in road stupor. But Rudi was wide awake. Far back, too far to see very well, was a shadowy shape that he thought might have been a midnight blue Continental.

They were on Route 84. At that hour, the only other traffic was an occasional tractor-trailer. The landscape was barren: high hills, long stretches of fallow farmland, abandoned houses. The exits were few and very far between. Rudi pushed his foot hard on the gas, and the van began to shake.

"Jesus, man, take it easy," Scratch growled. "You wanna blow us all up?"

"Go back to sleep."

Hearing the clatter of bad valves, the whine of protest from the van's ancient transmission, he slowed, and the car behind crept closer.

He smelled a noxious odor from the heat vents and shut off the blower. He felt a raw grinding, in the transmission and in the pit of his belly. Now that there was absolutely no one on the highway with them, the car behind seemed to grow bolder.

Rudi's imagination filled in the details that the darkness hid: battered fenders, torn roof, paint scarred and scabbed.

Terry was nodding inside his Walkman cocoon. Scratch muttered like an old wino. Rudi turned on the radio, but could get only static and ghost voices. The hills were too high; New York was at least fifty miles to the south.

He looked back, and the spectral car was clearer now. One headlight seemed to wink at him. Fighting to keep his cheeseburgers down, he opened the window a crack and sucked in a few lungfuls of frozen night air.

The car was steadily gaining. One intermittent light and a pale cloud billowing behind. Rudi pressed the accelerator to the floor again, murmuring, "Come on, come on," like a prayer. They were approaching a long incline, a mile or two to the top of a dusk-shrouded hill.

Now the Continental was only a few lengths back. He thought he heard the familiar thrum of the eight well-tuned cylinders. The car moved into the passing lane. "Oh Jesus, oh Jesus no." It felt as though he were driving into a powerful wind. The Continental's grille was a nasty grin and the headlights two throbbing eyes.

As it came up alongside them, Rudi looked over. Too dark to see anything. It moved now into his lane, crowding him. He smashed his fist on the knob at the center of the steering wheel, but the van's horn came out a sickly bleat.

Roaring like a locomotive, kicking up a cloud of early-winter snow, the Continental drifted within inches of the van.

Rudi yanked the wheel to the right and tore across the rough gravel shoulder. He heard a muffled bang and the flap-flap-flap of a blowout.

"Goddamn it, no. Not here."

Rudi brought the van to a stop and shut off the engine. The Continental's taillights disappeared into the lowering gloom and silence flooded the van.

Vince looked up, belched, then drifted back to sleep. Terry pulled one headphone back and said, "What the hell happened?"

"You did it, you fix it," Scratch growled.

Rudi got out and opened the van's back door. The jack

was there somewhere, buried under hundreds of pounds of amps and speakers, cables and instrument cases. "Goddamn it, goddamn it." Only one emergency blinker worked, a feeble red eye pulsing fitfully.

Rudi bent down to inspect the damage, then heard the hum of tires behind him and the purr of a small engine. He looked up and was pinned in headlights.

A Volvo pulled up: a nice, middle-class car, shiny, brand-new. Probably full of sleeping kids and an ordinary suburban couple on their way to visit the in-laws.

The electric window rolled down and he heard music: loud and angry. He heard his own voice on tape, wailing like a soul on the doorstep of hell.

A hand stuck out, hung limply for a moment, then dropped to the gravel with a thud. Rudi picked it up, like a gentleman picking up a lady's glove. A familiar face appeared. Big smile, gleaming eyes. "Get in," she said, making the two hard, everyday words into a seductive song. "Come on, Rudi, get in."

Scratch was wandering in the weeds, looking for a place to pee. Terry was nodding in time with some silent music.

"Get in. I'll make it worth your while."

Rudi felt the cold wind plucking at his jacket. No cars could be seen in either direction. The sky—real country sky—was as dark as he'd ever seen.

"You don't want to get me mad again, do you?" she said, her voice sweet and lilting. "I didn't like doing what I did, but she had it coming, grabbing you away from me like that. And those others at the club, well, they shouldn't have got in the way. You made me so mad. It's not good when I'm mad."

There was a long pause. The sky was so empty, so silent above him.

"I was just looking out for you, Rudi, taking care of you. I was taking care of us both. This thing we have together is too good to throw away on trashy girls like her."

Rudi looked back at the van. Oblivious, the others waited for him to fix the tire. He thought of the months to come, the years maybe, spent on the road with them. Cooped up in the van smelling of liquor, unwashed clothes, old cigarettes. Endless gigs in nameless towns. He thought of all the girls he'd met on the road, and they blurred together like ghosts. He could remember only a few names, a face here, a particular boozy laugh, the fists of an angry biker boyfriend, waking with no idea who he'd spent the night with.

At least Marlena was a sure thing. She really wanted him; this was forever. She needed him. In a way that Rudi didn't understand, she actually loved him. He'd spent more than a decade on the road. Maybe this was the thing he'd been looking for all those years.

The air was cold, and getting colder.

"I want to take care of you forever," she purred.

Rudi shrugged and tossed the hand into the ditch. "Shit," he said, took hold of the chrome handle, and pulled open the door. Marlena gave him a big kiss on the cheek and told him he could drive.

MR. PANTS

Gary Brandner

The scene backstage, as usual after a concert, was controlled chaos. With the air-conditioning turned off the air was heavy with dust, smoke (never mind the "No" signs), and the smell of sweat. The young roadies in their jeans and Brain Cancer T-shirts laughed and cursed as they tore down the sets and packed away sound equipment, lights, smoke machines, and the other accoutrements of a heavy metal concert. Big-shouldered security guards blocked off the squealing groupies trying to claw their way to the band members.

Farley Zmeckis wiped his palms across his red jacket and stared longingly at the nubile fans. His eyes bounced in rhythm with the ripe young breasts ready to burst forth into eager hands. His saliva flow increased with the plump red lips pursed to encircle a throbbing member. But the breasts were not for Farley's hands, the lips not for Farley's member. After a brush-by glance that revealed him as a nonmusician, the groupies ignored him.

Flourishing his employee pass, Farley was allowed past the squealing girls, through the phalanx of security guards to the dressing room occupied by Jojo Kingman, lead singer of Brain Cancer. Farley paused at the door to pluck out the sponge-rubber plugs that protected his eardrums. If the truth be told, which it was not about to be by Farley, he could not stand heavy metal. He detested the explosive percussion and the shrieking guitars. Most of all he hated the primal screams that passed for singing. Given a choice, he would rather listen to a chorus of leaf blowers. His darkest secret was that in the privacy of his bedroom he liked to listen to Harry Connick, Jr. He would never, of course, admit any of this to anyone. Not only would it mark him as hopelessly out of touch, it would cost him his job. And without the job, he would have no excuse to be near Valerie Mons.

He drew a deep breath and knocked on the door of the star dressing room.

"Fuck off," growled a scream-ravaged voice from the other side.

Farley's feet wanted to do just that, but his brain ordered them to stand fast. He had promised himself he would not falter tonight. He knocked again.

"Go the fuck away."

"Just a minute of your time," Farley said, embarrassed at the way his voice squeaked. "Please?"

"Oh, for shit's sake . . . come in, then, and get it over with."

Farley opened the door and entered. The dressing room was littered with costumes, makeup, fast-food wrappers, cigarette butts. The air stank of unwashed bodies. An open bottle of Wild Turkey stood on the dressing table. Jojo Kingman sat slumped on a bench before the dressing table mirror. His naked upper body was pale and soft, the pulpy flesh slick with sweat. Makeup was caked on his face, blue-black eyeliner smeared down across one cheekbone. The harsh light revealed a deep tracery of lines, discolored pouches under the eyes, loose flesh at the jaw. Kingman's hair was dyed an inky black, his eyebrows darkened.

Farley had seen rock stars up close before, and it always fueled his sense of injustice. This thirty-year-old wreck who looked twenty years older, who screamed his way through songs with no recognizable melody or lyrics, could have any woman anytime. Farley Zmeckis, who was nineteen and had a pleasant, unmarked face and a passable tenor voice, could not get within arm's length of the one girl in the world he wanted.

"Who the fuck are you?"

Farley told him his name. "I work here. I'm an usher."

"Good for you. There's a stack of glossies by the door. Take as many as you want and go away."

"I didn't come for a picture. I just want to ask you something."

The rock star coughed into a towel. "So ask and go."

"The thing is, I mean . . . you get all the girls you want. There's a crowd of them outside now who would die for you."

"So?"

"How do you do it? What's the secret?"

"Shit, man, I'm a star. Women love to fuck stars. That's your secret. Good-bye."

"But isn't there something more than that? I've watched at a lot of concerts. Not everybody has it, the thing that draws the girls. You do. A few of the others. Couldn't you give me a hint? Is there something you do that's special?"

Jojo Kingman turned on the stool and looked directly at Farley for the first time. "Why is this such a big thing for you?"

"It's my girl. Well, not really, but I wish she was. Valerie Mons. She's a cashier here. Maybe you noticed her?"

"Why would I notice a cashier?"

"Because she's the most beautiful thing I've ever seen."

"Yeah, right. And you want to fuck her."

Mr. Pants

Farley felt the heat of his blush. "Well, I mean . . . you know . . ."

"Do you or don't you?"

"Yes," Farley squeaked.

"So what's stopping you?"

"I can't get close to her. I've tried everything. I've been nice, I've been cool, I've given her presents, I've written her letters. Nothing works. Before I give up, I've got to know if there's something you know . . . something I could do that would make her notice me."

"As a matter of fact, there is," Kingman said suddenly. "Are you sure you want to hear this?"

Farley's heart leapt. "More than anything in the world!"

"Then pay attention." The rocker stood up and planted himself in front of Farley. "Look at me. What do you see?"

Farley found it impossible to keep his eyes off the lower half of the rock star's body. The fawn-colored pants clung to his pelvis and legs like skin. Tiny lights seemed to dart through the clinging fabric. Every mole and pimple on the flesh of Jojo Kingman was starkly revealed. Especially prominent was the cylinder that hung down along one thigh like a sausage.

"Well?" Kingman prompted.

"Your . . . your . . . your . . ."

"My cock. What's the matter, can't you say the word?"

Farley's mouth flapped. Jojo shook his head.

"So, everybody's got a cock, right? Yours is probably as good as any."

Farley recovered his voice. "Then what's the secret?"

"The pants, man, the pants. They're custom-made. Put on a pair of these and I promise you, the women won't leave you alone. That includes your . . . what's her name?"

"Valerie."

"Right."

Farley stared. Truly, the shimmering pants did look magical even there in the grubby dressing room. "Where can I get a pair?" he said in a small voice.

Kingman sat down. The wonderful pants stretched and

contracted with his movements, showing never a wrinkle. He scribbled in a spiral notebook, tore out the page, and handed it to Farley. It read:

> Mr. Pants
> 369 Moody Place

"Moody Place?"

"It's in Beverly Hills, off Rodeo Drive. You can't miss it."

Farley stared at the scrap of paper as though it were the formula transmuting lead into gold. "I don't know how to thank you."

"Just fuck off, and let me be. I'm tired."

Farley backed out of the dressing room, all but bowing as he went. He made his way through the security people and past the clamoring fans, then walked out through the auditorium, where the cleanup crew was shoving the evening's debris into piles. He climbed a flight of stairs to the accounting office.

Valerie Mons glanced up briefly, then back down at the figures she was tapping into a computer. The creamy hair swung softly, framing her heart-shaped face.

Farley swallowed hard. "Hi, Valerie."

She muttered something that might have been a greeting.

"Are you going to be through here soon?"

"No."

"Hey, I'm in no hurry either. Want to go for a Coke or something after?"

"No."

"Or, I give you a ride home?"

"I've got a ride."

"Maybe tomorrow . . . ?"

Valerie looked up again. A tiny frown line etched itself between her sky blue eyes. Her full cherry lips pouted in a way that made Farley's groin ache.

"Give it a rest, Farley. You're probably a nice boy, but you're not for me. You don't appeal to me. You don't excite me. I don't want to do anything with you. Not tonight, not tomorrow, not ever. Please, please, *please,* stop bothering me."

"Well, good night then." Farley left the office, clutching the scrap of paper in his fist. We'll see, he thought, we'll just see about that.

The next morning in Beverly Hills, Farley had no trouble finding Moody Place, which surprised him. Usually when somebody said, "you can't miss it," it was all too easy to do just that. But here it was—a short, narrow street, little more than an alley, leading off Rodeo Drive between Sunset and Santa Monica. Unlike the elegant shops of the famous street, the buildings along the single block of Moody Place were drab and nondescript. The only sign visible was a wooden panel hanging in front of number 369. Gold letters painted on a brown background spelled out "Mr. Pants." Heavy green draperies were pulled across the show window, blocking any view of what was inside.

Farley walked through the door into a dark, musty room unlike any store he had ever been in. There were no showcases, no mannequins, no merchandise display of any kind. The floor was naked concrete. The only frill was a series of eight-by-ten photographs of some of the most familiar faces in rock music; faces that had looked out from the cover of *Rolling Stone.* They were the screamers who attracted women like carrion drew blowflies. Among them was Jojo Kingman. Their eyes followed Farley as he crossed the cold floor to the rear, where a wooden counter ran from wall to wall. Behind the counter were bolts of cloth stuffed into cubicles of shelving. In the center of the back wall was a closed wooden door.

Farley's skin prickled. The place had a dank, unpleasant feel. With the legends of rock watching him from their photos on the wall, he stopped at the counter and cleared his throat.

"Anybody here?"

When there was no response, he tapped the nipple of a push-bell on the counter, producing a silvery *pingggg*.

After a painful thirty seconds, the rear door opened and an old man entered on silent feet. He was frail and hunched, with wispy white hair, a thin, crooked nose, and thick rimless glasses. He placed himself across the counter from Farley and stared at him silently through the distorting lenses.

"I—I was interested in buying a pair of pants."

"Of course," the old man snapped. "Why else would you be here?"

"A pair of your special pants."

"Special pants is all I sell."

"Uh, Jojo Kingman sent me? Brain Cancer?"

The old man did not react to the famous name. He leaned on the counter and ran his gaze over Farley, then turned abruptly and disappeared through the door. Farley's heart sank. Rejected again. As he started to back away from the counter, the old man reappeared. He held out his hands, over which was draped a pair of pants the color of rust.

"Try these on."

"Um, is there a dressing room?"

"You got something to be ashamed of?"

"Well . . . no." Farley took the pants from the old man. The fabric was soft as chewed suede, light as Japanese silk. It was strangely warm to his touch. In the dim light, flecks of gold seemed to dance among the fine reddish threads. He carried the pants over close to the curtained window. The golden flecks squirmed and glimmered like tiny living things. Farley wiped the material along his cheek. It was like the caress of a lover. The young-old faces watched from the photos on the walls.

With the blood pumping faster through his veins, Farley held up the pants for a closer look. They had no zipper, buttons, or closure of any kind. There were no pockets, no pleats, no belt loops, no cuffs. The velvety cloth was faintly elastic as he pulled it between his hands.

"You going to wear them or play with them?" said the old man.

Mr. Pants

Farley shucked his Reeboks, his socks, and his Bugle Boys. With a shy glance back at the old man, he peeled off his white Fruit-of-the-Loom briefs. The wonderful pants would have to be worn next to his skin.

He stood feeling foolish and exposed in nothing but his plain white T-shirt. He shook the pants out and stepped into them. They slid up his calves and caressed his thighs, soft as butter and warm as a lover's lips. He pulled them up so the waistband encircled his trunk, just below the navel. Perfect.

Hurriedly he put on his socks and shoes and looked down at himself. Farley sucked in his breath. Everything—*everything*—was revealed. The pants clung to his skin like rubber, yet felt like nothing at all. His sexuality surged and simmered in his loins.

"I'll take them."

"Of course you will," snapped the old man.

"How much?"

"How much do you have?"

"Will you take Visa?"

"No. Cash only."

Farley retrieved his wallet from the crumpled Bugle Boys and extracted the bills.

"I only brought fourteen dollars."

The old man held out a liver-spotted hand. "Give it to me."

Farley thrust the bills at him, gathered his old jeans and underwear into a bundle, and hustled out of the store, fearful that the old man might renege on the bargain. Not until he reached Rodeo Drive did he relax and slow to a walk.

He watched in the store windows as his reflection kept pace with him. He saw a young man carrying an untidy bundle of clothes, wearing a plain white T-shirt and . . . a pair of enchanted pants. Even in transparent reflection they glittered and hummed and moved like a part of Farley Zmeckis, yet with a life of their own. Never had he felt so confident.

When he stopped looking at himself, Farley saw the reaction of the women around him. Young, old, plain, beautiful—none remained unaffected. Those walking by broke stride and goggled at him. The women in cars slowed and rolled down their windows for a better look. Girls barely out of puberty ceased their giggling and gaped. Housewives out shopping, nannies pushing strollers, businesswomen on their way to lunch all stared openly, hungrily. There was no doubt what they were looking at. Their eyes burned with naked desire. Farley knew . . . he absolutely *knew* he could have any one of them, or all of them, right here, right now. All he had to do was crook a finger.

He smiled again at his reflection and ignored the women. First things first. He could always come back to Rodeo Drive. But right now, today, Valerie Mons was going to be his.

She was still in bed when he called, and it took some doing to talk Valerie into meeting him for lunch. He had to tease her with the promise that he had something to show her that would change her life. As he said this, he stroked himself through the marvelous pants, smiling a new, secret smile. Finally, as he knew she would, Valerie agreed.

Farley chose a back booth in a small Italian restaurant with candles on the tables and oregano in the air. Valerie arrived ten minutes late. She stood frowning, legs planted apart, arms akimbo, peering around the dim interior of the restaurant. In her snug white Calvins and pink jersey blouse, she looked as sweet and tempting as a birthday cake. When she spotted Farley, she strode back through the tables and came to a stop facing him.

"Well? Here I am. What's the big surprise?"

Farley slid out of the booth and stood up so she could get the full benefit.

"What do you think?"

Valerie's gaze dropped to the pants. Her eyes grew large.

"Oh, my God!" she breathed. "My God!"

Mr. Pants

Farley opened his arms, and Valerie floated into them as eagerly and naturally as though she had always belonged there. She pressed her lower body against him. His manhood swelled with pride and desire. The marvelous pants concealed nothing.

"Let's go somewhere." Her breath was hot in his ear.

"My place?" Farley could not quite keep his voice under control.

"Yes. Anywhere. Hurry!"

He eased her gently away from him, took her arm, and swept out of the restaurant. Behind them a wide-eyed waitress stood with the menu in a limp hand, staring in wonder at the retreating pants and the secret parts of Farley they revealed.

As he steered Valerie into his bachelor apartment, Farley remembered that he had not made the bed. Nor had he cleared away his breakfast cereal bowl or the dirty coffee cup. None of this mattered to Valerie. She headed for the rumpled bed as though drawn by a magnet.

"Would you like a soda or anything?" Farley asked, feeling he should make some small gesture toward romance.

"All I want is you inside me," Valerie said. "Please, Farley, do me now!"

Swiftly, she began to undress, stripping the jersey blouse over her head to free the full, buoyant breasts, ripping open the jeans and peeling them down her long, tanned legs. She stroked the crisp hair of her pubic mound.

"Here, Farley. Put it here."

He held the moment as long as he could, savoring his masculine power, her feminine need. Keeping his eyes on Valerie, he pulled off the T-shirt with cruel deliberation and laid it aside. He sat on a chair and removed one shoe, then the other, loving the way she stared. He stripped off the socks and stood just beyond her reach. He tucked his thumbs into the waistband of the pants.

No. He *tried* to tuck his thumbs in. There was no give in the fabric, no stretch to the waistband. He could not wedge so much as a thumbnail between cloth and skin. As Valerie moaned, he tried to roll the pants down his flanks using the flats of his palms. The pants would not move. He clawed at the bottom of one leg, hopping awkwardly as he tugged and scratched, vainly fighting for a grip.

"Come *on*, Farley," Valerie moaned from the bed. She rocked back and forth, succulent breasts swaying, her hand squeezed between damp thighs.

"I'm *trying*," he said through clenched teeth. The sweat spilled down his face and upper body as he clawed at the velvety pants, trying vainly to get a purchase with his fingers.

"Goddamn you, stop playing with me! I'm going crazy. Fuck me, Farley. *Fuck me!*"

"I'm not playing, damn it! I can't get the pants off!"

"Oh, Jesus!" Valerie scrambled off the bed and began fumbling into her clothes. "You rotten son of a bitch!"

"Wait, wait!" Farley cried. "Don't go!"

He ran to the tiny kitchen alcove, yanked out a drawer, fumbled through the contents, and seized a razor-sharp chef's knife. He tried to force the blade under the waistband of the pants, but succeeded only in nicking himself painfully in the stomach. He poked tentatively at the fabric that encased his thigh. The rusty material dimpled where the point of the knife touched, but the blade would not penetrate. Frantically he began to stab at the pants, heedless of the damage he might do to what lay underneath. He could feel the prodding of the repeated thrusts, but the blade never pierced the cloth.

The front door slammed as Valerie fled out of the apartment and out of his life. Farley sat down hard on the kitchen floor and cried. During the next two hours he tried without success to cut, snip, tear, rip, or ravel the glittery pants. Finally he staggered to his feet and out the door.

Shoppers on Rodeo Drive were startled as Farley, naked except for the enchanted pants, stumbled along, whimpering like a child. At each street sign he would clutch the pole and read the name through tear-dimmed eyes. Then he would moan and stagger on.

There was, of course, no Moody Place.

And no Mr. Pants.

When he collapsed, exhausted, in the doorway of a chic leather shop, he knew why rock stars scream.

DEAD LEGENDS

Rick Hautala

"Holy shit! What's this picture over here?"

With a swirl of his ankle-length, cotton print jacket and trailing a plume of cigarette smoke, Stuart Bonney walked boldly up to the framed photograph on the wall and tapped it with his thin forefinger. With a sweep of his other hand, he brushed the long shock of dark hair from in front of his left eye, but it immediately fell back into place.

"Hell, boy, that there's Jimi Hendrix, of course," Al Silverstein replied as he folded his stubby arms across his chest and gave Stuart a self-satisfied grin. "See right here? It's even autographed by him and the other two guys in the Experience."

"I *know* who it is, but do you mean to tell me Hendrix actually recorded here?"

"Uh-huh." Al gave his balding head an exaggerated nod, making his fleshy jowls jiggle like twin bowls of Jell-O inside his tight shirt collar. "Back in the sixties. They stopped in for a few sessions just before the Monterey Pop Festival."

"Un-fucking-real," Stuart said, his voice lowering to an uncharacteristic near-reverential whisper. "I can't fucking believe it. And you were working here back then?"

Al's smile widened, and he looked almost as though he was gloating. He was a short, rotund man who stood a whole head shorter than the rail-thin Stuart, but there was something about him that made him *seem* bigger . . . a lot bigger. Maybe it had something to do with his near-legendary status in the music industry.

"You have to remember, Stuie, that I *own* this goddamned recording studio, so of course I was here. For every goddamned session. I'm telling you, they were just starting to get some attention stateside—Monterey's what finally did it—but they laid down the heaviest fucking tracks I ever heard. None of them have ever even been released, of course."

"No shit," Stuart said, suitably impressed, but trying hard not to let his irritation show; *no* one had called him "Stuie" since he was a little kid.

"Oh, yeah," Al said, frowning slightly. "They, uh, they're all tangled up in the legal problems with Hendrix's estate. You know how that bullshit goes."

"Fucking A . . ." Stuart said. He inhaled and blew out a stream of smoke. "But don't tell me you still *have* 'em. Those tapes, I mean."

Al shrugged casually, a smirk lifting one corner of his mouth as his dark, deep-set eyes beamed. "I sure as hell do. They're locked away safe and sound in the studio vault along with a whole shitload of other stuff nobody will probably ever hear."

"No shit. Like what?"

"Why, I've got some unreleased material the Stones recorded here, back when that blond guy—what was his name, Brian? Yeah, Brian Jones—back when he was still alive. He did some *incredible* shit with a sitar. I can't remember the dates exactly, but it was sometime during one of their first North American tours. Hell, John Lennon came in and did four or five solo numbers back when he was out here on the West Coast, carousing around with Nilsson and those guys. I've got some tracks the Doors laid down just before Morrison went over to Paris, a few things by Stevie Ray—"

"No shit, you mean to tell me you've got some unreleased *Doors* material?"

"Almost half an album's worth. Four songs they started working on right after they'd finished *L.A. Woman.*"

"No shit," Stuart said, shaking his head in wonderment. "I never realized they had started on another project back then."

"Yeah, and about that time McCartney was supposed to come in for a few days, but he had to cancel at the last minute. Too bad," Al said, shaking his head.

Stuart took another deep pull on his cigarette, then exhaled a gray plume of smoke as he moved a few steps farther down the hallway to the next framed photograph. It was a black-and-white glossy of Jim Morrison, leaning with one foot against an amp. Scrawled across the bottom of the photograph, right across his black-leather-clad crotch, was Morrison's signature in gold ink. In the photo he had a whiskey bottle clutched like a baseball bat in both hands and was looking down at the floor, his head tilted so his long, curly hair covered most of his face, but Stuart immediately recognized the smirking curl on Jim's upper lip. When he was a kid growing up in Chelsea, Massachusetts, Stuart had practiced that sneer in front of the bathroom mirror night after night.

"I can't fuckin' believe you've recorded all these dudes, man, and no one's ever even *heard* about it."

"Well, I wouldn't say *no* one has heard about it. A few have," Al said, his voice lowering to an almost conspiratorial whisper. "This studio is just sort of a . . . a little trade secret, you might say. I don't have to advertise all that much because people pretty much hear about what we're doing here, and *they* come to *me.*"

"Yeah, I'll bet they do, but . . . I mean, shit, man, just look at the fuckin' pictures on this wall!" Stuart let out a loud gasp. "I mean, it's a fuckin' who's who of rock 'n' roll history."

"You betcher ass it is, Stuie-boy."

Stuart almost exploded.

Stuie-boy! No one *ever* called him that! But Al went on talking, not even noticing Stuart's irritation.

"And if we can work things out right between us, do you know whose picture I'm gonna put up on this here wall, right alongside the Lizard King and Jimi Hendrix and Janis Joplin?"

He smiled as he let his voice trail away teasingly, but Stuart didn't have to answer him; as far as he was concerned, he knew damned right well who it was going to be.

Stuart Bonney was the lead guitarist for Brokenface, a fast-rising hard rock group out of Boston. After a string of "almost-hits" from one label, their first album from Relativity Records had charted in the top fifty under its own steam last spring. It had gone all the way to number one after they'd toured last summer, opening for Pearl Jam, but it had stayed there only one week because U2's new album came out. Unlike most groups, who usually took a year or two to come out with a follow-up album, Brokenface had gone into the studio the day after the Pearl Jam tour ended in August to start recording *Zygomatic,* which they hoped to have in the stores before Christmas.

But there were problems.

The band wasn't at all happy with the way things were going with its current studio, especially with Ed Simmons, who had coproduced their first Relativity album. There was subtle but very definite pressure from the money men upstairs for them to come up with something that would hit the top ten as soon as it was released, and all Simmons kept saying was, "I don't hear a single here! Do you?"

Over the past few weeks, the internal pressure had been building steadily, at times threatening to unravel the entire band. That's why Stuart had taken the weekend off to drive from L.A. up to San Francisco. Like a lot of rockers, he had heard through the professional grapevine about Al Silverstein's Sharp Sounds Studios, and he wanted to talk things over with Al, see what was up. He wasn't all that serious, at least not yet; he was just sniffing around at this point, looking to keep his options open. Stuart wasn't all that easy to impress, either, having cultivated over the years an unflappable image of cool; but as he realized the roster of people Al had worked with over the last twenty years or more, he knew sure as hell that he was going to push for the band to come up here for at least a few weeks to see if they could get anything happening. It couldn't be any worse than the problems they were having now. And if things went *too* badly, Stuart was thinking about bailing out of the group anyway and starting work on his solo album.

Stuart continued moving slowly down the hall, puffing on his cigarette and exclaiming surprise over some of the other framed, autographed photos: Buddy Holly, Sid Vicious, Janis Joplin, John Lennon. Al kept up a steady stream of chatter, telling detailed stories about the legends who had recorded here and when, and emphasizing that most of the material had never even been released.

It wasn't until he was nearing the end of the hall that something struck Stuart as odd. Frowning, he looked carefully at a photo from a recording session with the original Pretenders. His mouth dropped open, and he almost said something, but then he kept silent when he realized the implications of what he was thinking.

"That there's Chrissie Hynde," Al said, his voice sounding unnervingly close and loud behind Stuart's back. "Boy, she's got one hell of a distinctive voice, doesn't she?"

"Umm, yeah," Stuart said, nodding absently as the thought that had come to him grew steadily stronger. "It's—ahh, it's too bad half the band had to go and OD."

He could feel Al, close to his shoulder, and took a quick step to one side, hoping to put a bit more distance between them.

"And how about *this* one of Stevie Ray Vaughan?" Al said, indicating the last photograph on the wall. "That's one helluva shot, ain't it?"

"Yeah, it sure is," Stuart said, but he was still distracted as the thought he'd had became more focused in his mind. Not only was this wall a history of rock 'n' roll, but it was also a nearly chronological photo history of the dead legends of rock 'n' roll.

"This one of Stevie Ray—it, ahh, it looks like it was taken . . . when was he . . . ?"

Stuart let his voice fade away as he tapped the photo with his forefinger, hitting it hard enough to knock it off kilter. Grunting softly, Al reached past him and straightened it while Stuart leaned down and buried his cigarette butt in the sand-filled ashtray on the floor beneath the picture.

"You were saying . . . ?" Al said.

His breath washed like tepid water over the side of Stuart's face, but in spite of its warmth, it gave Stuart a subtle chill.

"When was this, ahh, picture taken?" Stuart asked, aware of the slight quaver in his voice. He stared at the photo of Stevie Ray for what felt like several seconds, waiting for Al's reply as steadily strengthening rushes of cold squiggled up his spine.

"Not too long before the crash, actually," Al said simply, and then he sighed. "It was horrible, the way that happened, wasn't it?"

"Yeah," Stuart said.

Al's voice and heated breath were still too close for Stuart's comfort. He wanted to put a little more distance between him and Al, but he didn't want to appear too obvious about his discomfort, either. Stuart turned and looked at Al, but he found he couldn't maintain eye contact with the man for very long, so he turned back and stared blankly at the photograph. In the picture, reflected light, probably from the photographer's flash, made the guitar in Stevie Ray's hand look like it was blazing with white laser fire.

Carefully avoiding Al, Stuart started walking back down the hallway, checking every photograph on the wall as he went, trying to put them into chronological order. All of the pictures had obviously been taken here in the studio, most of them while the singers and musicians were in the studio actually working. As he neared the other end of the corridor, the thought that had been niggling at his mind became a firm conviction.

Every single one of these pictures had been taken shortly before the performer had died, a matter of weeks, if not days.

The thought gave Stuart a soul-deep chill like he hadn't experienced in a *long* time.

"Do you want to take a minute to check out the studio itself?" Al asked as he crossed the hall to a closed door. "We've got some remarkable state-of-the-art equipment, and the acoustics in here are absolutely unique. I guarantee that you'll get a sound in here that you won't find at any other recording studio."

He fished for a moment in his pants pocket until he produced a large brass key, which he inserted into the door lock. He smiled over his shoulder at Stuart as he turned it.

The moment Stuart heard the lock's tumblers click and saw the door swing open wide, a shudder went through him, and he felt suddenly weak in the knees. His lungs hurt from the breath he was holding, and his mind became a roaring, white blank as he followed Al into the spacious studio. He hardly registered what he was seeing as he scanned the room with its glassed-in sound booth spanning the whole length of one wall. Arrayed around the spacious room was a chaos of sound boards, instruments, foam-covered microphones, stacked amplifiers, folding chairs, tables, and a vast assortment of guitars and other equipment. Al was prattling on about something or other, but Stuart found it almost impossible to pay attention as he tried to process what he was thinking.

No way! It can't be, he told himself over and over. There's no fucking way there can be any kind of connection!

But there was no denying it. Every single one of the people whose photographs adorned the Sharp Sounds Studios walls had died not long after that particular picture had been taken. Another thing that struck Stuart was that, from what he knew about rock 'n' roll history, he'd bet his left nut most rock critics would agree that every single one of those pictures had been taken when the artist had been at the peak of his or her career. Maybe not their peaks in popularity, which in most cases had soared even higher following their deaths, but at least their *artistic* peaks!

The more he thought about it, the more obvious the connection became until he was absolutely convinced of this.

"So," Al said, gesturing around the studio with a wide sweep of his hand, "would you like to play a little something for me? See how it sounds?"

Startled by the question, Stuart looked around, blinking like a mole caught in the sunlight. He had been so engrossed in his line of thinking that he felt almost disoriented, as if he had no idea who or where he was or what he was supposed to be doing.

Al walked over to several guitars arrayed on foam-cushioned guitar stands. He selected one, a black-bodied Martin acoustic, and hefted it before handing it to Stuart.

"Come on," Al said, smiling and nodding eagerly. "I've heard your records, but I'd like to hear what you can do on your own. Tune it up and play a little something for me. I'll go into the booth and get the tapes rolling."

"I—I, uh, don't know, Mr. Silverstein. I mean, I'm not, uhh—" Stuart stammered.

His first thought was that he might be violating his contract in some way, especially if Al recorded it, but he pushed such objections from his mind as he sat down on a folding chair and adjusted one of the microphones so it was close to the sound hole of the guitar. He strummed the strings a few times and twisted the pegs until he was satisfied that it was in tune. He figured what the hell, he'd play "Find Me a Star," a song he had written a few years ago but was keeping from the band because he thought it was so damned good he wanted to save it for his first solo album, whenever that happened.

He heard a tap-tapping on the window of the sound booth and, looking up, saw Al leaning on both fists over the control board. Al raised one hand and touched the headphones he had put on his own head, then pointed down at the floor by Stuart's feet. Stuart looked around until he saw the set of headphones hanging on the microphone stand. He picked them up and slipped them on, adjusting the earpieces to fit comfortably.

"Can you hear me all right?" Al asked.

Coming through the headset, his voice once again seemed much too close for comfort, but Stuart forced himself to smile broadly as he gave Al a quick thumbs-up.

"The vocal mike's on, too. Just say a few words so I can check the levels," Al said.

Stuart cleared his throat and said, "Testing, one two. Testing, one two three."

"Okay, I'm ready to roll," Al said, smiling at him from the glass booth. "Just let 'er rip whenever you're ready, okay? One, two, three . . ." He pointed at Stuart. "We're rolling."

Stuart checked once more to make sure the guitar was in tune; then he began picking the opening chords of "Find Me a Star." As soon as the music started, filling the muffled silence of the studio with its rapid run up and down the strings, Stuart experienced at least a slight measure of relaxation. He loved playing guitar. Ever since junior high school, he had used music as a refuge, at first from the turmoil of living in the slums of Chelsea with his divorced mother and two younger brothers, but even after he had achieved a certain level of fame and had plenty of money to buy whatever he wanted. He truly found comfort and escape only when he was playing.

Turning his head away from the microphone, he cleared his throat and then began to sing, letting the words and tune carry him further away. His sudden irrational fears about the photographs in the hallway seemed to melt, and he was soon lost inside his song. The notes issuing from the guitar seemed to surround him like a gush of warm, soothing water; and his voice, in which he'd never had all that much confidence, seemed to sound infinitely smoother and richer in this room. He hit every high note with a precision and confidence he had never felt before. By the time he was into the last verse, his eyes were actually misting up.

As if for the first time, Stuart truly heard and felt the gut-wrenching longing and loneliness that were at the heart of his song. He heard it now as a desperate plea for a small measure of peace and tranquillity in his hectic life as a rock 'n' roll star.

The only problem was, Stuart knew he wasn't at the top yet.

Not really.

At least, not as far as *he* was concerned.

No, he still felt as though he was nothing but a rock 'n' roll wannabe who could still be impressed by pictures of the truly great dead rock stars—the *real* legends of rock 'n' roll. So what if his band's album had made it to number one? *Brokenface* had only been in the top spot for one week! Shit, that was nothing! Lots of groups did that and quickly faded away, never to be heard from again. Flashes in the pan. One-hit wonders. Now the pressure was on Stuart and the band to make a record that would get them back into the top spot and *keep* them there. If they didn't accomplish that, then in a matter of months they, too, could become nothing but an entry in someone's "Where Are They Now?" column.

Stuart hit the last chord and sustained it, letting it fade slowly away as his voice dropped off to a trembling, breathy whisper. For several seconds, there was perfect silence in the studio. After drawing a slow, shaky breath, Stuart heard the muffled *clap-clap* of Al's applause through the glass enclosure.

"Fantastic! Fan-fucking-tastic!" Al shouted, his voice sounding much too close and loud in the headphones.

As Stuart looked up at the man in the sound booth, he saw, or *thought* he saw, a spark of red light flash in the man's eyes. Stuart grunted with surprise, but his rational mind immediately told him that it was nothing but a reflection from one of the board lights. Whatever it was, it instantly brought Stuart's twisted train of thought roaring back even stronger, and with it came an even more frightening question: Who the hell is this guy, anyway?

Successive waves of shivers raced up Stuart's back and then broke over his neck like a surprise dousing of ice water.

"I'm telling you, man," Al said, his voice rasping with excitement inside the headphones, "that was unbelievable! Absolutely fantastic!"

Stuart started to stand up, but Al waved him back down into the chair.

"Stay right where you are," he shouted. "I'll let you hear the playback. I'll fool around with the mix as we go."

Stuart was feeling emotionally drained after singing the song. He slung the guitar to one side, slouched back in the chair, and closed his eyes. After a few seconds, during which he tried his best not to think anymore about the photographs out in the hall, the sounds of his guitar and voice filled the room. Once again, perhaps even more deeply than before, he felt that undefined sense of loneliness and hurt as he listened to the song he had just finished playing. And once again, it carried him away, reminding him just how hard he had worked to get where he was, and how much he still wanted to make it all the way to the top.

Maybe it was just the power of suggestion, but even in playback, Stuart thought his guitar playing and singing had a vibrant richness that he had never heard in them before. He couldn't help but remember what Al had said about how he could get a sound in this studio that was absolutely unique.

As he was sitting there with his eyes closed and his head swaying gently back and forth, a sudden flash of light startled him. His eyes snapped open, and looking up through the brilliant blue-white afterimages that zigzagged across his vision, he saw Al lowering a camera.

"Hey," Al said, smiling sheepishly, "I had to take at least one picture of you, you know? For posterity's sake. You never know when someone's gonna hit their peak."

Blinking away the afterimages of the flash, Stuart saw that Al's grin had widened into a hard, almost frightening smile that looked more like a pained grimace. Blue and white dots still swam crazily around in his vision as he stood up and pushed the chair away with the backs of his legs. The thought came back to him, screaming in his mind: *Who the fuck is this guy?*

"So, what did you think? How'd it sound to you?" Al asked excitedly.

"Uhh . . . unbelievable," Stuart said. His voice was wire-tight with tension. He felt a subtle loose trembling throughout his body as he started walking toward the studio door. Al was close at his side. Casting a sly glance over at the man, Stuart wouldn't have been at all surprised to see that same vibrant red glow in his eyes, but Al looked back at him with a steady, clear gaze.

"It sounded . . . absolutely fantastic," Stuart said softly, horribly aware of how shaky his voice must sound. When he shouldered open the door and stepped out into the corridor, his gaze was drawn against his will to the row of glossy photographs.

"And, hell," Al said, "that wasn't even with a good mix. Why, I've got a sound engineer, a guy named Dan Perez, who can jack that up so it sounds ten times better."

Stuart was speechless as he nodded absently. He suspected that Al wanted him to say something more about the quality of the sound, but all he could think about was the people in these photographs, and that they were all dead. Rationally, he knew that there was no possible way each of their deaths could be connected—in any way—to their having recorded here, but he couldn't get that thought out of his mind. Every one of them, from Buddy Holly on up to Stevie Ray Vaughan, had recorded here, and every single one of them had died shortly thereafter.

Stuart opened his mouth, desperately wanting to say something to Al about what he suspected, but instead he pushed open the door and stepped outside. The afternoon sun dazzled his eyes, making everything indistinct. It seemed so foolish, he thought, but he was suddenly afraid that, if he did agree to record in Al's studio, then he, too, might die before he got old.

But wasn't that the rock 'n' roll legacy? Live hard and fast, make a lot of money, fuck a lot of women, and die young!

The thought tantalized Stuart, and he told himself that even if this *was* the case, it might not happen right away. He had a long way to go before he approached the status of a rock legend.

But even if he had, what did it matter anyway?

The driving force behind Stuart's entire career had been that he was going to make it. Make it *big!*

If recording at Sharp Sounds Studios could somehow guarantee something like that, then maybe—Christ, *yes!* He was willing to take the chance. He'd pay Al Silverstein double, hell, *triple* what he was asking to use his studio!

"So," Al said, his face still split by a wide smile that made his teeth flash in the sunlight. "Do you think you and the rest of the band might consider coming up here to see what we can do?"

Leaning toward him much closer than Stuart cared for, Al seemed almost to be leering at him. Once again, for just an instant, Stuart thought he caught a flash of red light glowing deep in the man's dark eyes. Out here in the bright sunlight after being in the subdued lighting of the studio, Al's face seemed unnaturally white. He looked like a man who seldom if ever went outside during the daytime. Stuart tried not to read anything menacing into Al's words or tone of voice, but just contemplating the offer made him shiver inwardly in spite of the warmth of the sun. He didn't answer Al's question.

"Where are you parked?" Al asked, shading his eyes as he scanned the small parking lot beside the building.

"Over there," Stuart replied, nodding in the direction of the red Corvette that was parked in the shade across the street.

"Well, let me walk you to your car," Al said, stepping even closer to Stuart. "You know, you'll want to think about all of this very carefully. I don't make an offer like this to just *anybody*, you know."

Stuart bristled inwardly. He wanted to remind Al that his band's latest album, on which he had written the words and music for more than half the songs, had charted at number one. Sure, it had only lasted there for a single week, but there was no fucking way he could be considered *just anybody!* Not after all the years he'd dedicated to his career. But Stuart sensed that Al Silverstein wasn't the kind of person who would be impressed by anything Stuart had done. No, not a man who had actually been in the recording booth when Jimi Hendrix and Jim Morrison were recording.

Stuart didn't say anything as, side by side, they crossed the street. He fished the car keys from his pants pocket and unlocked the door. Looking past Al to the small, brick building, he silently weighed his options: Whether or not he should record here . . . and whether he should record with or without the rest of the band. At last, though, he raised his right hand, clasped Al's hand, and shook it firmly. He was struck by the man's cold, clammy handshake, but he pushed that thought from his mind and said, "Yes sir, Mr. Silverstein, I'd say we've got ourselves a deal."

A tight smile spread across his face, and his insides felt like they were vibrating at an unnaturally high frequency as he let go of Al's hand. A hard lump had formed in his throat, and no matter how hard he tried to swallow it, it wouldn't go down.

"You know, it might take us a couple of days, maybe a week or two to work out the details," Stuart went on, his voice sounding unusually tight. "But I'm telling you, man—"

Looking again at the studio building, he whistled between his teeth and shook his head as he tried to recall how his voice and guitar had sounded to him just moments ago in there. But the sound had already slipped away, and all he was left with was an urge to hear it again. If Al could make a whole album sound like *that*, then there was no fucking way it could miss.

"The way that playback sounded," he said, shaking his head wistfully. "Shit, man, you must work some kind of magic in here."

"Oh, we do," Al said, still smiling widely. "We most certainly do. And now you'll be one of the very select few who get to record at Sharp Sounds Studios."

Stuart froze for a moment and, licking his lips, said, "Hey, wait a second. You said a lot of famous people recorded in your studio."

Al nodded gravely. "Oh, that's absolutely true. A *lot* of them have, but—well, as you could tell from the pictures in the hallway, if I gave you a list of the names of everyone who has, you wouldn't be able to ask a single one of them what it had sounded like."

Stuart's voice wasn't much more than a strangled grunt when he cleared his throat and asked, "Why not?"

"Why not?" Al echoed. "Why, because every single one of them is dead, *that's* why. Hendrix, Lennon, Brian Jones, Jim Morrison . . . all of them. Dead. It's tragic, really, how so many rock stars are just starting to reach their peaks when they die."

"Yeah, but there—there's no way . . ." Stuart said. Shaking his head, he bit down on his lower lip. He closed his eyes for a moment, and all he could see in his mind was the line of framed black-and-white photographs on the wall in the corridor.

"But there can't be any connection, can there? Like . . . I

Dead Legends

mean, all those guys didn't die just because they . . . they recorded here. How could that be?"

Again, Al shrugged.

"I don't know," he said, his voice dropping to a low, gravelly growl. "Maybe there's no connection whatsoever . . . but then again, maybe there *is*. I guess it all comes down to how much you want it, and how much you're willing to risk."

Al had been smiling all along, but now his smile spread even wider, exposing the top and bottom rows of his wide, flat teeth, which made him look like he was about to take a bite out of something. Shadows from leaves overhead shifted across his face, making his skin look all ripply. Feeling weak in the knees, Stuart opened the car door and sat down behind the steering wheel.

"But you can rest assured, Stuie-boy," Al said, leaning forward with one hand on the opened door, the other on the car roof. "If by any chance you *do* meet an untimely death . . . well, just like all those other famous rock stars, you've already laid down one track here. And I'll be sure to put your photograph up right there on my studio wall."

Stuart straightened up and took a deep, shuddering breath.

"Yes sir, Mr. Bonney. You actually got to record a song in the Sharp Sounds Studios. At least you'll be famous for *that!*"

With that, he slammed the car door and gave Stuart a big wave before crossing the street back to the studio. Even when he was in the middle of the street with bright sunlight pouring down on him, his body seemed somehow insubstantial, almost like a shadow passing across the hot asphalt. Stuart shook his head before slipping the key into the ignition and starting up the car.

"Yes, goddamn it," he whispered, glancing at his reflection as he adjusted the rearview mirror. He shifted the car into gear, but instead of pulling out of his parking space, he pressed down hard on the brake pedal and jammed the shift back into park. His mind was whirling with crazy thoughts, and most of them were centered on a basic question Al had raised.

How much did he want it, and how much was he willing to risk?

There was no doubt about it, Al could get some incredible sounds. Recording here might mean there was no way in hell Brokenface could miss with their next record. He should feel happy—elated that Al had agreed to let the band record there.

But for nearly a full minute, Stuart just sat there, nervously drumming his fingers on the steering wheel as he considered what he might have just agreed to. His loudest internal voice was telling him that thinking he would die simply because he recorded at Al's studio was absolutely crazy. There was no possible way all those people's deaths could be connected with their having recorded here. But another voice in the back of his mind, much fainter but still demanding attention, was telling him that it might already be too late. He had already agreed to come up to Sharp Sounds Studios and record some more. If he followed through with those plans, it really might mean that he would die shortly thereafter.

A cold tightness verging on panic gripped Stuart by the throat as he considered all of this. Finally, he came to a decision. Turning off the ignition, he opened the car door and stepped back out onto the street.

The whole fucking thing is crazy! he told himself, but now he wasn't so sure he wanted to take that kind of chance. Although there were a few problems right now, things were going fairly well for the band. They were getting good airplay, and although their new album might not be ready in time for Christmas, things were coming along just fine. So why take a chance of messing it up?

His decision made, Stuart tossed his car keys once into the air and caught them, then slid them back into his pants pocket as he started across the street. He was so lost in his own thoughts that he never even saw the car that was heading straight toward him.

ROCKIN' ON HOME

Nat Gertler

"Let me spin a little story,
a tale that's short but tall,
about a lass, lovely and lost
with her back against the wall.
Sherley took a wrong turn,
and couldn't make it right,
but time and music solve things
caused by a foggy night. . . ."

Don't worry. I'll get back to playing shortly. But there's a story to this song, more of a story than can be squeezed into the three-minute, seventeen-second version that I'm elated to see climbing the charts. It may be important that the whole story be told at some point.

But it's just a story. It's just something I made up. Please, it's vital that you remember that.

This all started last fall. It was Saturday night, and I was in a restless mood without anywhere to go, so I went to see *The Rocky Horror Picture Show* at the Harwan. I hadn't seen it in a year, and I wanted to see some of the old gang there. Unfortunately, most of the people who made it through the dense, clingy fog to get to the theater that night were extremely young. I only recognized a couple of people who had been regulars when I used to go to the *Picture Show*.

The night wasn't a total loss, though. There was this one lady—twenty-one, twenty-two, long bottle-black hair draped over one green eye, her gangly body traversing the lobby in a gracefully awkward manner. One of the great things about the audience participation cult that has built up around *Rocky Horror* is that you're expected to talk to strangers. No one comes to *Rocky* when they want to be left alone.

"Come on in!" I invited. "Make yourself at home! It's your turn to take out the garbage!"

"Just my luck," she played back, "my first time and I have to do the chores."

"First time? Don't worry; I won't tell anyone you're a virgin. Hi, I'm Jason."

"Sherley," she replied. "I used to hang out with some kids from the High School for the Performing Arts, when I lived in Brooklyn. They were always raving about this movie, and when I was driving around with nothing to do and passed by here, I thought I'd check it out."

I took her down to a seat next to mine, and we spent the next two hours shouting obscenities at the film while people of various sexes danced in fishnet stockings in front of the screen. I gallantly shielded her from several water pistol attacks. It's always an interesting time—if you haven't seen the show, you should.

Afterward we headed to a diner for a quick bite, and we got a lot of talking done. It was amazing how much we had in common, how much in sync we were. She told me about her band, Death by Kisses. We'd both just signed record deals, within a couple days of each other. I write most of my own stuff, she writes most of their stuff. We both ordered scrambled eggs, putting ketchup on the toast and then piling the eggs on. I've never met anyone else who does that. It was that kind of freaky, everything-matches feeling. Felt wonderful.

So we finished our meal, and she invited me back to her place. Sherley claimed that there were no romantic overtones to it, but of course there were. And that I certainly didn't mind.

I almost lost her a couple of times, following her taillights through the dense, pervasive fog, but we made it to her apartment, safe and sound. She dropped her handbag and hit a button on the CD player with a single motion. She had stacks of those little CD drawers, and a big tape cabinet, and a few crates of genuine vinyl.

"Would you like something to drink?" she asked me. I didn't feel the need for anything harder than a ginger ale, and she said she had the ingredients for that. "What is this?" I asked her, meaning the music. It wasn't anything that I'd heard before, kind of a Led Zeppelinish ornate rock with some Jimi Hendrix energy to it. Whatever it was, it was good.

"It's Ziggy Stardust," she answered, handing me my glass.

I didn't understand. "What, is this one of the CD bonus tracks? I've got *Ziggy Stardust,* and it doesn't have this song on it. Doesn't sound like Bowie anyway."

She started talking swiftly. We were talking music, and this was clearly her topic. "This is Ziggy and the Spider's third album, the last one, *Man or Maniac?* I always thought it was a shame what happened to them. Weird B. Smith did some good experimental solo stuff afterward, but nothing could measure up to this. Ziggy was so out there."

"What are you talking about? I thought Bowie did only the one Ziggy album?" I was confused. When she asked "Bowie?" that only confused me a little more. I reached for the plastic CD case on top of the stereo. And that's when things got really weird.

It wasn't a Bowie album. It was an album *by* Ziggy Stardust and the Spiders from Mars. Gillis Strezkowski on bass, Weird B. Smith on keyboard, a bunch of other people on other instruments.

"These guys did three albums? Taking their name, taking their *names,* from the Bowie album? And if their stuff is this good, how come I've never heard of them?"

"Oh, of course you've heard of them," she said, laughing. "But who's this Bowie you keep referring to?"

"David Bowie! *The Rise and Fall of Ziggy Stardust and the Spiders from Mars* was his album."

"He did an album about the Spiders?"

"He created the Spiders! Made them up! They don't really exist!" It was like we were talking entirely different languages. She shook her head, as lost as I was, so I continued trying to explain. "David Bowie, while somewhat derivative, was a pretty big influence in the immediate post-Beatles scene."

"Post-who?" she asked, befuddled.

"The Beatles. The *Beatles! The White Album. Abbey Road. Sergeant Pepper's Lonely Hearts Club Band."*

At that, a spark of recognition lit her eyes. "Sergeant Pepper's Band! My parents went to hear them play a couple of times." She smiled.

I like to think I can communicate well, and when I can't make myself understood, I feel incompetent and get angry. I started turning away, frustrated, shouting, "There is no such band as Sergeant Pepper's! It's the—"

And that's when I saw it. Sitting in one of the crates of LPs, right on the end, was an album by the Sultans of Swing. Not a Dire Straits album, a genuine Sultans of Swing album. I started pawing frantically through her recordings. There were a lot of bands I didn't recognize, a few that sounded vaguely familiar, but there were also a couple of CDs by Bennie and the Jets (right next to one by Ruben and the Jets), a duped tape of Uncle John's Band, another dupe of Willie and the Poor Boys' *Greatest Hits* . . .

For a while I couldn't speak, I couldn't breathe. Reality had just done a major shift to the left. The more I tried to explain what was going on, the less sense it made. Sherley asked in a firm but polite manner if I was on some drug, but I wasn't, not that night. I wouldn't do a drug that would do this anyway. I like reality to stay just where it is, thank you.

I needed some time to think about this, to clear my mind, to not speak. Even more, I needed to hear some of this music. Sherley understood in a bizarre kind of way as I started to put things on the stereo. I played a keen, soulful creole track off of the Sultans of Swing record. Bennie and the Jets were glam rock, and not particularly impressive glam rock to boot, if the one song I heard was any indication. The others—well, it doesn't matter. These songs, these albums were real, they were there.

The only way that I could get Sherley to understand what it was that I couldn't explain was to get her to listen to some of the real music, the stuff that I knew. She was willing to follow me back to my place, which showed she had a lot of trust in a man who must have seemed crazy. We arrived at my apartment as the first glow of dawn was peeking out, and the fog was disappearing into little wisps.

I got out the Bowie album and put the title track on at a suitable volume. My neighbors would complain to me later, but I had more important things on my mind. She sat, transfixed, as the tale of ego trips and hard crashes was sung. When it was over, I moved the tone arm back to its resting place.

"Wow." That was her only syllable for about fifteen seconds. Then: "He captured what happened so perfectly. Shit, I wish I could write like that."

"That didn't happen. That never happened. He made it up."

She looked lost. I grabbed an Elton John "best of" collection off the shelf, and tossed it at her. "There. There's where Bennie and the Jets comes from. And here, here's a disc by the most popular band in recording history, *a band you never heard of,* with all your musical knowledge!" I winged *Sergeant Pepper's* toward her lap. "They didn't form in the 1940s. They weren't even thought up until well into the sixties."

She was shaken. I mean, she was *shaking*. She could tell I wasn't just jerking her around. I wish I had been. I mean, damn it, it's music! It's not supposed to hurt anybody.

"I've got to . . . to . . . to just get out of here," she stammered. "Just, just tell me how to get back to the theater. I can find my way home from there." I thought for a second that maybe it wasn't a good idea for her to drive in this condition, that maybe the best thing was for us to figure out what was going on. But sometimes it's best to let someone do what they feel they have to, and this was one of those times.

I watched the exhaust billow from the rusted tailpipe of her sedan as she drove away.

It'd been twenty-two hours without any sleep. I should have gone straight to bed, but I wasn't drowsy, and I wasn't settled. I put on some Chili Peppers and just sort of zenned out for a while. By the time the album was over, I'd convinced myself that my mind had been playing tricks on me.

Then Sherley came back.

Ragged streaks of cheap mascara were like a road map of her tears. Her face seemed to have aged ten years in the hour she'd been away. Her voice sounded hollow as she said, "It's not there. Nothing is there. Nothing I know is out there."

She'd tried to get home, and she couldn't.

"This isn't where I belong!" she pleaded. "This isn't my place! This is a world full of streets I've never been on and bands I've never heard of! And the books! I'll bet the books . . ." She started to scan my bookshelf. "No, I've never heard of any of these. I've never—wait!" Her eyes grew wide with hope as she grabbed my copy of *Venus on the Half Shell*. "This is by Kilgore Trout! I've *heard* of him!"

I didn't know how to cushion it. "Sherley . . ." I said.

She cut me off. "He doesn't exist, does he?"

"Kilgore Trout is a character, a writer, in books by a man named Kurt Vonnegut," I explained. "That book's just a pastiche of his work, by a guy named Farmer."

"Nothing, nothing I know exists. You people, you just

made it all up." She sat on the couch, staring in shock. For three hours, she didn't say a word, and I did not violate her silence. Then, mercifully, she fell asleep. I carefully carried her light form into the bedroom and laid her on the bed. Put. I put her on the bed. You have to be careful with words.

Even after everything, she looked gorgeous asleep. I stole one of my pillows, went out to the couch, and fell asleep almost instantly.

I woke up a bit before she did, and when I saw her stirring, I quickly made her some breakfast (breakfast being a relative term; the sun had already set before she awoke) and carried it into the bedroom. Her face blank, she sat up and sucked on the coffee for a while. Then she shoveled down some eggs and managed a strained smile. "Scrambled eggs. I've heard of those." A weak joke, but I took it as a sign that she was starting to figure out how to cope, so I smiled back at her.

When she had cleaned her plate, she put down her fork and began to speak in a detached, analytical tone. "I think it's clear that I come from another world, another place. It's a place that people from this place create or add to whenever they make fiction. It's a world of fiction. I come from a fictional world. I don't belong here. There's nothing I know here. I'm going to have to figure out how to get back, and I don't even know how to start. It may take a while. It may be impossible."

I didn't wait a beat. "You may stay here as long as you need to."

I was already falling in love with her.

The conversations in the days that followed were often very philosophical. How could we bridge this rift between worlds if we couldn't understand it? So we set about trying to get a grip on it. We considered the thought that both worlds were equally valid. Perhaps hers was the more real world, and what passed for creativity here was only the ability to pull information through from her world. That theory fell apart, however, when we realized that the more successful a piece of fiction was on my world, the more significant an effect its contents had on hers. Thus, Albert Hammond's creation "The Free Electric Band" was a little-known group on her world, while the long-term popularity of "Ziggy Stardust and the Spiders from Mars" made them her world's equivalent of the Doors. It seemed that our collective cultural subconscious imprinted itself on her world.

We thought that maybe my world was derived from yet another world, that maybe there was a world with a hit song about "Fleetwood Mac" or "Michael Jackson," and that's what made those folks big here. Thinking about that, I realized for the first time just how this must've shaken her faith in reality to the core. There had actually been something nifty about thinking that I, as a musician, was a sort of god, with the ability to create musicians on her world. However, the thought that I was just here because on some other world, some drummer was saying, "Hey, let's do a song about a guitarist with a receding hairline named Jason Caldwell," made me feel small and insignificant and artificial. It also didn't help solve our problem, so we abandoned that train of thought.

On the third day we made love for the first time. I think she just needed something that could make her forget her problem for a few minutes, and I was more than willing to oblige. It was good. Each time it was always at least good, but it was also hollow, because I always remembered that this woman shouldn't be here, that she graced my presence only because she had nowhere else to go.

After she'd been there a week, I had to start going to the studio. I'd promised the company an album and had already booked the studio time, investing in getting more time at a cheaper analog studio rather than going for one of the newer ones where they chop your music up into millions of little numbers and swear to you that it's still there. I wanted to compose in the studio, to keep my mind on the recorded sound, so the extra expense was worth it. Besides, I wouldn't have been any use at home; Sherley and I had run out of ideas, and were settling down to wait and hope and pray for the return of the mysterious fog that seemingly had allowed her to come here.

Every day I would come home and find her a bit more sullen. At first she tried going out and doing minor shopping and things like that, but it never worked. It always seemed that the world was mocking her, that there were always blatant reminders that this was not the world she had grown up in, that her world was derivative. She couldn't face that. The human mind is not equipped to deal with that.

So instead she spent her days at home, watching some television, listening to records that I had screened and verified as being free of cultural references. She watched mainly nonquiz game shows and sitcoms about families—things that, if they created anything in her world, would be things that she would not have encountered. Seven castaways stranded for years might have become newsworthy when they returned, but the family from *Family Ties* would have been just another family. I came home late one night to find her bawling her eyes out in front of *The Jackie Thomas Show*, because it's about the making of a TV series that is actually quite popular in her world.

The only time I ever saw her reacting remotely positively to any reminder of the situation was when she caught an "Itchy and Scratchy" short on *The Simpsons*, and even that was bittersweet.

And as I watched this vibrant, magic woman degenerate into a housebound couch potato, I loved her even more, because watching her slip away reminded me of what she truly was in her heart. I tried to convince her to do something, anything to regain her spark, but it was no use. I asked her to write some lyrics for me, to get her creativity flowing, but after staring at an unopened notebook for ten minutes, she threw it across the room.

"I can't!" she screamed. "Don't you understand? I'm just a marionette from another world, and now there's no one pulling my strings!"

I don't think that was the real problem. She'd just literally stopped believing in herself. She could have grabbed her own strings if she'd only believed.

Meanwhile, my album was almost done. It was coming out pretty good. A bit melancholy, but understandably so. Being with a woman who could be who you really loved only if she was somewhere where you couldn't be will do that to you. I only had one track left to record when I realized something.

I might be the only thing holding her to this world.

Movement between these worlds, these levels of reality, isn't something I'll claim to understand. It makes sense, though, that if I was constantly seeing her here (and I was the only one who knew who and what she was, remember), I was constantly reanchoring her here. If her world and her people are made up of the images of our minds, then my mind was keeping her what she was, where she was.

So I set her up in an apartment with shades over the windows and a year's supply of food. I left her there and told her to stay inside and not let anyone see her. She smiled because she understood and she pulled me in and we made love with true abandon for the first time, and when it was over I was crying like a hurt child. I walked out the door and she locked herself away from the world.

And then, to give her a push home, I went and I wrote this song. It may be the best thing I've written; I can't judge because I can't distance myself from it. There's a lot of myself in that song. And there's all of Sherley.

But how big a push does she need? Writing the song may not be enough to bridge the gap. It may need to be widely heard, to become part of the collective subconscious. I haven't dared check the apartment, because if she isn't gone yet, my seeing her could anchor her further. I like to believe she's home already.

Damn, I miss her.

So that's the part of the story that's missing from the song, the part that wouldn't fit on a track of a record. I wanted to tell it at least once. I wanted people to hear it. It might be important.

But it's just a story. It's just something I made up. Please, it's vital that you remember that.

> "She's belting out a hot tune
> and the kids all sing along,
> then they play into the evening
> when nothing could be wrong.
> The music had gone missing
> but now it's here to stay;
> Someday soon they'll all forget
> that Sherley went away.
>
> Sherley's back with Death by Kisses
> The band that packs 'em in,
> and things could not be sweeter
> since Sherley's home again.
>
> Sherley's home again."

THE UNDEADLIEST GAME

Bill Mumy and Peter David

The toilet stall was shuddering rhythmically around Connie, pounding in time to the cadence of the hand clapping and foot stomping out in the open-air amphitheater. Over and over, like a jackhammer, the word was repeated. A single word, like a chant, like a mantra: *"Rave! Rave! Rave!"*

And Connie, feeling as if she were on the power trip of her life, thought to herself, You get to wait, you bastards. You poor mindless, foot-stomping dumbfucks. Because Rave ain't goin' out there until I'm done. God, what a trip. You think you're giving them what they need with your applause and hotel keys and shit you throw onto the stage. And it's nothing. It's all show. Because when it comes to choosing between what you give and what I give, it's no contest. . . .

Connie was crouched in front of Reb. Her face was obscured by the long, sandy brown hair that hung around her head like a damp mop. She was crouched in front of him, the toilet jamming into the small of her back and one knee of her tatty bell-bottom jeans mashing an old cigarette butt. Her multicolored glass beads (or as her mother called them, her goddamn hippie beads) clattered noisily around her neck.

Reb was looking at the ceiling, the back of his skull tapping lightly and repeatedly against the door of the toilet stall. It was impossible to tell whether it was in time to the clapping from outside or the rhythmic strokes of Connie's ministrations. His eyes, however, were starting to roll up into his head, and his fingers were wrapped around a long strand of Connie's hair. His back was arched, and he was starting to stand on his toes.

"Yeah," he whispered. "Do it, yeah . . ."

Connie replied, "Mmm-hmm." Since her mouth was otherwise occupied, there wasn't much else she could say at that moment.

There was a pounding on the door outside that somehow managed to make itself heard over the sustained whooping and shouting from the crowd. "Reb!" shouted a hoarse voice. "Let's do it!" The voice belonged to Billy Bob, the fat drummer of Tidal Rave. The band, in response to the floor-shuddering exhortations of the crowd, was ready to play its third and final encore of the night. "Hey, Reb!" shouted Billy Bob again. "You coming?!"

"Yes!" shouted Reb, the back of his skull slamming so hard against the stall door that it left a dent in the metal. His fingers flexed convulsively in Connie's hair. It hurt Connie like hell, but it was a delicious sort of hurt.

"Good!" called back Billy Bob.

Reb sagged against the door, his muscles momentarily failing him. Connie released his sagging erection with satisfaction and patted it smugly. "Now you can entertain the rest of the troops," she said.

She looked up, waiting for Reb to saying something affectionate. Something appreciative. Something—

"Jesus," he gasped, pulling his breath together. "Don't just sit there and stare. Help me get my pants up."

He loves me, she thought self-righteously.

His leather pants crackled as she helped him pull them up. But she paused, studying something that had caught her eye before. She hadn't had time to really look at it, though, considering the speed with which events had gone.

It was a beautiful tattoo on his left thigh. She had never seen anything like it—the tattoo, that is. A hairy, sweaty, male thigh; those she had seen tons of. One did not become what amounted to a professional backstage rock groupie without experiencing more than one's share of male anatomy.

The tattoo was six inches high, a purple and black silhouette of a woman's profile. And it was crying a single, blood-red tear.

"That's a far-out tattoo," she whispered. "Where—?"

And then it was gone, obscured by the trouser leg pulled over it. "Yeah," he said brusquely. "You can take a picture of it later."

And then he was gone, the stall door slamming open.

Connie fished around in her handbag, pulled out a cigarette, and lit up. She stayed there for a minute or so, taking long, grateful drags. She smiled slightly as she heard the roar of the crowd. The band had obviously taken the stage. *If only you dweebs knew,* she thought. Then she rose, peeled the cigarette butt off her knee, and walked out of the backstage bathroom. She grabbed a beer from the ice chest; the ice had melted, and she wiped the cold wetness from the bottle with the trailing end of the "Tidal Rave" T-shirt she was wearing.

She moved to the wings offstage and watched as Tidal Rave ripped through an extended version of "She's Not You, But She'll Do," one of their biggest hits. The sound onstage that blazed through the band's monitors was so different from what the audience heard. Connie swallowed the last drop of the Heineken, her fourth so far tonight. She

The Undeadliest Game

fondled the green bottle and smiled at the moon as the band rocked the crowd into a satisfied frenzy.

And the night was filled with magic. . . .

It was the first time Connie had ridden in a limo, but she didn't want Reb or anyone else in the band to know. She drank champagne and smoked the potent joint being passed back and forth as if she were born to it.

She sat on Reb's lap the entire ride back to the hotel. And it didn't bother her at all that he fondled her tits in front of the other guys the whole way there. In fact, she was proud of it. And she smirked in secret pleasure at their amused and envious glances.

Connie was making a name for herself in the inner circles of touring heavy rock bands. She was considered the cutest, sweetest, best piece of teenage ass in Little Rock. She couldn't handle piano or guitar, but she was a virtuoso in other respects.

Despite her experience, though, there was something different about Reb. There was an intensity burning in his midnight blue eyes. His black hair was thick and wavy, and he had a mustache with ends that hung down just below his chin. She admired his long neck, with the Adam's apple that bobbed up and down furiously as he sang.

And she worshiped his body . . . lord, did she love it. She admired it now, in the hotel room, as he stepped out of the shower. Lying naked on the bed, Connie put aside the fat joint she had just fired up and snagged the Polaroid camera from its perch atop Reb's metal suitcase. "Tell your tattoo to say cheese," she said, and giggled as the camera flashed.

Reb grinned. "I got a treat for ya. Be right back," he slurred, and strolled into the living room of the spacious suite. When he returned he was holding a large, ornate metal chalice. His semi-erect penis swayed confidently as he walked. He was wiping his lips, apparently having just downed a healthy quaff from the chalice, and he handed it to Connie. "Have a drink, babe. A fine brew, for special occasions."

She was surprised at the chalice's weight as she took it. Unhesitatingly she brought it up to her talented lips and swallowed. The liquid burned as it went down, and seemed to permeate every pore. "Mmmm! Delicious, Reb!" She turned the chalice slowly in her hands, studying it. "And look at all the far-out engraving and jewels and shit! It's like something out of King Arthur, y'know?"

"Yeah, I guess." The bedsprings creaked as Reb stretched out on the king-size bed.

Connie covered him like a blanket. "That was tasty, Reb," she said invitingly. "But I'm still not full." She worked her way down below his waist, and now she was giving the concert. . . .

And then the moon floated down into the hotel room to get a better look at her. Connie felt distantly, dimly surprised . . . but not as surprised as she should have been, given the unusual nature of a lunar body showing up in a hotel room. And it was colored wrong . . . blood red . . .

And then she heard the moon singing to her, or was it talking? Or was it laughing? And was she moving? She was aware that Reb was no longer under her . . . that she was under him, but that was fine, and he was moving around inside her and it felt so damned good, except, the weirdest thing, he was standing off to the side. And the rest of the band was there, too. The moon was bouncing along across the tops of their heads, humming that odd tune, and it was like one of those old "follow the bouncing ball" cartoons. And sure, it was weird, but then so was life. It was no weirder than that, and the pleasant buzz in her head made it all oookayyy. . . .

"Slut! *Whore!*"

Her mother's hand moved so quickly that Connie never even saw it coming. One minute it was at her mother's side, hanging there limply, and the next, *wham,* it was across her face.

Curiously, the impact didn't bother her all that much. She

The Undeadliest Game

was still feeling rather numb, as if her brain were awake but her body hadn't responded to the alarm clock yet. If anything, she found the noise of her mother's shriek and the sound of skin slapping skin to be far more of a nuisance.

"Whore!" her mother shouted again. Mom was a head shorter in height, but towering in her wrath. "You come staggering in here, now, at 8 AM! What have you been up to all night? No, you don't have to tell me. You were out with another rock group, weren't you?! *Weren't you?!*"

She started to swing her arm again, but this time Connie was ready for it, taking a step back so that the swing was a clean miss. "Yeah," she said, her own voice sounding as if it were coming from a hundred miles away. "Yeah, I was. Why shouldn't I?" she added defiantly. "You don't care about me or what I do."

"Yes! That's right," snarled her mom. "I've stopped caring. I've had to stop caring, because if I cared, I'd be dying thinking about what you do! You're killing me, Connie!"

Don't gimme ideas, thought Connie grimly, rubbing her temples.

The hell of it was, Connie didn't remember precisely what she'd been up to all night. She'd lapsed into some sort of . . . of utterly whacked dream shortly after hitting the sack with Reb. When she'd woken up, she'd found herself back in her own car in the arena parking lot. Everything else was a blur of ridiculous images and dim feelings that were fading fast.

Connie's father was planted in front of the television, as he so often was these days. The accident at the loading dock that had put him on disability also seemed to have taken the fight out of him. Once upon a time, he would have been at his wife's side, haranguing their wayward daughter. On the one hand, Connie was happy that the odds were more even. On the other hand—although she hated to admit it—she missed her old dad. Just a bit.

Dad was fixated on some game show as if it were the word

of God coming down in flaming letters. Connie's mother, meantime, was wringing her hands. Whenever she did that, Connie felt like replying in kind by wringing her neck.

"What's going to become of you?" wailed her mom. "Dear God, I've tried to give you morals, values . . ."

But Connie was suddenly tuning her out, because a news bulletin had interrupted the game show, and she was positive that they'd mentioned the name of the group.

"Rock and roll fans have new cause to grieve," Chet Huntley was saying. "The recent breakup of the Beatles upset many, certainly, but it was nothing in comparison to the news of the tragic plane crash early this morning that took the lives of the hard rock group called Tidal Rave. Billy Bob Batson, Reb Jonny, Mad Dog—"

She didn't hear the rest of the report, because she was screaming too loudly. It sounded like the voice of a different person—high-pitched, caterwauling, as if her soul had just been torn away.

And she heard her mother shouting, "Good! Good! Was that who you were with? *Good!* I hope they burn in hell! I hope they all do, and—"

Connie turned and smacked her. It was a lousy move, her fingertips barely brushing her mother's face. Nevertheless, her mother's eyes filled with tears, her face going slack with shock at the notion that her daughter would retaliate in such a primal, furious way.

And her mother laid a curse on her. The worst, most vicious, most effective curse that a mother can utter.

"I hope," she whispered harshly, "I hope that someday you have a daughter who treats you just like you've treated me."

Wind pulled down the torn-out newspaper ad for Dark Academy that she'd stuck to the refrigerator with a banana magnet, and pressed it close to her breast. She wondered how it was possible that a minute could always be a minute, a day always be twenty-four hours, and yet the week leading up to the Dark Academy concert had been, quite simply, the longest week in her eighteen years of life.

Wind was of medium height, with the same sort of almost catlike eyes that her mother sported. Unlike her mother, though, who hadn't changed her hairstyle significantly in, like, twenty years, Wind's flaming red hair—the one substantive thing her father had left her before he had ditched them both—was short and permed. She was fortunate to have skin unmarred by blemishes and full, rich lips.

She spun in place, scarcely able to believe the concert date had arrived. Finally, finally, fi-na-lee—

Her pirouette stopped short as her mother stepped into the kitchen doorway. She gaped.

"Oh, God, Mother . . . no . . . you can't be serious."

Connie looked down at her outfit, then back up at her daughter. "What?"

"You're—you're not coming along. I thought you were out in your garden. Pruning and hedging and whatevering."

"So I finished and I changed. So?"

"Yes! Changed! Into those . . ." Wind gestured helplessly. "Those . . . those *things*."

"What?" Connie said again. She ran her hands proudly down her hips. "It's my concert clothes. They still fit great. What's the point in keeping your body up if you don't strut it once in a while?"

"But, *Jesus*, Ma!" wailed Wind. "You look like something out of *Hair*"—a positively ancient movie she'd caught on cable the previous week. "Those bell-bottoms! Those beads! This isn't going to be a costume party! Christ, I saw pictures of you wearing them back in the seventies, and they were *already* out of style." She stomped her foot. "Do you *have* to come?"

"No," Connie shot back a bit impatiently, "but I want to come! First off, you've been playing their CDs so much that you've got me interested in checking them out myself. I like their grooves." Ignoring her daughter's pained expression, she continued, "Secondly, my darling, I lent you the money for the tickets, remember. I could use a night out. Besides, if you were at least going with some friends . . ."

"I don't *have* any friends," said Wind, sinking into a chair.

Oh, here we go again, she thought. The "my mother is the world's biggest embarrassment" speech again. Somehow Connie just didn't feel up for it.

She pulled off the hippie beads and tossed them on the counter, then leaned against the oven. "I'll lose the beads. Okay, kid? That's my final offer."

Wind blew air out impatiently. "You know what you're doing, don't you. You're trying to recapture your youth . . . and I'm getting caught in the trap."

Connie was clearly unmoved by Wind's incisive, albeit petulant, analysis. "Concert's in an hour, Your Highness," said Connie mildly. "What's it gonna be?"

"Fine. Whatever." Wind sighed. "Go looking however you want. Go stark naked, if you feel like it."

"Mmm," said Connie. "Now, *that* takes me back. . . ."

The crowd was on its feet for almost the entire set. Dark Academy was headlining the Sports Arena for the first time. They'd been on the road as a supporting act for two summers straight, but their second album, *Prove It,* had produced two big video singles, and now they were roaring through the world as top of the bill.

Wind was having a great time. Connie's feet were getting sore, but she stayed up and moved to the groove, which assaulted the stadium at earsplitting volume.

"You know, the best thing about these guys," Connie bellowed in between songs, "is the way the rhythm section plays together. Very tight! But I'm not wild about that singer."

"Really?!" Wind looked stunned. "Of the five of them, Whiley's the most popular! But I like the bass player, Val, the best! He's . . . God, when I think of him, it makes me—"

The Undeadliest Game

And then she suddenly became aware that this was her *mother,* for crissakes, and she promptly clammed up.

But Connie didn't want to let it go. For the first time in ages she felt a connection, not only with her daughter, but also with the girl she herself used to be. Back in the days before the lousy marriage and the series of chicken-shit jobs and the realization that, more and more, her mother's reflection was staring out at her from the mirror.

"Like mother, like daughter," Connie told her.

Wind turned and stared at her. "What do you mean?"

Connie shrugged nonchalantly. "Bass players were what did it for me, honey. Of course, in my day, it was a lot easier to do something about it. . . ."

If Connie had sprouted antlers, she could not have gotten a bigger look of surprise from her daughter. It gave her a flash of the old self-confidence. And now Wind was actually grinning in a conspiratorial fashion.

"Do something . . . like what?" she asked. Lord knows she'd heard her mother talk about the old days, *ad nauseam*. But she'd developed a knack for tuning Connie out because, well, who really cared about the *old* days? Now, though, it actually seemed like it might be applicable to Wind herself.

"Well, back then nobody worried about AIDS. Casual sex wasn't a danger, and I don't mean to rub it in, but don't let anyone tell you it wasn't fun, because I had a fuckin' great time with some touring musicians who passed through town. And, of course, it was a snap getting backstage."

"A snap?"

Connie looked at her daughter in amusement. "You planning to repeat everything I say?"

"I mean . . ." Wind cleared her throat. "If I, y'know . . . *wanted* to get backstage, how . . . hypothetically, I mean."

"Hypothetically . . . it helps that you're drop-dead gorgeous and over eighteen with a body to die for." Connie smiled lopsidedly. "So nature gave you a leg up. Hypothetically, you understand . . . if I were you, I'd head for that blue door there. You see it?" She pointed. "Just left of the beer stand. The one with 'Do Not Enter' all over it. Well, they count on those signs to do ninety percent of the work for 'em. Once you go through that door, the dressing rooms are just around the corner, a couple of doors on the right."

Wind was gaping at her mother's calm, confident manner.

"There's usually a musclehead kid sitting at that door," continued Connie, "and the list with all the backstage passes and names is kept around the corner at the main backstage entrance. You just act like you've already been there all night. Tell him you left your purse with your pass in the dressing room or something. Tell him you're—what's the bass player's name?"

"Val." Wind said it like it was poetry. "Val McCloud."

"Tell him you're Val's old lady, and you got tired of standing in the wings and went out to hear the mix from the back, and forgot your purse. Be a little pissed off at him for asking, and show yourself off at the same time. That'd get you in . . . hypothetically, of course."

She saw Wind looking nervously at the stage door, and back to her mother, as if trying to screw up her courage, while at the same time seeking some sort of . . . what? Approval?

Why are you doing this? a voice demanded inside Connie's head. What are you pushing her into? For her? For yourself?

She ignored the voice, stopped thinking. Instead she fumbled in her purse and pulled out a couple of condoms. "If you're going to go, go before they finish the set. Be there when the band comes offstage. You want to be Val's girl? Then tell yourself that's what you are. Be Val's girl. As soon as you see him, kiss him. Act like you belong with him. Tell him he was great. Hand him a beer." She was speaking faster and faster, in almost a breathless whisper, and yet she was still making herself heard above the thundering of the crowd. "Squeeze his nuts, but not too hard, and whisper something to him . . . maybe how much you want him, and then just give him a look that tells him that this is his lucky night. But no needles—no damned needles, you understand? And if you do see it through, it damned well better be using these, understood?" She pressed the Trojans into Wind's hand.

Wind was staring at her mother as if with new eyes. She didn't say it, but the question was clear in her face: *Why?*

"Because I'm not my mother, damn it," Connie said in response to the unspoken word. "I swore when I was your age I wouldn't turn into her, and I won't, goddamn it, I *won't*. Here's cab fare if you need it. Do you want your bass player?"

There was only a moment's hesitation, and then Connie saw some of her own wildness in her daughter's face. She felt as if they were connecting for the first time since . . . Jesus, since Wind was in diapers. Wind nodded vigorously.

"Then go get him," Connie said.

Wind was on her way as fast as her namesake. Connie watched her go, watched her worm her way through the aisles and down to the blue door. There was a moment's hesitation, and then she saw Wind square her shoulders, move with that old-time confidence. Move through the door.

And part of Connie was singing in triumph.

And another part—a smaller part—was dying. . . .

The tall, lanky, long-haired bass player had his arm around Wind. Val lay next to her, those elongated, strong fingers that pumped a powerful throbbing tone out of his bass idly fondling her breasts. Their naked bodies were pressed against each other, to savor that last bit of heat before it dissipated completely.

Some part of Wind's mind still couldn't quite accept it. Her mother had been right. Right about everything. About sneaking in. About how her self-assured pose (and a pose it had been, nothing more) had been enough to draw Val to her like a moon snagged into orbit around a planet. No, not a planet—a star. He'd called her his star, his nova, the center of his universe. And who cared if, in all likelihood—all right, in all certainty—it had been pure heat-of-the-moment bullshit. He'd said it, even if he hadn't really meant it.

Her mother had been right.

Jesus.

Things had not been so hot between Connie and Wind lately—lately meaning since sometime after Wind's second birthday. But it had gotten particularly bad of late. Her mother had been hanging over her constantly, stifling her. It seemed lately as if, whichever way she turned, there was her crazy, overaged-groupie mother.

It was . . . it was so damned pathetic. Her mother was this huge, aching embarrassment, and there was no way that Wind had been able to make her realize that. No way to get her to back off, to stop prying into Wind's affairs, to stop prattling on and on about the good old days as if driven by some inner demon to communicate every moment of twenty-some years ago as if anyone gave a shit. . . .

"You okay?" Val was rubbing her shoulder, looking mildly surprised. "You went all stiff."

"I'm fine." She smiled gamely. Because, damn it, this time . . . this time, her mother had been right. Give the crazy old bitch credit where it was due.

Val looked down in obvious disgust at the condom that now hung limply on his penis, looking about as attractive as a deflated balloon. He'd made a face when Wind had pulled it out of her pocket. "Babe," he'd said swaggeringly, "if there's anyone in this world you don't have to be worried about snagging a deadly disease from, it's me." But, damn it, her mother had been right about all the other stuff. There was no reason to assume that she'd been off target about this particular caveat.

Still, now that the immediate fun and games were over, she wanted to help him maintain *some* degree of dignity. "Let me take care of that," she said, indicating the condom with a tilt of her chin. She headed to the bathroom, stepping over the clothes that lay strewn on the hotel room floor. A

The Undeadliest Game

moment later she was cleaning up her rock star with a hot washcloth.

Val turned on the bedside lamp and lit up a Marlboro. As the harsh light invaded the room, Wind paused.

"That felt good, babe. Why'd you stop?" asked Dark Academy's bassist as he produced a series of smoke rings that pranced around Wind's nipples.

"I'm just looking at your tattoo, Val. It's really great. It's so . . . emotional."

"Oh. Yeah." He sounded bored.

"Have you had it long?"

"Yeah. A long time."

"Wow," she sighed as she toweled him off some more. "It's the neatest tattoo I've ever seen."

And she traced its outline with the long nail of her right index finger, following the outline from the top of the purple profile of the woman's silhouette all the way down to the single, blood red tear that fell on her dark cheek. . . .

The moon was singing that same old song now . . . but it was discordant, shrill, ripping through her mind. And there was laughter now, faces rippling through, and a hardness beneath her that felt like . . . like the coldness of stone. She felt an aching in her joints and tried to stretch, but her hands were tied, she couldn't move, and they were coming for her. And there was some sort of odd stench filling her nostrils, filling her *soul*. . . .

Connie woke up, hearing a scream from a distance, and it took her a few confused moments to realize that the scream was coming from her . . . at which point she closed her mouth and, lo and behold, the screaming stopped.

She looked at the old Felix the Cat clock that hung on her wall. It was 4:09 AM. She thought about the Beach Boys for a second.

Her extra-large men's Rolling Stones Sticky Fingers T-shirt was plastered to her. She drew her knees up, pressing them against her breasts.

Wind wasn't home yet. She knew it instinctively—which didn't stop her from padding to her daughter's room and opening the door.

The room wasn't much different from her own of twenty years or so ago. Posters on the closet door and wall: Dark Academy, Guns 'n' Roses, and Albert Einstein riding a bicycle. Still plenty of dolls and stuffed animals tucked away on shelves and piled on Wind's four-poster queen-size bed. But no eighteen-year-old beautiful daughter safely tucked in and sleeping.

That dream . . .

She ran her fingers through her sweaty hair . . . and then, for no reason she could understand, she touched the back of her neck, just below her skull. The skin was rough there, had been for ages. As if it had been scratched, or even clawed.

She hadn't had that dream in years. It had started happening right after Tidal Rave had crashed and burned, and she would wake up screaming. And she could still see, in her mind's eye, her own mother standing framed in the doorway, saying, "Good! Good! Have some of the nightmares that you've given me!"

Fat lot of help she was.

The dream had faded so long ago—almost, it seemed to Connie, out of a sense of spite. It was as if her subconscious mind didn't want to give her mother the satisfaction of seeing Connie in distress.

But her mother was long gone. And Tidal Rave was long gone.

And the dream was back, with a vengeance. As if some sort of alarm had gone off in her subconscious, trying to warn her of . . .

Of what?

Something that was going to happen? Something that already had happened, but her mind refused to accept or understand? Something . . .

"Wind," she whispered. "Oh, baby . . . please come home safe."

The Undeadliest Game

But she had the anxious feeling that there would never be safety again.

It had taken every ounce of self-control not to come running downstairs when she'd heard the front door open and close at a little after 6 AM. She had, however, felt a sense of relief sweep over her, and that relief had swept her back to sleep, a blissful slumber that didn't end until a little past noon. Connie staggered downstairs, rubbing her eyes, to hear the crackling of eggs frying up in a pan. She stepped into the kitchen and there was Wind, fresh as the morning, looking up from the stove. "Over easy?" she asked.

Connie half-smiled. "According to the guys, I was."

She resisted the urge to run across the room, to hug her daughter to her. To—as childish as it sounded—count her fingers and toes, just as she had when Wind was born, to make sure that she was okay. Instead she sauntered across the kitchen, her tattered bathrobe swishing around her muscular calves. Plopping down in a chair, she said, "So . . . ?"

"So what?" replied Wind.

"Don't get cagey with me, young lady. Did it work?"

Obviously Wind was thinking of stringing it out, but she wasn't a talented enough game-player to stay quite that blasé. "Yeah . . . it worked. Like a charm."

"Everything?"

*"Every*thing," said Wind significantly.

And something else within Connie died. But she couldn't say exactly what.

"Congratulations," she said evenly. "You're now—"

(A whore! Slut! Bitch!)

"—one of the privileged few," she finished, trying to slam the door on her mother's voice. Feeling she should do something, she got up and went to Wind, hugging her. She reached over and turned off the stove.

"Mother!" Wind protested. "I was making you breakfast."

"Yeah, well . . . you can't cook for shit. That's how I know you're my daughter. So . . ." And she pulled Wind over to the other chair, sitting down across from her. "Tell me *every*thing."

She did. Wind told her everything. Every glorious moment. Every subterfuge. Every second of discovery. Connie kept smiling even though her face was hurting, and nodding until she thought her head was going to plop off her shoulders.

("Are you happy, whore? You've turned your daughter into a slut just like you. Just so you could continue your slutty pleasure vicariously through her, you've ruined her, you've—")

". . . and a tear that looked like blood . . ."

That snapped her concentration back to the fore. She looked at her daughter, blinking furiously. "Go back. What? What were you talking about?"

"Val's tattoo," said Wind, puzzled. "Weren't you listening?"

"Just—" She forced a smile. "Bear with your old mom. What'd it look like?"

Wind described it, in detail. And she watched her mother become more and more pale as she did so. "Mom, are you okay? What is it?"

And the moon was singing, and Reb was laughing, and the others were there . . .

("Slut! Whore! If you won't listen to me, listen to yourself—!")

"Hon . . ." She was fighting to keep her voice steady. She took Wind by the shoulders and said, "Promise me you won't go back."

"What?"

"To Val and the others. I—I just have this feeling. That's all. Maybe it's silly."

"It *is* silly," said Wind with conviction. "And I am going back. Tonight."

"No."

"But they invited me—"

The Undeadliest Game

"No!" And now she was shaking Wind firmly. "You won't go back there!"

Wind brushed her arms aside, and Connie felt a flash of amazement at the strength in her daughter's arms. Wind stood up. "Why the hell not?"

"It's . . . it's nothing I can explain. Woman's intuition, okay?"

"No, not okay! Mom, what the hell is going on?"

"It's . . ." She tried to find words to articulate what was mostly a gnawing dread. "Look . . . there was this group, Tidal Rave—"

"Oh, God, Mother, not more war stories about—"

"Listen to me, goddamn it!" Connie fairly roared. "You wanted to know, and here it goddamn is!"

And she told her everything. Everything that she could remember, at any rate, for it was twenty years gone, and much of that time was a haze for her. But there were some things she remembered. She remembered that growling bass player, and that tattoo. She remembered the goblet, and the limo ride, and the cold, and a sharp stabbing pain, and the laughter, and the moon singing that song.

She spoke quickly, desperately, trying to get through to her daughter. Trying to connect.

But as she spoke she saw, with growing concern, the skepticism on Wind's face. She wasn't convincing her. If anything, it seemed as if she was losing her.

"There's something wrong," she concluded forcefully.

"Mother"—Wind was trying to remain patient, but not doing a terribly good job of it—"this is so fucked up it's not even funny. So he's got the same tattoo. So what? There's probably some guy in L.A. or Chicago or Frisco or who knows where, and it's his specialty. So what?"

"Wind . . . please don't go back."

"I promised."

"Promise me, damn it! I'm your mother! I count for something! I count! I order you not to go!"

"You *order* me?" Wind was incredulous. "What're you, nuts? I'm overage—"

"And oversexed! You're thinking with your glands! You're so anxious to get him in you and be a rock slut that you won't even listen to—"

Wind slapped her, fiercely and unexpectedly. And Connie reacted automatically, swinging back and hitting Wind so hard across the face that it spun the girl around. She bumped up against the stove, and her hand brushed against the still-hot frying pan. She yanked her hand away, giving a small shriek.

Connie took a step toward her, contrite. "Wind—"

But Wind wouldn't hear it. She spun away, clutching her hand and shouting, "You are *such* a fucking hypocrite! You give me all this bullshit about how great the old days were, and how wonderful you were, and all this garbage! And you bust your ass to make me like you because of some whacked hang-up you've got with your mother—and as soon as I do start to act like you, you go nuts on me! What's the matter, Mother? Don't like what you see? Too much of you in me? Well, that's your tough luck! I'll do what I want and go where I want, and you can't fucking stop me!"

But Connie wasn't even listening to her. She had yanked open the junk drawer near the phone, which was stuffed with all sorts of old photographs and shit. Connie's definition of being organized was knowing the general vicinity of where something was. She rummaged through, desperately trying to screen out Wind's diatribe, and yanked out a fistful of photographs.

"Look here!" she said. "I can't find a picture of the tattoo, but this is Reb—this guy here." And she was shoving pictures into Wind's face. Wind caught a brief glimpse of some old-time rocker's nutso expression, but she hadn't the patience to look at any more. There was no way she was going to feed her mother's wacko paranoia. She backhanded the pictures out of Connie's grasp, sending them tumbling to the floor.

And she stormed out with the speed and ferocity of her namesake, ignoring her mother's shouts.

* * *

"I want to carve myself a slice of your l-l-l-l-l-love!" screamed and shouted Whiley Coyote, the lead singer of Dark Academy, as he pranced around the stage wearing a pair of torn, skintight black leather pants and red ostrich boots. His fiery red hair swung back and forth like a swarm around his entire body as he leapt and fell and screamed and clawed and whipped the delighted audience into a teenage frenzy.

Wind watched from the wings backstage. She was now officially one of the privileged few. She held two beers: one a Miller Lite that she sipped, and the other a long-necked bottle of Budweiser to give Val when he finished the set. Or whenever he strolled offstage to sneak a kiss and a cool sip.

As the band finished "Slice of Your Love," Rudy Valenz, the lead guitarist, changed guitars for his next number. And while his roadie was switching Val's instruments, Wind noticed that he was looking at her. She blew him a kiss, and the bass player cocked his head and grinned at her.

It was a weird, lopsided, freakish, nightmarish grin. As if a portion of his mouth was dead.

It sent a shiver through Wind's soul. She had to turn away and retreat to the dressing room.

There was something about that grin . . . something that reminded her of the same demented smile she'd seen in that pile of photographs her mom had shoved at her.

Her mother, the crazy bitch . . .

"Oh, don't be ridiculous," she said to no one in particular. She popped a strawberry into her mouth from a backstage tray, and headed back to the wings to watch the rest of Dark Academy's set.

The limo ride back to the hotel had been one of the headiest experiences of Wind's life. A light rain was pattering down on the windshield, and the driver—making idle chitchat—had been saying something about how it was expected to get worse.

Wind had paid no attention to chitchat. She had sat in Val's lap, laughing and stroking his stubbled chin, and the rest of the band had been eyeing her hungrily. But Val had put a possessive arm around her and snickered, "She's mine, boys. All mine."

All his.

She lay back on the bed in Val's hotel room, curled up and smiling. She hadn't gotten undressed yet. She was having too much fun watching Val walking back and forth across the room, a cellular phone pressed against his ear, making some sort of deal. Yelling at his agent about something or other. She loved it. Val didn't take any shit from anybody. She took mental notes, planning to apply his way of handling things to her own situation with her nutty mother.

Val tossed the phone down, then turned to face her. He grinned that spooky grin of his as he peeled off his shirt. Then he pointed at her, making a pistol of his finger, and said, "Wait here."

He went out of the room for a moment, and when he came back—

He was carrying a chalice. A large, silver chalice.

His face fell as he saw her expression—one of confusion and nervousness. "Something wrong, babe?"

"Ummm..." She looked around, as if trying to find someone who wasn't there. "Ummm..." she said again.

"Wind"—and now there was an unpleasant edge to his voice—"Wind, what's going down here?"

She pointed uneasily at the chalice. "What, uh... what do you want me to do? With that?"

"Got a brew in here just for you," he said, speaking with renewed confidence. "Take a sip. You'll love it."

"I, uh..." She slid off the bed. "I gotta go."

"Where the hell do you think you're going?"

"Away. Out. I don't know."

He blocked her way. "Out where?"

There was a warning screaming in her head. The warning had her mother's voice. That alone should have been enough reason to ignore it, but she found that she couldn't.

"Val," she said tightly, "if you feel anything for me, get out of my way."

He smiled that bizarre, lopsided smile of his. "And if I don't?"

"If you don't get out of my way?"

"No. I mean if I don't feel anything for you."

She hesitated only a moment, then abruptly faked to the left before moving to the right. The move, however, did not fool Val for a moment. He snagged her wrist, and they struggled for a moment. With a sweep of her hand she knocked the chalice out of his grasp, and it clattered to the floor. A thick, viscous red liquid spilled out, seeping into the carpet and staining it permanently.

She lunged under his outstretched arms and this time made it all the way to the door. She yanked it open, but before she could get out into the hallway he snagged her by the hair and pulled. Her head snapped back and it hurt like hell as she lost her grip on the doorknob. The door swung back but didn't quite close, giving her hope that she could yell and attract some attention. But he clamped a hand over her mouth.

"You shouldn't have tried to run," he whispered harshly into her ear, dragging her toward the bed. "This could have been fun. This could have been a lot of fun. You stupid bitch. You stupid, stupid—"

Suddenly it got a bit darker in the room. Val turned, glancing toward the table lamp that was next to the door. The lamp wasn't there anymore.

And then it crossed his field of vision, smashing him between the eyes and sending him reeling. Blood poured from the vicious wound that had been ripped in his forehead.

"Let her go, you bastard!" shouted Connie, and she swung the lamp again. It cracked against the side of his head, sending him pinwheeling back and crashing to the floor.

Wind vaulted over him as Connie stood there, her hands trembling, gripping the lamp even tighter. Her hair was slicked down and her clothes were sticking to her body. Apparently the chauffeur had been right, the rain was getting worse.

Val was moaning on the floor, clutching his forehead. Wind was at Connie's side now, staring at Val in confusion and revulsion. But Connie was calm, lord, was she calm now. "Hello, Reb," she said.

Val looked up at her, and there was no mistaking that reaction. He wasn't just responding to her voice; he was answering *to that name.*

"Remember me?" she said icily.

And he dove forward, snagging the trailing cord from the lamp and yanking as hard as he could, pulling it from Connie's grasp. The lamp crashed to the floor, shattering, and the two women shrieked and bolted from the room.

They pounded down the hallway, Connie grabbing Wind by the wrist and pulling her along. Wind was stunned at her mother's speed; Christ, the old woman could run. Connie thought her own arm was going to be yanked out of the socket.

"Get back here!" the infuriated Val/Reb howled behind them, but they ignored it. They ran, ran as fast as they could. They didn't even pause for the elevator, instead bolting down the stairway. They were three floors up and they covered the distance in death-defying sprints, slipping, sliding, tumbling down the stairs. As they reached the ground level they heard the third-floor door explode open, and Val shouted down after them, "You can't get away! *You can't get away!"*

The admonition did not slow them down in the least. They burst out of the exit door into the parking lot and had run ten yards before Connie skidded to a halt.

"Shit! Where am I parked?"

"Where are you parked?! *Where are you parked?!* Jesus Christ, Mother! You always do this! I *hate* when you do this! I—"

The exit door burst open, and Val was standing there, fists clenched, face twisted, mouth in that smile/snarl.

They ran.

He came right after them.

The Undeadliest Game

The rain poured down, and lightning ribboned across the sky as if God were snarling. Connie and Wind charged across the service road that led into the hotel, and Val was right behind them. And he was waving something.

A knife. A dagger.

Connie felt a tingling at the back of her neck, could feel the point piercing. Could feel the blood trickling out, drip, drip, drip . . .

Ahead of them an overpass crossed the major highway that ran past the hotel. The rain was coming down in sheets, and Connie stumbled. Wind caught her, and now she was trying to pull her mother forward. Connie's hand went to her chest, her breasts heaving.

And Val was right there, *right there*, and he swung the dagger at Connie. She dodged it as the point ripped across her sleeve, and staggered back and slammed against the concrete fence at the edge of the overpass. Below her the headlights of passing cars played across the asphalt.

He came at her again, and she caught the thrust of his wrist, putting all her strength against him. But her strength was far less than his, and the knife point inched down toward her face. He grinned lopsidedly—

She twisted, shoving the knife upward, and it slashed across the underside of his chin. His blood spurted out in a pulsing burst, splattered on Connie's face. She blinked, choked, made a noise of disgust. And Val didn't even seem to notice. There was still that idiotic grin.

Abruptly the grin was replaced by a look of confusion. Wind, her upper body also decorated with Val's blood, was directly under him, and she lifted his feet off the ground and shoved upward as hard as she could. The move was enough to overbalance him, and with a scream Val went over the edge of the overpass.

He plunged toward the highway, arms flailing. He did not, however, quite make it to the asphalt. Just before he hit, his plunging body was intercepted by a Mack truck. It smashed into him, truncating his scream, not to mention his body.

The driver hit his brakes, the mighty truck's tires squealing in protest. But it wasn't nearly enough, and Val's body was completely ground up beneath the massive tires of the truck.

Connie and Wind looked on in horror, and then dazzling bolts of purple lightning struck from the skies. And they heard a scream such as neither had ever heard. A scream they recognized from the deepest depth of racial memory, filled with terror and evil and everything that mankind tried to forget about itself. There was a blinding display of light that seemed to come from everywhere.

Connie felt it filling her, permeating her being, and there was that same hideous odor coming back to her from all those years ago. That odor of burning. And the world seemed to turn red all of a sudden, and it seared against her soul the way a flashbulb leaves an imprint on the retina. But unlike that photographic sensation, she knew deep in the pit of her spirit that this imprint would never, ever go away.

There was utter silence between the two women the rest of the way home. Every so often they would cast glances at one another. And each was convinced that she knew precisely what the other was going to say:

I warned you, Wind! I warned you and told you, but you wouldn't listen. A mother's feelings count for something. But you—you wouldn't believe me, and I had to save your sorry ass, you stupid little bitch, was what Wind *knew* her mother was thinking. And she hated her mother for it.

But she would have been wrong.

And Connie . . . she knew, beyond any question, that Wind was thinking, *I could have handled it, Mother! I had everything under control! You butted in when I didn't ask you to, and you actually tailed me to the hotel, Jesus, Mother, you actually followed me. And besides, you made me do it, you got me into that situation. You forced me into it, you practically dared me, and it's all your fault.*

And she would have been wrong.

But neither spoke, so neither knew.

Connie went straight to the bathroom once they got home

and showered, showered for what seemed ages. Finally, though, she got it all off, and headed for her bedroom. Wind followed her into the shower, but they did not speak as they passed in the hallway.

They lay in their respective beds, and the storm had not abated—had, in fact, gotten stronger, louder. Connie listened, counting seconds between the flash of lightning and the crack of thunder in order to get an idea of how close it was. There was a blinding flash, and she barely made it past a second before the world was exploding around her. She lay in terror, certain that the lightning was going to rip right through her window. She sat up, looking across the room at her wall mirror, and when the lightning erupted around her once more, she saw two things.

She saw her reflection in the mirror . . . and there was the blood she'd washed off. It was all over her face as if water had never touched it. Permeating her skin, permeating her mind, dear God, it was all through her.

That was the first thing.

The second thing wasn't much better.

It was the one that Wind had called Whiley. He was standing *that close,* so close that she could touch him. She wanted to scream, to leap out of the bed, to go for the phone, to go for his throat—something, goddamn it. But she sat there, paralyzed. She wanted to scream, but her vocal cords were constricted.

"I remember you," said Whiley Coyote. His voice was surprisingly soft, almost sweet. "Yeah . . . yeah, I do. Back when Val was going by Reb, and I was—what was it, now? Oh, yeah. Billy Bob." He winced. "It wasn't my best time. What can I say? But I remember all of you girls, throughout the decades. Val never did, but that's the way he was. We never liked him, really—you gotta understand that. In fact, we're kind of glad he's gone."

He took a step toward her, and now she could see clearly that he was holding something: the chalice. Gleaming in a distorted light. She tried to scamper back on the bed, but her body blissfully ignored all the commands that her brain was screaming.

"Okay, look," Whiley continued, as casually as if he were striking up a conversation in an elevator. "This was your basic satanic deal, cut years before you ever ran into us. Five of us, bartering for immortality and bitchin' rock careers. We started out in the fifties as Jimmy and the Generators."

There was an air of unreality about it, because—insanely—she was fascinated. She heard herself saying, "Holy . . . you did 'Boppin' with My Baby?' That was one of the first records I ever made my mother buy me!"

He grinned, looking disconcertingly boyish. "Thanks."

"And then you guys kinda . . . disappeared."

"Yes," he said, frowning. "We discovered that although the rise up is fun, the inevitable downhill slide is that much longer when you're immortal. So after that we decided that each new group would go out with a bang."

"What do you mean?"

"Easy. We'd get hot, work ourselves up until we figured we'd just about peaked, and made tons of money. Then we'd fake our deaths, live high until the money ran low and we had an itch to perform again. We love performing live—the studio just isn't enough, y'know?"

She nodded numbly. It was the first motion she'd been able to make.

"The blood, well . . . that helps keep us in the pink, y'know? But we like to be subtle—investigations can be such a hassle, y'know? So when we took you, for example, we opened up a vein right back here, on your neck, where your hair would cover it. You were so drugged up you didn't feel it. Just a little blood, that's all. Then we patched you back up, sent you on your way." When he saw her expression, he rolled his eyes. "Yeah, okay . . . we all took our turn with you. But that's before we knew the type of girl you were, who you'd turn out to be."

He suddenly leapt through the air, and landed squarely on her bed. "Here's the deal," he whispered. "With Val the asshole out of the picture, we have room for a new band member. But only one: The deal's for five at a time. The incredible advantage of this offer, of course, is that you live forever—provided you don't do something stupid like get yourself turned into roadkill, like Val did. And if you come aboard, your youth will be restored. You'd be a bitchin' choice, Connie. Course . . . so would your daughter."

Her eyes widened in horror.

"But we leave that up to you," he said. "Can't take you both. Won't take either of you, if neither of you wants it. I mean, hey"—and he grinned lopsidedly, his eyes glowing slightly reflecting the lightning, or maybe on their own— "hey, just because we're devil-worshipers doesn't mean we're bad guys."

And finally she broke from her paralysis and lunged toward him—

And the lunge snapped her awake.

She looked around. Everything was exactly the same. The storm was still thundering its fury outside, and there was her room, and—

And she screamed. The chalice was right there, right there on her nightstand.

She rolled off the bed, grabbed it, and stumbled, slipped, recovered, and made it down the stairs. The chalice glittered in her hands as she bolted outside, into the garden. Her gardening tools lay scattered about because she hadn't bothered to put them away, and she grabbed a shovel and started digging furiously. The rain matted her hair, and as she dug she saw that Val's blood was indeed still on her hands. It had reappeared like a determined canker sore, but she ignored it. All she was concerned about at the moment was getting rid of this thing, this hideous object.

She felt a burning in her skin that the rain was doing nothing to cool, and a pounding in her head. Her mother was starting to shriek at her again, but she blocked it off as her shovel overturned dirt as quickly as she could. She dropped the shovel, about to throw the chalice in so that she could give it the grave that it deserved—

And she saw her reflection in its gleaming sides.

She looked like some sort of demented harridan. Her makeup was washed away, her hair shapeless, spots of blood speckling her face that, in the darkness, looked like age spots. . . .

Live forever . . . youth restored . . .

She looked down into the chalice. There was a liquid there that she could swear hadn't been there before. The falling rain splattered in it, and it would be so easy. . . .

And there were other voices now, whispering to her, encouraging her . . .

"Give it to me!"

That voice was most definitely not in her head. It was from right behind her, and she spun to see Wind standing there.

She was holding the shovel.

"Give it to me, Mother. *Now!*"

Connie understood in a heartbeat. As the thunder crackled, she knew that Whiley, or perhaps another of them, had appeared to her daughter as well.

Both had made the same offer.

One opening. One possibility . . .

There were other warnings now, her mind alive with the screaming voices. But the thunder pounded them all away.

"It's mine," said Connie intently.

"You *bitch!*" shrieked Wind, her eyes wild, her mind overwhelmed. "You *had* your chance! You had more than enough chances! You fucked up everything! Your marriage! Your life! Me! Everything! Why the hell should you be rewarded for that!"

It wasn't her daughter talking. She was positive. Wind wouldn't say that, think that. Wind wouldn't be there shrieking at her like a demented banshee. It had to be something else, something pushing . . .

Pushing—

Wind pushed her. Connie staggered back, and rage seared through her mind, wiping away any thoughts except those of unadulterated fury.

"Because I earned it! I deserved it! I put up with my

mother, with you, with forty years of bullshit! And this time, goddamn it, I'm going to do it right!" And her body was burning everyplace where Val's blood had splattered on her, but she wasn't noticing it anymore. All she saw was her daughter's gaze fixed on the chalice.

Wind came at her with the shovel, swinging it clumsily but viciously. Connie stumbled back. She bumped up against a spade, put the chalice down quickly, and grabbed up the spade.

The sky roared its approval around them as the two women swung and slashed at each other. Connie struck Wind a glancing blow, and blood welled up from Wind's nose. Wind stabbed brutally forward, the shovel hitting Connie in the side, knocking the wind from her and—she couldn't be sure—possibly bruising or breaking a rib.

They shrieked epithets, years of bile and hurt and pain spilling out. Everything that had ever gone wrong in their lives they unleashed on each other, blamed on each other. Their pulses pounded in their temples, their eyes burned with rage, and they staggered through the mud and dirt, swinging and missing and connecting and screeching and groaning and cursing until they were unrecognizable as themselves. Until they were like two demons, two beings spat up from hell.

And the lightning cracked. . . .

And with both of them poised to strike with simple gardening utensils now become tools of destruction, one of them saw the other illumined in the light, for just a moment—saw her in a light that purified the other, made her remember what they were, and who they were. Made her remember the bond that could never be broken between mother and daughter, no matter all the machinations of hell. . . .

And she hesitated, gaining control of her senses for a moment.

It was the wrong moment.

Because then sharp metal, wielded by the other, struck her head with such force that it practically tore off the top of her skull. She stumbled back, dead before she hit the ground, and drops of her blood showered into the chalice, mixing with the liquid that was already there.

The one living woman in the yard stood there for a moment, her chest heaving. For the briefest, briefest of moments, the atrocity of what she had done became clear to her.

But there was one more flash of lightning, and one more burning sensation from the blood that decorated her body, and then all regrets were burned away.

She grabbed up the chalice and drank greedily of its contents.

Everyone agreed: The new band was a winner. The Funkamentals were going to make it big.

The audience was going wild, waiting for their appearance. And now Sarah and Nicole, the number-one morning DJ team in the area, were introducing them.

Sarah strutted around the stage in a leather biker jacket and skintight Levi's tucked into knee-high cowboy boots. "Awright, you honkers! Are you tough enough tonight to really rock?!"

"Yeah, sure, Bud!" shouted back the crowd, repeating Sarah and Nicole's trademark line.

Nicole, the other half of the self-proclaimed "bitching monarchs of morning," stalked the stage in a black leather miniskirt. She was decked out in black leggings, spiked high heels, and at least twenty silver bracelets. "Well, then, let's hear you give it up for the newest, the nastiest, the band that everyone in the country is talking about! We had 'em on our show this morning, and you've all heard their single, 'Take It Out or Break It Off.' We're proud to bring you—in their first major appearance here—the *Funkamentals!*"

The Funkamentals roared onto the stage and, as they started their set, the crowd did what crowds were supposed to do: yelled, stood up, clapped, cheered, whistled, danced, and cheered again.

It's funny how trends come and go. Lately the in thing

The Undeadliest Game

seemed to be trashy versions of the 1960s. Everyone in the Funkamentals was groomed as if he or she had walked out of a Kennedy cocktail party in 1962. Except for their exaggerated stage makeup, and the fact that the mysterious female lead singer wore no shirt under her jacket.

And under her pillbox hat, mingling with the fine brown hair that curled around her chin, you could see an odd thing: a single, blood red tear—the last souvenir from a dead rocker that wouldn't come off despite years of scrubbing—rolling down her cheek.

And tonight, the moon was out to sing along with the chorus. It might have been a new song, but the moon knew the words by heart.

THE RED SAX

Graham Watkins

You ever look inside one of those things, man?" Eddie Parker demanded. "After you been playing it for a week or two, you ever take off the reed and look inside the mouthpiece?"

Charlie Watt leaned against one of the amplifiers and stroked the tenor sax that was hanging from his neck with real affection, as if it were a living thing. "Why, sure," he answered, grinning a half-lidded southern grin. "Hell, I play the fucker, don't I? Every goddamn day of the fucking world, I play the fucker. Reeds don't last forever. You gotta replace the fuckers. And sometimes you gotta clean out the mouthpiece and the neck, too."

Eddie made a face of disgust. "Then you know what I'm talking about. Those things are gross, man. I gotta tell you, I don't know how you come in here night after night and put that thing in your mouth. I just don't know." He ran his fingers quickly over the Roland keyboard in front of him; a

The Red Sax

flutelike sine wave decorated with a brassy spike grated from the big JBLs at the sides of the stage. "You hear that?" he asked. "That's music, man, that's good clean music." He shook his head. "I started out on sax, I played one for years. The goddamn thing grossed me out, just grossed me out, every time I looked inside the mouthpiece or neck. Man, I couldn't take it. All that goddamn slime in there, I just couldn't take it. Every time I went to put the goddamn thing in my mouth, all I could think of was that slime. So I said fuck it, I took up keyboards. I ain't never been sorry."

Charlie grinned, ran a riff on the keys of his Selmer Mark VI without blowing it. In the quiet of the still-closed bar, the keys thumped back up against their stops. "Music," he said, "ain't supposed to be clean. Music's supposed to be dirty. When you blow sax, when you do it like it's supposed to be done, you're blowing your whole fucking soul down that fucking pipe. That's what that stuff inside the mouthpiece is, that green and gray slime, those ol' fuzzy black spots that show up when you let it get real good and dirty. They're parts of you, man, parts of your fucking lungs and your mouth and your tongue—parts of your fucking soul. It's bound to be dirty. You ever know anybody whose soul is all nice and clean? Shiiittt . . ." Coming to stand beside Eddie, he ran his fingers over the keys of the Roland; his touch was as expert as the keyboard man's. "You can't put none of your soul in this thing, man," he declared. "This is a fucking computer; all it knows is pitch and envelope, and that's all you can get out of it." He shook his head vigorously. "Sorry, man. You're good with this thing, but I gotta tell you: You ain't no *mus*ician, you're a *tech*nician. That's all there is to it. Just like Manny when he runs the sound board; a *tech*nician."

His mouth tight, Eddie keyed the Roland's memory to echo some programmed riffs and added a double counterpoint with both hands. "You're a prick, Charlie," he said sourly. "You're a goddamn arrogant prick. Hear you tell it, you're the only goddamn musician in the band."

"Ah, hell no," the saxman argued. "No, Jerry and Margie,

they sing, that's music." He pushed his long hair back, rolled his eyes to the left, considered. "Hack's guitar, that's music—well, he gets a sort of a something out of it that's close to music, anyhow. Joe, well, shit. Anybody with any rhythm can sit and whang on drums, there ain't nothing to that, nothing. Same with Sammy's bass." He shrugged in an exaggerated fashion. "But hell—we need 'em all to get the sound. Even Manny. Even you."

"Shit," Eddie commented. "You're so full of shit I can't understand how come you don't drive off the audience with your stink."

Charlie was unfazed. "Ah, well, I ain't seen 'em running for the doors, Eddie. Look, let's cut this shit; we came in here this morning so you could get some backgrounds for my solos worked up. Let's get after it, okay? The others'll be here pretty soon—" He glanced at his watch. "Shit! It's past noon, we been here a fucking hour!"

Eddie didn't answer; instead he started playing, hitting a high note and using the bend to take it down to a low growl before cutting into a chord pattern that fitted one of Charlie's own compositions, a tune he called "Greasyfinger Love," an audience favorite—and a song their band, the Gates of Darkness, had recorded on its soon-to-be-released first album, the album they all hoped would get them out of these grimy little clubs and onto the concert circuit.

For a few bars, Eddie played on alone; then Charlie cut in, his tenor sometimes soaring and lyrical, sometimes harsh and growling. With a hard-eyed determination, Eddie kept a focus on what he was doing with the Roland, but all the while he knew that Charlie was, at least in a way, right. The man could make his sax moan, he could make it weep, he could make it laugh. Eddie's synth could manage only a pale imitation of those emotions at best, a mere suggestion of them.

His fingers on automatic, his mind wandered as he played. Things had been easier in the last two bands he'd played with; one of them, a metal-oriented group, hadn't used any horns at all, while the other had had a distinctly mediocre

The Red Sax

saxman who played mostly background, whose rare solos were uninspiring. But those bands had been headed nowhere, and Eddie felt his considerable keyboard talents were being wasted on them. Finally, he'd gotten the break he'd been waiting for: Gates of Darkness, a band most people in the local music crowd felt was destined for the big time, had suffered a rather common disaster—their keyboard man, a close friend of Eddie's, had managed to off himself with an OD of snort, allowing Eddie to move smoothly in. For him, it was a dream come true—when the band moved on, he'd be moving with it.

But that didn't mean that all was well with his world. A good deal of what he'd just told Charlie was, he acknowledged to himself, lies; he'd long ago fallen in love with the sax, fallen in love with the sounds the great ones could get out of it, people like Coltrane, Getz, Desmond, Adderley, Mulligan, Clemmons, Junior Walker—and, okay, Charlie Watt. Yes, the filth inside grossed him out, but that wasn't what had stopped him. He would've been willing to lap that slime out and gulp it right down if it could make him play like the Cannonball.

What had stopped him was that he couldn't make it sound like any of his idols, no matter what he did. With his fingers there wasn't a problem; he could finger with anybody. But, try as he might, he couldn't develop a good lip or good breath control. Worse, he had only a moderately good ear for pitch; with a keyboard, that wasn't much of a problem—mostly you just whack a key, and the machine puts out the right frequency. If you do bends and you miss it a little, you just keep bending around there and the listeners—especially those who know how fast and accurate you are with your fingers—assume you're doing it on purpose.

With a horn, though, you can be a little off all the time. Most people won't notice—as far as most audiences are concerned, you can be a semitone off and they won't notice—but the people who count will.

He said nothing more, but his sourness continued throughout the afternoon's practice and on into the evening's performance. At times it distracted him to the extent that he botched his part—not so badly that the listeners were aware of it, but badly enough to earn him glares from Charlie and the other band members.

And, to make matters worse, Sara wandered in. Wandered in halfway through the first set and, even though the place was packed, managed somehow to get herself a table right in front of him, where she could sit and stare at him fixedly. She was one fucking fantastically beautiful broad, he told himself, but he sure didn't want to see her face in here tonight.

Still, during the break, he had to go sit down with her, he had no choice, anything else would've looked weird. Her old man, Nate—the Gates' former keyboard man—had been one of Eddie's closest friends, and he hadn't been in the ground for two weeks yet. To ignore her would've looked weird.

"You're fucking up a lot, aren't you?" she asked bluntly as soon as he sat down. She seemed to be trying to drill a hole in his head with her ice blue eyes. "You sure don't sound like Nate up there, but shit, I know you can boogie down, I've heard you and Nate when you used to get together and jam. Something got you freaked, Eddie?"

He closed his eyes for a moment, took a deep breath to calm himself. "Cut me some slack, Sara," he begged. "Hey, I've only been playing with the Gates a week. I—"

"You play with them ten years, you're not gonna be Nate," she shot back. Turning her head toward the empty bandstand for a moment, she drummed her fingertips on the Formica tabletop. "Tell me about it again, Eddie," she said. "About the night Nate died. You were with him that night, tell me about it again."

He made a sound halfway between a sigh and a snort. "Goddamn, Sara," he complained, "I musta gone over it a thousand times, between you and the cops. They're satisfied; how come you aren't?"

Again, the ice stare. "Maybe it's because I don't buy it,

Eddie. The cops, they didn't live with Nate for six years. The cops didn't fuck him just about every night. They didn't know him like I did." She sighed and again looked away. "I'm not saying Nate never did any drugs, Eddie; hell, I know better than that. But he was careful, he was real careful. He knew how many rockers go down like that, he used to talk about it all the time, used to say he didn't want to go down like Hendrix or Morrison or the keyboard man for the Grateful Dead."

"But that's what he did, Sara. That's the fact."

"Yeah, that's the fact, all right. That much I'll buy. What I want to know is why."

"Well, shit, how am I supposed to—"

"It was your stuff, wasn't it, Eddie? You didn't tell the cops that."

He snorted again, then laughed. "Well, shit, Sara! Yes; yes, it was my stuff, I brought it over. I can tell you that; you expect me to say that to the cops?"

She shook her head. "Was it straight stuff, Eddie? Good stuff?"

"The best. You know that. The autopsy didn't show up a thing in his system except the cocaine, that's what they said snuffed him. Goddamn, he was my friend, Sara! You think I'd pass some spiked shit off on him?"

Her eyes were colder than ever. "I don't know," she told him. "I don't know if that's what went down or not. I do know this, Eddie: You knew the Gates were headed up. You wanted in, you wanted in bad. I think you found a way to take my old man down, that's what I think."

"Goddamn, Sara! Listen to what you're saying here! You're saying I fucking murdered him for his gig!"

She nodded vigorously. "Yeah. That's what I'm saying, all right. Somehow—I just don't know how, Eddie, that's all. I don't know how you talked him into snorting so much of that shit. Why don't you just—"

She stopped speaking, looked up; Charlie stood grinning down at her. She smiled back, somewhat forlornly. Turning a chair around, he sat down at their table, resting his arms on the back. "You doin' okay, hon?" he asked her gently, his face serious now.

She pursed her lips and nodded, this time only a little. "Well, you know," she allowed. "Life goes on, you gotta go on. I miss the shit out of Nate, though."

"Yeah, me too," the saxman agreed. He glanced at Eddie. "Ol' Nate, he could work a keyboard. He didn't fuck up."

"Well, goddamn!" Eddie almost shouted in frustration. "I don't know what you expect—"

"He expects," Sara cut in, "for you to play your part, to hold up your end. It's the least you could do, you bastard, after you killed Nate to get this gig!"

Charlie gave her an exaggerated wide-eyed look. "He did?" he asked. "He offed ol' Nate, just to get his gig?"

Once more, the vigorous nod from Sara. "Yes," she declared. "He did, I'm sure of it, I—"

"I did not!" Eddie snapped. "It was an OD, pure and simple—"

"Well, now, I can't say," Charlie cut in. "Maybe you did and maybe you didn't. I don't see where we can do much about it if you did." Sara opened her mouth to protest; Charlie silenced her with a wave of his hand. "We got other reasons," he went on, "to get rid of you, Eddie. You're fucking up, we can't have that. I think maybe tomorrow I'll talk to the guys about it, and we'll—"

Eddie felt as if his stomach had fallen to some point down near his ankles. "You can't!" he snarled. "You can't! We're making that live recording tomorrow night, you know the tour manager wants to hear—"

"Don't matter," Charlie said as Sara's smile grew wider and more relaxed. "Like I said this afternoon, for the keyboards we only need a *tech*nician, not a *mu*sician. Ol' Fred Hammond, he's a fine *tech*nician and he's worked out with me, he—" He stopped, swiveled his head toward the bandstand where Manny, who was making some adjustments on the PA, was working perilously close to the stand where his Selmer rested. "Watch the sax, man," he called.

"Be careful about my baby. You dent her, it's me who's gonna bleed." Manny nodded; reassured, Charlie turned back to Eddie. "Anyway, ol' Fred, he knows our stuff. He'll do fine." He shrugged. "Now, I don't know if we can get ol' Fred for tomorrow; we'll hafta see. But you, my man, I just don't think you're gonna work out." Using the same wave as before, he dismissed any further objections. "You'll get paid for what you do," he said, his voice now as cold as Sara's eyes.

At that point he dismissed Eddie altogether and turned his attention to Sara, talking to her as if the other man did not exist, offering to take her home after the show.

Getting up so suddenly and violently that he almost overturned his chair, Eddie left them and went to the bar. "Scotch," he snarled at the bartender. "Straight up." Gulping the drink, fuming, he looked back over his shoulder at the couple at the table. You goddamn arrogant asshole, he told Charlie silently. Not only do I have to put up with you humiliating me with your playing, but now this, now you and that bitch are going to kill the dream for me. Turning again, he spun the glass slowly on the bar. No, he told himself, no. Later, maybe, he could try to talk to Charlie again, see if he could be dissuaded. He'd heard him offer to take Sara home, heard her accept; that meant he'd be over at Nate and Sara's old pad after the show. Charlie, he was sure, would be pretty much drunk; he always was, it was routine. Maybe then Eddie could get through to him, get him to change his mind.

You have to try, he told himself glumly. It's all you have.

For the remainder of that evening's show, Eddie focused himself totally on his playing; he allowed nothing to distract him, he made no more noticeable errors. Afterward he stood at the bar and watched Charlie and Sara leave together; as soon as they were gone he went out to his car and headed for Nate's old pad.

He'd rather hoped to get there before they did, or to arrive at about the same time. That didn't happen; on his way he got caught in a traffic jam caused by an accident, which cost him about twenty minutes. After passing it he drove on, grinding his teeth, hoping that Charlie wouldn't simply drop Sara off and leave. Not likely, he kept telling himself. Not likely, but possible.

His fears were groundless; as he pulled up in front of the ramshackle apartment building where Sara still lived, he saw Charlie's Chevy parked out front. As always, he checked the street before getting out of his car—this was hardly a good area, it was hard to say who might be hanging about. Seeing no one, he got out, bounded up the stairs, pounded on the door.

It was Charlie who answered, and it was obvious, instantly, that Eddie hadn't needed to worry about him leaving too soon: He was dressed only in a towel. In his hand was a pint bottle of Rebel Yell, almost empty. "Eddie?" he asked, slurring the name. "What the fuck are you doing here?"

Eddie pushed his way in; Charlie staggered a little to catch his balance. "We gotta talk, man," he said urgently. "We gotta talk. Look, you ain't talked to any of the guys about what you said, have you?"

"You mean about dumping you? Nah. Not yet. Practice tomorrow." He shook the bottle at Eddie threateningly, still weaving on his feet. "It don't matter none, though. You, my man, are history. Now, get the fuck out of here! Can't you see I'm busy?"

"No, man, come on," Eddie pleaded. "Let's talk, let's just talk, I can't—"

Drunkenly, the saxman swung the bottle at him; it was coming rather slowly. "Get out, motherfucker!" he yelled.

Without difficulty, Eddie reached out, grabbed his arm, took the bottle away from him. "Come on, Charlie," he begged. "Come on, man, talk to me, there's a way—"

"Fucker," Charlie snarled. He lunged at the other man, swinging his fist wildly.

It was, Eddie told himself, reflex. Just reflex, nothing more. Charlie was swinging at him, he struck back—and he still had the Rebel Yell bottle in his hand. It caught Charlie's temple, and the bottom half of it shattered; then the saxman was falling, crystal bits of glass along with droplets of amber bourbon and red blood spinning in the air around his head. As if seeing it in slow motion, Eddie watched him go, watched his head hit the corner of a table with a sickening, crunching thud. Then he was on the floor, twitching, his eyelids fluttering, and blood was pouring from his mouth, nose, and ears. The towel had fallen off; Charlie had a partial erection, but even so a little fountain of urine sprayed for a moment.

Eddie couldn't believe it, couldn't believe it had happened. Stunned, paralyzed, he was still standing over Charlie's body when Sara, also clad in a towel, burst in from the bedroom. Expectedly, she screamed.

"You bastard!" she shrieked at Eddie after her initial howl. "You motherfucker, you killed him!" Dancing around, she raged at him. "This time you've done it, Eddie! This time you've gone too far, this time you're going away! By God, you just wait till the cops get here, you just wait! You killed Nate to get in the band and now you've killed Charlie because he was going to see to it you got kicked out! Just you wait—" She stopped, apparently realizing that, in her neighborhood, the police weren't going to be coming just because she'd screamed—screams around here at night were like gunshots, commonplace. "I gotta call 'em," she muttered, and rushed for the phone.

"Sara," Eddie said as she picked up the receiver. "Sara, hang that up." He took a few steps toward her.

"Fuck you!" she spat. "I'm going to—going to—" Again she stopped: this time because she'd realized that he was coming toward her and that he still had the jagged-edged bottle in his hand. The ice blue eyes very wide, she gingerly replaced the phone. Eddie could almost see her mind working, high gear. "Uh—put that down, Eddie," she said uncertainly.

Eddie, too, was thinking fast. This, a voice was telling him, is different, this is real different. You didn't mean to kill Charlie, any more than you meant for Nate to die. Sure, you fed him lines of nearly pure coke while you snorted powdered sugar and taunted him; sure, you hoped to put him out of the way for a while so you could have your chance; and that he died—well, that really wasn't your fault, was it?

But now, this is different. You do Sara and it's different. You know what you're doing, all the way.

But if you don't do Sara . . .

"Hey," he said, "I'm not going to hurt you. We just have to figure this out, that's all. I didn't mean to, you know . . ." He kept advancing on her.

"Yeah, yeah," she said hurriedly, although her expression made it obvious that she remained terrified. She kept backing off. "Yeah. An accident, that's what we'll tell the cops. It'll be okay, Eddie."

He kept coming, cornering her against the wall where the bedroom door frame jutted out a foot or two. Evidently afraid that running or fighting might trigger violence, she let him put a hand on her shoulder; she smiled at him tremulously.

And, deliberately, she dropped her towel.

He glanced down at her; wonderful, just wonderful, better than he'd imagined, and he'd been sure she had a great body. Grinning, he laid a hand on her breast. She sighed and her smile became steadier; he understood what she was willing to do to save herself. She was sure of herself, too, sure of her looks, sure of what they were going to get her.

He didn't take that away from her. While she still had that look of confidence on her face, he drove the raw edge of the broken bottle into her belly, as hard as he could.

Her eyes and mouth flew open; she didn't or couldn't scream, all she did was gasp, shudder, and clutch desperately at his shoulders. Eddie twisted the bottle savagely, drove it deeper, twisted it again. Her blood, red-hot, was squirting all over him. He kept at it, twisting and pushing and tearing even as her body started sagging; he didn't hate her even though she had been causing him trouble, he didn't want to hurt her, he just wanted to get her dead, get it over with.

The Red Sax

Holding on to him as if he were her last hope, she slipped on down and collapsed in a huge pool of blood; for a moment after her body had stopped trembling, Eddie stared at that still-spreading red slick, unable to believe there was so much.

As he stood staring, trying to figure out what to do next, he heard a groan and looked back at Charlie. Unbelievably, the man was not dead! He was squirming around, trying to pull himself up but not succeeding. Eddie ground his teeth. You're committed, he told himself. No backing out now. Holding the bloody bottle, he went to the saxman, knelt beside him.

"Motherfucker," Charlie hissed. "Bastard!" Eddie grabbed his hair, jerked his head back, moved the bottle toward his throat. Charlie had to know what was coming, but he didn't try to fight. "Don't you . . . touch . . . sax," he grated. The glass touched skin, blood appeared. "Don't . . . !" he gurgled as it sank in. "Red . . . red . . . !"

Eddie didn't know what he was talking about and didn't care; he pressed on, laying Charlie's throat wide open, watching the spraying blood cut off any further words.

When it was all over, he locked the door and sat down for a moment to collect himself. There wasn't a problem, he insisted mentally; there hadn't been nearly enough noise to cause folks around here to call the cops, there'd really been only the one scream. He'd been here a million times, the cops knew that; except for the bottle itself, fingerprints weren't a problem. He knew, too, how they'd see it: Charlie was a rocker, Sara's old man had just ODed; the cops would see a drug deal gone bad. All he had to do was clean his prints off the bottle, clean himself up, and get rid of these clothes—Nate had been about his size, he could take something from the closet, he doubted that Sara had gotten rid of it all yet. Feeling that everything would be okay, he rushed off to the bathroom, taking the bottle with him.

"We're just fucked," Hack was moaning. He held his head in his hands. Charlie's and Sara's bodies had been found, the band already knew what had happened. "Just fucked. Nate ODs and now Charlie gets himself snuffed! I can't believe this shit, I just can't!"

"Well, I'm gonna miss him, too," Eddie said carelessly. "But hey, life goes on. We got that recording to do tonight—"

"How the shit are we gonna do that? This concert promoter wants audience reaction to 'Greasyfinger Love' and some of the other tunes Charlie wrote! Charlie's fucking dead, man! His solo, man, it was the soul of that tune!"

"So? So we get another—"

"Man, there ain't no sax players around here like Charlie!"

Eddie grinned. "Hey, I can blow a sax. I'm out of practice, but—"

Hack sneered. "Like Charlie? Shit!"

"No, gimme a chance. Look, call up—oh, Fred Hammond, maybe, see if we can get him to do the keyboards. I'll blow the sax."

The guitarist—and the other band members—still looked dubious. "You got a sax, Ed?" Margie asked him. Her eyes were red; she'd been crying, on and off, ever since they'd gotten the word about Charlie and Sara.

He glanced at her. "No. But Charlie's Selmer's still in the back room, ain't it? Shit, he wouldn't care."

"Let him try," Manny put in. "What've we got to lose?" He turned to Eddie. "Go get it," he suggested. "Let's see what you can do."

He did; he took the Selmer out of its case, hooked it on the neck strap, adjusted it, examined it. Most of its surface still retained the shine of lacquered brass, but the thumb hook and the register key were well-worn, far down into the metal. With a new expression of distaste he stared at the mouthpiece, at the tooth grooves in its upper surface. Unable to help himself, he sniffed it, and he thought for a moment he was going to throw up; it smelled, quite literally, like a dead dog. But, almost desperately, he stuck it between his lips and began wetting the reed. After he'd tuned it to the Roland, the band began to play, and he joined in.

The band members were, it was obvious, amazed; but they could not have been more amazed than Eddie himself. Long out of practice, he'd expected to struggle at first, but that did not happen; it all came back, smoothly, easily—and much better than ever before. Almost—so everyone said when the tune had ended—almost as good as Charlie himself.

"Maybe you were right," he said wonderingly as Hack rushed off to phone Fred Hammond. "Maybe you were right, Charlie. Maybe you did blow yourself into this thing." He smiled, happy as a child. This was it, he told himself. Like Charlie had said, real music. Real. Maybe in some weird way it was Charlie's soul coming out of the Selmer, but he didn't care, not really. It was coming out and he was the one who was getting it out. He could not help crinkling his nose at the smell, and now there was an even worse taste in his mouth, but he still didn't care. Tonight, tonight it was going to be like he'd always dreamed it would be, and he'd put up with anything for that. He surely wasn't going to take the risk of cleaning out the sax, not yet.

Throughout the practice, nothing happened to upset his euphoria; Fred was found, the keyboards were covered; in spite of all the disasters the Gates of Darkness was ready to make its tape, ready to move on. Nine o'clock came, the audience filtered in, Manny began his taping; still all went well, as well as before or better. Eddie admitted—he could admit, now—that Fred was an even better keyboardist, an even better *tech*nician, than he was.

But he, he was Charlie's equal; he was now the *mu*sician he'd always wanted to be. That's what the band said, that's what the audience said, that's what the club's owner came to tell him during the first break. The best was yet to come, he said confidently. Yet to come.

And it did come. Second set, second tune: "Greasyfinger Love," the showcase piece Charlie had written for himself.

Jerry and Margie went through their vocal, he trilled a background; then, at last, he stepped forward, center stage, for the long solo that made up the middle of this tune.

Ten bars in, the audience was going nuts and Eddie was in paradise. He made the Selmer shriek, made it moan, made it howl, made it cry; he ran chromatic scales at a blinding speed, he dazzled his listeners with the crispness of his totocotici articulations. After a while, he shifted away from the rock stylings that Charlie had always used; he went to a Getz whisper, to a Desmond lyric, to a Mulligan bellow, to Coltrane atonals, and back again, and the audience loved it all. From there he changed to a classical mode, he screamed out a Prokofiev theme and turned it on its head, turned it sideways, inside out. All manner of music, all types of stylings, came out of the sax. Eddie felt he was floating at some great height over the stage; he could not remember ever having felt like this.

He felt so good, in fact, that he failed to realize that the solo was going on a bit long, that the other band members—dazzled though they were—had begun to look at him curiously. The moment, he thought with a mental sigh, was over. He started to wind down, to turn the song back over to the vocalists for the finish.

He only got halfway down, though, before blooming again into a new phase of the solo, a much more frenetic phase than before. The band, startled, faltered; the audience came to its feet, cheering wildly, and after a moment the band members rejoined him. There was a wildness in the club that Eddie had never before seen, a rawness, and he was at the heart of it.

And he couldn't stop. He wasn't playing the saxophone, after all; instead, it was playing him. If he tried to keep his fingers still, the keys popped up and down regardless; if he tried not to blow it, it sucked air out of his lungs. Fighting it—which to the audience looked merely like a frenzied dance—he tried to pull his mouth away, but the instrument's mouthpiece and reed seemed to have developed hundreds of tiny teeth, recurved like a snake's, that held him

The Red Sax

fast. He fought to remove his hands from the keys; invisible tentacles seemed to have sprouted from each one, winding around his fingers, holding them where they were.

For minutes that soon stretched into an hour, he fought the horn—to no avail. On he played; he was becoming so exhausted he was sure he would fall, but in some way the sax seemed to be keeping him on his feet. Heavy dark pains were developing in his abdomen and chest as his lungs fatigued but were pushed on nevertheless. One by one, the other members of the band wore down and dropped out, leaving him playing a cappella. Still he could not stop. He felt a tearing in his chest, looked down at the Selmer. Very quickly the pads stained red; a fine spray of blood began blowing out of the tone holes whenever they were open.

Turning himself a little—his first voluntary action in quite a while—he looked over at Manny. The soundman gave him a sign, his thumb and forefinger closed in a loop, and grinned. He was getting it, Eddie told himself, he was getting it all. Tears of desperation and pain flowing down his cheeks, he faced the audience again, and he played on. Glancing down at the horn, he saw that now fragments of gray and pink tissue were fluttering around the tone holes and sticking on the pads. It wasn't going to stop, he could see that; it wasn't going to stop until the Selmer had sucked his insides out of him, until there was nothing left of him but a husk.

And, understanding that, he began to relax, to enjoy himself again. There were, he told himself, worse ways to go. As far as the audience was concerned, as far as the band was concerned, and—most important—as far as the tape was concerned, he was making music, he was making some of the best music ever made. They would all see him as, at last, a real *mu*sician.

Of course, Eddie himself knew better. But he tried not to think about it.

HE'S HOT, HE'S SEXY, HE'S...

A. R. Morlan

The Miami Herald, June 26, 2000
Local Historians to Settle Morrison Death Rumors
(Special to the *Herald*)

Ever since his death was reported in early July of 1971, friends and fans of the former Doors lead singer Jim Morrison have expressed doubts about whether or not the poet-musician actually did die in a bathtub in Paris. These doubts are mainly due to the absence of hard evidence supporting the news of his death—including the lack of an autopsy, scant paperwork concerning his death, and, perhaps most tellingly, the numerous supposed "sightings" of the singer in Europe over the past thirty years. Those who claim that the troubled musician did indeed die on July 3, 1971, feel that his remains should be allowed to rest undisturbed. However, other interested parties have been quietly pursuing the possibility of disinterring Morrison's remains, for both historical and as-yet-unspecified legal reasons. According to an unnamed source in the Miami Police Department, these legal reasons may concern a number of still-unresolved paternity suits, as well as the infamous University of Miami "exposure" incident. . . .

The Miami Herald, June 27, 2000
(from the arrests/legal column)

Jean Zidor Desire, aka Papa Zidor, 45, cruelty to animals, disorderly conduct, resisting arrest; paid $596 cash bond, sentencing to be determined.

AP wire service, Saturday, July 1, 2000

Noted historian Wallace Davis arrived in Paris today, along with a team of fellow historians and relatives of the late rock and roll musician James Morrison, for the official exhumation of the infamous frontman for the Rock and Roll Hall of Fame (1993) group the Doors. Dr. Davis's only comment about the upcoming exhumation was: "Once we establish that the deceased is, in fact, deceased, it is to be hoped that that determination will forever quell the ongoing and most unfortunate rumors which have surrounded his heretofore uncertain and highly controversial demise, as well as clear up certain unresolved legal matters. . . ."

UPI wire service, July 2, 2000
(caption of a photo depicting a portion of the graffiti near the grave of Jim Morrison at Pére La Chaise cemetery, reading: "Leave Jim Alone!")

FANS OF ROCK STAR PROTEST IMMINENT EXHUMATION

Colonel McClaren, Agent to the Undead: *The Life and Extraordinary Times of Papa Zidor,* Edward Pike, Pocket, 2006
(excerpt, p. 56)

. . . Of course, once news of the Morrison "incident" (as it was initially dubbed by an unusually reticent and politically correct press) leaked to the major wire services, nationwide attention was focused on the admittedly eccentric version of Laveauian[1]-style voodoo practiced by *houngan* Papa Zidor and his followers prior to the Paris "incident." While *houngans* (male and female; voodoo is a religion that allows for both priests and priestesses, which further backs practitioners' claims that it is a "true community religion") around the United States and the West Indies immediately decried Zidor's actions, publicly stating that the concepts of zombies and possession for evil purposes are not part of the "true" practice of voodoo, which is itself more of an amalgamation of Roman Catholic beliefs and various African tribal beliefs with an emphasis on benign possession of the faithful by *loas,* or gods, Papa Zidor himself had a very different view of both the Paris "incident" and the eventual outcome resulting from the "incident":

"You make [a] man a god, then that *loa,* he [is] able to possess anyone . . . even himself. That is [a] natural thing. It is common in voodoo. *Houngan* draw *veves,*[2] and *loa* [he or she] come. Faithful play the drums, drink the cane drink laced with sacred herbs, and sing, and dance, until the *loa* come. Go into anyone, ride them like horse, only inside. Way it is in voodoo, way [it] will always be. No need to *make* zombie, no need to give drug to person, let them die, then bring [them] back. [The "incident"] not anything like that. Those who say Papa Zidor do this, [they] are wrong. Him

---

1 Marie Laveau, the priestess who started the New Orleans style of voodoo, which utilized elements of black magic in the worship.
2 Symbols of a *loa* drawn on the ground with cornmeal flour.

loa, it come before that July. It was out there, waiting. I only bring it to original home.

"And I never kill [the] original home. And I never keep it preserved. *Nature* do that, not Papa Zidor. Ask nature why she do that. I just summon *loa*. . . ."

MTV, *The Day in Rock*, July 4, 2000

". . . In more unsettling news, according to still 'unofficial' reports, the exhumed remains of legendary Hall of Fame rocker Jim Morrison were said to be missing. Just last Saturday, music historian Dr. Wallace Davis and a team of 'rock' historians arrived in Paris to conduct an official, state-sanctioned exhumation of the late musician, scheduled for July 3, the anniversary of Morrison's death. Details have been sketchy ever since the remarkably intact coffin was removed from Pére La Chaise cemetery. According to some eyewitness reports, the coffin was actually opened at the gravesite, while other witnesses claim that the unbreached casket was taken by hearse to Dr. Davis's undisclosed headquarters in the city. Whatever the condition of the casket was on Monday, it has been reported today that the remains somehow 'disappeared' overnight, even though sources claim that the casket itself is still in Dr. Davis's possession, albeit in an 'unoccupied state.' French officials, mindful that Morrison's gravesite is currently Paris's fourth-largest tourist attraction, have the matter under investigation. In more upbeat news, the . . ."

Paris Match editorial, July 5, 2000

. . . Must we all fall victim to "historical curiosity"? This unfortunate incident, in which the remains of a beloved and revered cultural figure have been—to quote the historian in charge of this ultimately dubious project—"misplaced temporarily," has only served to bring shame upon the adopted resting place of one of the heroes of popular music.

And is this fair? I do not think it is so; while certain members of the government allowed this to happen, this sad incident in no way reflects the wishes or desires of the people of Paris, or of the world. For the sake of historical inquisitiveness, the mortal remains of this man have been spirited away, for reasons and purposes unknown—leaving the mystery of his death thirty years ago all the more unanswerable. . . .

Weekly World News, July 17, 2000 (distributed July 10)
What Really Happened to the Lizard King—An Exclusive, Eyewitness Report
(Special to *Weekly World News*)

The Paris police may be keeping quiet about it, and "rock historian" Wallace Davis may be uneager to let Morrison fans know the truth, but according to the bizarre eyewitness description of the events of the night of July 3, 2000, the remains of the legendary rocker were in an almost "lifelike" state of preservation, or so claims Olivier Dupree, one of the gravediggers who helped to exhume the late rocker's coffin. In an exclusive *World* interview, Dupree firmly maintains that "when Dr. Wallace [Davis] opened the casket, there was no . . . smell. No hint of decay. I couldn't see the face, but I saw legs, and folded hands no less intact than my own. When he saw that, Dr. [Davis] closed the coffin, and hurried it to the waiting hearse. But I have attended other exhumations, and have seen other bodies buried a far shorter time than [Morrison's], and never have I not smelled the odor of decay and death. . . ."

A History of Rock and Roll, Dr. Wallace Davis, Time-Life Books, 2012
(Dr. Davis's notes regarding the July 2000 Morrison exhumation)

. . . Whether the remarkable preservation of the deceased was due to some naturally occurring phenomenon, e.g., the known preservative qualities of some modern, preservative-added foodstuffs, or due to some inherent quality of the ground itself, the fact remains that this individual's body was in an almost uncorrupted state, akin to that occasionally found in exhumed members of the Catholic church prior to sainthood being bestowed on them. The exact cause of this almost perfect preservation will need to be determined by medical examiners more skilled in pathological dissection than are available to me today. Further examination of the remains will be postponed until tomorrow, when a team of U.S. pathologists will arrive. . . .

What *Really* Happened to the Lizard King

. . . Mr. Dupree's observations in and of themselves are telling evidence of Morrison's lifelike state of being on July 3, but the scene witnessed by a pair of American college students, Peggy Wolk and Clay Mathers, indicates that far more sinister forces were at work that muggy Paris night than simple body-snatchers. Wolk and Mathers were walking past the Hôtel de Lauzun just after eight o'clock when they witnessed a lone male suspect drawing "odd-looking" branching, complex geometric figures on the sidewalk with what looked like yellow sand taken from a burlaplike sack nearby. Mathers used his 35mm camera to snap a picture of the strange "sand-drawing" (see below). Experts on variant religious practices identified the symbol as a *veves*, which is used in voodoo ceremonies to summon pagan gods, or *loas*. According to Wolk, the man was "obviously drunk or stoned; he smelled sort of sweet, like raw sugar, and was singing and muttering to himself while he was working. Clay asked him what he was doing, but the guy just mumbled something in some sorta French-sounding dialect and kept on working with that sand." (Experts identified the "yellow sand" as cornmeal, commonly used to draw *veves*.) Interested, but too wary to stay close to the singing man, Wolk and Mathers crossed the street and then observed the individual. He was reportedly joined "by maybe five, six other people like him, y'know, island types, and one had a drum, and the rest brought bottles of liquor, and they started this weird dance on the sidewalk, but when we saw that they had this live chicken, we figured the heck with it and split," said Mathers. What makes the students' story important to the Morrison incident is the timing; according to Wolk, the "weird dance" began at approximately twenty minutes after eight, the approximate time that Dr. Davis and his team left the disinterred body of Morrison alone in one of the chambers of Davis's as-yet undisclosed Paris headquarters. No one from Davis's team checked on the body (which was still in the casket) until the next morning, when the remains were discovered to be missing. And at approximately eight-thirty that evening, a policeman broke up the "weird dance." The official police record relates that while most of the individuals ran off (including the man drawing the *veves*), the police officer did speak to one woman who claimed to be "summoning" someone, but otherwise refused to comment on the night's events.

While the police still deny any foul play in regard to the whereabouts of the dead rocker's remains, reporters for *Weekly World News* have determined that the man photographed by Clay Mathers is a well-known Miami voodoo priest, or *houngan,* called Papa Zidor (aka Jean Desire), who was recently arrested in Miami for . . .

Excerpt from *Colonel McClaren,* p. 67

. . . got out of Paris with his "charge" before the theft of the body was discovered the next morning, using a passport he'd forged prior to leaving Miami on June 29. How Zidor knew that Morrison's body would, indeed, be uncorrupted and intact prior to the actual exhumation is still a mystery; all Zidor would say (either then or now) was that "it is the duty of the *houngan* to protect sacred secrets." It has been speculated by other *houngans* (those not allied with the New Orleans voodoo sanctuaries) that Zidor made spiritual contact with Morrison during a series of ceremonies held in Miami in late May and early June of that year; as several participants from those ceremonies later related (after they'd broken away from Papa Zidor following official public disclosure of the "incident"), they'd seen Zidor create *veves* similar to the one published in several tabloid papers that July . . . *veves* theretofore unused in any voodoo ceremony performed by Papa Zidor. In fact, those *houngans* (both traditional and those aligned with the Laveauian voodoo) contacted by this author didn't recognize that particular pattern as being associated with any known *loa.*

Furthermore, at least two of the participants in Zidor's ceremonies, one each for May and June, reported being "wildly" possessed by a *loa,* yet once the possession was withdrawn, no one would tell them exactly *which* god had been "riding" their bodies, for Papa Zidor refused to identify that new *loa,* and the actions of the *loa* were not familiar to the other participants. Regardless of whether or not this unknown *loa* was, indeed, a spiritual manifestation of the late rock star, Zidor was confident in the knowledge that he could not only summon the spirit of the man in Paris, but that he could also provide a suitable—and, most significant—*permanent* "home" for that particular *loa.* . . .

Rolling Stone headline, 1981

Jim Morrison—He's hot, he's sexy, he's dead

Rolling Stone headline, 1991

The Doors: The Making of the Myth

Rolling Stone headline, 2001

Jim Morrison—He's hot, he's still sexy . . . he's undead

60 Minutes, "Resurrection of the Lizard King," Sunday, January 14, 2001

STEVE KROFT: I realize that once a person dies, their soul technically "belongs" to no one except perhaps God, but—

PAPA ZIDOR: There you go, there you go. Inflict *your* belief on *my* faith. For me, for my believers, soul is the soul. *You* are ones who proclaim this man "god," *you* are ones who kept him alive after he die. What happen when I contact his *loa* is act of nature. I hold ceremony, one, two times, he come. Is simple as—

KROFT: But according to my sources, in the religion of voodoo, in order to summon a *loa,* or god, one must perform certain steps asking that *loa* to come, that specific *loa,* who is summoned through music—

ZIDOR: Yes, yes, that is true—

KROFT: —through the use of ceremonial drinks, through . . . certain animal sacrifices—

ZIDOR: Again! There you go again! I see . . . I see that wiggle of distaste in your voice, see it in your eyes. Animals are sacrificed to the *loa* so *loa* can bless offering of holy meat, which is to be given to poor at such ceremony—

KROFT: As I *was* about to add, so that the viewers would understand, too. Mr. Desire, we're not here to ridicule your religion. But, as you well know, the result of your ceremony before the Hôtel de Lauzun last July was the . . . reanimation of the gentleman sitting next to you. A man who was . . . *dead* for thirty years, who had only been disinterred that morning—

ZIDOR: Am I the man who did *that* to him? Ask my followers, I do not haunt the graveyards, I do not give the potion which creates the zombies!

KROFT: Mr. Desire, I wasn't accusing you of grave robbing. I just would like to know why you brought it upon yourself to, in essence, give life back to Mr. Morrison here. Or, more to the point, why you felt *you* had the right to do this.

ZIDOR: I am only instrument of the *loa.* I am no god. I give *no life.* (rises from chair)

KROFT: Okay, okay, I didn't say you were. But there's still the question of Mr. Morrison. He's obviously quite . . . alive, listening to us, watching the whole conversation, yet only six months ago he was . . . *dead*. Lying in a casket in a cemetery in Paris. Obviously, he didn't reanimate *himself*. If that had been possible, he would have done so sooner—

ZIDOR: In a coffin with no air? With no food? No, no, these things, they happen for reason. I contact *loa*, other man, he do the digging up.

KROFT: Let me put this another way. . . . Ever since July 3, you have been accompanied by Mr. Morrison here, but has he in any way expressed a desire to *maintain* this . . . unusual existence? Was this whole event *his* doing, *his* idea?

ZIDOR: (smiling) You the question man. Ask *him*.

KROFT: Well, Jim? Can you tell the viewers what really happened to you? How you came to be here?

MORRISON: Uhm? Sorry, I was watching your cameraman over there. He's got this . . . I dunno, *look* on his face. (smiles at camera) Could you, uhm, repeat that last question?

KROFT: What really happened to you that night? How did you come . . . *back?*

MORRISON: (closes eyes, shakes head) Steve . . . if I knew, I'd tell you. It was like . . . drifting off and waking up. Too fast to contemplate. I . . . (glances at camera, smiles, and shrugs)

-- CUT TO COMMERCIAL --

CNN *Headline News*, July 16, 2000

. . . We have this breaking news from Miami, Florida: A local *houngan* of the voodoo faith named Jean Zidor Desire has just called a news conference in regard to the disappearance of the recently exhumed body of—just a moment, we're switching to a live feed. . . .

(Zidor seated behind a bank of microphones in the Miami Hilton conference room.)

ZIDOR: I will answer your questions in a minute, as soon as my companion arrive—ah, come here, Jim.

(Cameras pan to left of screen, where a dark-haired man of medium height emerges into camera range; sounds of surprise from unseen audience.)

MORRISON: (walking up to Zidor, then standing behind microphone) Hello . . . my name's Jim—

(Overlapping voices, cameras moving in for close-up.)

Excerpt from *Colonel McClaren,* pp. 80–81

Zidor's July 16 news conference was a stroke of inspired genius; by publicly showing his "companion" to the assembled members of the press, and furthermore demonstrating that Morrison was acting of his own free will and was able to speak for himself, Zidor circumvented the possible negative reaction of the police and other authorities. Instead of being labeled a mere body snatcher, Zidor was dubbed a "resurrectionist" by the press. Although the passport he'd used to bring Morrison back into the United States was forged, the fact that he brought his "companion" back to the very city where he was still wanted on indecent exposure charges proved (in the eyes of the world) that Zidor's intentions were not as dishonest as they originally appeared. The fact that Morrison willingly returned to Miami makes it difficult to prove that Zidor was, in fact, holding an unholy "power" over the revived Morrison.

Even after learning that the charges had been dropped[1] in regard to the pending prison sentence, Morrison still chose to remain with Zidor, a fact that eventually brought up the

---

1 Even though the outstanding prison sentence had been under appeal at the time of his death, due to the statute of limitations being seven years for indecent exposure, it was decided that "above and beyond Mr. Morrison's nebulous legal status, i.e., officially dead or officially alive," the 1970 charges would be dropped, with that course of action deemed "most humane," due to "time served."

suspicion that Zidor did, indeed, have some sort of hold over Morrison (an extreme example of this was the *60 Minutes* segment devoted to the affair in 2001).

Morrison himself emphatically denied these charges. In a letter to the editor of the *Miami Herald*, he wrote:

"During my past life this last century, no man, no woman, was my master, a situation which *continues to this day*" (italics Morrison's). He further stated that the decision not to contact members of his former band, his former associates, and his family was "based solely on the desire on my part not to further disrupt their current lives any more than they have already been disrupted by disclosure of my current circumstances."[2]

In addition to the *Miami Herald* letter, Morrison wrote similar letters defending Zidor's peculiar actions on his behalf to *Rolling Stone*, the *Wall Street Journal*, *Time*, *Newsweek*, and other magazines and newspapers that had either tacitly or directly criticized Zidor for resurrecting and "maintaining" Morrison in his highly unusual and "unnatural" state of being; the content of these letters, while specifically addressing the individual claims and/or charges brought by the publication in question, all dealt strongly with his (Morrison's) free will in all "decisions and actions undertaken after July 3, 2000, by myself in my behalf."[3]

---

[2] Morrison did contact the above-mentioned people by viewphone shortly after the July 16 press conference, mainly to prove that he was indeed who he claimed to be and not an impostor; what was actually said during those twenty-six records-substantiated phone conversations (which lasted from five to fifty-six minutes) has remained a mystery. However, no one called during that time later came forward disputing his claim to be James Douglas Morrison, even if each person has steadfastly refused to reveal what was or wasn't said by Morrison at the time of the call.

[3] This statement, of course, does not take into account Zidor's possession of the forged passport to which was affixed a thirty-two-year-old photograph of Morrison, nor does it take into account the time *prior* to July 3, 2000, and *after* July 3, 1971. At no time was the literal fact of his death in the last century discussed by Morrison, a most curious omission at best, but an ominous one at the worst.

At no point did Morrison choose to address the improbability of his "current circumstances," however. . . .

Rolling Stone #987, 2001

"View from 'the Other Side': Fame, Rock, Drugs, Death, and Rebirth, Paul Ridgeway reporting

. . . but in just as many ways, Jim Morrison never *did* leave the scene. Page through almost any issue of this magazine since his death in 1971, and you'll come across his name or that of his group, be it in actual articles, features, reviews, or whatnot, or be it in the classifieds section: Wannabes and would-be hangers-on hawking everything from the relatively benign posters and bootleg concert films to the somewhat tackier eight-by-ten glossies of his grave to the "actual" transcripts of his infamous Miami trial for indecent exposure during a 1960 University of Miami gig.

True, it's difficult for the average "live" person today to fully comprehend what sort of culture shock Morrison may be going through right now—but no one can deny that he has been an inactive participant in almost every phase of the music industry during those years he's been "away." . . .

AP wire service, Monday, March 5, 2001

The last of the ten pending paternity suits against Jim Morrison was dismissed today in a Los Angeles courtroom based on the negative results of DNA tests. The plaintiff's lawyer was quoted as saying, "How does anyone know what being dead for thirty years did to his DNA?" Lawyers for the defendant countered with evidence that the defendant's DNA is consistent with that supplied by other living relatives. . . .

He's Hot, He's Sexy, He's . . .

Excerpt from *Colonel McClaren*, p. 102

Zidor soon found that he needed a great deal of money in order to offset his newly revived companion's massive legal fees. While Morrison was legally entitled to a share of the publishing rights from both his own books of poetry and the lyrics to the Doors catalogue, his will had been specific about leaving all of his worldly possessions to his former common-law wife, who, when she died in 1974, left all of her inheritance to her parents, who eventually shared the money, property, and other inherited goods with Morrison's family; therefore Morrison in effect had no specific right to those monies and property which had already been legally willed to others.

Zidor, however, discovered that Morrison himself was a valuable commodity; while the former singer now refused to have anything to do with the music industry (a field he had been contemplating leaving prior to his death, possibly in favor of a career in the movie industry), he wasn't averse to giving readings of his prose works, or to lecturing—a fact Papa Zidor took full advantage of at the earliest opportunity. . . .

Handbill posted outside the USC Fine Arts Center, week of April 1–7, 2001

FOR ONE WEEK ONLY
April 8–April 14
Live and in Person
Jim Morrison
reads
selections from
"The Lord" and
"The New Creatures"
7:00 PM nightly
Tickets $25 in advance
$30 at the Door

UPI/AP wire services, Monday, May 7, 2001

In a rare joint statement of policy, the Vatican and the assembled leaders of the U.S.A's voodoo sanctuaries (including the New Orleans Laveauian sanctuaries) have issued a decree declaring the practice of reanimation to be a "sin against God, Man and Nature," and further stating that such "animated beings" are not considered, in their view, to be truly "human" beings. . . .

MTV, *The Day in Rock,* Monday, May 7, 2001

". . . responding to today's unusual 'joint statement of policy,' Morrison had this to say": (switch to taped feed)

"I can't say that this comes as a surprise. I mean, it's not like I'm *not* used to being condemned for things I didn't do. . . ."

Excerpt from *Colonel McClaren,* p.106

. . . It was around this time that the nickname "Colonel McClaren" was given to Papa Zidor,[1] due to his incessant booking of his erstwhile "client" into concert halls and universities across the United States. While it soon became apparent that Morrison's patience with the increasingly rapturous audience members was growing short (during one gig in Portland, Oregon, during the first week in June of that year, Morrison stopped his reading to ask his listeners, "Assholes, are you really *listening* to me, or just getting off on being in the same room with a guy who was dead long before you were born?"), Zidor continued to book him into whatever venue he could find—as long as the advances were good. This soon attracted the attention of the ACLU and other groups . . .

---

1 From Colonel Tom Parker, Elvis Presley's manager, and Malcolm McClaren, who managed the Sex Pistols and Bow Wow Wow.

He's Hot, He's Sexy, He's . . .

MTV, *The Day in Rock,* Monday, July 2, 2001, also repeated on CBS, CNN, NBC, and ABC evening newscasts

". . . and in what was a not-unexpected announcement, legendary rocker and revived poet Jim Morrison announced that he is canceling all further speaking engagements as of this week. While a recording gleaned from the best of his poetry readings and lectures will be available in stores within the next two months, Morrison announced that he has no further plans to 'perform' in public, although he is still open to granting interviews and, quote, 'maintaining contact with my "true" fans and associates,' which is thought to be an affirmation of his continuing loyalty to Jean Zidor Desire, also known as 'Papa' Zidor, the man who was responsible for the sudden and unexpected reemergence of Morrison on the . . ."

Rolling Stone, July 2001, interview with Jim Morrison conducted by Brian Preston

Back when I was younger, perhaps in the early nineties or so, I had this dream about Jim Morrison and his common-law wife, Pamela Courson. In it, neither of them had died during the seventies, but the years hadn't been good to either of them. In my dream, Pamela had become the all-encompassing Mother figure to Jim, the role she'd begun to play during his last days in Paris, when she was picking out his clothes and trying to help him get his act together, only in this dream she was a little older, a lot grayer, and somewhat fatter—and she was guiding a grayer, chunkier, and *quieter* Jim around like he was senile . . . or worse.

That's basically all there was to that brief, intense dream —Pamela leading Jim down these stone steps set into a cliffside, and him just *letting* her lead him. And what freaked me during that dream was how quiet Jim was, how resigned to every little thing he was, as if the farce of a trial in Miami and all the petty legal hassles he'd been enduring for the past few years had finally broken him, left him empty. And then I woke up.

Not long after that, I read about Val Kilmer's dream of Morrison with his brain exposed as he talked to the young actor who was going to play him in Oliver Stone's biopic, and how freaked Val was over seeing this guy's brain-on-drugs . . . but *my* dream still shook me.

That's why I drove slowly to my first meeting with Jim Morrison; I was afraid that I'd find the dream-Jim being led by the arm by his surrogate-companion, Papa Zidor. But once I approached the Miami home of the now world-famous *houngan* from Anse-a-Veau, Haiti, my fears frittered away, for I saw Morrison standing in front of Zidor's screened-in wraparound front porch, smiling and waving at me. He even opened the car door for me after I parked my rental Saturn, telling me as I walked with him up the wide, shallow porch steps, "I'm glad you got here before the photographer. I wanted to show you around the place before we got to talking."

While Morrison showed me Zidor's place (aside from a couple of corner shrine-like jumbles of candles, potions from the local botanical, and statuelike dolls which Morrison assured me were "nothing like the voodoo dolls used in bad movies. See those pins? They're used to symbolize holy messages for the spirits, not to hurt people," the house was uniformly neat, with a large, well-stocked library dominated by several comfortable reading-style chairs), I studied this again-living legend of my own youth. While he's been on earth (and in it) for almost fifty-eight years, Morrison could pass for roughly thirty or so; his features are a little heavier than those captured in Joel Brodsky's landmark photo session, and his blue eyes (now adorned with barely perceptible contact lenses) are a little more hooded, while his still-longish brown hair is heavily flecked with gray.

But he's still as animated, still as articulate as he was prior to his death in 1971, albeit somewhat more . . . distant. While exceptionally polite, and open to my casual questions about the house and its voodoo-related contents, I quickly sensed a certain sense of alienation about the man; not a rejection of *me*, or even of his surroundings, but an aura of *apartness* nonetheless.

Once the tour of the house was finished (his manager/mentor Zidor was nowhere to be seen), we made our way back to the front porch. By that time the photographer had arrived, and while she was busy weaving back and forth with her Nikon, waiting for the right tilt of the head, the right expression to capture for the magazine layout, I turned on my tape recorder and began.

ROLLING STONE: Jim, I hate to ask this first, but it's what the readers want to know. What was it like, being—

JIM MORRISON: Dead? Oh, God. . . . I know this sounds like I'm evading the question, but I have *no* idea. It's like, uhm, I was *there*, but can't recall any of it. And that's what's so unbearable . . . the having been there but not remembering any of it. Realizing that a major chunk of my time on earth was spent . . . *somewhere* is the most painful thing, especially when there's evidence that I was in a, you know, *active* mode wherever I *was*. Because of what happened with Jean's followers, all that. He *knew;* otherwise, he wouldn't have . . . although sometimes I wish he hadn't, after all I'd gone through to experience it and all . . . I just wonder what I was *doing*, what I was thinking. . . . I must've been thinking, been reaching *out*. . . .

RS: Have you ever found out anything about why your . . . *you* remained as you were before? I think that's the thing that's had people puzzled the most; that you were still uncorrupted—

JM: (laughing) "Uncorrupted"! What a word choice! *That's* ironic. . . . Getting to your question, though, no, no one knows why. They had to do some DNA testing on me, for legal reasons I can't talk about due to the appeals process and all, but nothing out of the ordinary was found then.

RS: You're aware that what happened to you isn't an isolated occurrence? That certain saints—

JM: Don't bring up *that* mess, okay? I certainly don't think *they'd* (makes sign of the cross) enjoy the comparison!

RS: (laughs) True! Getting away from the circumstances surrounding all of this, how has the readjustment period been for you? Getting used to society, all the changes.

JM: (with a frown) That's where things start to get to me, finding out how little some stuff has changed, you know, with the racial tensions, and the Middle East mess, and . . . I don't mean to put down anyone, but it appalls me how little people *think* anymore. I thought some of my audiences were so fucking stupid, but I see the kids now and . . . God, the people up on the *stage* are even worse than *I* supposedly used to be, and the kids out there just keep egging them on. . . . I get to wondering; If they're what's considered "cutting edge" or whatever you call it now, what the hell were they after *me* for? I never intentionally injured a fan, or did half the things these clods just get away with.

RS: About ten years ago Axl Rose had some major run-ins with—

JM: (waving his hand) Yeah, I read about him. I also read about how insulted he was when that Oliver Stone compared him to me. Actually, I'm insulted that I was compared to *him*.

RS: Speaking of Stone, what did you think . . .

JM: Well . . . he meant well. I was glad *he* did the film, and I'm happy to see he made it in Hollywood, but it was such a weird experience . . . sort of like seeing the tapes of that eighth annual Rock and Roll Hall of Fame induction, when that guy, what's his name—

RS: Eddie Vedder.

JM: —okay, him, did "Light My Fire," and I was sitting there thinking, What the fuck would they have done with *me* if I'd been around for that? Ridiculed me for losing my voice, or for having a fat gut? Actually, though, not to sound bitter or anything, I couldn't help but think, The other guys *didn't* need me after all. . . .

RS: Well, under the circumstances, y'know, they had no choice.

JM: Yeah, I realize that, but still, after hearing that Vedder guy, and finding out that the actor who played me did some of the singing himself, I felt so . . . I dunno, *fungible*. . . ."

Excerpt from *Colonel McClaren*, p. 127

. . . When asked why he had such an interest in reuniting the *loa* or spirit of Morrison with his disinterred body, Zidor explained with unusual candor, "When I a boy, coming to this country on the big boat from [my] homeland, this rock and roll thing, it mean a lot to me. The rhythm, the . . . power of it, and then there were the words, especially words like from Morrison. . . . He say [a] lot to me, to other[s]. Not words just sung, like other song, but words to *me*. He like god, even when alive . . . not because he [was] good man always, but [he] wanted to be good *inside*. I felt it in music, felt it in words. That's why I draw *veves* to summon [him?], based on power of words and music. Because of the good in there.

"And when he come walking down [that] Paris street that night, he smile at me, say 'Hello' like I'm old friend. Jim, he like *every*one 'less they cross him. Always was nonprejudice[d] man, still was when I know him. Maybe that why he leave again, because people prejudice[d] against *him*. . . ."

AP/UPI wire services, Monday, December 10, 2001

James Morrison, former lead singer of the 1960s rock group the Doors, and lately the subject of intense religious and public controversy due to his physically revived status, was found dead on the eve of his fifty-eighth birthday this past Friday by his mentor and companion Jean Zidor Desire. Morrison had shot himself in the heart with a handgun; according to his written wishes, he was cremated, and his ashes were scattered over the Pacific Ocean. He left a brief note exonerating Zidor, which stated that "a legend has its own life, surpassing that of the being who created said legend—in such circumstances, the presence of said being becomes superfluous. My legend has always lived, may it continue to live unaided and unaugmented." Zidor had only this comment for the press: "Jim never die in first place, how can he really die again?"

Excerpt from *A History of Rock and Roll,* p. 325

... I don't know if we really learned anything from the second life and death of Jim Morrison, other than that his *first* life and death were momentous enough to forever assure him his place in musical and cultural history; perhaps the legacy of his second life and final days is that we *are* incapable of truly listening to and learning from anyone, no matter how much they try, or how intent they are upon their chosen mission in the arts and letters. ...

AP wire service, December 2001

For the first time in the history of Paris, a non-French landmark has become the number-one tourist attraction. The empty tomb of singer Jim Morrison has surpassed the Louvre, Versailles, and even the Eiffel Tower as the most-visited spot in France. Said one tourist spotted near the empty grave, "It's just the only way to be *close* to him anymore. ..."

OI BOY

Mike Baron

*D*onahue was on when Richie woke. Richie's tongue tasted like a used sweatsock and his head felt like someone had kicked in his temples. Without raising himself he swept his hand across the cluttered nightstand and found the amber plastic pill bottle. Empty. He'd washed down the last white cross around midnight with a shot of tequila. His stomach screamed. He needed water, food, and some hair of the dog.

Richie sat up and planted his black Ft. Lewis Go Devils on the floor with a thunk. He hadn't even managed to peel off his boots before collapsing on the sprung sofa that served as his bed. On the little silver screen across the one-room basement apartment, Donahue shoved his microphone in the face of a fat, middle-aged bitch wearing too much makeup. She had a question for one of the wives whose husbands had had sex-change operations.

"Faggot asshole," Richie snarled without much conviction, hurling a shirt at the screen. He'd been so blotto the previous night he hadn't even noticed the TV was on. He probably hadn't even locked the door, not that he had anything to steal, or that anyone would try to steal it. Richie had a rep in his East Seattle neighborhood. He wasn't afraid to rumble and he didn't back down. He ran with the boys of the National Front.

And he played in a rock and roll band. It was the cherry on top of the sundae of the American dream. Never mind that he'd been shit-canned the previous month from his job at a paper recycling joint because the fat Jew could hire two Koreans for the price of one white man, or that he was behind in the rent for his pisshole of an apartment. His unemployment checks hadn't started yet, and he didn't even have a line of crystal meth to prop up his eyelids, much less to hustle to the chickenhawks down on the strip.

Richie had a hangover like a jackhammer in a phone booth, he was out of work, had no immediate prospects and no old lady. His life was like a Merle Haggard song. He popped a Guns 'n' Roses cassette into his stolen boombox and staggered to the bathroom mirror in rhythm. Fuckin' Axl Rose used to be a real man before the MTV weepies taught him how to suck dick and sing for the rain forest, he thought.

Richie examined himself in the cracked mirror partially obscured by a large skull decal advertising Thrash boards. He had a nasty welt under his right eye, and both eyes were sunk so deep in their sockets, they looked like they needed prying out with a screwdriver. His earrings were intact, the little silver skull and the sterling Maltese cross, both dangling from his left ear. He vaguely remembered some kind of hassle last night, someone getting in his face. The bros would fill him in at the club. He'd have woken up in jail if he'd done any serious damage. His two-day stubble matched his buzz cut so that most of his head appeared to be covered in a stiff bristle.

He jammed a finger down his throat and forced himself to heave into the toilet. He always felt better after he heaved. Do it before you eat, that was his motto. He half expected the silly-ass bitch from upstairs to pound on his floor because of the music, but then he noticed the sunlight streaming in through the high west-facing windows and realized it was late in the afternoon. She was probably making her daily constitutional to the park with her dog, Sniffer. One of these days, when he moved up and out, he'd break into her apartment and fix Sniffer a little treat—a mixture of ground chuck and ground glass.

Richie felt better after he'd showered. He put on a clean Aryan Nation T-shirt, dirt-stiffened jeans, his stompers, and black leather, chrome-studded, fingerless gloves, then slid a commando boot knife into the right boot. The boys from the Front had promised him a nine down the line. Maybe after tonight, when they realized what he and his band could mean to the movement. I mean, he thought, they already know I'm a kick-ass, front-line warrior in defense of white Christian America. But they *don't* know I can sing.

Everyone was going to be there: Aryan Nation, the Klan, the John Birch Society, the White Panthers, even some of the New Age yuppie groups like States' Rights and the National Heritage Coalition.

Sure as shit there would be big money in the hall tonight. If they liked what they heard, they'd come up with the bucks for White Heat to cut an album. And if they liked what they saw afterward, when Richie and the boys went down on Aurora Street near the bay, they'd give him his nine and promote him to lieutenant in the New Aryan Army. He'd heard there were secret initiation rites with beautiful black hookers dressed as slaves.

It was dusk by the time he emerged on Rusk Street. His entrance was underneath and to one side of the main entrance to a very crummy apartment building that was rapidly filling up with niggers, wogs, and spics. Excuse me, thought Richie, I meant people of color. Maybe he wouldn't poison the old lady's dog. Maybe he'd torch the whole fucking building. Do the neighborhood a favor.

It was late March and a stiff wind blew in off the bay as Richie tripped down the street toward Dan Dunn's, the only decent Irish workingman's bar within walking distance. He stopped in a Burger King and scarfed down a Whopper after carefully checking the contents to make sure the Arabs in the kitchen hadn't jerked off on it. He passed one Jap car after another. One night, coming home from Dunn's with a gut full of malt liquor and a head full of coke, he'd torn the aerial off a Toyota and used it to customize every gookmobile on the street.

There were still a few stragglers out, and a bus moved down the street. It was the most important night of Richie's life. He'd formed White Heat as a means of personal salvation, to lift himself from the slough of despair and to show the way to other God-fearing white Americans. Richie had taken the name from the Cagney movie. Cagney was his kind of guy—he didn't take shit off anyone. Sometimes when the band was deep into its groove, that's how Richie felt—like Cagney on top of the refinery at the climax of *White Heat.*

Top of the world, Ma!

An Ur-punk freezing his skinny ass off in baggy shorts and an Arrested Development T-shirt rumbled his way down the cracked concrete. Fucking sandy-haired nigger, you couldn't tell what race the little mongrel was. Richie made as if to step aside, then stomped down hard on the board's nose as the kid drew near, sending the little fucker into a parking meter.

Kid never skipped a beat. He scooped up the board, ran into the street, threw it down, and jumped on it, flipping Richie the bird over his shoulder.

Dan Dunn's was a corner establishment painted battleship gray with chrome yellow trim around the corner door. Years of grime had reduced the yellow to a faded school-bus color. The interior smelled like beer and damp wood, and the lights from the video games were the brightest thing. That and the big Bud display over the bar, six Clydesdales dragging that silly-ass wagon around and around and around.

The jukebox was playing Nirvana. Even here you couldn't get away from that puke grunge shit. Richie would love to personally help Kurt Cobain find the vein. He'd give him a hot shot that would shut him up forever. White Heat was an oi band, and even though oi had grown out of the Brit punk tradition, it traced its lineage equally to heavy metal. And one thing you had to say about those heavy metal fuckers, they could play. They didn't just strum chords. They didn't wallow around the beat. Every note was fucking right on, punched out like a rivet on an assembly line. That's how White Heat sounded. Heavy metal with a message, made in America.

Garrick, the pasty bartender with the Errol Flynn mustache and Irish accent, asked him what he wanted. "Gimme an Oly. You seen Marv?" Marv was his speed connection. Malt liquor by itself wasn't going to do it.

"Aye, mate. I expect him shortly." Garrick had a conspiratorial air and liked to hint that he was somehow connected with the IRA.

After draining the Oly in one draught and ordering another, Richie looked around. There were three other patrons in the bar, a couple of grizzlers in a wall booth smoking pipes and playing chess, and a kid who'd just got off construction. You could tell from his mud-covered boots and the tool belt hanging over the back of his stool.

Richie pulled out his folding green. Eight bucks. Barely enough to cover his bar tab, much less enough Dexedrine to get him through the night. And he'd need some of that fine China White to smooth out the jangles. By the time Marv slithered onto the stool next to him, he had three bucks left.

"My man," Richie exclaimed, doing the white power shake. Marv was a hanger-on and a poser, but knew where to score righteous crank.

Marv wore a bandanna to keep his greasy locks out of his face. His nose was two sizes too big, red and running. He looked like a rat. "Whatchoo need, bro?" His beady eyes danced around the bar, everywhere but on Richie.

"Marv, I'm a little short. Can you spot me five whites and a gram of China, and I'll catch up with you later?"

"What's later, bro? I'm a businessman. I got commitments to keep."

"Hey, man, like the gig at the hall. You gonna make it?"

"Oh, yeah. Wouldn't miss it. How much you got?"

Richie showed him the three. Marv wiped his nose and tried not to look disgusted. "Tell you what, bro. I'll just slip you this here one white cross, gimme the three, you catch up with me at the hall. You got the skank, I got the crank."

The hall was only a couple of hours away. But Richie had an idea. He was not without resources. He popped the white cross into his mouth without looking at it, washing it down with malt liquor. His heart began to pick up the pace and his eyes grew big. Oh yeah, the power was in him now. His hands clutched as if holding his bass and he unconsciously began to air-walk the rhythm booming out of the Wurlitzer in the corner. The problem was, some faggot-assed hippie was playing Fleetwood Mac.

Fleetwood Mac! Time for Richie to hit the road, before Sting started singing about saving the rain forest. One more dustup in Dunn's and they wouldn't let him back in.

It was dark outside and there was a light drizzle containing a taint of the sea, a hint of rotten fish. To get to the hall, Richie had to traverse three long loser commercial blocks, discount clothing, used furniture, pest extermination, a natural gas dispatcher, a bodega that was the only thing open, and five or six boarded-up storefronts decorated with gang graffiti. Richie had done some of the decorating, defacing the crude scrawl of the local branch office of the Los Angeles Crips, replacing it with the white power symbol.

Someone had torn down all the posters he'd put up yesterday advertising White Heat's gig. Mother*fuck*ers. Must have been the apes in the jungle. Richie wished they'd go back to the jungle—that's what white power was all about.

Little lights danced at the periphery of his vision and the streetlamps reflected up at him from beads of condensation on the sidewalk. He passed the bodega on the other side of the street, hearing a snatch of Spanish and some laughter. Fucking spics, why didn't they learn American if they wanted to come here and slop up welfare?

Past the bodega the street arched downhill toward Humphrey Boulevard, where he could catch the Amstel Avenue bus to the hall. A hundred yards ahead, underneath a steel awning framing the entrance to a plumbing supply house, someone was playing a guitar. Richie couldn't believe it. What kind of porous-brained idiot would stand on a side street in the rain singing?

Amazingly, he had an audience. Even at that distance and in the rain, Richie could make out the long hair, ponytails, fringed leather jacket, and pile of rags of a pair of hippies, lost in a time warp for thirty years. He heard the clink of silver as they tossed some coins into the busker's open guitar case, and his mumbled thank-you. They moved on to the end of the street and disappeared around the corner.

The singer continued, although he thought he was alone. Singing that drippy folkie hippie shit, that wimp music that made Richie want to smash things. Sometimes he had fantasies about fucking Sinead O'Connor up the ass. But first he'd make her wear a wig.

As Richie drew near, the folksinger glanced his way and saw him for the first time. The moron smiled like he'd just been waiting to sing and play his songs for someone like Richie. In the pale and diffuse light from the corner lamp, Richie could see a thin young man with dreadlocks and a Zapata mustache wearing a Mexican peasant blouse, baggy trousers that quit above the ankles, and huaraches. His skin had an olive tint. Richie didn't know if he was a spic, a sand nigger, or a fucking Hottentot. Maybe he should ask the man for his green card.

Smiling ingratiatingly, the busker strummed his cheap

Gibson hollow-body and started singing that stinker by the Jefferson Starship, the one about how white men are no damn good, but the yellow man, a fucking prince!

Richie glanced in the guitar case. Must have been at least twenty dollars there. Where the fuck did this parasite get off, singing antiwhite songs and getting rich? The fool mistook Richie's rictus grin for approval, because he promptly segued into a Culture Club ditty, the one by the screaming fag queen with the pink spiked hair that always had the opposite effect its lyrics intended. It made Richie want to hurt the singer.

"Where you from, man?" Richie asked, high as a government surveillance satellite, breaking up the chorus. The singer strummed a few more chords but, sensing he was losing his audience, stopped, smiling.

"I am from Romany, brother," he replied in a soft European accent.

"No, man, you ain't from Rome, see, 'cause they don't wear no fucking dreadlocks in Rome. You're some kind of sand nigger or Indian, ain't you?"

The singer smiled quizzically and for the first time looked a little nervous. "I don't know what you mean, brother. I am from Romania. I am Radolfo Azore." He proffered a delicate hand with perfectly finished nails and three large rings. Richie took the hand and examined the rings. Radolfo tried to tug free, but Richie tightened his grip.

"Look at this shit. You wearing a month's rent on your hand, shaking down honest Americans for this hippie-dippy shit, what are you, some kind of poofter? What's this, some fucking makeup?" Richie seized the singer by his long, curly locks and pulled his face forward for a better look in the dim light. Sure enough, the Romanian appeared to be wearing some light lip gloss, rouge, and mascara.

"I knew it." Disgusted, Richie shoved the man forcefully back into the alcove, slamming him against the iron-grated door. A flash of gold chain leaped up from the neck of the peasant blouse.

"Please, sir, I am a harmless street singer," Radolfo said

before Richie backhanded him across the face, the metal pyramids on his fingerless gloves tearing off a triangle of lip. Richie glanced up and down the street. Nobody. A bus passed down on Humphrey.

Goddamn, payback was good.

He stood the singer up with one hand and sank a thudding fist into his stomach. Richie could swear he could feel the man's backbone. Probably a fucking junkie who didn't eat right. Groaning, Radolfo sank to the stoop. They were enclosed on three sides by the entrance to the plumbing supply store, a display of faucets, meters, and elbow joints visible through the filthy glass.

"Fucking foreign faggot fuckwad," Richie chanted, methodically kicking the man in the ribs with his steel-tipped boots. Crunch. There went a rib. There was blood everywhere from the mouth wound.

Panting and sweating, Richie stopped. The singer lay in the corner moaning softly, covered with blood. Richie quickly grabbed the guitar case, scooping up the money. He examined the guitar. A piece of shit, not even worth hocking. With a quick glance up and down the street, he smashed it over the singer's head.

He was about to leave when he remembered the gold chain. When he grabbed for it, some kind of amulet got stuck in the shirt's crude cotton weave. Richie yanked. It was about the size of a silver dollar, a butt-ugly piece of pewter with a red stone set in the middle. He was about to rip the works over the singer's head when Radolfo's hand closed over his with surprising strength. The man's brown eyes bored into his with unholy intensity as he spat a single unpronounceable syllable at his tormentor.

Richie backhanded him savagely across the face, then smashed a fist down on his nose. "Oh, yeah?! Oh, yeah?! Go back where you came from, whatever the fuck you are."

But Radolfo wasn't going anywhere. Radolfo was dying. Richie had enough sense to get out of Dodge. He wiped himself off as best he could and then, because it was a nice night for walking and he was filled with energy, he decided to walk to the hall. It was only three miles. He checked himself in a storefront, but the blood was hardly noticeable. It looked just like his usual outfit.

The club was on Ranier Avenue, separated by a glass-splattered parking lot from a carpet wholesaler and across the street from a liquor store. Many years ago it had been a supermarket, but it had been dormant for eight years when the Brotherhood purchased it as a meeting hall, blocking off the big display window out front. It served daily as a youth club and gymnasium, and a martial arts training hall for members of the elite White Panthers. On weekends, it was a social hall, an arts ball, an experiment for Seattle's Next Big Thing: oi rock.

Rock that reaffirmed these United States as a white Christian culture, the way God intended. The Brotherhood was building its own studio in the back, preparatory to releasing its fledgling CD on the White Power label, a sampler that would include some of the top Seattle oi rockers.

White Heat would have at least three songs on that album, more than any other group. Richie had dedicated himself to that end, establishing White Heat as the official house band, waiting for just such an opportunity as tonight.

He felt a little hollow by the time he reached the club. A big skinhead with a Harley logo tattooed on his forehead guarded the door, his jacket bulging over a shoulder holster.

"Yo, Moose."

"Password, Richie."

"Yo, Moose. I only known you for three years. Why for we got to go through this horseshit every night?"

"Password, Richie."

Fuck. They'd given him the password last night at Dan Dunn's after the third shot of tequila. He stood there staring at his boots while Moose gazed serenely out at the lights of the city, visible through the alley between buildings across the street.

Mnemonic association. Wealth. Money. Richie-rich, no,

that wasn't it. But he was close. Reich, that was it. As in Fourth Reich.

"Fourth Reich."

Gaze still fixed on the distance, Moose swung open the metal door. The interior smelled faintly like a gymnasium. The overhead fluorescents had been replaced with indirect lighting hidden in fake wood wainscoting. The place had been redecorated to resemble an American officers' club somewhere in Southeast Asia circa 1966. Several rows of folding chairs had been set up toward the back of the hall, near the entrance, for those who wanted to sit and soak in the dulcet tones, but most of the tile floor remained open for the nightly skeez as patriotic boys worked themselves into a fervor to the beat of their favorite oi bands.

A man in combat fatigues dispensed liquor from a portable bar to the left. There were about twenty people standing around, mostly young punks and skins waiting for the action. At a round table near the back there was a group of five men dressed in simple two-piece suits, with simple ties. They had short, neatly combed hair and athletic bodies. Those would be the representatives of the National Front, including a Brit.

The Brits had money. Word was, they were backing the huge media blitz, including the recording company. Benno, White Heat's drummer, was onstage taping down his kit. Seeing Richie, he stood and waved him over. Benno wore a denim vest so that the audience could see the tattoos that covered most of his muscular torso. He was a living testament to white power. He'd gone into Walla Walla six years ago on a drug bust, a pale white kid scared shitless, and come out a stone killer in the service of the Aryan Nation. Benno taught self-defense classes during the day.

They did the power shake.

"Benno. What the fuck happened last night? Where did I get this?" Richie gestured to the slash under his eye.

Benno laughed, revealing teeth like untended tombstones. "Shit, man, you don't remember? We was walking down by the dock after the gig and there was that candlelight vigil where we beat that gook to death last spring. Some fuckin' Hebe in a beard did that to you before you pushed him into the bay."

Richie rubbed his head. Little sparks exploded all around the edges. Where the fuck was Marv? Richie needed rocket fuel. He had to have altitude and room to maneuver. "No, man, I was really fucked up. You got any crank?"

"No, man, Benno don't do that shit. Got some righteous reefer, you want to get mellow. No? Didn't think so. Hey. Hey. What's this faggot chain around your neck?" Benno's hand snaked out and grabbed the gold chain, pulling it up from beneath the Aryan Nation T-shirt. "What is this, a disco thing?"

"No, man, I took it off some fucking gypsy or something on the way over."

"Yeah, man. Just, if you like break into the Bee Gees or something, ahmina haveta cut ya." Benno grinned to show he was just kidding. Sort of.

Joe the bass player and Mook the rhythm guitarist came up on the stage and began setting up. The hall was filling. There were now about fifty people buzzing around. A voice would occasionally rise above the din with a stinging denouncement of some liberal special interest group or another.

The dex was making Richie jangly. He needed to snort some smack to smooth it out, but had to settle for a tequila. As he stood near the entrance with his unplugged Fender in hand, a man got up onstage and introduced the speaker, the organizer of the States' Rights Coalition from Decatur, Alabama. As the speaker droned on about the need for free choice in schools and the right to own handguns, Richie reviewed the night's playlist in his head.

They'd start with "National Front," which Richie hoped would become the theme song of the movement. Da-da-da-DUM, the bass line pounded in his head. His hands arched over the steel strings and he picked out the lead, audible only to his ears.

Oi Boy

He was aware of a presence on his left. Marv. "How you doin', bro? You lookin' for me?" Marv's breath stank of beer and stomach acid.

They went into the men's room to do the deal. The hall actually had a women's room, but since no woman had set foot in the hall for many years, the room went unused. Richie had often mused that all they had to do was take the fucking women's sign off the door to double their bathroom capacity.

The gypsy had done well for Richie, who had enough long for five white crosses and a gram of China White, which he did off the stained porcelain sink. By the time he emerged from the rest room, he was up among the clouds. A different speaker stood on the stage ranting about the mongrelization of the United States. About a hundred and fifty white men were on their feet, stomping and hooting their approval.

The speaker was Ian Faith, the representative from Britain's National Front. "I've been asked to introduce a rock and roll band," he said, pausing for the shouts of approval. Richie felt proud. His people loved him.

"As you know, in England we have a new musical movement dedicated to the proposition that ours is a country founded by white people, and that we can do naught but suffer from the unchecked immigration of those who do not share our values, our love of God, family, country, and hard work!"

The crowd was going nuts, hands slapping Richie on the back as he made his way down one side of the room toward the stage.

"Rock and roll is an American invention," the speaker continued, "but it took the British invasion to put you Yanks on the right track. It's a tradition that hasn't changed, and I'm very pleased to introduce to you some of your local boys who've taken the inspiration from our own oi bands to forge a new musical movement. Boys, here's White Heat!"

No music was sweeter to Richie's ears than the applause of that group of men as he plugged his Fender into the amp.

He was in the sky looking down. His mates were ready. The playlist was taped to the floor in front of him. Signaling the count, they broke into "National Front."

For an instant the crowd picked up the beat and started skeezing, but then they stopped, confused by the cacophony issuing from the stage. Something was wrong, horribly wrong. While the rhythm section was pounding out the chords to "National Front," Richie was playing another song in another key. And he couldn't stop. It was as if each hand had its own brain and they weren't responding to central. He tried to stop but couldn't. As the rest of the band fell out, Richie stepped up to the microphone. What the fuck was happening here? Just before he opened his mouth to sing, he felt the thump of the amulet against his chest as if it had its own heartbeat.

The awful words came out. Boy George, the poofter with the mascara, his most famous song. That same simpering invitation to smash the singer in the face that had reached number two on the *Billboard* charts in 1983, when Richie was twelve years old. Yeah, they did want to hurt him.

Gypsy.

Curse.

He couldn't stop his ass from twitching. Part of him seemed to observe the situation from up near the ceiling, taking pride that, as a solo, he had a pretty full sound.

Mook was screaming at him. Benno threw his sticks to the ground and stood up like he was ready to do some serious butt-kicking. The crowd, which had at first fallen silent, now began to shout and mutter.

Richie wanted to explain that it wasn't his fault, he was the victim of a gypsy curse. All he'd done was try to protect the shores from the tide of foreign filth!

He sang the whole fucking song. There was a moment of silence. The crowd had moved in close, angry at this mockery of their most sacred symbols. They were waiting for an explanation.

"What the *fuck* are you doin'?" Benno demanded.

Oi Boy

Richie tried to speak. He tried to tell them about the gypsy and the chain around his neck, the amulet pounding its alien rhythm to his soul. He opened his mouth to speak.

He began to sing a medley of Judy Garland songs. That's when the crowd surged forward.

TRACK EIGHT

John F.D. Taff

"Aww, man. I been lookin' all over for that."

Dave turned to see a scruffy headbanger, wearing tattered blue jeans, a black T-shirt with the word "SKULL" on it, and an armless jean jacket. An invisible cloud of old beer and stale smoke seeped from him and hung in the air around him.

Dave looked again at the CD he had flipped to in the used-CD bin, noticed that the headbanger's T-shirt matched the CD's artwork.

"SKULL," the cover screamed in sharp, iron letters that dripped blood. The jacket liner pictured four long-haired, spaced-out-looking kids leering over a nubile young woman writhing on a stone slab. Definitely heavy metal.

The man looked at Dave expectantly, as if he might return the CD to the bin, and Dave was struck by his strong resemblance to one of the band members on the album cover. But the disheveled man looked more burnt-out

Track Eight

than the only slightly post-teenage musician pictured on the liner.

"Skull, huh? Are they any good?" Dave asked him.

"Oh, man. Are they any *good?*" The man threw his hands up in disgust, turned, and disappeared into the crowded store as quietly and suddenly as if he had never been there.

Shaking his head, Dave took two bills from his wallet, handed them to the girl behind the counter, then pushed his way to the parking lot.

After an hour in the late afternoon sun, the air whooshed out in a dry gasp as he opened the car door. He threw the bag onto the passenger seat and slid in, starting the ignition and the air conditioner with one motion.

As he waited for the car to cool, he dumped the CDs onto the seat. He opened the Skull case. The song titles read like a lexicon of heavy metal: "The Blood of Satan," "Hellfire and Damnation," "Virginacide," and the particularly interesting "Fuck the Pure/Puree the Fucks."

Oh, well, he told himself, he'd spent more for less.

He pulled the disc off the center spindle. It was slightly warped, and its edges were blackened, as if singed. It was hard to tell if it had been manufactured like this as a novelty or if the disc was damaged. He slid it into the mouth of his car's CD player, not sure whether it would play. It did.

Traffic was heavy, and by the time he pulled onto the freeway, the first seven tracks on the disc had played. None of them grabbed him. The album was poorly produced, real garage-band shit. And like the song titles, the lyrics were pretty standard, heavy metal love/death/Satan/hell stuff.

Dave's free hand moved to eject the disc, but stopped as the first notes of the eighth track began to play. This was not the same caterwauling he had heard before. This song was pretty good.

Dave picked up the cracked jewel box and pulled out the liner notes. "The Fire of Love." He listened to the lead singer slur:

"The fire of love has cast a glow
A soul's mirror to the fire below
The fire of love will catch up with you
And burn your body and soul through and through
And no one knows
Who the fire of love will burn tonight."

And then a low chorus of voices, accompanied only by a synthesized wind, took up a chant that raised the hairs on the back of Dave's neck.

"Carl Unger, Carl Unger, Carl Unger . . ."

He stabbed the search button, and the machine obediently gurgled back ten seconds.

"Carl Unger, Carl Unger, Carl Unger . . ."

"Carl Unger?" He laughed. "That's weird."

Like Dave, Carl was an auditor at the regional IRS office downtown. Dave knew him in the vague way workers at large offices know each other.

He played back the section of the song several times before he ejected the CD and put it into his briefcase. He'd play the song tomorrow for Carl on the portable CD player he kept in his desk. That'd be sure to get a laugh.

"Died?" echoed Dave with all the conviction of someone who doesn't know what else to say. "How?"

A small group of people were huddled in a loose knot around the coffee machine in the office's cluttered lunchroom.

The receptionist broke into a series of hiccuping sobs, and another of the auditors answered, "From what we've been told, the heating pad he used for his bad back short-circuited and burned the house down." He shrugged. "No smoke detector."

"Died," Dave repeated, fighting a shiver that splashed the coffee in his cup. "I was just thinking about Carl last night. Jesus."

Track Eight

He stood there in silence with the group for a few minutes, until it became too uncomfortable.

Back in his office, he closed the door, glanced at the clock. Eight-fifty. In ten minutes his first appointment would be here, nervous and defensive. He opened his briefcase, and the Skull disc slid out onto the desk.

He opened the case, held the disc to the light. Rainbows arced across its surface like oil on water. Dave thought it felt warm.

Plopping the disc into the Sony player pulled from his desk drawer, he clipped the thin headphones over his ears, fingered the skip button until the digital counter read "8."

As the lyrics of the first verse faded and the synthesized wind began, Dave turned the volume up a notch and closed his eyes. There was another brief passage of wind, and the lyrics of the second verse picked up where the first had left off.

No chanting chorus.

No "Carl Unger" repeated over and over.

Dave opened his eyes in confusion. He flicked the button to the "scan" mode, and the disc gibbered back.

Nothing.

He scanned forward, thinking that the spot was deeper within the song. It was not. The cut was a short one, and Dave scanned into the first twenty seconds of track nine— "Whipped Cream and Leather"—before he realized that it was not there anymore.

It was there last night, he thought. I know, I heard it.

Before he could listen to the track again, his phone beeped.

"Dave, the Millers are here," sniffled the receptionist.

He put the player away, took a big swallow of coffee, gagging a bit on its bitterness, and punched the intercom button on his phone.

"Send them in."

That evening at home, he went first to the stereo. It was high-end equipment, with all the bells and whistles.

And it was one of the few pieces of furniture in his apartment.

Long, narrow shelves lined every wall of the apartment, stuffed with hundreds, thousands of CDs and the thin paper spines of albums. Discs and records also lay stacked on his coffee table, on the tops of speakers. They were scattered in heaps on the floor, spilled from the end tables at either arm of the couch.

The cartridge to his disc player slid out like a morgue drawer, and he dropped the Skull disc into it, hit the track selector until the little LED sticks gathered into an "8," glared red.

Music filled the room. The instruments seemed cautious and subdued in this song, unlike the blaring guitars and screaming lyrics of the other cuts on the album. The lead singer's voice, somewhere between Jim Morrison's rambling and Joe Cocker's incoherence, was subdued, almost reverent, and spoke the words as if they were purest poetry.

Wind howled loudly from the speakers, rattled the windows.

And the voices chanted:

"Melvin Simons, Melvin Simons, Melvin Simons . . ."

Dave frowned. He had not really expected to hear "Carl Unger" again, much less another name.

Another name he knew, for that matter.

He scanned back to the section.

"Melvin Simons, Melvin Simons, Melvin Simons . . ."

"Oh, come on," he muttered in confusion. "This can't be right."

As he reached for the scan button again, though, he froze, and his heart lurched in his chest.

He rushed to the phone. This is crazy, he thought. What am I gonna say? His hand hesitated on the phone; then he punched the number.

"Hello," came a thin, hurried voice.

"Ma?"

"David? Is that you?" she asked huskily.

"Is everything all right?"

"They just took Uncle Melvin to the hospital. He was smoking in bed, and . . ." She paused to hitch in a sob. "The doctors don't think he's going to make it."

"Oh, my God."

He hung up the phone and shivered.

Words can't change on a compact disc, he thought. It's impossible.

He walked numbly to the stereo, picked up the Skull CD case. He opened it, pulled out the liner notes.

"For more information on Skull, write: Screaming Monk Records, Akron, Ohio."

"I think I'll give them a call tomorrow," he decided.

"Screaming Monk Records," the voice answered after nearly a dozen rings.

"Hi, I've got a question about one of your bands," Dave said. He was calling early the next morning from the office.

"Which band is it? We've got a few," said the woman, an edge of frustration readily apparent in her voice.

"Sorry, it's Skull."

"Are you with the police or the fire department?"

"Uh, no."

"Listen," she sighed, her voice dropping in volume and pleasantness, "if you motherfuckers from *Rolling Stone* call one more time, I swear to God that I'll—"

"Whoa, whoa, wait a minute," interrupted Dave. "I'm not with *Rolling Stone*."

"Then who're you with? *Spin*? *Creem*? I mean, Christ! They're not even cold yet!"

"I'm with the IRS," Dave intoned in his best government bureaucrat voice.

"The IRS? If this is some kind of sick joke—"

"No joke. You can check if you like."

"Uhh, sorry for tearing into you like that." Dave heard

her blow out hoarsely, and he got a mental picture of a haggard, hard woman smoking furiously, jamming the cigarette into the corner of her mouth with a shaking hand. "What can I do for you, Mr. . . . ?"

"Dave Beggs. I'm with the regional office. I've got the 1988 paperwork for the corporation known as Skull Inc., a rock band under your management, and I've got a few questions." The lie, he figured, was just enough.

"Well, you know, it's kind of funny, in a sick sort of way. They say you can't avoid death and taxes. The first already got them, and the second is coming in for what's left." She laughed bitterly.

"I'm sorry, is there something I'm not catching here?" he asked, feeling awfully sure that there was.

"They died about three weeks ago."

"Died?" he asked, for the second time in twenty-four hours. "How?"

"Fire," she answered simply. "They recorded in some industrial space downtown. Real weird place. Evidently, a fire started and swept through the entire building just like that." She snapped her fingers. "All of them died, plus the recording engineer, their manager, and a couple of techies. Too bad, too. They were cutting some new tracks for their next album. Word was it was great stuff. Never finished anything, though." She paused. "Why is the IRS concerned about how they died?" Her voice was low again, full of suspicion.

"I have a personal interest in the band. I just bought one of their albums," answered Dave. He glanced at the disc lying near his coffee cup.

"Oh, yeah?" she asked, obviously not believing him. He heard the click of a cigarette lighter.

"Honestly, I'm an IRS accountant, and I like Skull," he said. "Why's that so hard to believe? I'm holding their compact disc right now."

There was a sharp intake of breath. "You fucking asshole! All right, *who* is this?"

Track Eight

"I told you, Dave Beggs with the IRS. Why? What did I say?"

"Skull never cut a CD! They never had the money. Everything they did is on tape or vinyl. Everything! You fucking slime!" She slammed the phone down hard enough to hurt his ears.

As he turned to hang up the phone, he had another idea. He dialed again.

"Sonic City Records. This is Doug. Can I help you?"

"Hi, it's me," said Dave.

"Hey, dickhead, whattaya want?"

"Do you know anything about a group called Skull?"

"Sure, heavy metal. One-hit band. They had a single about a year ago, called 'To Hell with It All.' Kept the zitty headbangers happy for a few weeks. Why the sudden interest in a second-rate heavy metal band?" asked Doug.

"Do you have anything in stock now?"

"I don't know, probably."

"Any CDs?"

"Nope. Their label didn't cut any CDs for them. Care to tell me what's up?"

"What would you say if I told you I have a Skull CD? Bought it the other day at that used record store," Dave said.

"It's a bootleg, gotta be."

"Maybe." Dave turned the battered plastic case over and over in his hand. "But there's something else."

"Like what?"

"You'd never believe it." Dave laughed rather harshly. "Up for a few beers and pizza at my place? Say, seven?"

"Sure. If you've really got a bootleg Skull CD, it'd be worth some money. I mean, it's not an original Beatles master, but it'd be unusual."

"Yeah, you'd be surprised."

"Okay, I've been here for an hour, man. When are you gonna show me this Skull disc?" asked Doug, sloppily folding the last slice of pizza and tucking it into his mouth.

Dave flopped onto the couch, tossed the case to Doug.

"This isn't a professionally produced disc. I've seen bootleg CDs before, but . . ." Doug said, opening it and removing the disc. He handled it gently, looked at it closely. "Man, this doesn't look like any CD I've ever seen, bootleg or professional." He rubbed at a few of the dark smudges. "Looks like it's been burned or something. Does it actually play?"

"That's Skull," agreed Doug, grimacing a moment later. Dave skipped to the next song, played the first few minutes.

Doug shook his head in wonder. "Well, it's Skull all right. That stuff is all on their last album," he said, pulling a pack of cigarettes from his shirt pocket, lighting up.

"You haven't heard the strangest part," said Dave.

As the music of track eight began, Doug's face twisted in confusion. "What's this?"

"It's called 'The Fire of Love.'"

Doug slid a paper bag out from under his jacket hanging over the arm of the couch, withdrew the LP version of the Skull album, and quickly read the playlist.

"There's no song by that name on the record," he said, puffing on his cigarette and shaking his head.

"Well, plenty of artists put an extra track on the CD that's not on the LP or tape," offered Dave.

"Sure, but that's their label doing that. If this is bootleg, where'd this cut come from?"

Dave had no answer. They waited for a moment, a long, agonizing moment when Dave was sure that nothing was going to happen. Sure that he'd look like a fool.

"Wendy Ziner, Wendy Ziner, Wendy Ziner . . ."

Wendy? Dave's heart skipped a beat at the mention of her name. They'd broken up nearly eight months ago after three years of dating. He leapt to the stereo, played the section again.

"Wendy?" Doug asked. "You pullin' my pud, man?"

"No, this is no joke. The evening before last, it said 'Carl

Unger,'" Dave said. "The next morning, I learned that Carl was dead...."

"Who's he?"

"An accountant in the office. Last night, it said 'Melvin Simons.' My Uncle Mel. He died late last night."

"C'mon! You expect me to believe that what it says changes from day to day? You're hearing things. Besides, it's probably just something they cut recently."

"I called their label, Screaming Monk. The woman told me that the band all died a couple of weeks ago in a fire. Before they had a chance to finish anything new."

"Yeah, I read about that in *Stone*." Doug leaned back on the couch, exhaled a cloud of smoke. "But, Dave, man, I think you've been crunching numbers too long."

"No, really. I mean, it sounds crazy. But if this CD is a bootleg, why did someone go to all the trouble to release a bunch of songs that are already out? Except for one song. One song that shouldn't exist. Look, my Uncle Mel is dead, Doug. Carl Unger is dead. Maybe we should call Wendy." Dave started to rise from the couch.

"Wait a minute! Are you nuts?" Doug caught his shoulder, pulled him back. "It's been nearly a year. She's gonna think you're pathetic! You really think she's gonna buy this shit?"

"No." Dave paused, shook his head. "I guess not. You don't believe it, do you?"

"Come on! It's a coincidence. It just sounds like her name."

"Yeah, right. And last night, it just sounded like 'Melvin Simons,' who just *happened* to die. And the night before, it just *happened* to sound like 'Carl Unger,' who also was good enough to croak."

Doug didn't say anything for a minute. "Okay, look. Since Wendy probably wouldn't want you calling, I'll touch base with her tomorrow. Okay, man?"

"Sure," said Dave.

"Look, it's getting late. Why don't you get some z's, have

some coffee in the morning, and audit the hell out of a few people. You'll feel much better." He retrieved his jacket and the Skull LP. "I'll call you tomorrow."

As he opened the door, Doug turned to Dave. "You know, that disc's worth some money—especially with the extra track. Want me to call a few dealers I know, get some prices?"

"Nahh, think I'll keep it for now."

"Okay, talk to ya tomorrow."

"Shit, man," came Doug's quiet and deflated voice through the phone the next morning. "I called Wendy's place today. . . ."

"Yeah?"

"Cops think she left a greasy pan on a burner, left the burner on. She's dead."

"Oh, God," whispered Dave, cradling his head in his hands. "Oh, my God."

"It's just not possible. I can't buy it." There was silence for a moment. "I should've let you call."

"Forget it," Dave advised. "Don't you think I know how crazy it sounded? And don't you think I'm kicking myself right now for not calling her anyway? I mean, you didn't hold a gun to my head."

"What now?"

"I'm going to get rid of it. There's something wrong with this disc. Really wrong. The people who died were people I knew . . . loved. Maybe that's why the person who owned it before sold it."

"How're you going to do it?"

"I don't know. I guess I'll take it home tonight, think about it."

"Why don't you burn it?"

Dave shuddered. "I don't think so. Somehow, I think that'd just make it worse." In his mind, he saw the disc melting limply over a crackling log, looking like a Dali painting. Thick, acrid smoke drifted lazily up from it, coalesced into a large, dark form.

Track Eight

"Well, call me when you decide."
"Sure."
"Positive you don't want to just sell it?"
"Positive."

After work, Dave walked to the parking garage, feeling the disc slide back and forth inside his briefcase. He climbed into the car, threw the briefcase onto the passenger seat. He backed the car out of the parking space, wound down the corkscrewing ramp of the garage.

"What a night for heavy traffic," Dave said, fidgeting in his seat. He was anxious to get home, to dispose of the disc.

He'd break the disc into small pieces, feed the pieces into the garbage disposal, grind them into silver confetti. Then he'd turn on the water and wash the whole mess into the sewage system.

He relaxed as his car accelerated up the entrance ramp to the highway, merged smoothly into the moving traffic. From this vantage point outside the city, he could see the sun sinking below the horizon, a feral, half-lidded eye.

Ten miles from the exit to his apartment, he began to wonder whose name would be on the disc tonight. It was the first time he'd thought of this since he'd decided to destroy the disc, and it surprised him.

He looked at the closed briefcase.

Go ahead, a voice inside his head whispered. You're going to get rid of it anyway. Aren't you the least bit curious?

He was curious. He hesitated, reached over to the briefcase. Its brass latches snapped loudly in the closed car. With one hand, he took out the disc, looked at its cover for a moment, opened it.

The disc felt hot in his hand, its surface like smooth, warm water. He thrust it into the car's CD player, skipped to the eighth track.

His finger shook over the stop button.

Wind roared through the car, distortion crackled through the speakers.

"D—"

He stabbed the stop button convulsively.

"*D—*"

The player's readout flashed "8—2:46" at him in angry yellow numerals.

Holy shit! It's going to say my name next.

How do you know? asked the voice. Play the rest.

NO!

His hands shook so much that he was forced to pull the car over to the side of the highway. A bridge stretched across the river directly in front of him. He steered as close as he could to the guardrail, giving the cars in the lane closest to him as much room as possible.

Outside the passenger window, he saw the last rays of sunlight fall onto the river.

That's it, he thought. The river!

He'd throw the disc off the bridge, out and over the river. Then, down. Down. Into the water.

He snapped the disc forcefully into its case, looked into his side mirror, waited for a lull in the traffic.

Opening the car door, he stepped out, holding the jewel box like a Frisbee.

He approached the guardrail, cocked the disc back in his hand.

Behind him on the highway, Verill Jordan was fumbling for the cigarette lighter in the cab of his eighteen-wheel tanker. He took his eyes off the road for a second, lit his Camel.

Dave turned toward the truck, saw nothing but white light.

Verill's truck smashed into Dave's car, which struck the bridge's concrete abutment, scraped alongside it.

The tanker struck the abutment, too, its trailer jackknifing onto the highway.

Dave's car twisted against the abutment, flipped over, crushing Dave beneath its bent frame, dragging him nearly fifty yards.

Another car struck Verill's jackknifed trailer. Fumes from his last load of gas erupted in a ball of flame. The fire ballooned into the night, engulfed the truck's cab, exploded over Dave's crumpled car, burst the windows in a spray of safety glass.

Traffic continued squealing to a halt for several more minutes. Cars in the oncoming lanes slowed. Several drivers attempted to help survivors.

There were none.

Flames licked at the bridge's rusting arches, billowy arms of dark, oily smoke reaching between them into the early evening sky.

And orange light sparkled on a compact disc that had popped free from its broken case and rolled off the highway, lying like a piece of wreckage. The weeds around the disc quickly blackened, wisps of smoke curling from it.

Doug pushed his hands farther into his coat pockets. He shuffled from foot to foot where he stood, clutching the yellow plastic ribbon that marked the edge of the police line.

The fires were long out, but the heavy fumes of burnt rubber and oil hung in the air, hurt his eyes. A wrecker was busy with what was left of Dave's car.

Thank God, Doug thought, I was not here to see them drag away what was left of Dave.

The whirling blue, red, and orange lights of the emergency vehicles rippled over the dark surface of the river.

From the corner of his eye, he saw a smaller flash of blue. Among the rank weeds and garbage, a small object that reflected the lights.

He walked slowly to it, plucked it from the weeds.

It was a CD. And it was so hot that he had to juggle it between his hands until it cooled.

He wiped a thin, waxy film of ash from it.

Skull.

He slid it nervously into his pocket and left the scene of his friend's death.

Once home, he turned his stereo on, dropped the CD into the player.

One. Two. Three. Four. Five. Six. Seven.

Track eight.

Doug settled back onto the couch, expelling a long, forceful sigh. He wondered what had happened to Dave, why he had stopped on the bridge. Was he trying to get rid of it right there?

Why was he so afraid of this disc?

He pulled a lighter and a crushed package of Marlboros from his pocket, knocked a cigarette onto his hand.

He wrinkled his nose in disgust. Something in the apartment really smelled, stank like rotten eggs. Better open her up and air her out tomorrow, he thought.

The CD's wind swept through the apartment, and the silence following it was filled with voices. Voices whose chants seemed to echo from the caverns of hell.

He fumbled the cigarette into his mouth, lit it, took a puff. As he sucked in the smoke, he realized what the smell was.

Gas.

The explosion blew the cigarette out, propelled the door into the hallway, the windows into the night.

The last thing he heard was the stereo calling his name.

GRAVEYARD SHIFT

Jeff Gelb

Rusty Nails was bored. *I went to broadcast school six months and spent $2000 for this?*

He was the air personality of the midnight-to-five shift at classic rock WMCR. But jocking the graveyard shift meant few breaks for commercials, since most advertisers favored daylight hours and audiences to sell their products to the Cleveland market. Instead, Rusty played lots of uninterrupted music sweeps, but even those were controlled by a computer music selector system, making free choice obsolete.

Worse still, there were hardly any phone callers. The few times he'd filled in for daytime jocks, he'd been astonished and delighted by the amount of action on the request line, which had lit up virtually nonstop. Overnights were another story. He was lucky to get three requests an hour, most for Lynyrd Skynyrd or Led Zeppelin, which were guaranteed to come up on the music scheduling system anyway, and an occasional obscene phone call.

It was a brainless job, Rusty admitted to himself, and, worse, a boring one. He sighed as he reached for the Jethro Tull *Aqualung* CD. It might have been great music at one time, but Rusty had stopped counting after playing "Locomotive Breath" 143 times since he'd started at the station two years ago. Didn't these jerks ever get tired of hearing their favorite songs? God knew he did.

No doubt about it. I'm stuck in a rut. He'd gotten into radio because he was a rock music fan who'd never learned to play an instrument. To stay close to the music, he'd gone to a broadcast school in Cleveland and had landed the overnight gig with the help of the school's placement program. He'd started his radio career with tremendous excitement, but it was obvious now that he was not going to advance any further at this station. It was time to move on, check the *Radio & Records* job classifieds, pack his few things, try a new market and hopefully a new shift.

The request line lit up. Rusty shook his head, assuming it was another teenage, acne-scarred all-night gas station attendant waiting to hear Aerosmith's "Sweet Emotion" for the millionth time. *Fuck it. I just won't answer the phones tonight.*

When he'd started his radio career, he'd hoped to meet the girl of his dreams on the request line. Naturally shy, he'd never dated much, so he'd counted on the request line to provide him with an endless stream of available women to meet, date, and screw if he was lucky. Perhaps he'd even locate his life's mate. He'd heard numerous stories about radio groupies who would call jocks on the air, arrange meetings, and then fuck their brains out.

It hadn't worked out that way. His first radio groupie had been a girl named Greta who gave the term "bag lady" new meaning when he met her after his shift at her apartment and wished she'd been wearing a bag as he screwed her anyway. He'd gotten crabs three days later, which, he felt in retrospect, served him right.

The second groupie was a married woman who had actually been quite attractive. But she'd kept a diary, unbeknownst to Rusty, which was found by her husband, a career navy vet who'd confronted Rusty after a shift. He'd expected the guy to pop him, but it turned out she'd done this sort of thing before. Rusty was the last straw, the navy guy said. Sure enough, a month later she'd called him to say she was getting a divorce, and would he like to see her again. But the whole experience had weirded him out so much that he'd given up on finding sex—or anything more permanent—by phone. Normal women just didn't call radio station deejays in the middle of the night.

He jerked awake when the studio speakers went dead as "Aqualung" ended. He'd purposely blared the music at nearly top volume in case he fell asleep during the songs, which he sometimes did, the dead air acting as his alarm clock. One time he'd slept through half a Hendrix CD at earsplitting volume and had not received a single phone call, let alone a complaint.

He pressed a button and the Rolling Stones began a song he used to love but had long since grown tired of. The phone light was still pulsing.

"Gimme a break," he muttered to the phone, but "You Can't Always Get What You Want" was 7:28 and he was bored out of his medulla. He picked up the phone.

"'MCR."

"Hi." Female. Breathy. Deep. Cultured. Probably weighed three hundred pounds on a good day.

"Can I help you?"

"Is this Rusty?"

"No, this is the engineer. He's busy right now. You want to request something?"

"Oh." Disappointment. Rusty felt a tinge of guilt but stuck to his guns. "Well . . ." she breathed, "how about asking him to play Kate Bush's 'Wuthering Heights'?"

He laughed. "You got a chance!" The last time he'd played that song, as much as he personally loved it, was in college, where even the word "playlist" was illegal.

"Rusty?"

Oh, shit—he'd blown it. Oh, well. "Yeah."

"You lied to me. You said you were the engineer." She paused. He said nothing. "I hate liars," she finally continued. "My boyfriend's a liar."

Oh, God, here we go. I'm gonna get her whole life story. On the other hand, she is *a Kate Bush fan.*

"Look, we don't play Kate Bush."

"Oh." She sounded genuinely depressed.

The Stones song had 5:30 to go. What the hell. "If you like Kate Bush, you must like Peter Gabriel."

"I love him!" Her voice brightened, and Rusty decided he definitely liked it. "Do you have 'Shock the Monkey'?"

"No, but I have 'Sledgehammer.'" He winced as he said it; that was his least favorite Gabriel song but the only one in the station's music system.

"Oh, could you play it? It'd mean the world to me . . . to know someone cares."

He glanced at his computer screen, typed in the title. The song wasn't due to come up for three days, during the midday shift. Fuck it.

"Sure, I'll play it next."

"You will?" You'd think he'd offered to buy her a diamond ring.

"No sweat. And . . . you take care, okay? Things'll work out." The doctor is in, a nickel a session, he thought.

"I doubt it," she said, then gasped. "I—have to go now. He's coming back to the room."

She hung up before he could ask her name, but he played the song anyway, skipping the next song on his computer list to accommodate the playing time for "Sledgehammer." He half expected his program director to call to ask why the hell he was playing the song, but the red phone light stayed dark. "Sledgehammer" sounded better than usual that night.

Rusty picked up the request line the rest of the night, but she didn't call back. A week later, she called again.

"Hi."

"Hey!" So what if she weighed three hundred pounds. Talking to *anyone* made the nights go faster. "Where've you been?"

"Working out."

That got his attention. "Really? Where can you work out in the middle of the night in Cleveland?"

"Oh, my boyfriend has one of those home gyms. I use it sometimes when he's out. He'd kill me if he knew I used his equipment, but I want to keep in shape—for him."

"That's nice of you," he gulped. The three-hundred-pound image had melted and was now replaced by the face and body of his favorite Victoria's Secret catalogue model.

"So where's the bodybuilder right now?"

She paused and he heard her sigh. "He said he was going to play cards with his pals, but I don't trust him. Last time he said that, he came back smelling like perfume."

"Mmm." He hated the guy already. How could he leave such a gorgeous girl all by herself at night? If she were *his* girlfriend, he'd never leave her side. "So . . ." *Here we go again. I shouldn't do this. It's none of my business.* "What do you look like in a leotard?"

She giggled, a very pleasant sound that brought a smile to Rusty's face. "Why do you want to know?"

"Oh, just wondering what kind of girl calls a lonely deejay in the middle of the night."

"You're lonely, too?"

"Hey, I'm ready to kiss the janitor, and he's not my type." She laughed, and he felt himself starting to really care about this girl.

"Can you play me a song?"

"Name it."

"Pretenders? 'Brass in Pocket'?"

"Great choice!" And probably not set to come up for a month. The Pretenders were passé. "I'll play it next."

"Thanks, Rusty. You're . . . really a nice person."

He could feel his heart beating a little faster.

"Why are all the nice people so lonely?" she asked, then hung up before he could respond.

He slammed his fist against the countertop. He'd forgotten to get her name.

"It's Kendall. Kendall Lake."

He'd asked her name as soon as she'd called again, a week later. "Nice name."

"Is your real name Rusty Nails?"

He laughed. "Hell, no, it's Rusty Leisenberger, but no one would hire me with a name like that. So the PD gave me this one. It sucks, doesn't it?"

"It's kind of cute." She paused. "Are you?"

"Am I what?"

"Cute, silly!"

"Oh." He looked at his reflection in the glass window between the studio and the outer office. He was losing his hair and was twenty pounds overweight from not exercising, but he wasn't exactly Quasimodo either.

"Well, my mom says I'm the handsomest guy in Cleveland, outside of my dad. How about you?"

She paused. "I hear Tom coming. I'll call you again."

"Kendall—" But she was already gone.

Shit, I'm hooked on a woman who might look like Mr. T on a bad day. Nevertheless, he answered every request line call till she called again, over a week later.

"R-Rusty?" She sounded like she was crying.

"What's wrong?"

"N-nothing."

"Hey, c'mon, it's me, remember? Your friend? What happened?"

She sniffled. "Tom found out I'd been using his equipment."

"Yeah? And?"

"He . . . hit me with one of the barbells."

"Jesus Christ! Are you okay?"

"I will be."

"Why do you put up with that kind of shit? I'd clobber the guy."

She paused, then started whimpering softly. "I have nowhere else to go. My parents are both dead, and I have no brothers or sisters. I'm trying to make enough money to move out on my own. And anyway, sometimes he's nice to me."

"Yeah, when he's not beating you." Rusty was beet-red angry. At Tom, for beating her. At Kendall, for putting up with the asshole. Most of all, at himself, for realizing how much he cared about her. He'd promised himself: never again. He still didn't even know what she looked like, fer crissakes.

"Listen, if he pulls that shit again, you call the cops, okay?"

"I have to have a place to live."

She's trying to trap me into asking her to move in with me. I don't even know this girl. His defenses were going up. She'll just end up hurting you, he thought. You don't need the headaches.

"Yeah, well, you take care, okay?" Silence. "Can I play something for you, make you feel better? How about some Kate Bush?"

"Not tonight. I just wanted to . . . know you were there."

She hung up. "Damn!" he shouted at the empty studio.

She called again in a week. He was playing "Voodoo Chile" at full volume and missed her first few words. By the time he turned down the monitors, he realized she was crying again.

"Kendall, calm down. What's wrong? Did he hit you again?"

"Rusty, I'm scared."

"Why are you whispering?"

"Tom came home drunk and smelling like . . . another woman. I accused him of sleeping with someone else, and he told me he had and it was none of my damn business anyway. Then he starting throwing some of the weights at me. I locked myself in the bathroom with a cordless phone. Rusty, I'm scared."

"Kendall, call the police."

"No, he'll kill me if the police come."

"Then I'm calling the police. Where are you, Kendall? Where do you live?"

"No, Rusty, don't." There was a loud crash in the background.

He jumped as she screamed into the phone mouthpiece, and then the phone went dead.

Shit! He stalked the studio like a beast in heat. There was no way to help her—he just had to hope she'd be okay.

Please, God, let her be okay.

The next several weeks were maddening. He attacked each request phone light like a starving man, only to be disappointed by another simpleton begging for his favorite song. Where was she?

He realized he'd fallen in love with a voice on the phone, despite all his defenses. It no longer mattered to him what Kendall looked like.

He found himself in a tremendous depression, fearing for her life, imagining the worst things her boyfriend could have done to her.

By the fourth week Rusty had taken up smoking again, and he was on his second pack of the shift, the studio now a foggy eye-tearing soup, when she called.

"Kendall? Is that you? We have a bad connection. Thank God you called. Where the—" He literally had to bite his tongue not to curse at her for not calling. He stamped out the cigarette in the crowded ashtray. "Are you okay?"

"He . . . hurt me, Rusty. He hurt me real bad. I couldn't get to a phone, and I . . . couldn't talk for a while."

Rusty envisioned his phone-call lover with a heavily stitched lip, maybe a broken arm.

"You would have been proud of me, though," she continued. "I . . . defended myself."

"What'd you do, hit the dumbbell with a dumbbell?" She laughed. "Hey, that's better. Where are you?"

"I'm . . . with him. He's next door."

"For God's sake, Kendall, get out of there. You can . . . stay with me till you have the money for a place of your own." *Did I just say that?* Maybe later he'd regret it, but at that moment, it seemed the right thing to do.

"Rusty, I can't—"

"No arguments, Kendall. I've thought about this a lot, and I really want to be with you."

"But you don't know how I look."

"I don't give a shit. I—I care about you. And I want to offer you a new chance for a good life, away from that asshole Tom and with someone who will appreciate you for who you are."

She laughed softly. "For who I am," she echoed, and was silent. "I can't," she said finally. "I just called to say thanks, and good-bye."

"Kendall, no! Please let me at least speak to you. Tell me where you are. Let's meet and talk. If it doesn't feel right, you can walk away, and I won't argue. Kendall, give me a chance. Please. It means the world to me."

She was crying softly. "I've got to go. I hear him banging on the wall. He knows I'm talking to you."

"Jesus, Kendall, just let me see you for a minute, will ya?"

She paused. Was he getting through to her at last?

"I . . . okay."

She blurted out an address he'd never heard of. He feverishly wrote it down. "I'll come by right after my show. Wait outside so he doesn't see us. And Kendall." He wanted to say it aloud. "I love you."

"I love you, too."

She hung up.

The rest of his show was a blur. During a long song he ran outside to his truck and brought a map back up to the studio. The address she'd given him was in a small town about twenty miles east of Cleveland in an area he'd never visited. He figured he'd get to her place just before the sun came up.

He wasn't overly concerned about her insistence that he

let her make her own choice once she saw him. He studied his reflection in the glass. He didn't look *that* bad. In the past few weeks, he'd actually gone on a diet, dropped the gut, and started combing his hair in a different and more up-to-date way. Maybe she wouldn't run away screaming.

And once he'd met her, he was fairly certain he could win her over. Not just by his appearance, but by his resolve to give her a better life, a life with someone who truly cared.

In return, he would finally win the woman of his dreams.

He rechecked the address. With daylight still half an hour away, it was hard to tell for sure that he'd found the place. It was a Victorian house at the end of a cul-de-sac in the middle of nowhere. There were no streetlights, so he brought out the portable flashlight he kept in the glove compartment of his Toyota pickup.

He stepped out of the truck and shone the flashlight at the old house, which was unlit. She must have fallen asleep. He stepped lightly onto the porch that fronted the house and was about to tap at the door, hoping to wake her but not Tom, when he noticed he was at the wrong address—the number was off by one digit.

Confused, he turned around and aimed the flashlight at the surrounding property. No other houses were in view, but there was a dirt road he'd missed before that led into a fogbound field.

He imagined she would be waiting for him there, where Tom wouldn't find them together. He walked into the fog, his flashlight doing little to illuminate the area around him.

"Rusty." It was her whisper. Breathy. Deep. He felt his heart literally skip a beat; he'd always assumed that was just a writer's cliché.

"Where are you?" he answered in a stage whisper.

"Turn off your light."

Her voice was coming from somewhere just beyond his vision. "Don't be paranoid. I can't even see you—there's no way Tom could see us."

"Rusty, please. Turn off the light."

He did, surprised that he could see about as well without the light. And then he saw her shape, not more than six feet away, obscured by the dark and the fog. She wore a shawl.

"Kendall! Thank God you're here. Did you know you gave me the wrong address?"

She laughed softly. "No, I didn't. You just missed the sign." She kept her distance from him. "Remember your promise. You've seen me. Now . . . I have to leave." The last words were choked out; she was obviously trying not to cry.

"No, Kendall, just listen to me. I know you hardly know me and I know I'm no Mel Gibson, but—"

"It's not that, Rusty. You're a very sweet man and I meant what I said on the phone this morning. But it won't work between us. It can't. Not now. Not since . . ." Her words trailed off into the fog.

He was straining to see the features of her face, but they were too obscured. He blinked to see her better, but it was as if she was being viewed through gauze.

"Kendall, what . . ." He felt his heart racing now, his stomach flipping as he detected tiny forms falling from her shawl, twisting on their way to the moist ground.

"I have to go. Remember me, Rusty." She turned and ran into the fog.

Cursing, he followed her. His feet crushed the small, white, wriggling forms that had fallen from her garments.

He'd lost her to the fog. "Kendall!" he shouted, and thought, Fuck Tom if he hears me! In desperation, he switched on the flashlight and followed the sick trail of twisting white worms to two fresh mounds of earth.

No.

At the head of each mound was a new grave marker. One said Kendall Lake, the other Tom Reeves. The death dates were identical—two weeks prior to Kendall's last call to Rusty.

Rusty was fired for breaking format that night, after playing "Wuthering Heights" for four hours straight, hoping the phone would ring one more time. It did not.

INSPIRATION

Don D'Ammassa

Lisa Stone left the stage while the final notes of her closing song were still echoing, allowing the security people to hustle her through the wings and along a planned route to the side entrance where a car waited. She'd agreed to the tighter arrangements reluctantly, unwilling to accept that she was the potential target of a deranged killer, but unable to dismiss Ted Troia's theory that she had been quietly stalked by a psychopath throughout her career. To date, only the people around her had suffered, but there was no way to guess what might happen in the future.

In any case, it was virtually impossible to shield her if she persisted with the concert tour. Rock stars, like politicians, actors, and other celebrities, sacrificed security along with privacy when they attracted the public's attention. After writing scores of interviews and articles, Ted felt very little sympathy for the rich and famous. But Lisa Stone was different.

Inspiration

Ted left the theater on his own, took a taxi back to the hotel where Lisa was staying. He smoked a cigarette outside before entering and taking the elevator to her floor. The security men nodded when he stepped out of the elevator and let him pass without comment, recognizing him, smirking among themselves. Ted pretended not to notice.

"Oh, there you are, Ted. C'mon in. I thought you'd gotten lost."

"Heavy traffic." He closed the door behind him, tried to hide his disappointment when he realized they weren't alone. Dean Campbell, her business manager, was sitting at the far end of the suite.

"Dean's not too happy with me. Seems I'm being fiscally irresponsible again."

"You *do* pay me to look out for your financial interests, you know. It's not really fair to complain when I'm just trying to earn my salary."

"Who's complaining?" Lisa switched to her innocent waif look, and Ted marveled at how well she could manage it. Thirty-five years old, but she still looked twenty, at least until you got up close. And very few ever had that opportunity. "I value your opinion, Dean, but that doesn't mean I can't make my own decisions, or that we'll always agree."

Ted shook his head, uncomfortable, and crossed to the wet bar, started to mix himself a drink.

"Maybe you can make her see reason, Ted." Dean had tried more than once to recruit Ted as an ally, a role he had so far resisted. "She wants to do the Chicago concert for free."

"Not for free," Lisa protested. "I just want the money to go to charity. It's not as though I need it."

Campbell shook his head. "Your cash-flow projections for the next several months don't look good. Even with the concerts, you're in an earnings trough that won't see an upturn until your next album is ready, and you just told me that won't be for at least six months."

"I need to write the songs," she said mildly.

"All the more reason to bank the money while you can."

Campbell wet his lips with his tongue, looked toward Ted for support. "Lisa, your net worth has been steadily declining, and the last royalty statement was well below our projections. Do you have any idea how much money you've given away?"

"Dean, I'm tired of arguing about this." There was a sudden hint of steel in her voice, and Ted recognized the erosion of Lisa's patience. "I have plenty of money to live on comfortably, even if I retired right now, which I don't plan to do. You've known me since before I cut my first record and that's long enough for you to be able to understand my reasons. So let's drop the subject."

For a second it looked as though Campbell might persist, but instead he nodded, then quickly stood up. "All right, boss. Whatever you say. I'm too pooped to argue about it. In fact, I'm calling it a night. Catch you tomorrow."

Ted waited until Campbell was gone before speaking. "You were a little hard on him. He's very devoted to watching out for your best interests. And he does have a point."

Lisa threw herself down onto the couch, arched her head back. "God, Ted, not you, too? You of all people should understand why I give the money away, why I have to."

"I know that you feel guilty about your success, and that you've been trying to buy absolution for imaginary sins for most of your career. That doesn't mean I agree."

She sighed. "Mix me a drink, will you?"

He already had. He crossed and handed it down, then eased onto the couch beside her. Lisa sipped slowly, her eyes closed, waiting for the neat brandy to burn its way to her stomach.

She wasn't a particularly beautiful woman, and there was nothing special or unique about her voice. Indeed, her first album had done well only because of the hit single, "Old Magic," and the second foundered so badly that her career might well have ended before it was truly launched.

If her kid sister hadn't been killed, Lisa would probably have ended up as a waitress or a hairdresser.

Inspiration

It sounded callous phrased that way, but it was still the truth. Lisa and Kari had been very close; their parents had died in an airline disaster and Lisa had been largely responsible for raising her sister. They were almost inseparable, even while Lisa was on tour.

The mutilation murder had been particularly gruesome; the teenager had been literally torn apart, their hotel suite drenched with blood. Her assailant had carried off the corpse, or most of it anyway, not even leaving enough behind to allow a positive identification of the remains.

Profoundly shocked, Lisa had shut herself off from the world for months, emerging finally with the score for "Kari's Song," still one of the most frequently played singles in rock history. Two months after its release, Lisa had signed a contract for another album, but with the stipulation that her entire share of the proceeds be donated to a variety of charities.

"It was my last gift to Kari," she'd explained to Ted during one of their early sessions. "To make up for all the things I might have done for her if she'd lived." But Ted had sensed the truth even then, that Lisa felt guilty, probably because she'd spent that terrible evening anonymously visiting one nightspot after another, instead of returning directly to their hotel suite.

"If you'd gone home, you would have been just another victim," he'd suggested later, after they'd grown more intimate. "You shouldn't feel any responsibility."

"You don't understand. It's not a rational thing, but that doesn't make it any less real."

If they'd ever caught Kari's killer, Lisa might have been able to set aside the pain, but the police had never even had a solid lead.

"Hey, Ted! Where are you?"

He came to himself, realized he'd been drifting among his thoughts, felt the warmth of her hand on his arm. "I'm right here," he said, and proved it by leaning forward into her embrace.

* * *

But later, lying beside her in the oversize bed, Ted couldn't sleep. Three weeks earlier he'd pointed out the suspicious pattern of tragedy in Lisa's life, the possible existence of a sinister enemy, relentless, ruthless, and clever enough to have escaped detection, at least until now.

Lisa had dismissed it as coincidence and bad luck, but with a hint of panic in her eyes that Ted interpreted as evidence she'd already entertained similar suspicions of her own.

"Kari's Song" had quickly become one of the most popular rock singles of all time, but its companions on the album of the same name had ranged from so-so to forgettable. A follow-up album barely made gold, and the recording company delayed and eventually canceled the next. Lisa was reduced to doing backup vocals for bigger names, like Brian Sparrow.

Financially, she was self-sufficient, having banked the proceeds from a brief but popular concert tour, but her career as a major voice in rock appeared to be over. She became romantically involved with Sparrow, and after a brief, hectic courtship, the couple married in a secret ceremony. Their daughter, Kelly Marie Sparrow, was born ten months later, and Lisa announced her retirement from the music business. Prematurely, as it turned out.

Three days after their third anniversary, Brian Sparrow was run down by a hit-and-run driver in Seattle while returning from a fast-food restaurant with a bag of burgers and fries. The driver was never identified, although the vehicle, stolen earlier that day, was found parked in an alley not far from the accident scene.

Lisa had retreated from the world, renting a château in Switzerland to keep the public at a distance, quietly converting all of her late husband's holdings to cash and donating the proceeds to a long list of foundations, funds, and worthy causes. Shortly after the last of the money was gone, she returned to public view by debuting a new song at a benefit concert. "Death Is a Dream" wasn't quite as successful as "Kari's Song," but the story of a young girl and her ghostly lover was the hit of the show, and resulted in a new record contract.

Restless, Ted slipped out of bed, careful not to disturb Lisa. They'd started sleeping together only a few weeks earlier, much to the surprise of both of them. The earliest interviews had not gone well; Ted had been unable to maintain his usual objectivity. He'd been one of Lisa's biggest fans ever since that first hit single, "Old Magic," worshiping her image of purity and vulnerability from afar. Reality hadn't always lived up to his image of Lisa Stone, and the disparities had sometimes been unsettling and a source of tension.

Lisa's popularity was well along one of its periodic slides downward, a situation that made it difficult to find a publisher willing to consider the biography in progress. But it was a project Ted considered important, and the proceeds from his last best-seller provided the opportunity to indulge a longstanding ambition.

And now they were lovers, and Ted was wondering what might happen when the book was done, when he no longer had an excuse to follow her around the country. He didn't like thinking about it.

The barriers had started to go down while Lisa was discussing her personal tragedies. Apparently she'd never really talked to anyone about the deaths before. When Ted felt sure enough of himself to confide in her his suspicion that she was the focus of a subtle conspiracy of violence, Lisa resisted at first, but once past the initial shock, she'd admitted that he might be right, that she'd wondered occasionally if such a horrible thing might be true, always dismissing her fears as paranoia.

Chicago was not a roaring success, in Ted's opinion, probably because of a mediocre selection of songs. He would never admit it aloud, but too much of Lisa's music sounded alike to him, rock Muzak, monotonous lyrics, simple riffs and melody lines strung together almost randomly. When Lisa was inspired, she was one of the best, a larger-than-life figure who'd captured his imagination when they were both much younger, a grip that had loosened but not fallen away during the years that followed. Her lesser work vaguely embarrassed him.

Something disturbing happened in the hotel that first night.

Lisa was depressed by the way things had gone during the Friday show and was worried that Saturday would be even worse. Ted knew the signs well enough to distance himself, and retreated to his own room that evening.

By two in the morning, he realized he wouldn't be able to sleep. Rather than waste time turning restlessly in bed, he got up, booted the laptop, and began editing the draft of Lisa's autobiography-in-process. It was the chapter dealing with her daughter's kidnapping while they were in Dallas.

This was the most difficult part of the book, for both of them. Like everyone else in the country, Ted had followed the twelve-week ordeal in the papers and on television. Lisa had offered to pay any amount of money, of course, but the kidnapper never responded, just kept mailing the twelve-year-old's severed fingers, one every few days, each small package mailed from right inside the city, once from the branch office adjacent to the hotel where Lisa was staying.

Then, on the last day, the head. They never caught the kidnapper, never even found the rest of Kelly Marie's body.

Images of mangled flesh kept intruding on his thoughts.

Ted pushed his chair back and stood up, unable to separate his emotions from the words he was reading. Much of the story had been reconstructed from contemporary accounts, necessarily since Lisa still had difficulty speaking about that period of her life, and he was just filling in gaps now.

He dressed quickly, small angry movements, and left the room. The elevator arrived quickly, brought him to the lobby, where a sleepy counter clerk nodded as he passed.

Ted walked the nearly deserted streets for just over an hour, then returned to the hotel, hoping that sleep would not continue to elude him. But a few seconds after unlocking his door, he returned to the lobby, barely controlling his fury as he disturbed the desk clerk's nap.

"Someone's been in my room," he said quietly. "I think you'd better call the police."

Hotel security replaced the smashed light fixtures quickly, but the officer in charge refused to allow Ted to examine what remained of his belongings until an evidence team had gone over everything thoroughly. Not that there was anything worth salvaging.

His clothing and few personal possessions had been savaged almost beyond belief. Not one item, not even a sock, had survived intact. Each article of clothing had been torn into strips, along with towels, sheets, and blankets, even the shower curtain. His luggage had been crushed flat, the electric razor shattered and dropped into the toilet. Worst of all, his laptop was a total loss. Fortunately, he'd backed up his work earlier that day, and the diskette was in Lisa's room. At worst, he'd lost a couple hours of work, easily reconstructed.

Significantly, two hundred dollars in cash that he'd left on the dresser had been ripped in half and dropped on the floor rather than stolen.

The hotel's security officer insisted that the door lock was functioning properly, and since Ted had left the door to the balcony open, it was assumed that the interloper had managed to jump from one balcony to another, or climbed up or down from one of the adjacent floors.

"I don't understand it," admitted the investigating officer from the city police. "It would take someone with a hell of a lot of nerve to swing from one of those things to another, particularly as windy as it is up here. And a thief who was smart enough to get hold of a duplicate key would have taken the cash, probably the computer as well. This destruction . . . it's just crazy."

They gave him another room for the balance of the night, but he lay fully dressed on the bed, waiting for daylight.

* * *

Lisa knocked on his new door at nine the following morning. He let her in, surprised that she had broken precedent by coming to him, noticing that one of her bodyguards had posted himself outside.

"Ted, I just heard what happened. What's going on?"

He shrugged, too tired to think clearly. "Just one of those things. Don't worry about it; everything's replaceable."

She stepped close, wrapped her arms around his back, pressed her cheek against his chest. "Things like that scare me. Too many of the people close to me have had awful things happen to them. I don't want you to be the next to die."

"Does that mean I've finally convinced you that this isn't just my imagination?"

"I don't know what to think anymore. Even the chance that you're right frightens me."

"I'm hardly important enough to be a target, in any case."

"You're important enough to *me*. I've needed someone I could talk to about things for a long time. But if I've put you in danger . . ." She didn't finish the sentence.

"I'm a big boy, Lisa. I walked into this with my eyes open. If we take some precautions—"

"I just find it so hard to accept." She stepped back, her hands clutched so tightly together it must have been painful. "I've never had very many people close to me, and none of them seem dangerous. Dean's tedious at times, but I can't believe he'd ever hurt anyone. It bothers me even to think that way about people, particularly the ones I love. And now I suspect everyone, even Randy."

"He's been your drummer for a long time, hasn't he?"

"Forever. We met when he was a studio musician and I was cutting demos. Dated a couple of times, nothing serious. Brian never liked him much, but he stuck by me through the bad times." Suddenly there were tears in her eyes. "Ted, please don't think I'm a terrible person, but I'm really getting frightened. These horrible things happen to people around me, and all I can think of is, what if that were me? What if I'm next? Who's going to write *my* song?"

He stepped forward and put his arm around her shoulders. "As long as you're with me, nothing bad is going to happen."

"You don't think last night was bad?"

"Well, if you can write a hit inspired by the trashing of my hotel room, it will have been worth it." He regretted the words as soon as he said them, but he was tired and his internal censor wasn't on the job. "Kari's Song" and "Death Is a Dream" had both been megahits, but "Part of Me Is Part of You," released a year after Kelly Marie's death, had surpassed both within weeks of its release. If Lisa had been willing to keep even one-tenth of the money it had earned, she would have been a very rich woman. But as before, she gave away the lion's share of the proceeds.

Ted felt her body stiffen and spoke quickly, hoping to divert her attention. "Hey, as long as we're both up at this ungodly hour, why don't we do actual breakfast in a real restaurant? No room service."

Some, but not all, of the tension dissipated. "I thought you didn't want me out in public places?"

"Hey, at this time of the morning, no one'll believe it's really you. Particularly if we find some greasy spoon no self-respecting rock star would ever be caught dead in."

"All right." She unwrapped herself from around him, sounding considerably more cheerful. "You're on. But what about the Terminator?" She cocked her head toward the door, beyond which the bodyguard was no doubt prowling restlessly back and forth.

"Send him on an errand," Ted answered recklessly. "What the hell, you only live once."

Saturday night's audience was somewhat more enthusiastic, and the entourage moved on to Detroit in higher spirits. Then Milwaukee, Toledo, St. Louis, and Atlanta. Lisa remained tense and her performances were erratic, the reviewers were less than kind, and the audience reaction was generally polite but often restrained.

"Maybe you were right; maybe I should cut this tour short," Lisa remarked more than once.

Ted knew it wasn't just the security problems that were bothering her. Lisa was not like most rock singers he'd met. The money was almost incidental. But she was deeply devoted to her music; it was important to her that what she created meant something to people, that it touched them on some level, and she seemed to draw strength from the response of her audiences. In rare bitter moments, she complained that her reputation rested on three very sad songs, not the more exuberant singles like "Fire Up Your Love," "City Girl," "Hot Spots," or "Traffic Jam," and Ted nodded sympathetically, without admitting that Lisa's favorites of her own work struck him as so much fluff.

"Why don't people like happy songs?" she'd complained more than once.

"Maybe because most people aren't really happy. You've shown them how to take the tragedies of their lives and turn them into something beautiful, and they respond to that transformation."

"But music is supposed to be uplifting, not depressing. A way to escape from all the bad stuff."

"You can't really escape unless you're willing to face the unpleasantness first." He'd been mildly drunk at the time and felt he was being profound. Later, sober, he wasn't so sure. But Lisa had seemed satisfied with the explanation, or at least she hadn't pursued the subject any further.

There was a three-week layover in the tour and, for security reasons, they were spending a few days incognito at a quiet inn in Managansett, Rhode Island. The band members and technicians were elsewhere, visiting family, getting laid, or just taking a therapeutic break. Originally they'd all been booked into a small resort in New Hampshire, but Lisa had canceled the arrangements after having a mysterious spell of weepiness that had erupted into a major fight with the drummer, Randy Whitehall.

Inspiration

"I think he hates me, Ted," she'd confided in bed that night. "You should have seen the look in his eyes."

Ted hadn't been able to think of a constructive answer, and the next morning he helped her switch the reservations. Except for the two newly hired bodyguards, none of the members of their entourage knew where Ted and Lisa were spending the layover. Dean Campbell had sulked and gone off without announcing his destination.

Ted had been making good progress on the final draft. With any luck, he'd be finished by the end of the year, well ahead of schedule.

"Ted, I'm going away for a day or two."

"What? Where?"

The two of them were eating in the inn's dining room, the bodyguards sitting at a table just out of earshot. She reached over and pressed her fingers against the back of his hand, mutely reassuring.

"Don't worry, I'm not going far. I just need to get away from all this." She gestured vaguely. "From everyone who knows me. Even you." Her hand touched his arm gently. "No big deal. One night and I'll be back."

"If I've been pushing things too fast—"

She shook her head, cutting him off. "No, nothing like that." Her face softened. "Don't worry, Ted. I mean, I still feel the same way about you I always have, maybe even more so. It's just that I . . . I need to get away, just for a day or two, and get some perspective."

"We haven't made any commitments to each other," he answered slowly. "You're certainly free to do what you want." It sounded stiff, but he couldn't help being resentful.

"Ted, stop it. I don't like it when you play the hurt lamb. If you don't realize how I feel about you by now, then you're a lot denser than I think you are." She turned away, and her eyes were bright with unshed tears. "It's hard for me to talk about this, Ted, hard for me to feel . . . affection for people, or to admit it anyway. Whenever I've had something like that in my life, someone always takes it away."

"I'm sorry, Lisa. I'm just being foolish. You're taking Arnold and Rambo with you, aren't you?" The bodyguards' real names were Nathan Moore and Lester Wade, but Ted and Lisa had rechristened them. Lisa had fired the Terminator in a fit of hysteria one evening, apparently after he'd made some oblique comment about her vulnerability to attack that she'd interpreted as a threat.

"I suppose I ought to, but it wouldn't be the same."

"No supposing about it. They can't protect you from a distance."

"I'll think about it, Ted. But I think I'll be safer if no one knows where I am." There was a tone in her voice that he knew all too well. Don't push me on this, it said.

"I suppose it'll give me a chance to get some work done." He tried to keep the tone light despite his misgivings. "No distractions."

She was already gone when he got up the following morning, and neither Rambo nor Arnold had seen her leave.

Ted spent most of the day working, and when he turned off his new computer that evening, he tossed the last of his handwritten notes into a drawer. It was after nine, he hadn't eaten yet, and the dining room was too formal for his mood. Instead, he walked to the nearby downtown area, found a small, not particularly clean diner, and had one of the best bowls of chili he'd ever tasted. A half block away stood a dimly lit bar, where he drank more than usual in celebration of his misery, but what the hell, he wasn't driving and he didn't have to get up early in the morning.

It was after midnight when he finally returned to the inn. The front desk was unoccupied, the dining room closed, and only the night lights were on. Ted climbed the stairs on unsteady legs and after three tries was finally able to work the lock. With a self-deprecating laugh, he stepped inside.

He turned on the lights as the door clicked shut and then something slammed into the side of his head and he fell into darkness.

* * *

Inspiration

Nausea hit him even before the pain. The taste of bile was strong and bitter, and his head throbbed angrily. And that wasn't the only place that hurt. There were lines of fire around his ankles and wrists, where they'd been tied to the arms and legs of a chair.

The gag in his mouth didn't help much either.

He was in his own motel room. The new laptop was right where he'd left it on the small desk, and his replacement luggage was visible in the rear of the open closet. There was no one in sight, nothing out of place.

Until someone stepped out of the bathroom.

"How are you feeling? I was afraid I might have hit you too hard. If you had a concussion or something and never came to, everything might have been spoiled."

Ted didn't answer, couldn't have answered even had he not been gagged. The shock of realization was too great. He'd been right. He was face to face with the mysterious person who'd dogged Lisa's career almost from its outset, preying on those she loved, and the discovery might well be his last accomplishment. Even wrapped in a dark raincoat, a scarf concealing the face, his attacker could not disguise her gender.

It was not just any woman. It was Lisa Stone.

"I know this must be very confusing, but it's important that you understand why this is happening. Otherwise it'll all be for nothing. Remember the lines of 'Old Magic,' my first hit? The bit about 'sacrificing everything for love'? Well, that's the secret I learned, that's where I get my inspiration."

She paused, as though waiting for a reaction he couldn't possibly have given. "You remember when I told you about how I'd never had a pet when I was a kid? Well, that was a lie." Lisa moved to the desk, began pulling open the drawers and emptying them, books, newspapers, magazines, loose papers, spilling them all onto the floor.

"Just before they died, my parents bought us a kitten, and when they were gone it was the only thing Kari and I had left besides each other that we really loved. But I needed to write songs, good songs, ones that would move people, and I realized that the only way to draw out my talents, use them to create something beautiful and enduring, was to feel those emotions directly. You can't pretend to be sad or happy or anything and expect to translate false feeling into real art. And the purest emotion of all is grief, loss, separation from those you love, and I knew that I could turn tragedy into beauty, but only by experiencing it. I had to sacrifice something I really loved in order to free my creative soul. The choice was Kari or the kitten, so it was really no choice at all."

She kicked the papers around the room, then crossed to the dresser, out of Ted's line of sight. When she was visible again, she was carrying something in one hand. Ted's lighter fluid. He knew he should struggle, try to attract attention from outside the room even if he couldn't actually pull loose from his bonds. But he was frozen, unable to summon the will to act, pierced to some deep, secret inner place by sudden knowledge.

"I thought having help with that one big hit would kind of kick-start my career, that it would open the door to the creativity I knew was there within me. But things didn't work out. I needed to find another inspiration, and there wasn't much to choose from. I've never been very good about making friends, and when it came down to it, Kari was the only thing left in the world that I really valued. It's a tribute to her as well. I tried to make her understand that, right at the end, but I don't suppose she ever really did."

Lisa began spraying the lighter fluid around the room, elongated arcs dark on the paper, less obvious on the blankets, curtains, wallpaper.

"Brian wasn't as hard, but Kelly was the worst of all. If I hadn't realized how much could be drawn from her pain, I might have held back, and the world would have been poorer for it. And back in Chicago, when things were going so badly, I realized that I loved you and that here was another chance to achieve marvelous things. But you weren't in your room when I came to visit you and at first I was so furious I couldn't think, but afterward I was glad you weren't there, because it wasn't time yet and I might have ruined everything by acting too soon."

The lighter fluid was almost gone now, the last few drops trickling out.

"I know it seems unfair to you, but actually I'm giving you all a kind of immortality. Your songs will still be played long after we're all dead and gone, maybe forever, you know? It's my final gift to each of the people I love, in return for what you've given me. I just wish you could hear the song I'll write in your memory."

She threw down the empty container, then raised her other arm. Ted's cigarette lighter, bright red against the palm of her hand. Suddenly, she was close to him, leaning forward to plant a single kiss in the center of his forehead.

Then she was moving away, across the room to the door beyond which the deserted hall held no promise of rescue.

"I really do love you, Ted. I just thought you'd like to know. It wouldn't work if that wasn't true."

A tiny flame dropped from her hand to the floor as she left to write the greatest song of her career, a song Ted Troia would never hear.

SHOCK ROCK JOCK

Rex Miller

He was very short. Outrageously attired in black and silver leather, the outfit accenting every pound. His red hair fell below his shoulders, giving his eyes a sort of hairy halo. The eyes gave no clue of his myopia; they were light blue-green and when the light caught them they flickered with intelligence.

"Yeah," he was telling someone over a telephone, "I'm wigged, man. Yeah—I'm outta my fuckin' mind with the deal. Very, very happy. What can I say? Who deserves it more, though—eh?" he brayed into the phone. "I gotta go, Elaine. Listen—one thing—can't you please do something about those pricks at Paralyzed?" He used his pet name for the top studio in town. "Who the happy fuck do these schmucks think they're dealing with, for shit's sake? I gotta get the thing put together by next Monday. . . ." He listened briefly to his agent's response.

"Okay. Sounds good . . . Later." He hung up the phone.

"Don't ever let me do another fucking deal with these nutcases." He looked at Rick Bauman, his writer/producer, who was seated a few feet away writing on a yellow legal pad. "If I say the word 'movie,' just pull out a fucking gun and do the deed. Shoot me right there, it'll save so much goddamn aggravation, you know? Buncha friggin' creeps in suits, man." He shook his head. "All these gay boys running around the lot in their French jeans and BK high-tops—looks like a pickup game at the Y—they're the heads of the freaking studio, for crissakes!"

"Break's over," the engineer warned, his finger up, then pointing.

"This woman goes into a store and asks for D cells. Not D *cups*—Rick, my producer, was starting to get a boner—D *cells,* you pervert. So anyway, she says, 'Gimme some D-cell batteries.' The clerk says, 'Oh, D-cell batteries? Come this way. . . .' And she goes, 'If I could come *this* way, I wouldn't need D cells!" The three people in the room broke up as the man with all the hair cued the engineer for the spot cluster. All across the U.S., major market stations were dropping in their own local commercials for everything from auto parts to strip clubs. The program being broadcast live was the top-rated radio program of all time, starring the king of all "shock jocks," Bobby O'Toole, who'd been a rock jock in the seventies but had eventually become so popular he no longer played music on the program. People only wanted to hear one thing on his show—chin music; the outrageous stuff that came from the mighty mouth of Bobby O'Toole. There were plenty of imitators, but there was nobody like him. You hated him or you loved him, but you knew you were listening to a unique, nonderivative mind at work.

"Here we go," the engineer warned, waiting for the outcue of the spot. O'Toole did his show with the same two people every day, and they'd both been with him for a zillion years. His engineer, Buddy "All Day" Long, was an incredible production man. He'd been a jock in some Midwest shithole when he and O'Toole had started working together and become friends. Rick Bauman essentially produced—and sometimes wrote—the show, but for O'Toole that was mostly just cutting stories out of the morning papers and lining up celebrity guests.

"Good morning. This is *The Bobby O'Toole Show*. It's 'whatever happened to . . .' time. Whatever happened to: Judy Geeson and Judy Carne? Martha Graham and Graham Kerr? Peter Max and Peter Drucker? Weird Al Yankadick and Al Sharpton? Clive Barnes and Clive Brooks? John Sununu and John Gotti? Well, hell, we *know* what happened to him—but what about John-Boy, John John, and Jon Bon Jovi? Remember Pee Wee Reese and Pee-wee Herman? Michael Eisner and Michael Medved? Sandra Dee and Dee Snyder? I'll just say some names—if anybody knows what happened to these people, call your local station or write me in care of the Kotch Radio Network in Los Angeles. Here we go: Tawana Brawley? Morgan Keyes?

"Oh—you don't remember her? All right, Morgan Keyes was one of those half-assed actresses who was a sex symbol for about *ten minutes*—literally—one of those bimbos who just come and go and you never hear their names again. There were several actresses named Morgan there for a while—like Morgan Fairchild, Morgan Brittany, Morgan Keyes—she was a total nothing. Remember, Rick? She was on that stinker *The Love Barge?* God, whatta piece of dreck." Listeners could hear off-microphone laughter. "Well, listen to this: According to the *Midnight Inquirer*—and I'm quoting now for all you butthole lawyers listening—'Two years ago I had an affair with Morgan Keyes. We were both doing a lot of drugs at the time, but she was totally into the Los Angeles junk scene.' Now, what guy do you think said that in the *Inquirer?* . . . Dig it: not a guy but a *woman*. The admitted lesbian Sonny Collins, the jazz singer! No. I swear to you. Morgan Keyes was a lez! I *knew* it back when she was on that stupid show. I told my wife—dollars to donuts she's a friggin' *lesbian*. Can I tell 'em or what? Now we learn this big sex symbol is a queer and this wonderful role model is a damn *junkie*. Is this unreal? Folks—it's too creepy.

"Let's see what's going on in the news. Harry Polsky, the big record producer for Blue Vista, formerly a top A&R guy with Geffen, has just been signed on to 'coordinate' the Shotgun Roadies' Clam-Scarfin' Tour. Polsky is, of course, the Dealer to the Stars, so by coordinator we can assume he'll be coordinating their crack buys. Maybe he can get some for Morgan Keyes, who I *always* clocked as a damn basehead. I mean, remember how she was always such a spaz on the show? She had to be a complete bust-out *stonie*, right? Now we know. It's in the paper so it's gotta be true.

"The drugs, that's one thing—but all these guys were sitting around fantasizing about making it with Morgan Keyes, and the bitch only likes other bitches." Off-mike laughter. "Bitches in britches . . . Anyway, what else in the show-biz crap? Okay, here's the famous dancer/singer/former cheerleader Paula Kelly, she's dating Van Arthur the heavy metal creep. See, look, all these stories are tied together: Van Arthur buys his drugs from Harry Polsky, probably, and we'll probably find out in the *Midnight Inquirer* tomorrow that Sonny Collins, Morgan Keyes, and Paula Kelly did three-ways! Man, if I hear that, I'm hanging it up. That's it for me. Not Paula Kelly—she's so nutty I'd eat the peanuts out of her Shalimar Bar. I better not find out *she's* a dyke junkie, too. Oh, man!

"Let's go to the phones—Buddy's signaling we got a live one. Who? . . . Morgan Keyes? Oh, I'm sure. Are you friggin' around with me on the air here?"

"No way—she's pissed, too." The engineer's voice was audible in the distance.

"You're on the air. Who's this on the line?"

"This is Morgan Keyes."

"You're live on *The Bobby O'Toole Show,* do I have your permission to put this call on the air?" He instantly recognized her voice, but was wary, as a few clever impersonators had fooled him in the past.

"Yes, and I want to tell you that your filthy mouth is disgusting. Where do you get off, saying such things about me on national radio? You don't know the first thing about me. You don't know me at all."

"Hey—I know all about you from the papers. Did you or did you not have a lesbian affair with—"

"Just shut that mouth. What I did in my personal life is no business of yours, and if some paper said that, well, they better be able to prove it in court, and so had your radio station."

"So you're threatening to sue me and the *Midnight Inquirer* and Sonny Collins, too?" He laughed.

"That's the most disgusting trash—"

"Not only a *lez* but you were a junkie, too, right? I mean, are you gonna deny you were in rehab for addiction only recently? Your picture's in the paper, lady. You look like death warmed over. Of course, you didn't look all that good to begin with, in my opinion."

"Why would you want to hurt me and hold me up to ridicule in this way? I never did anything to you. I don't even *know* you, and you're attacking me in public with these awful accusations."

"Hey, you're a big girl—defend yourself. Tell America, are you a dyke or not? Were you a junkie dyke? Simple yes or no."

"That's the most—"

"Are those your real breasts or were they implants? And when you had a lesbian affair, just answer this—were you the man or the woman? I mean, did you get on top or—"

The line went dead.

"The lesbian dope addict Morgan Keyes just hung up on me because she did not want to admit she may have had hooter jobs, and that she liked to play the daddy when she and Sonny Collins did their thing in the sack. I personally never thought much of Morgan as an actress—she was god-awful, in fact—but I would watch an episode of *The Love Barge* if she and Sonny would make the beast with two backs. Hey, speakin' of sixty-nine—this is *The Bobby O'Toole Show* from the flagship station of Kotch Radio Network, Kotch for your crotch over K-Pulse, ninety-eight point six!"

"What do these popular entertainers have in common: Uncle Miltie, Forrest Tucker, and Bobby O'Toole?"

At her small cottage in Canoga Park, Morgana Kester, nee Morgan Keyes, sat in the kitchen, not moving, trying to understand what had just taken place. Had she hallucinated this nightmare? She heard the heavily accented, abrasive voice ask over the radio: "They're kings of comedy? They have six-letter names? They have fourteen-inch schmeckles?" His producer and engineer laughing loudly filled the air. "Wrong! It's television, you dummies. Each man was or is a biiiiig hit on the tube. In the latest sweeps *The Bobby O'Toole Show* killed. So, if you only listen and don't watch, you're only getting half the buzz. Turn us on over Kotch TV every Friday night. The show that owns nine major markets from coast to coast now owns Philly, too! In the latest Arbitron, I'm solid number one in Philadelphia!"

Morgana Kester couldn't take any more. She turned off the radio and crumpled the letter she'd been writing to a partner in an entertainment law firm in Beverly Hills. She picked up the phone and dialed the lawyer's number instead.

An apology on the air and a written expression of remorse would no longer do. She would sue this evil person. Get him where it hurt—the wallet. The attorney was out of the office. She slammed the phone down in disgust, showered, finished dressing, and opened the front door. From the door she could see her car parked in the driveway. Someone had just spray-painted the word FAG across the side of her car!

She felt a pain in her arm and chest and staggered back into the house. "Oh, my God," she thought, "I'm having a heart attack."

* * *

"I just don't understand this," she said to her counsel.

"I know," the suave man said, making a little sympathetic tsk-tsk noise as he shook his head. "Just appalling! I'm afraid it just goes with the turf."

"Goes with the turf? He's calling me names on the radio! Why can't we at least file a lawsuit? Get an injunction against him—"

The lawyer patted his snowbird do. "You're a public figure to the extent that you worked as an actress and were seen on television by the whole country, and while privacy is protected by law, this guy can always fall back on the time-honored 'satire' defense. The court has upheld the right of media to satirize—a few print cases that come to mind are the *Mad Magazine, Hustler,* and *National Lampoon* cases. Each is different from the others, but the case law is the same, basically. Media can satirize, and that's sort of what he's doing by extension."

"But how is it satire to read something out of a paper and then—"

"No. I hear you, dear. What I'm saying is, it would be *adjudicated* within that sort of a contextual envelope, and you not only would probably not win—how could you prove malicious intent when he was only repeating something in a public record?—but moreover, and understand I'm playing the devil's advocate for you, what if you lose? If the decision goes against you, he'd surely countersue. Not only do you call even more attention to yourself, but you stand every chance in the world of looking like someone out to get even with a nuisance suit, or—worse—like you're trying to get damages under false pretenses. It's a legal minefield."

"You mean someone can call you any name they want on radio or TV or in the papers, and you can do *nothing?*" She couldn't believe any of this. He kept saying the same thing in different ways. Legal double-talk. Meanwhile here she was with smeared paint on the side of her car, a pain in her chest, and whatever hope she might have had for breathing life back into her career suddenly evaporating—all because of this . . . terrible man.

The pain in her chest hadn't been a heart attack after all, just a bad case of heartburn. She was feeling better—the pain had faded—and she'd finally got her Honda looking decent, although she could tell the door had been repainted. Had she not succumbed to the temptation of turning his show on again, everything might have been different. But four days later she was driving her car on the freeway and heard her name again. The ridicule was so unfunny, so gross, and so totally without meaning that it hurt her even more than the first time.

"It's that time of the month and . . . oh, *noo!* Your best dress is ruined. Don't let a bad monthly accident put a curse on your activities. When it's that time again and regular protection isn't enough, you need BIG BOB!" The hated radio voice boomed the words in echo. She knew it was a mistake to keep listening, but she couldn't shut it off. "Big, maximum protection with triple-thick panty-guards to keep you safe at those special times. Need extra safety? Industrial-strength protection? Go with the flow and go for . . . BIG BOB!" Rude laughter exploded out of her car radio like so much broken glass.

"When it's your heavy-duty time again, don't take a chance, put BIG BOB in your pants." Her chest felt so funny. That heartburn again. "Coming soon—new Blue Bob for water sports." More raucous hoots. "And don't forget—BIG BOB will plug up the hole in any leaking dyke—just ask Morgan Keyes!"

Morgana Kester pulled her Accord over and tried to catch her breath, too sick even to flick the station off. Mad L.A. traffic kamikazed around her. They found her that way, still alive but very ill, when the CHiPS summoned the paramedics. She was hospitalized for "a mild coronary and nervous exhaustion," according to that bastion of the First Amendment, the intrepid *Midnight Inquirer*.

She'd become an addict once again, but this time to a radio voice. Even flat on her back in the hospital, she had a small radio beside her. She was listening when she heard him begin "sacking" her. When he wanted to punish someone he sacked them.

"I see where they're kicking more gays and lesbians out of the military. Boy—that's tough on the *rear* admirals, eh? Speaking of lesbians, we send our get-well wishes to recuperating Morgan Keyes at Cedars Sinai. The ugliest yenta ever to appear on *The Love Barge!* Morgan, why not do all of show biz and the rest of America a favor: Look, you weren't that great to begin with, but after rehab . . . whew! How's about putting a sack over your head, and Sonny Collins can breathe easier!"

That day it arrived with some wilted flowers, "from your secret admirer": a copy of *Heather Has Two Mommies* and a little anatomically correct female doll with a tiny sack over its head. It didn't even bother her.

Two weeks went by, and O'Toole "did" her over the Kotch TV Network—for all of America to see. They'd taken the hit record "I Can't Ever Wait to See Your Face" by Sonny Collins and restructured it just enough so that the melody was altered, but anyone could tell what tune he was mocking.

The cast of *The Bobby O'Toole Television Show* performed it dressed as flamboyant gays and lesbians, the theme apparent in the title, "I Can't Masturbate and See Your Face." The skit involved hooker-types wearing near-topless bikinis and sacks. While it was offensive in the extreme, the program's ratings went up even higher.

The following Monday morning, in the middle of the O'Toole radio show, Rick Bauman shoved a note across to the star of the show. Buddy "All Day" Long had just taken a call from Morgan Keyes, who sounded excited and wanted to brag about what had happened to her after she'd gotten out of the hospital. Apparently she'd landed work as a result of all the publicity.

"—those friggin' creeps at the FCC are totally irrelevant. . . . Speaking of friggin', guess who's on our telephone line? Morgan? 'Zat you?"

"Yeah! 'Zat you, Bobby?" Her voice was bright and sexy, filled with warmth.

"Yeah. Hey! How's my favorite has-been washed-up actress/slash/dyke-junkie?"

"Your favorite dyke-junkie is pretty fine, actually, thanks to you!"

"Me?"

"Yeah. As you know, after your favorite show, *The Love Barge*, sunk, I couldn't get arrested. You also know I went through rehab for a drug problem, etcetera. When I heard you ragging me about it, I went a little cuckoo—but guess what? It's turned everything around for me. I've landed a part in a pilot for a TV series, and I'm up for a big feature film—how about that?" She'd rehearsed the lies with great care.

"Wow! That's great. But you better learn to act first. Also, get some plastic surgery—unless you plan to work with a sack over your face."

"Very funny!" She giggled musically. "I saw you on TV, you naughty boy. Anyway, that's why I'm calling. You're always on my case about what a dog I am and all. I want to see if you're a real man or if *you're* a fag, a closet fag—you know, since you put so much stock in heterosexuality. I want to make you a bet."

"What? You wanna bet me whether I can get it up while I'm watching you and Sonny Collins strap on the peter-cheaters?"

"No!" She bit her lip during the laughter, but kept the smile in her voice. "I want you to have me on your show. Right there in the studio. I know you saw me when I was looking like forty miles of bad road, but—"

"Forty miles? You looked like an entire interstate highway of ugly. The Ugly Route One!"

She laughed again. Really sounding like she was enjoying being on his show. "I didn't look good, I'll admit. Okay—

but here's the deal, Bobby baby. You like to play the role of Mr. Honesty, so here's my offer: Have me on your show. Look at me now that I'm well. You tell your national audience whether or not, in your opinion, I'm a good-looking woman. Don't lie, you have to tell the truth—right?"

"Right."

"If you say I'm not a good-lookin' chick—seriously—I'll quit show business. Right then and there. But if you have to honestly admit that I look good, I want you to apologize publicly on the air. Are you man enough to do it?"

"Wait a minute now. If I *don't* think you look all that good—"

"Yeah."

"You'll get outta the business?"

"You have my word."

"When do you want to do it?"

"Your show. You say."

"Tomorrow too soon?"

"You got it."

"You got a deal. Hold on. I'll put my producer on, and you guys can work out details."

"See you in the morning! Be ready to eat your words."

"Don't count on it."

"Twenty fuckin' bucks says the bitch don't show."

"Man, I love easy money," his producer said, grinning and pointing. Just turning the corner of the long hallway from Security, Ms. Morgan Keyes was being escorted in the direction of the studio.

"Son of a bitch." O'Toole covered his mouth so she couldn't read his lips. "Looks like she borrowed one of Jackie Collins's old gowns." They laughed. The low-cut dress was ludicrously out of place. "Dyke's got her push-up bra on." The spot ended as Morgan Keyes was being quietly escorted into Studio Two.

She silently locked the studio door as O'Toole prepared to

take the microphone again, Bauman's finger on his smiling lips in the "shh" sign. She smiled and nodded.

"Good morning, gays and straights, ladies and gerbils, nutbaskets and fruitcakes. This is the number-one—"

The explosion was louder than she'd been expecting and she almost dropped the gun when she fired the first shot. The .38 plus-P load struck producer Rick Bauman in the chest from less than four feet away. She shot engineer Buddy Long in the head. In ten cities across the United States, in hundreds of small towns and communities that listened to Bobby O'Toole over their nearest Kotch Radio Network affiliate, millions of Americans heard him say "This is number-one—" punctuated by two cannon blasts.

"Please," they heard him say. "Please—whatever you want. Listen, I—" Was it one of his outrageous gags?

"Shut up you filthy-mouthed *scum!"* A woman's sharp tones audible, but from a distance.

Clicks of steel.

"Oh, Jesus—" But no expletives followed. It sounded more as if someone were praying. Crazy Bobby.

She finished putting handcuffs on the long-haired man. The blood on Buddy Long and Rick Bauman seemed as unreal as movie ketchup.

"Please, they're too tight. Please!" Bobby begged in his nice, resonant baritone. She had one half of each pair of cuffs secured to each hand, the other ends firmly attached around the steel supports of the studio chair. She took rope out of the huge handbag she was carrying and quickly—and rather inexpertly—bound his feet together at the ankles, having to put the gun down for a second at one point, then securing the feet to the chair itself. Listeners heard him whisper "Help" twice, close into the microphone. Everyone undoubtedly assumed this was a typical O'Toole bit.

He had no idea what to do. Obviously she'd conned her way in. There was no TV show pilot, no movie, no career. His mind raced a mile a second: rehab, heart attack, *money!* There was always a key.

"Listen," his audience heard him say live, "I'm quite wealthy. I will gladly pay you what—"

"Just sit there and shut that evil mouth of yours." She smiled—that was the most frightening part. When she smiled, he saw the pent-up rage, and something else that scared him.

"Oh, *please* I'm *begging* you—"

She was getting more tools from the bag.

"Don't talk," the woman said. "I've heard enough of your words to last me a thousand lifetimes." Her words over the air were not as loud now. "You're a bad man. You hurt folks and you don't care. You say anything that comes into your head. Well, you're going to lose the thing that makes you who you are. The thing you love the most." She looked him up and down. He shuddered and began to cry as she reached over and unzipped his trousers. "You're going to lose the thing that gives you your *power.*"

"PLEASE DEAR GOD I'M SORRY WHATEVER I'VE DONE TO HURT YOU PLEASE GIVE ME ANOTHER CHANCE, LET ME MAKE IT UP TO YOU SOMEHOW, IT'S JUST AN *ACT*—I'M A GOOD PERSON—I—" Two dead or dying men beside them, and all he could think of was his own life.

"Hush, now. You be a man for once. Be your last chance to talk like a *man,* if you understand my meaning. You're evil. You think you're so funny, but your humor hurts. Now you pay. Pay with the symbol of your power."

She spread her instruments out across the control board counter in front of them, and when he saw the things he bucked like an animal.

Straight razor, sharp medium-size tin snips, needle and thread, large heavy-duty surgical forceps.

"I've had some training," she said pleasantly. "You won't bleed to death if I can help it. I don't want you dead." She took the straight razor and—beginning at his fly and working her way up—began to slice his clothing from him. He fainted instantly.

Morgana Kester, whose single lesbian experience had

found its way into the sleazier annals of popular culture, whose rehabilitation from substance abuse had rendered her vulnerable, whose hopes for career, health, and any shred of dignity had been cruelly denied, forced her way in with the big hospital forceps and got a powerful grip on what she wanted.

She wasn't going to cut it *all* off anyway—just part of it. Take enough that he couldn't use the evil thing again. How fittingly perfect. Without further preamble, she picked up the tin snips and began sawing through Bobby O'Toole's evil tongue.

THE SONGWRITER

Jesse Sublett

They were a hundred ninety miles from Oklahoma City when the right rear tire went flat. Having been on the road long enough to have a system worked out, the band members immediately set about performing their assigned tasks: Keef operated the jack, Mick replaced the tire, Charlie stayed in the van and rolled a joint. Bianca stayed in the van, too, using the opportunity to paint her nails or write a letter to Mom. Everyone in their places, just like onstage.

Mick sang and played lead guitar. Bianca played bass, sang background, and did anything else she could within the somewhat limited scope of her musical abilities to prove she was more than just Mick's girlfriend. Charlie played drums. Keef wrote the songs and played rhythm guitar. That was the way it had been ever since the four of them started out in Charlie's parents' garage back in Austin, Texas, almost five years ago.

But things had been uneasy lately. Keef hadn't written a

new song in almost three months. During that same period, however, Mick, who previously hadn't written anything that couldn't be inscribed on a latrine wall while taking a piss, had experienced an awakening of his own songwriting muse. Though his three new songs were clearly inferior to Keef's, the boost to the singer's ego was tremendous. And this shift in band dynamics (Mick up, Keef down) had emboldened the singer to make the following decree: "When the band gets a record deal, and it's only a matter of time once we get that demo tape recorded, I get 25 percent of any cash advance we get, right off the top. After all, it's *my* band." That's what Mick had said after the gig last night, and no one had said a word.

"Well, you can stick your 25 percent and that baby blue Stratocaster of yours up your pretentious ass," was what Keef would have told the singer, had Keef not been in the middle of this creative dry spell. But he was, so he didn't, and he could just hear Mick's likely response: "You've got writer's block anyway, Keefy boy, so what's there to argue about?" But writer's block was a concept Keef didn't dare let himself believe in. If you were in fact a *writer,* he thought, you *wrote.* Like plumbers plumb, painters paint, preachers preach. To not do the thing that defines your existence, thought Keef, means death. And writing had always, it seemed, defined Keef's existence.

Once Mick had the lugs loosened, Keef levered the jack up higher, watching as Mick tucked some of his long hair behind one ear so it would quit getting in his eyes. Keef's feet crunched on the loose gravel of the roadside, making a sound like eggshells being crushed. Keef wondered if Mick's skull would sound like that if the jack post was yanked loose from the bumper claw, causing the van to crash down on his head.

Or would it be more of a liquid sound, like a ripe tomato hitting the ground?

Bianca peered at the truck-stop menu, thinking about how hard it was to keep your weight down and your complexion clear when you are in truck stops all the time. They were always the same: little pictures of burgers and fried things on plastic-coated menus, waitresses calling you "hon," signs on the cash registers like "The bank doesn't serve breakfast, so why should we cash checks?"

"I'll have one poached, a grapefruit, and coffee," she told the waitress. Pointing to the place in the booth where Mick would sit when he returned from the rest room, she added, "He'll have the Spanish omelet and a large orange juice."

The waitress nodded, smiling as if she were pleased with Bianca's choices. God, thought Bianca, what an insignificant thing to smile about. The waitress leaned forward. Keef was mumbling in a low voice. Several seconds later, Bianca realized he was ordering. "I guess I'll have iced tea, French toast, and bacon," he was saying. "And, uhm, maybe a glass of iced tea."

"You want two iced teas?" said the waitress.

Keef turned red. "Oh. No, just one."

Mick, returning to the table, said, "Heads up, Keef. Can't even order breakfast without screwing up."

"Two eggs over easy, sausage on the side, whole-wheat toast," said Charlie. "And one iced tea. I'll take his extra." He nudged Keef.

Keef just looked down at his menu. The waitress cleared her throat to get his attention. Charlie finally jabbed Keef with his elbow. "Lemme out," he said. "And give her the menu."

Keef let Charlie out, shoved the menu at the waitress.

Bianca watched Mick as he shook his head, giving her a discreet wink as he said, "You're burned out, man." Mick reached over and flipped an imaginary light switch on the side of Keef's head. "See?" said Mick. "Click, click . . . nothing happens. Burned out."

"Fuck off, Mick," said Keef.

Finally, a sign of life, Bianca thought as Keef sneered and Mick settled back in the booth, grinning. She hated it when the guys picked on each other. Did all bands act like this?

The Songwriter

When a band got more successful, she wondered, did they stop being petty to each other, or just get meaner?

Worrying about it wasn't doing Keef any good. Neither was the treatment he was getting from the guys. Especially Mick. After all, like he said, he was the leader of the band. But if someone else wrote all the songs, then what gave him the right to call all the shots? It was like if an armed robber had to ask you to loan him bullets. And being the bandleader didn't give Mick the right to say it was "his band," either. Like he owned them. Like he sat down one day and made them up in his mind, like a song.

Spikes of sunlight ricocheted into the songwriter's eyes from a hundred chrome bumpers in the parking lot. The truck stop was too bright, too noisy, an unwanted diversion from his private world. Keef sat there, letting things seep in, but not letting anything out.

Before, writing songs had always been effortless, like breathing. It was funny, the way other people labored and strained to write songs, agonizing over each line, each little melodic hook. Because Keef's mind was full of music, always. If he got up and walked to the bathroom, a little voice in his head or the whistle in his throat would chime a dreamy little phrase. By the time he'd walked ten steps, there would be an answering phrase. Then an accompanying countermelody, or a fragment in the relative minor, and that could make a bridge.

When Keef hummed to himself, he was a one-man band. He envisioned the drum parts, bass line, melody. Parts and counterpoints. If a guitar or piano was within reach, he'd bash it out, and if a tape recorder was handy, throw the whole thing down in one sitting. He'd written as many as six songs in a day. A hundred a year, usually, and he could easily have written more.

It was the same way with lyrics. The English language is a wonderful thing, thought Keef. So many sounds, cadences, rhythms. Listen to a truck driver talk, catch that waitress barking her meal orders to the cook. It's music. You didn't have to have something to say, just a way to say it. Songs were always saying the same things, over and over; what made them different was the way the things were said. Keef had no trouble picking up voices, sounds, and ideas, putting them together until they made a statement, in a voice that was undeniably his own.

That's the way it was, the way his mind worked. The way he saw it, there was all this music out there floating around like dust motes in the air on a lazy summer afternoon, and you just reached up and grabbed some of it and rolled it around, and you had a song. He was proud of his ability, but then again, he was past thinking it was a big deal.

Just as long as he got the proper respect for it.

Just as long as Mick realized he needed Keef worse than Keef needed him. But Mick didn't realize that, and that was becoming painfully obvious. He was a typical guitar player/singer. Egomaniac with a capital E. Thought everything hinged on him. Thought everybody who came to see the band only paid attention to him. Where would he be without my songs? thought Keef.

Look at him. Sitting there in the booth, eyeing every skirt that comes in the place. He's so dumb, thought Keef, he doesn't know I killed him back there on the side of the road, letting the weight of the van squash his head like a ripe tomato. As easy as writing a song, he'd made the asshole cease to exist.

It was comforting, that thought. More than that, actually, his knowledge of Mick's defunctness gave Keef a warm feeling, an inner glow. Like when you've written a song in your head but you haven't played it for anyone yet. It's still a song. What had his grandmother always said as she raised him? "Sin in thought is the same as sin in deed," she'd said, clacking those damn sewing scissors together that rang in his head, gratingly off-key, and with that stern pucker on her lips. Like the taste of sin was like a green lemon. Well, it doesn't taste like that to me, thought Keef. It tastes like victory.

Keef got up to go to the rest room, feeling better than he had in a long, long time.

The scene was typical. The band had played it a thousand times before. The cowgirl walking by their table. Looking like she'd been poured into her jeans. Walking like she didn't give a fuck who noticed. Staring straight ahead but a bit sullen, as if any second she might turn around and tell you to fuck off or *Go ahead, take a picture, it lasts longer and you might not get your ass kicked.* About three steps behind was the guy who'd deliver the ass-kicking: a tall redneck in faded Levi's, cowboy boots, and western shirt with a round snuff can in one of the snap pockets.

Mick studied the girl's jeans as if they held a hidden meaning. His eyes slowly wandered over them, from cuffs to knees, thighs, hips, crotch—where the button-fly ran down between her legs, making a hard-edged crease.

The redneck shot Mick a dirty look before sliding into the booth next to the girl. That look was a warning shot. Mick averted his gaze quickly, pretending he'd just been gazing at the wall behind the redneck's head. Just then Keef and Charlie returned from the rest room. The redneck gave them all a disgusted leer.

Charlie just shook his head and gave Mick a look that said, *You'll never learn, will you?*

Mick said, "Watch this, Charlie." He reached over and flicked the imaginary light switch by Keef's head. "Click, click . . . See, Charlie? Nothing happens, man."

"Real funny," said Charlie.

Keef exchanged a half-lidded glance with Charlie, then turned toward the window. Like he thought he was better than the rest of them, thought Mick. He hated when the songwriter did that. Why couldn't he take it? Why didn't he just try to blend in, to be one of the guys instead of acting like he was better? To be in a band, you had to go with the flow, even when everybody else was riding you. Sure, it got a little sadistic, but that's how it was.

And it was the bandleader's job to set the flow. Because if

he didn't, a band was just a bunch of guys flailing about, everybody trying to force his own personality on the thing —no defining identity. When you heard a song on the radio, it didn't matter who wrote it, or if the singer was the best singer in the world or if the guitar player was the hottest guitar player in the world. If that music didn't come pouring balls-out from the speakers with a personality that you could say, "Oh, yeah, I feel like I know this guy" . . . then it was no good. That's why some bands made it, most didn't. And Mick was determined to make it.

That's what he was trying to let Keef know. If you want to play with me, play *with* me. If not, hit the road. Because every band's got to have a leader.

Charlie realized that, he thought. Bianca, too, even though she was sitting there on her cute little ass, frowning with those full pouty lips, and inside her cute little head topped off with that bubble of red hair she was wondering why guys in bands were so cruel to each other. Cruel, shit. Go with the flow. Or flow on out.

Charlie was nodding his head, grudgingly going along with Mick, drumming the tabletop with his fingertips. He was tired of sitting—sitting on his drum stool for two hours last night, then sitting behind the wheel and driving for four hours this morning, and they were three more hours from Oklahoma City. But he liked driving, watching the countryside go by in a blur, hands on the wheel, in control of something.

You could measure a day in miles. You could measure a day in cigarettes. You could slice it all up into little bite-size chunks: fifty miles to the gig, two hours till we eat again, half hour till load in and sound check. Then back to the motel to shit, shower, and shave. The gig: eighteen songs, divided up into parts—measures, bars, beats.

It gave you a weird perspective, sitting behind the drums, behind the guitar players. From there you saw mostly the other band members' backs. Past the edge of the stage, the audience. You saw more, and you weren't doing fancy moves trying to dazzle everybody while you played some cool riff on your guitar.

From his drum throne, Charlie controlled the basic engine of the songs: the tempo, the pulse of the verses and choruses, the little spaces between the parts in which less was always more, giving the audience a chance to anticipate what was next by delaying it just a little, giving them a bit of a tease.

Charlie's fingers kept drumming. He wished the food would arrive.

"Hey, Keef, seemed like you were in the john for quite a while," said Mick. "Your writer's block affecting your bowels, too?"

Keef shook his head, glaring briefly at him.

"I got some prunes in my bag if you need 'em," said Charlie. "Might loosen everything up, you know?" Charlie playfully popped Keef on the arm, trying to get him to lighten up.

But Keef didn't lighten up. He just sulked. Why didn't Keef just snap out of it? Charlie thought, exasperated. Because when he sulked, his guitar sulked, too. His timing was off, a little too much behind the beat, right on top of the drums, throwing everything off. And you just can't have that, unless you're a garage band.

And Charlie wasn't into that.

He watched as Mick winked at Bianca. She winked back. She's gotta go along with her boyfriend, thought Charlie, even though she hates the friction. Because she knew she wouldn't be in the band unless she was Mick's girlfriend. She was cute, but there were lots of better bass players out there.

What could you do? They'd have tonight off, and maybe Keef would write something and get out of his funk. Maybe, thought Charlie, he could score some heroin in OKC. Take the night off. Let that white pony drive for a while.

Being in a band is a constant source of irritation. On the one hand, you have several people around at all times that you can consider friends. People to laugh at your jokes, to share your problems and observations of the world. But on the other hand, you have their problems, too. You have all the irritation of other people's ups and downs, and no privacy. No privacy to be in a bad mood on your own. So if they're there to share it, and they're a part of the problem, they must, in one fashion or other, be a part of the solution.

They're sucking up all I have to give and then they're stomping on the shell of what's left, thought Keef. They're screwing with the songwriter in me, they're tearing up the fabric of my universe.

You ask for it, you're gonna get it, he thought.

All the ideas about the way to do it were tied up in the people themselves. They were nothing more nor less than the sum total of the various factors that made them who they were, and those self-defining variables determined the transactions they conducted with the world around them. So you just sat there and grabbed at the ideas that were floating around in the universe and . . .

It's easy, thought Keef.

Mick has a big head. But some things are bigger, obviously. A van is bigger. Gravity is stronger.

It's easy.

Keef felt himself being transported back to that place on the side of the road where the band had stopped to fix the flat tire. He coasted over the scene with the wings of an avenging angel, a lilting melody in A minor. He saw himself kicking the jack out from under the van, the van crashing down on Mick's head. It was easy.

Like writing a song.

"Hate Thing," said Bianca. The words seemed to tumble out of the big lips like a drunk rolling out of bed.

"Oh," said Charlie, long, slow, with vibrato, "I feel it."

Acknowledgment spread quickly around the table, like flu in an office building. "Hate Thing" was part of the band's private language, a typical phenomenon observed in small groups of people thrown together for extended periods of time.

"It's rolling in, I guess," said Mick. "Good ole Hate Thing."

"Hell-o-baaaby," went Charlie, mimicking the Big Bopper's delivery in "Chantilly Lace." Charlie gave it his best baritone roll: *"Hell-o, Hate Thing."*

Bianca sipped her coffee, somewhat pleased with herself. "I think it picked up our trail when we had that flat tire. It's like a rattlesnake waiting by the road sometimes."

"I think it just likes those old straight interstates like I-35," said Charlie. "So boring, nothing to look at for hundreds of miles. Makes a three-hour drive seem like an eight-hour drive."

"Hate Thing," said Keef. "I thought I saw it back there. *Hate Thing,"* singing now, soft and hoarse like Marlon Brando imitating the Troggs, *"I think I hate you."*

Bianca nodded. Like a hangover after a bad gig, like the leering face of a club owner who offered to pay the band a bonus if that cute little bass player would blow him, the Hate Thing was with them, hanging in the air like a dead man's fart.

The waitress checked the food in the window against her ticket. Looked like everything was there, except for the toast. She'd come back for that. Over at table 13, she could hear almost every word the members of the rock band said.

They talked in their private code, repeating things over and over, adding nuances as they volleyed back and forth, like the way something was said was more important than what was said. But she guessed that that was true with everybody, especially people who traveled together. And they looked like they'd been traveling a long time. They looked sick of each other. They looked sad, too, like they were missing something. Maybe the food would pick them up.

She stacked the plates on her arm: French toast and

bacon, poached egg, number three, Spanish omelet. A lot of food for just a few skinny kids. She turned and looked over her shoulder at them.

It seemed like there had been only three of them when they came in.

Keef took a turn driving. Charlie rode shotgun. Bianca and Mick sat behind, and all the gear was in back—Fender guitars, Marshall amps, Gretsch drums—typical gear for the typical struggling American rock 'n' roll band.

Keef leaned on the steering wheel, seeming to look far in the distance, miles ahead of the bug-spattered hood of the van, where the road stretched on and on in front of them for eternity. Charlie leafed through his address book, checking to see if he had a dope connection in OK City. His OK City people were filed under K, and that made sense to Charlie. Mick fanned through a *Rolling Stone,* making cynical comments about the bands they featured, as if every other band's success infringed upon his own. Bianca just sat there, wishing she could sleep, but she couldn't, so she stared out the window, hypnotized by the gray texture scrolling underneath the chassis of the van.

"Oh, gross," she said. "Ugh."

They passed something flat and bloody, a lump of fur with bare flesh and entrails splattered out on either side, baking on the hot asphalt.

Keef and Charlie caught it in the rearview mirrors. Mick turned around and leaned across Bianca's lap to see it.

"Road kill," announced Charlie.

"Road kill number ten this week, isn't it?" said Mick. "Looked like a fox, or maybe a raccoon. Do they have foxes in Texas?"

"Gross road kill." Bianca shuddered.

"Hate Thing," said Keef.

Just north of Denton they had another flat. By the time they rolled into OK City, the sky was as black as the inside of a pocket in a black velvet coat.

* * *

The Songwriter

It almost seemed like a big mess sometimes, Keef's mind. A blues riff undulating like a slimy water moccasin cutting through murky swamp water, a hip-hop drum pattern ping-ponging around some dark alley. The wanton ululation of a tortured saxophone. Random thoughts, pictures, sounds. Sometimes he said wait a minute, and made them all come together and face front, but most of the time he just hung out and waited to see what floated to the top.

"Sin in thought is the same as sin in deed," his grandmother had said, one of the millions of things she'd said, always chattering away, clacking those damn scissors, making that sour face. She'd refused to let Keef buy a guitar, forbidden him to play his music loud, saying it interfered with her sewing. Always in his face, his mind, saying "No." Then she'd died, screaming and oozing blood. They'd sent Keef away to a school, and there he'd finally gotten his guitar, which gave his thoughts form, and gave those forms a world to inhabit freely and with purpose.

It's all been done before. People write songs, they don't create them. There are only eight whole notes in the scale, only so many ways to put them together, especially in rock 'n' roll. It's so easy, thought Keef, it's all been done before. Those ideas and sounds are already there, I just reintroduce them to each other. Hi-ya, E major, meet B minor.

It was the same with the band. He wasn't doing anything to them. They were doing it to themselves. The way you live is the way you die. Keef lay back on the motel bed in the room he was sharing with Charlie. He lay quietly, thinking how easy it was, waiting for the wheels of the universe to turn. They turned and there was nothing you could do about it.

The sound they made as they turned, lubricated by the solvent of time, was nearly imperceptible. As Keef strained to hear it, that comforting sound, there was another sound, echoing from a deep recess of his mind.

Scissors, finely honed, clacking.

* * *

Charlie had been gone more than three hours, but he had finally scored some heroin. He let himself into the room, hoping that Keef the sulker was asleep. The lights were on, the TV on with the sound off, the songwriter lying in bed with his legs draped over the side, his feet touching the floor, eyes closed.

Charlie went to his suitcase to get his works, slipped them into his shaving kit, and headed for the bathroom, like he'd done, what, once or twice a month for the last eighteen months he'd been on the road. He wasn't worried about getting hooked. He knew how to control it, and would never allow anything as insignificant as a drug to control him. He took the paper bindle of heroin out of his pocket and dropped that in the shaving kit, too, and pushed on the bathroom door—

"Marianne called," said Keef.

"Oh, shit," exclaimed Charlie. Keef was sitting upright, like a damn ghoul that had come back to life.

"What's wrong, Charlie? You look pale."

"You startled me, damn it. I thought you were asleep."

"No. I was just, you know, thinking."

Charlie started to go on into the bathroom. He put the shaving kit down on the toilet tank, then heard Keef's voice again.

"I'm glad I wasn't asleep," he was saying.

"Why?" said Charlie, sticking his head back out the door so he could hear better. When he looked at Keef, he started wishing he'd just done the junk at the dealer's place, then drifted home. He just wanted to blot everything out for a few hours, float on the big cloud. Being tired and sad and broke and looking at the songwriter's big dopey face was enough to make anyone want to shoot heroin. Especially after all that had happened.

"Because she said it was important," said Keef. "Said for you to call when you got in, no matter how late."

"Shit," said the drummer, shuffling back out of the bathroom. He plopped down on the bed, picked up the phone, trying to get the image of her face in his head before he heard her voice. When she said hello, he was still trying.

The conversation was surreal, unsatisfying: another awkward tangle of emotions over long distance, stretched taut, the meaning wrung out of them. He was dimly aware of Keef getting up and using the bathroom while he was on the phone. He didn't worry about Keef messing with his stuff. Charlie said a final, *"Goodbye . . . miss you,* too . . ." thirty minutes later, never getting around to asking why she'd called.

Charlie was back in the bathroom, the door shut and locked. The songwriter lay in the dark, listening to the riffs and voices in his head, listening for the sound the drummer would make when he fell over.

Charlie had the worst connections in the world, and no business sense to boot. If he went to the store to get beer, he'd pay champagne prices for the local swill. If he went down to Washington Square in Manhattan, he'd pay thirty bucks for junk that had been stepped on so many times it wouldn't get a grasshopper off the ground.

But Keef, ironically, looked like a junkie. People were always giving him the stuff, especially at some of the clubs they played. And the last time they'd been in Laredo, a generous fan had treated Keef to a dime bag of Mexican Black Tar. It was dark and gooey and it was strong, a good three to four times stronger than anything you'd normally get on the street—way stronger than anything Charlie ever dabbled with.

Charlie would just think that the stuff he'd bought had picked up some humidity and gotten gooey on the way back to the motel. After cooking it up in his spoon, he'd fill his spike up and boot it and . . .

A slippery, rubbery walking pattern on a standup bass skipping the root notes on the one-beat, a string quartet, the low moan of a Hammond B-3. Something light and jazzy, flutes maybe. Keef lay back on the bed, staring up at the textures in the spray finish of the ceiling, and waited, trolling the darkness. Lots of ideas, lots of patterns, but nothing concrete that begged pursuing. It's all been done before, he thought.

Then, after a bit, a muted thump and a rush of cool air, accompanied by the sound of wings taking to flight.

Bianca sat on the bed, wondering when it was all going to hit home. She wondered if the worst was over, or yet to come. She wasn't even sure how she felt. Once she thought she heard herself screaming, then realized it was all in her head. Maybe, she decided, she really had been screaming and had only convinced herself that it was her imagination. Staring up at the sea of nipplelike extrusions on the cottage cheese ceiling, she imagined that they were a vast army of tiny white soldiers; she felt conquered, blank, erased, she wished someone would come into the room and tell her what she was supposed to feel, tell her what she was supposed to do. This wasn't like anything she'd ever experienced in her short life.

The worst part so far, she thought, had been sitting in the van all that time, waiting for the highway patrol and ambulance to get there. Charlie and Keef wouldn't let her out because they didn't want her to see Mick with his head smushed under the van, so she'd just sat there and sat there for what seemed like a month, imagining what it would look like, and all she could think of was that poor animal she'd seen back on the road with all the life and identity squashed out of it.

She wasn't sure if she'd loved Mick, but she knew she didn't want to romanticize their relationship just because it had come to such a sudden, grotesque end. But despite herself, she kept trying to imagine what he'd felt in his last seconds—the sound of the bumper claw coming off and the van, all three or four thousand pounds of it, just dropping down, surrendering to gravity, right on his skull.

She wondered if his eyes had popped out of his head.

She was shaking. She felt a jolt, like an electric shock. No

The Songwriter

pain, no nausea, just the spasmodic contraction of bundles of muscle. She felt the emptiness, like a stone falling down into a deep damp well, never hitting bottom. The room's ugliness screamed at her. The orange comforter on the bed, the ridiculously vapid watercolors on the wall, the depressing dark veneer on the fake furniture—God, she thought, to sit in a room like this alone forever would be the worst thing that could happen to a person.

She buttoned her blouse and got up and went out and knocked on the door to Keef and Charlie's room.

Keef opened the door, and it struck her that he looked awfully clear-eyed and lucid.

"I'm lonely," she said. "Could you keep me company for a while?"

"Sure," he said. He got his key off the dresser and shut the door behind him, putting an arm around her as they went to her room.

"It's just you and me now," he said as they lay on the bed on top of the covers, arms wrapped around each other tight, their clothes becoming damp from their combined body heat. She didn't ask about Charlie, where he was or why he didn't count. Drummers often got left out of things.

They talked, but it was the silence that stretched between the words that spoke most clearly. Eventually they kissed. They held each other tight, white-knuckled, surrendering to raw need. The cold and numbness receded from her body, and the symphonic chaos of his mind found her deep well of emptiness, fell into it, and filled it up.

They shed their clothes like snakes shedding old skin.

As Keef thrust deep inside her, her thoughts abruptly swept back over the events of the day, compressing them, jumbling them out of sequence like a French movie she'd seen once. She thought back to the breakfast at the truck stop, one like so many they'd stopped in before, saying the same things, thinking the same thoughts. It was as if her life had become an endless tape loop, no yesterdays, no tomorrows. . . . She saw Mick sitting there at the table at the truck stop, needling Keef again. . . . But she knew he hadn't really been there. He was dead, lying on a slab in a town along the interstate.

Suddenly her body was wracked with convulsions, and she wasn't sure if she was about to come or cry and didn't care. This was here, this was now. She'd sort it out later.

The room was dark and his body was raw. The dampness of the sheets enveloping them had turned cold, but the warmth of her body next to him was nice. He closed his eyes and listened.

Silence.

He bolted upright, disengaging her arm and leg where they were knotted with his own. He strained to hear, but nothing.

No music. No instruments sounding lonely mating calls out in the outback of the universe, waiting for an answer, waiting for someone to link them up and turn them into a song.

He took a slow, deep breath, tasting the cool air, hearing the shushing sound of his bare body on the sheets, the low hum of the air conditioner, and nothing else, except his breathing.

He looked down at Bianca, her long red hair spilling out over her pillow like liquid, her bare shoulder smooth and soft. She'd been a part of Mick and therefore a cog in the machinery of the Hate Thing that had been draining his energies and giving nothing back except nothing. Now she'd gotten next to him and drawn out his energy and his sex. She lay there so quietly, coiled in the sheets like a saxophone riff undulating through tendrils of smoke in a darkened nightclub.

But as he closed his eyes and waited for the pictures and ideas, nothing came. He felt nothing from her. No tug, no pull. No melody.

Now what?

He was alone.

The Songwriter

Really alone. So quiet.

He drew his knees up and together and locked his arms around them and sat there, rocking. Then she stirred, moving a bit under the covers, sighing. After a moment she raised up and pressed her warm breasts on his back, put her arms around him and squeezed and made a small sound deep in her throat.

And that stirred something.

The nothingness was suddenly full of shapes, movement. People from a million walks of life, crisscrossing paths and worming their way around and through each other's lives, pulling and tugging and tearing at the fabric of his existence. They fed on each other, hungry parasites, fucking each other to death, gnawing each other's genitals because they couldn't gnaw their own, never satisfied until they had sucked their victims into empty shells that caved in from the weight of their emptiness.

"Keef . . ."

He saw bankers, lawyers, gas station attendants. Disgusting in their blissful insolence, leaving behind tunnels like ants in an ant farm, worm tracks in the dust. Postal workers, accountants, waitresses, soldiers. Didn't they know they were leaving patterns? His universe was filled again, teeming with patterns and voices swirling like dust motes in an old warehouse.

"Keef . . ."

Doctors, policemen, housewives, factory workers. Musicians. Young, old, yuppies, criminals. The married, the lonely, the hunters, the hunted. They were the notes of symphonies waiting to be written, waiting to assume their places in the inevitable cycle of nature.

He wasn't a killer. He just knew how to put things together, let things happen. He saw the patterns and he knew. He'd never made a conscious decision to become a songwriter, he'd never made a conscious decision to become a killer. Not that he could recall, anyway. It was just his gift. The universe has a place for everything, and he had his.

"Keef, are you writing a song?" Her voice was soft and

comforting, though it seemed to come from a place a million miles away. She held him close, waiting for an answer.

"I'm working on something," he said.

She lay back in his arms, listening to his breathing slow to a gentle rhythm, like tidal waves caressing a shore. He understood, she thought to herself. She thought of his grandmother, who'd been brutally murdered with her own sewing scissors, the killer never apprehended. Poor Keef. The grief she felt now was probably nothing compared with what he'd experienced as a young boy. No wonder he was so quiet, so withdrawn. What a price to pay for creativity, she thought, a price that can never be paid in full.

Odd, how safe she felt in his arms.

ROCK 'N' ROLL WILL NEVER DIE

Max Allan Collins

Zombies staggered toward him from either side, but Peter Lee—resplendent in leopard spandex, his bare chest lean but rippling with muscle, his golden hair brushing his shoulders, a pentagram medallion swaying from his throat—showed no fear.

The sound of his thin, high voice—loud as an air-raid siren—rent the air as he banished them: "Go to *hell!* Go to *hell!* Go to *heeeeh-laaaaaaa!*"

Behind him on individual platforms, the black-spandex-clad, rather anonymous-looking musicians of his backup band, Coven, their features obscured behind Satan-red facial makeup, hammered the droning final chord; the drummer on this central, highest of platforms unleashed a torrent of rhythm, his hands a blurring flurry as he went around his endless drum kit.

The audience was on its feet, screaming, chanting, *"Pee-*

ter, *Pee*-ter, *Pee*-ter," fists waving, horned-finger symbols thrusting.

On stage, Peter Lee—shrilly repeating the final phrase (and title) of his hit song "Go to Hell" into a headset microphone that made him look rather like a satanic rock 'n' roll air-traffic controller—ran to the stack of Marshall amps, climbed them to where the Uzi was waiting.

Even with the organized cacophony of the band's final chord, and Peter's own earsplittingly amplified voice, the sound of the Uzi was a thunderous, frightening thing. In the smallish rock star's hands, the Uzi smoked, spat empty shells, and rained apparent death on the zombies staggering from either wing of the stage.

The Uzi's metallic chatter and the sight of the zombies twisting and turning, doing a death dance to the metal music, blood squibs exploding lavishly, splashing the stage, the musicians, the amps, the hanging skull props, and the first several gleeful rows, served to fuel the audience's fire. They imitated the death dance of the zombies, pouring into the aisles, knocking into each other until some of the blood on the crowd wasn't just from the squibs, pounding each other in this variation of slam-dancing that had grown up spontaneously on the tour for Peter Lee and Coven's first album, *Hell Hounds*.

College radio had loved them once—*Spin* called *Hell Hounds* "a dope parody of speed metal laced with Hammer horror-flick imagery." *Rolling Stone* had coined the term splatter-rock to describe Peter Lee's blood-drenched horror-spectacle rock shows, adding, "Lee makes Alice Cooper look like Alice in Wonderland."

But when *Hell Hounds* went to number one, particularly after it went platinum, the critics changed their tune; five years and five albums later, *Spin* was regularly deriding them ("bloody boring") and *Rolling Stone* had called *Into the Abyss* "sheer embarrassment—unintentional self-parody from the self-styled Splatter-Rockmeister."

The crowds, however, still loved Peter Lee—he sold out arenas and auditoriums in every major city in the United

States, and Lee had done huge European and Japanese tours as well. His popularity was at its peak, and tonight's Chicago show made Peter Lee—his tanned body splattered with stage blood as he strutted triumphantly off into the wings, waving a fist in the air as he went—feel immortal.

In the dressing room, his stage makeup was washed away by a local makeup artist, a prissy boy in a lacy white shirt.

"Hey!" Peter said. "Watch it!"

"Watch what?"

"Quit bumping up against me. Just take off the fuckin' makeup. That better be cold cream you're wiping on me."

"Bitch," the makeup artist said, and continued.

When he was alone, after he'd showered and got into his street clothes (jeans and a vintage Stones T-shirt), Peter stared at himself in the makeup mirror. He was only twenty-six, but the lines around his eyes and mouth made him look a decade older. Too much booze. Too much coke. He shuddered, lighting up a Camel.

Thank God for the Betty Ford Clinic, he thought. Now his only vice (aside from the Camel between his lips) was the one no doubt lining up, waiting outside the dressing room. If he wanted to last in rock 'n' roll, he had to take care of himself; no more substance abuse, and between tours he'd have to keep up the daily workouts with his trainer.

Nobody lived forever, not even in rock 'n' roll, but Peter Lee wanted to outlast his contemporaries. Five years at the top was an eternity in this business; but he was determined to join that small circle—Jagger, McCartney, Elton John—who remained superstars into their forties and even fifties.

His road manager, Edward, a dissipated, bloated-looking, thirty-five-year-old Britisher in a black satin shirt and white leather tie and black leather trousers, poked his face in.

"They're waitin', luv," Edward said.

"How many?"

"Joey screened 'em down to half a dozen. Choice ones." But Edward's voice betrayed boredom. This ritual took place every night after the show.

"Show 'em in."

The groupies crowded into the dressing room; the scent of perfume and pot and perspiration made a heady cocktail for the nostrils that sickened and excited Peter. He never tired of the smell of them, or the look. Skinny, long-haired Joey, his personal assistant, knew Peter's type: slender, dark-haired, not too busty, not too flat, no silicone. Every night when the little group assembled, whatever the city, whatever the country, they might have been sisters, giggling, squealing with delight, their albums in hand, or their eight-by-ten glossies or possibly a *Rolling Stone* or *Spin* cover clutched in slender, black-nailed fingers.

Even the clothing was similar. Peter had told an interviewer with *Sassy* magazine what his ideal woman wore—torn jeans, a leather jacket, and a halter top—and ever since, that had been the groupie army's uniform; they were lined up, this latest little battalion, beaming before him with the scarlet lipstick glistening on full lips, the heavy eye makeup, the pale powdered complexions, all reflecting his public pronouncements of feminine perfection.

Willowy young women in black-leather biker jackets, Samantha Fox torn jeans (not just their knees, but portions of thigh and ass showing through the fashionably torn places), cupcake breasts high and barely covered by bandanna halter tops.

"You are so cool," they would say. Funny, after all these years that word was still around: "Cool."

And his response still worked just as well: "You look so hot."

They would flush with pride and excitement; every night it was the same, as he moved in and around and through them, signing their albums and pictures, rubbing against them, looking them over, choosing a victim.

Usually it was just as simple as picking the prettiest one; there was always a prettiest one.

Tonight, however, it was different.

One of the young women stood just a little taller; that was the one real difference between her and the other leather-jacketed, torn-jeaned, bandanna-haltered girls. That was the only thing that truly set her apart.

Except for her eyes.

Huge eyes, deeply brown, heavy mascara only emphasizing incredible long, real lashes. Her eyes—fathomless eyes—pierced him, held him. Hypnotized him.

"You are so hot," she said to him coolly.

"What's your name?" he asked her, about to sign her *Hellgate* album, Peter's latest.

"Marya," she said.

"Like in *Dracula's Daughter*," he said.

"What can I say?" She smiled; her teeth were sparkling white. "My mother loved horror movies."

Their eyes locked; he felt dizzy.

"Marya," he whispered, "can you stick around?"

"Thought you'd never ask. . . ."

Joey rounded up the other girls, who were to be ushered into the dressing room of Coven for more autographs and, for those girls who were interested, other fun and games. Passing along his rejects was a crumb Peter regularly tossed his bandmates.

When Peter and Marya were alone, the groupie found the zipper of his fly and teasingly lowered and raised it.

"Now?" she purred.

"When else?"

"I thought you might ask me back to your hotel."

"I—I'm wasted, babe. I gotta crash."

"I understand. Are you too tired to . . . ?"

"No!" He unzipped himself and fished out his already engorged dick. He was throbbing. There was something special about her. Something beyond sexual. . . . Not a bad line for a song, he noted, storing it away: *something beyond sexual*. . . .

"I'll just turn out the light," she said, and moved fluidly to the door.

Streetlight was filtering in through a wire-mesh window, so he could see her return to him, moving like a shadow in the blue near-dark, to lower herself to her knees, take his member between her cool hands, and place her warm, bruised lips around its head. Her big eyes stared up hypnotically at him as she slowly, sensually swallowed the sword of his dick, right down to the pubic bone, nuzzling her pretty nose in his hair, making a sound that was part purr, part growl.

It sometimes took him forever to come. As blasé as he had become about this act (and fucking was worse, fucking barely interested him anymore) he sometimes had to work these poor little groupies till their hair was dripping unbecomingly with sweat and their eyes were filled with discomfort and their jaws ached; he would reward their dedication with the usual spuzzle in the yap, and the less experienced of them sometimes choked, which was their problem, he figured. If they didn't have any more self-respect than to go around sucking some stranger's cock, who gave a fuck if they choked and died?

But this was different. Marya was no inexperienced kid, halting, fumbling, awkward, treating a man's dick with the delicacy of a glutton gobbling a bratwurst. No—this young woman could take him all the way down into her throat, and the lubrication was incredible, the warmth, the satiny smoothness of it, jarred only slightly by an occasional nick of her teeth.

Less than a minute had passed when her rhythmic bobbing motion increased speed, sucking, sucking, sucking the soul out of him, and he exploded in her mouth, and she kept sucking, but slowly now, gently, bringing him to an easy, semilimp finish, smiling up at him with a naughty whitesmeared smile, which she greedily licked at, her pointy pink tongue getting every drop of him, savoring every morsel.

The last girl had choked and spat him out and damn near puked. Real fucking romantic.

But this Marya . . . she was still staring up at him dreamily with wide, brown, hypnotic eyes, swaying as she pumped him gently, licking at every last droplet she could milk.

He helped her to her feet and held her in his arms; he

didn't want to kiss her—that would be gross. But he wanted to hold her, an emotional gesture that wasn't just rare, it was a first. These groupies were human Kleenex for him to beat off into. This young woman was . . . she was something very different, very special.

"Maybe you *could* come to the hotel with me," he said.

"Not this time," she said, and smiled in a sweet-nasty way, her big eyes slitted seductively; she pecked him on the cheek.

Then she was gone, flicking on the light as she left, and he was standing there with his dick hanging out.

He was tucking it away when Joey ducked back in.

"*That's* a sweet little piece," Joey said, raising an eyebrow.

"You get a good look at her?" Peter asked.

"Yeah, sure. So?"

"So if you ever spot her again at one of my shows, bring her around after."

"But you never use the same bitch twice."

"Rules are made to be broken," Peter said, quoting the opening line of one his biggest hits.

"Fuckin' A," Joey said, with an upward thumb gesture, and went back out.

Peter slipped into his studded leather jacket and waited for the security guys to come around to usher him to his limo in the alley. By now, he would normally have forgotten the face, form, and most certainly the name of the groupie who'd been granted his nightly gift.

But tonight, all he could see in his mind's eye was Marya: her face, her semen-streaked smile, the mesmerizing gaze of those big, long-lashed brown eyes.

"What am I," he said to himself, "in love?"

And laughed harshly.

But it caught in his throat, and he choked for a second, like those poor groupies did so often.

The next night, in Peoria, he rushed backstage for his shower and was toweling off when Joey came round.

"Is she here?" Peter asked.

"Who?"

"Marya! The girl from last night!"

"Oh. No. But tonight you got a sweet little corn-fed crop to choose from—"

"Forget it," Peter said, and threw his towel on the makeup table. "Just fuckin' forget it."

Joey looked at him like he was nuts, shrugged, and went out.

Peter was morose when he slipped into the bubbling whirlpool in his suite at the Marriott. Tired as he was from tonight's performance, he remained tense; even the churning water, the hot sprays, couldn't unloosen his knotted muscles. He thought about the liquor in the minibar in the outer room and considered falling off the wagon, just this once, just tonight, just to relax. . . .

"Hope you don't mind," a sultry voice purred.

He looked over his shoulder; through the fog of steam he saw her there—an apparition? A mirage? Had he fallen asleep in the hot tub, and was he even now drowning below its cauldronlike surface?

She was naked, a slender, faintly muscular, high-breasted vision, pale as a ghost, the darkness of her trimmed pubic triangle a stark focal point; her similarly dark, pixie-cut hair framed a face whose features were indistinct, but for the large brown eyes and the mischievous scarlet slash of her smile.

"Marya . . ." He was smiling like a kid on Christmas morning, only this gift was already unwrapped.

She slithered into the hot tub, leaned luxuriously back against the edge opposite him, her peachlike breasts bobbing on the bubbling surface.

"How did you get in here?" he asked breathlessly.

"Does it matter? Maybe I flew in the window."

"I didn't think you were at the gig tonight."

"I wasn't. Couldn't get tickets. But anyway, it wasn't your *show* I wanted to see . . . it was you."

She glided over and wrapped her lithe body around him, enveloping him, her mouth on his, tongue searching greedily.

Her breath was hot on his face. "I hope you didn't give it away to one of those little groupies tonight."

"No . . . I was hoping to see you."

"Saving up for me?" Her smile dimpled one cheek. "I thought you might."

Then she disappeared below the surface of the foaming water, and her lips locked onto him under there, and she began working him. . . .

It was ecstasy, but it was going on and on, and she wasn't coming up, and he pulled her to the surface. "Are you crazy? Do you want to drown?"

"I could never drown drinking you, Peter." She brushed back her wet black hair; her face streamed with droplets of water. She was radiant. Glowing. "You give me life."

And she disappeared below the surface and sucked him and sucked him, and he felt himself gushing into the warmth of her oral embrace.

She rose from beneath the water, shaking her head regally, her smile luminous.

He felt drained.

But he finally felt relaxed, too.

She stayed the night, and they slept a little, and she sucked him dry two more times; and they talked.

Pillows propped behind her, her pert breasts standing up though the nipples were flattened, she asked, "Have you always been fascinated by death? And horror?"

"I suppose," he said. "But not the real thing. You never met anybody more squeamish."

Her smile turned crinkly. "No kidding? The rock star who's famous for rock-concert bloodbaths?"

He laughed a little. "I'm afraid so. Maybe that's why I was so attracted to horror movies. . . . I remember seeing a bad car accident when I was a little kid. Dead people scattered around on the highway... bloody limbs..." He shuddered.

"How did you happen to see that? Was your family just driving by?"

"No. My father was a driver's ed teacher. He thought... he thought I should learn at an early age about the dangers of the highway. Some of my earliest memories are those gruesome driver's ed movies—remember those?"

"Sure! Highway carnage! We always looked forward to 'em."

"I liked them, too. Every kid likes stuff like that. But my dad thought I ought to see the real thing, so when there was this bad accident out on the highway, he took me there."

She winced. "Jeez. How old were you?"

"Eight. Nine, maybe. A fat lady was pinned in one of the cars, wedged inside the front seat, arms flailing up out of the broken windshield, and she was covered with blood and she was screaming...." He shook his head, trying to banish the image. "It was awful. Ever since then, even the slightest cut, just the sight of blood, sickens me."

"Amazing. But your shows splatter the front several rows of your audiences with blood every night! It's worse than a Gallagher concert!"

"Stage blood," he noted. "I've always been able to separate fantasy from reality, Marya. Fantasy is safe. Reality isn't."

"So that explains the fascination with horror."

"Right. I read *Famous Monsters* and *Fangoria* as a kid. Listened to Alice Cooper and Black Sabbath records. Bought reprints of fifties horror comics. Collected videotapes of the Universal and Hammer horror movies."

"That's why you changed your name."

He grinned at her. "You are good—where'd you get that, the *Sassy* interview? Yeah, 'Peter' for Peter Cushing and 'Lee' for Christopher Lee."

"Your favorite Hammer horror stars."

"Besides, my real name just doesn't cut it."

She smiled wickedly, folding her arms across the pert breasts. "Oh, I don't know . . . I think Daryl Beesley has a certain ring."

He laughed once. "The ring of nerddom."

"You? A nerd? Never."

He didn't know what it was about her—the luminous eyes, perhaps—that made him open up so; he never talked about himself like this to anybody, particularly not a woman. Particularly not some cocksucking groupie, which a part of his mind kept reminding him she was. . . .

But he heard himself saying, "I was the nerd to end all nerds. A four-eyed, friendless, comic-book-collecting geek."

"What happened?"

"I went off to college on a scholarship, to Athens, Georgia. I dropped out of school the second semester, 'cause by that time the band was formed and we were making some noise. I developed a whole new persona . . . and we got signed to a record deal, or rather I got signed."

"The band you were playing with wasn't Coven?"

"No. The record company wasn't interested in them, just me. We put together a band consisting of mostly session guys, though they had to have decent stage presence. The focus has never been on the band—just on me."

"Where it belongs."

"Well, I do all the songwriting, I front it . . . they're just paid employees. If one of them starts getting too much press or too much attention or his head starts getting big"—he drew a finger across his throat—"off with it."

"That's why there's been so much turnover in the band, then."

"Right. Marya, in show business you got to watch people every minute. It's full of bloodsuckers. Fucking leeches!"

Her smile turned teasing. "You don't like bloodsuckers?"

"No."

"Maybe that's because you don't understand a simple scientific fact."

"Such as?"

She smiled wryly. "Semen and blood are identical, chemically speaking."

"No kidding?"

"No kidding. So maybe you don't want me around, if I'm going to be doing this. . . ."

And she drew back the covers and buried her head in his crotch.

A few minutes later she was looking up at him, licking white droplets, catching every one, saying, "From that goofy grin on your face, I'd say you've decided to make an exception in my case. . . ."

When he woke up the next morning, she was gone. He found her note by the open window, the slip of paper rippling in the fall breeze, held down only by a gold ring with a black stone.

"Obsidian," her note explained. "The stone of the night. Think of me then. This gift is in thanks for the love gifts you've given me. Your scream queen, Marya."

He put the ring on the fourth finger of his left hand; a perfect fit. He could see himself in the shiny stone.

When he went east with the tour, Peter didn't expect to see Marya again, and for a time he didn't. He tried to resume his practice of nightly anonymous groupie blowjobs, but at first it took him forever to come, and finally he couldn't get it up at all. She had ruined him. Marya, with her come-hungry mouth sucking like a warm, moist vacuum and those huge hypnotic eyes staring up slavishly at him, made these girls seem like the amateur night they were.

It turned him surly, and backstage in Pittsburgh, when he arrived early at sound check, he caught two of his roadies in his dressing room in faggot flagrante delicto.

Billy had his pants around his knees, and Arnie was on his knees in front of him.

"Jesus!" Peter exploded. "In my own goddamn dressing room! You're fired! Both of you! Fucking fired!"

Embarrassed and humiliated, these two who Peter had

figured for your normal macho males fled his dressing room in shame and near tears. It made him sick.

Edward tried to reason with him. "You can't fire them over this, luv. It's terribly . . . politically incorrect."

"Yeah, right—like my show is on the Political Correctness A-List already!"

"Luv . . . it's none of our business what these lads do in private."

"Well, their privates were doing it in my dressing room, so they're fuckin' fired! And don't talk about unions to me, either! Get rid of them—pay 'em off."

"Honestly, Peter. Your homophobic attitudes are so . . . backward."

"Get rid of them, Edward, or I get rid of you next."

"Anything you say, luv."

The show was sluggish that night; there were missed cues, some squealing feedback, forgotten lyrics. Some of it was him, some of it was his off night rubbing off on everybody else. Backstage, he lit into his techies, then headed for the dressing room and showered and sat naked at his makeup mirror, staring at a face that seemed goddamn old to him.

Joey peeked in.

"Don't you fucking knock anymore?" Peter spat.

"Sorry. I, uh, got somethin' for you."

"I told you. Next time I'm in the mood, I'll tell *you*. I'm bored with these hollow-cheeked little whores. Got it?"

"You're not bored with this one, Pete."

"Go the fuck away, Joey."

"It's her. Your dream date."

"Marya?"

Joey smirked and nodded, his greasy shaggy hair swaying.

"Give me two seconds, then show her in."

He slipped into his jeans and stood waiting.

She wasn't wearing the groupie uniform tonight. She wore a black zip-up-the-front jumpsuit that clung to her like skin; her pixie hair was moussed up, her scarlet lips pulled back over brilliant white teeth.

"You need me tonight, don't you, Daryl?"

He grinned at her. "If anybody else called me that . . ."

"You'd kill 'em? A squeamish nerd like you?" She turned off the light switch. "C'mere, big boy. . . ."

He went to her and they kissed; then she slipped to her knees, found his zipper, and this time he had no trouble getting up, or painting the inside of her throat white, either.

In his hotel suite, they lounged in another whirlpool, the air pleasantly steamy, foggy, his arm around her.

He bit at her ear playfully. "Didn't expect to see you on the East Coast."

"Some of us star-fuckers get around."

"Don't say that."

"What?"

"I don't like to think of you with other guys."

She shrugged. "I don't mind you being with other girls. Or women. Or even guys."

"Don't say that!"

"What?"

"Guys." He shuddered. "I just had to bounce a couple of gay boys."

"Ah . . . you mustn't be prejudiced. It's just another alternative lifestyle. It doesn't make you *bad,* when you have an alternative lifestyle. You're not exactly *Saturday Evening Post* material yourself."

"I don't want to talk about it. It's unnatural."

"Is it unnatural when I do this?"

And she bobbed her head beneath the surface of the churning water and found him and sucked him again; he didn't think he had anything left in him, and he ached as he spewed into her. She came up and seemed to be savoring him, rolling him around inside her mouth.

"Nothing unnatural. It's sweet," she said, pink tongue licking white dabs off scarlet lips. "Well, actually . . . salty." And she giggled.

This turn of conversation disturbed him, and he crawled from the hot tub, found his towel, dried off, and headed for the bedroom. She snuggled naked against him.

"You're still wearing my ring," she said.
"Never take it off."
"You'd think you were in love or something."
"Maybe I am."
She looked at him, touched his face gently with black-nailed fingertips. "What do you want most?"
"What do you mean?"
"In life. What do you want most?"
"To stay young, I guess."
"To live forever?"
He laughed shortly. "Sure. Like they say, rock 'n' roll will never die. Unfortunately, a hell of a lot of rock stars *do*. And most of the rest of them would be better off if they would."
"What do you mean?"
"I mean, rock's a young man's game. Didn't you ever notice I don't do drugs or booze? You think that's 'cause I'm clean-cut? What did you say before—a *Saturday Evening Post* kind of guy? Is that what you see?"
"Not really."
"Right. I abstain, and I work out with weights, just trying to beat this fucking age thing."
"But you've had a wonderful ride. How long is it since *Hell Hounds?* Four years?"
"Five."
"That's a long time at the top, in your business."
"Tell me about it. The thing is, I've got the chops, both performing *and* songwriting, to stay at the top indefinitely. But to the next group of kids coming up, I'm going to start seeming like an old fucking geezer. Particularly if I *look* like one. . . ."
"Have you considered plastic surgery?"
"Do I look that bad already?"
She smiled gently. "No. But when the time comes . . . why not?"
"Go under the knife? Have you forgotten how squeamish I am? I hate the sight of blood—particularly my own!"
"They'd put you under."
"I'd freak. I'd completely freak. Or I might wind *up* a

freak, like that queen Michael Jackson. They've carved enough off him to make it the Jackson Six."

"Poor Peter," she said, stroking his face. "Poor, poor Peter. . . ."

He looked at her to see if she was making fun; but there was no irony in her expression or her tone.

"Maybe there's a way, my sweet," he thought he heard her say before he drifted off to sleep.

When he woke to sunlight streaking between hotel-room shades, he found her gone again. No note this time. No gift . . . other than the lingering memory of her.

On the rest of the East Coast leg of the tour, no sign of her. He began, after shows and into the night, getting the shakes, the likes of which he hadn't had since the Betty Ford Clinic.

At his hotel room in Newark, the private detective he'd hired in New York two weeks before came around with a hangdog expression. He was a balding, mustached man in his fifties with a paunch and a cigar; the only thing private-eye-ish about him was the rumpled trench coat.

"I couldn't get much of anything on her," he said, sitting on a couch in the outer room. "Other than what you already know."

"What do you mean?" Peter asked from the minibar, where he was opening a bottle of nonalcoholic beer.

"Her description and her name, well, she's well known backstage at most rock shows. If there's a dick in rock 'n' roll she hasn't sucked, I'd like to see it. So to speak."

Peter hated to hear that. Hated to! "You couldn't trace her?"

"Hell, man—you don't even know what town she's from! You first ran into her in Chicago, and I did some rudimentary checks there, but that's a big pond to locate a little fish in—if it's even her pond!"

"I know, I know."

"One thing odd, though. . . ."

"What's that?"

"I was checking out this auditorium in Jersey City, and

there was this oldies show. The night before, they'd had Guns 'n' Assholes or somebody, you know—the latest dipshits on the block. No offense, but rock 'n' roll has sucked since the Beatles broke up."

"Was there a point you meant to make?"

"Oh, yeah! The afternoon I was poking around there, they were getting ready for an oldies show. Some guy with one of those old British acts—Kinks or Gerry and the Pacemakers or Herman's Hermits or somebody—overheard me talking to the stage manager. He said he knew Marya Morrison from the old days."

"What?"

"Said there was a chickie named Marya Morrison who did the groupie circuit back in the sixties. She was one of the original Plaster Casters . . . you know, hippie chicks who would dip a guy's dick in plaster of paris and make themselves a swell souvenir."

"Marya couldn't be that old. That's ridiculous."

He shrugged. "Maybe it's her mom. Anyway, this chick back in the sixties was also named Marya Morrison and she was described by this Brit as being able to 'suck the chrome off a Bentley.'"

"Just a coincidence."

"Probably. Anyway, you've used up your retainer. You want me to keep digging?"

"Think you can find anything else?"

"Probably not—but I'm always willing to take a client's money."

"Thanks, but no thanks."

Peter showed the detective out and went back to his near-beer. He sat sipping the flavorless stuff, doing the math in his mind: If Marya was, say, sixteen in 1968, she'd be in her forties today . . . was that possible?

No, he told himself. He thought of her smooth, pale, flawless skin: *No.*

The last show of the tour was at the Coliseum in L.A., and the house was packed; he spotted Marya in the front row and it sparked the most enthusiastic performance he'd mustered in weeks. The zombie finale had been expanded for this venue, and the blood-splattering of his Uzi send-off sent the front rows into a frenzy. They swayed and shrieked down there, splashed with red, although among them Marya was more composed, smiling mysteriously, her huge hypnotic eyes locked on him like brown lasers.

Backstage, in his dressing room, they showered together—she had to get the red stage blood off herself, after all—and she got down on her knees in the shadowed stall, but for once her magic didn't work.

She followed him, dripping wet, out of the shower; he toweled off, his back to her. He glanced in the mirror, didn't see her, and turned suddenly.

"Where'd you go?" he said.

"I'm right here." She moved to him, took the towel, and dried herself, gazing at him soulfully. "What is it? What's wrong?"

"Nothing."

"It's something. Tell me, Peter."

He shook his head. "I can't stand the thought of it . . . you with other men."

She touched his face, petted him with the backs of her knuckles. "There are no other men but you, Peter."

"Do you mean that?"

"Of course I do. Take me home with you?"

He took her to his place in the Hollywood hills, and they swam in the moonlight in his pool, naked, free. In his outdoor hot tub, the stars above them, they kissed, held each other.

"I've never even made love to you," he said.

"Sure you have."

"I've never been inside you."

"You've been inside me many times."

"In your mouth. But not . . . *inside.*"

She shrugged a little, smiled a wry half-smile. "I figured you were . . . afraid of AIDS. A blow-job from a groupie isn't as risky as fucking her."

"Don't!"
"What?"
"You make it sound so harsh. So awful. I love you, Marya. I want to spend my life with you. I'd spend eternity with you, if I could."

Her wry expression faded, and something yearning and even tragic seemed to cross her perfect features, her pale face.

"Do you mean that?"
"You know I do."

He made love to her on the silk sheets of his round bed, driving himself into her, savagely, tenderly, and she was silken inside, she was wonderful, but at the moment of climax, with her on top, she ducked down and drank his seed greedily, using her hands to gather what her lips had missed, licking it off her fingertips, her tongue searching, seeking every morsel of it, until her smiling face was wet with only her saliva.

"You are an oral little thing," he said with a half-smile and raised eyebrow.

"Hope you don't mind," she said.
"How old are you?"
"What?"
"How old are you?"
"Old enough."

He was dreaming about the accident, the one his father had taken him to, dreaming of the fat woman trapped in the car, trying to squeeze out of the broken glass; there was blood everywhere, and the sound of pain, screams of agony, but suddenly the woman in the car wasn't obese, not grotesque in any way: She was Marya, and he could see himself in the dream, going to her, helping her out of the twisted wreckage, pulling her up through the broken glass of the windshield; but as he took her into his arms and she put her arms around his, his neck grazed the broken glass and he felt the puncture, and the spurt, the spurt of blood. . . .

Then he was underwater, and Marya was locked in his

arms, entwined with him, he was in her, and he came and came and came, in an endless orgasm as vast as the sea that enveloped them. . . .

He woke and she was still in his arms, but in bed with him, her face buried in his neck; it had been a dream.

Only his neck felt wet, and it hurt, as if the puncture had really happened.

He lifted her off him and her scarlet mouth was running with red, and her brilliant white teeth were dipped with red, her canines extended and razor-sharp. Her eyes had an animal gleam. The sound from her throat was not a purr, but it was catlike, all right. . . .

Then he gasped and passed out.

When he woke with a start, before dawn, she was not in bed beside him.

Two such strange dreams—a dream within a dream. Very Brian De Palma, he thought. He rose but felt weak, his legs wobbly. Naked, he stumbled to the bathroom.

He threw water on his face, then noticed that his neck—where he had dreamed the glass punctured him—ached; he touched it with his fingertips and felt the two wounds.

But when he went to look in the mirror, he could not see his own reflection.

He backed up, looking at his hands, looking down at himself; the gold ring's shiny obsidian stone stared back at him blankly. Was he still dreaming?

"You're not dreaming, Peter," her voice said behind him.

But her image was not in the mirror either.

When he turned, she was standing behind him in the large marble bathroom. She wore a black negligee. Her high breasts, her long legs, her slender shape looked unreal, dreamlike in their perfect beauty.

"Come with me," she said, and extended a hand to him.

Negligee fluttering in the gentle wind, she walked him out into the night—actually, the early morning hours—and they stood looking down at the lights of Hollywood. The night was a glittering thing, jewels scattered on black velvet.

"You asked my age," she said. "I'm sixty-five."
"What?"
"I was a bobby-soxer when I drank from Frankie. I wore a poodle skirt when I took the King's love potion. I was a hippie chick when—"
"Stop! This is insane!"
She stroked his face, smiled sweetly. "Peter, in all those years, you're the first man I've wanted to share eternity with. You're the first man worthy of the gift."
"Gift?"
"You'll be a star forever, now. You're like me."
"And what are *you*?"
She looked away, as if shy. "A nervous girl who was seduced many years ago by an older man. A squeamish girl who can't stand the sight of blood. I was a virgin until last night."
"Virgin?"
"I've never bitten a neck before. The cruelty of it, the thought of blood . . . I've nourished myself by dropping to my knees, accordingly. The chemical content of semen and blood are identical—remember?"
"I'm supposed to believe that you're a—a vampire?"
"And so are you. And we're a team now. Forever. You don't have to worry about aging. You may have to change your persona as the years go by. Music will change on us, as it always does. But you'll make adjustments—as I have."
"I'm a vampire," he said derisively. "Right."
"Did you see yourself in the mirror? You're a horror fan, Peter: Think about it. No—we're together now. But you'll have to be . . . understanding. As will I."
He pulled away from her. "What the hell are you talking about?"
"The chemical makeup of your semen has changed, Peter. It's as dead as you are. I need to seek sustenance elsewhere. We can make love, but we can't feed each other."
"This is fucking nonsense. Are you high? Ohhh! Owww . . . what's wrong with me?"
"It's dawn! Quick. Inside!"

The burning pain racking him convinced him, at least for the moment, of what she was saying.

"To the basement!" she said.

"This is California! There is no basement."

Soon they were cowering in a closet. Light came in from under and around the door, but not sunlight. Head spinning, he wondered if the dream—this nightmare—would ever end.

"If you are to survive," she told him as she huddled in one corner, he in the other, "you'll have to overcome one of your aversions."

"What the hell do you mean?"

"Either you overcome your squeamishness about blood," she said, "and seek your supper like most vampires. . . ."

"Or?"

"Or you'll have to get it like I do. I'm sorry, my sweet. You'll have to . . ." She made an O of her mouth.

"Never!"

"You don't have to decide just yet," she said, and she moved close, snuggled next to him. "You won't have to come out of the closet till nightfall."

DRUMBEATS

Kevin J. Anderson and Neil Peart

After nine months of touring across North America—with hotel suites and elaborate dinners and clean sheets every day—it felt good to be hot and dirty, muscles straining not for the benefit of any screaming audience, but just to get to the next village up the dusty road, where none of the natives recognized Danny Imbro or knew his name. To them, he was just another White Man, an exotic object of awe for little children, a target of scorn for drunken soldiers at border checkpoints.

Bicycling through Africa was about the furthest thing from a rock concert tour that Danny could imagine—which was why he'd done it, after promoting the latest Blitzkrieg album and performing each song until the tracks were worn smooth in his head. This cleared his mind, gave him a sense of balance, perspective.

The other members of Blitzkrieg did their own things

during the group's break months. Phil, whom they called the "music machine" because he couldn't *stop* writing music, spent his relaxation time cranking out film scores for Hollywood; Reggie caught up on his reading, soaking up grocery bags full of political thrillers and mysteries; Shane turned into a vegetable on Maui. But Danny Imbro took his expensive-but-battered bicycle and bummed around West Africa. The others thought it strangely appropriate that the band's drummer would go off hunting for tribal rhythms.

Late in the afternoon on the sixth day of his ride through Cameroon, Danny stopped in a large open market and bus depot in the town of Garoua. The marketplace was a line of mud-brick kiosks and chophouses, the air filled with the smell of baked dust and stones, hot oil and frying *beignets*. Abandoned cars squatted by the roadside, stripped clean but unblemished by corrosion in the dry air. Groups of men and children in long blouses like nightshirts idled their time away on the street corners.

Wives and daughters appeared on the road with their buckets, on their way to fetch water from the well on the other side of the marketplace. They wore bright-colored *pagnes* and kerchiefs, covering their traditionally naked breasts with T-shirts or castoff Western blouses, since the government in the capital city of Yaoundé had forbidden women to go topless.

At one kiosk in the shade sat a pan holding several bottles of Coca-Cola, Fanta, and ginger ale, cooling in water. Some vendors sold a thin stew of bony fish chunks over gritty rice; others sold *fufu,* a doughlike paste of pounded yams to be dipped into a sauce of meat and okra. Bread merchants stacked their long baguettes like dry firewood.

Danny used the back of his hand to smear sweat-caked dust off his forehead, then removed the bandanna that he wore under his helmet to keep the sweat out of his eyes. With streaks of white skin peeking through the layer of grit around his eyes, he probably looked like some strange lemur, he thought.

In halting French, he began haggling with a wiry boy over

a bottle of water. Hiding behind his kiosk, the boy demanded eight hundred francs for the water, an outrageous price. While Danny was attempting to bargain it down, he caught sight of a gaunt, grayish-skinned man walking through the marketplace like a windup toy running down.

The man was playing a drum.

The boy cringed and looked away. Danny kept staring. The crowd seemed to shrink away from the strange man as he wandered among them, continuing his incessant beat. He wore his hair long and unruly, which in itself was unusual among the close-cropped Africans. In the equatorial heat, the long, stained overcoat he wore must have heated his body like a furnace, but the man did not seem to notice. His eyes were focused on some invisible point in the distance.

"Huit-cent francs," the boy insisted on his price, holding the lukewarm bottle of water just out of Danny's reach.

The staggering man walked closer, tapping a slow, monotonous beat on the small cylindrical drum under his arm. He did not change his tempo, but continued to play as if his life depended on it. Danny saw that the man's fingers and wrists were wrapped in scraps of hide; even so, he had beaten his fingertips bloody.

Danny stood transfixed. He had heard tribal musicians play all manner of percussion instruments, from hollowed tree trunks to rusted metal cans to beautifully carved *djembe* drums with goatskin drumheads—but he had never heard a tone so rich and sweet, with such an odd echoey quality as this strange African drum.

In the studio, he had messed around with drum synthesizers and reverbs and the new technology designed to turn computer hackers into musicians. But this drum sounded *different,* solid and pure, and it hooked him through the heart, hypnotizing him. It distracted him entirely from the unpleasant appearance of its bearer.

"What is that?" he asked.

"Sept-cent francs," the boy said in a nervous whisper, dropping his price and pushing the water closer.

Danny walked in front of the staggering man, smiling

broadly enough to show the grit between his teeth, and listened to the tapping drumbeat. The drummer turned his gaze to Danny and stared through him. The pupils of his eyes were like two gaping bullet wounds through his skull. Danny took a step backward, but found himself moving to the beat. The drummer faced him, finding his audience. Danny tried to place the rhythm, to burn it into his mind—something this mesmerizing simply *had* to be included in a new Blitzkrieg song.

Danny looked at the cylindrical drum, trying to determine what might be causing its odd double resonance—a thin inner membrane, perhaps? He saw nothing but elaborate carvings on the sweat-polished wood, and a drumhead with a smooth, dark brown coloration. He knew the Africans used all kinds of skin for their drumheads, and he couldn't begin to guess what this was.

He mimed a question to the drummer, then asked, *"Est-ce-que je peux l'essayer?"* May I try it?

The gaunt man said nothing, but held out the drum near enough for Danny to touch it without interrupting his obsessive rhythm. His overcoat flapped open, and the hot stench of decay made Danny stagger backward, but he held his ground, reaching for the drum.

Danny ran his fingers over the smooth drumskin, then tapped with his fingers. The deep sound resonated with a beat of its own, like a heartbeat. It delighted him. "For sale? *Est-ce-que c'est à vendre?"* He took out a thousand francs as a starting point, although if water alone cost eight hundred here, this drum was worth much, much more.

The man snatched the drum away and clutched it to his chest, shaking his head vigorously. His drumming hand continued its unrelenting beat.

Danny took out two thousand francs, then was disappointed to see not the slightest change of expression on the odd drummer's face. "Okay, then, where was the drum made? Where can I get another one? *Où est-ce qu'on peut trouver un autre comme ça?"* He put most of the money back into his pack, and stuffed the remaining two hundred francs into the fist of the drummer; the man's hand seemed to be made of petrified wood. *"Où?"*

The man scowled, then gestured behind him, toward the Mandara Mountains along Cameroon's border with Nigeria. "Kabas."

He turned and staggered away, still tapping on his drum as if to mark his footsteps. Danny watched him go, then returned to the kiosk, unfolding the map from his pack. "Where is this Kabas? Is it a place? *C'est un village?"*

"Huit-cent francs," the boy said, offering the water again at his original price.

Danny bought the water, and the boy gave him directions.

He spent the night in a Garouan hotel that made Motel 6 look like Caesars Palace. Anxious to be on his way to find his own new drum, Danny roused a local vendor and cajoled him into preparing a quick omelet for breakfast. He took a sip from his eight-hundred-franc bottle of water, saving the rest for the long bike ride, then pedaled off into the stirring sounds of early morning.

As Danny left Garoua on the main road, heading toward the mountains, savanna and thorn trees stretched away under a crystal sky. A pair of doves bathed in the dust of the road ahead, but as he rode toward them, they flew up into the last of the trees with *chuk-chuks* of alarm and a flash of white tail feathers. Smoke from grass fires on the plains tainted the air.

How different it was to be riding *through* a landscape, he thought—with no walls or windows between his senses and the world—rather than just riding *by* it. Danny felt the road under his thin wheels, the sun, the wind on his body. It made a strange place less exotic, yet it became infinitely more real.

The road out of Garoua was a wide boulevard that turned into a smaller road heading north. With his bicycle tires humming and crunching on the irregular pavement, Danny passed a few ragged cotton fields, then entered the plains of dry, yellow grass and thorny scrub, everywhere studded with boulders and sculpted anthills. By seven-thirty in the morning, a hot breeze rose, carrying a honeysucklelike perfume. Everything vibrated with heat.

Within an hour the road grew worse, but Danny kept his pace, taking deep breaths in the trancelike state that kept the horizon moving closer. Drums. Kabas. Long rides helped him clear his head, but he found he had to concentrate to steer around the worst ruts and the biggest stones.

Great columns of stone appeared above the hills to east and west. One was pyramid-shaped, one resembled a huge rounded breast, yet another a great stone phallus. Danny had seen photographs of these inselberg formations caused by volcanoes that had eroded over the eons, leaving behind vertical cores of lava.

The road here, too, was eroded, a heaving washboard, which veered left into a trough between tumbled boulders and up through a gauntlet of thorn trees. Danny stopped for another drink of water, another glance at the map. The water boy at the kiosk had marked the location of Kabas with his fingernail, but it was not printed on the map.

After Danny had climbed uphill for an hour, the beaten path became no more than a worn trail, forcing him to squeeze between walls of thorns and dry millet stalks. The squadrons of hovering dragonflies were harmless, but the hordes of tiny flies circling his face were maddening, and he couldn't pedal fast enough to escape them.

It was nearly noon, the sun reflecting straight up from the dry earth, and the little shade cast by the scattered trees dwindled to a small circle around the trunks. "Where the hell am I going?" he said to the sky.

But in his head he kept hearing the odd, potent beat resonating from the bizarre drum he had seen in the Garoua marketplace. He recalled the grayish, shambling man who had never once stopped tapping on his drum, even though his fingers bled. No matter how bad the road got, Danny thought, he would keep going. He'd never been so intrigued by a drumbeat before, and he never left things half finished.

Danny Imbro was a goal-oriented person. The other

members of Blitzkrieg razzed him about it, that once he made up his mind to do something, he plowed ahead, defying all common sense. Back in school, he had made up his mind to be a drummer. He had hammered away at just about every object in sight with his fingertips, pencils, silverware, anything that made noise. He kept at it until he drove everyone else around him nuts, and somewhere along the line he became good.

Now people stood at the chain-link fences behind concert halls and applauded whenever he walked from the backstage dressing rooms out to the tour buses—as if he were somehow doing a better job of *walking* than any of them had ever seen before. . . .

Up ahead an enormous buttress tree, a gnarled and twisted pair of trunks hung with cable-thick vines, cast a wide patch of shade. Beneath the tree, watching him approach, sat a small boy.

The boy leaped to his feet as if he had been waiting for Danny. Shirtless and dusty, he held a hooklike withered arm against his chest; but his grin was completely disarming. *"Je suis guide?"* the boy called.

Relief stifled Danny's laugh. He nodded vigorously. *"Oui!"* Yes, he could certainly use a guide right about now. *"Je cherche Kabas—village des tambours.* The village of drums."

The smiling boy danced around like a goat, jumping from rock to rock. He was pleasant-faced and healthy-looking, except for the crippled arm; his skin was very dark but his eyes had a slight Asian cast. He chattered in a high voice, a mixture of French and native dialect. Danny caught enough to understand that the boy's name was Anatole.

Before the boy led him on, though, Danny dismounted, leaning his bicycle against a boulder, and unzipped his pack to take out raisins, peanuts, and the dry remains of a baguette. Anatole watched him with wide eyes, and Danny gave him a handful of raisins, which the boy wolfed down. Small flies whined around their faces as they ate. Danny answered the boy's incessant questions with as few words as possible: Did he come from America, did black boys live there, why was he visiting Cameroon?

The short rest sank its soporific claws into him, but Danny decided not to give in. An afternoon siesta made a lot of sense, but now that he had his own personal guide to the village, he made it his goal not to stop again until they reached Kabas. "Okay?" Danny raised his eyebrows and struggled to his feet.

Anatole sprang out from the shade and fetched Danny's bike for him, struggling with one arm to keep it upright. After several trips to Africa, Danny had seen plenty of withered limbs, caused by childhood diseases, accidents, and bungled inoculations. Out here in the wilder areas, such problems were even more prevalent, and he wondered how Anatole managed to survive; acting as a "guide" for the rare travelers would hardly suffice.

Danny pulled out a hundred francs—an eighth of what he had paid for one bottle of water—and handed it to the boy, who looked as if he had just been handed the crown jewels. Danny figured he had probably made a friend for life.

Anatole trotted ahead, gesturing with his good arm. Danny pedaled after him.

The narrow valley captured a smear of greenness in the dry hills, with a cluster of mango trees, guava trees, and strange baobabs with eight-foot-thick trunks. Playing the knowledgeable tour guide, Anatole explained that the local women used the baobab fruits for baby formula if their breast milk failed. The villagers used another tree to manufacture an insect repellent.

The houses of Kabas blended into the landscape, because they were *of* the landscape—stones and branches and grass. The walls were made of dry mud, laid on a handful at a time, and the roofs were thatched into cones. Tiny pink and white stones studded the mud, sparkling like quartz in the sun.

At first the place looked deserted, but then an ancient man emerged from a turret-shaped hut. An enormous cutlass dangled from his waist, although the shrunken man looked as if it might take him an hour just to lift the blade. Anatole shouted something, then gestured for Danny to follow him. The great cutlass swayed against the old man's unsteady knees as he bowed slightly—or stooped—and greeted Danny in formal, unpracticed French. *"Bonsoir!"*

"Makonya," Danny said, remembering the local greeting from Garoua. He walked his bike in among the round and square buildings. A few chickens scratched in the dirt, and a pair of black-and-brown goats nosed between the huts. A sinewy, long-limbed old woman wearing only a loincloth tended a fire. He immediately started looking for the special drums, but saw none.

Within the village, a high-walled courtyard enclosed two round huts. Gravel covered the open area between them, roofed over with a network of serpent-shaped sticks supporting grass mats. This seemed to be the chief's compound. Anatole took Danny's arm and dragged him forward.

Inside the wall, a white-robed figure reclined in a canvas chair under an acacia tree. His handsome features had a North African cast, with thin lips over white teeth and a rakish mustache. His aristocratic head was wrapped in a red-and-white-checked scarf, and even in repose he was obviously tall. He looked every bit the romantic desert prince, like Rudolph Valentino in *The Sheik*. After greeting Danny in both French and the local language, the chief gestured for his visitor to sit beside him.

Before Danny could move, two other boys appeared carrying a rolled-up mat of woven grass, which they spread out for him. Anatole scolded them for horning in on his customer, but the two boys cuffed him and ignored his protests. Then the chief shouted at them all for disturbing his peace and drove the boys away. Danny watched them kicking Anatole as they scampered away, and he felt for his new friend, angry at how tough people picked on weaker ones the world over.

He sat cross-legged on the mat, and it took him only a

moment to begin reveling in the moment of relaxation. No cars or trucks disturbed the peace. He was miles from the nearest electricity, or glass window, or airplane. He sat looking up into the leaves of the acacia, listening to the quiet buzz of the villagers, and thought, "I'm living in a *National Geographic* documentary!"

Anatole stole back into the compound, bearing two bottles of warm Mirinda orange soda, which he gave to Danny and the chief. Other boys gathered under the tree, glaring at Anatole, then looking at Danny with ill-concealed awe.

After several moments of polite smiling and nodding, Danny asked the chief if all the boys were his children. Anatole assisted in the unnecessary translation.

"Oui," the chief said, patting his chest proudly. He claimed to have fathered thirty-one sons, which made Danny wonder if the women in the village found it politic to routinely claim the chief as the father of their babies. As with all remote African villages, though, many children died of various sicknesses. Just a week earlier, one of the babies had succumbed to a terrible fever, the chief said.

The chief asked Danny the usual questions about his country, whether any black men lived there, why had he visited Cameroon; then he insisted that Danny eat dinner with them. The women would prepare the village's specialty of chicken in peanut sauce.

Hearing this, the old sentry emerged with his cutlass, smiled widely at Danny, then disappeared around the side wall. The squawking of a terrified chicken erupted in the sleepy afternoon air, the sounds of a scuffle, and then the squawking stopped.

Finally, Danny asked the question that had brought him to Kabas in the first place: *"Moi, je suis musicien; je cherche les tambours speciaux."* He mimed rapping on a small drum, then turned to Anatole for assistance.

The chief sat up, startled, then nodded. He hammered on the air, mimicking drum playing, as if to make sure. Danny nodded. The chief clapped his hands and gestured for

Anatole to take Danny somewhere. The boy pulled Danny to his feet and, surrounded by other chattering boys, dragged him back out of the walled courtyard. Danny managed to turn around and bow to the chief.

After trooping up a stairlike terrace of rock, they entered the courtyard of another homestead. The main shelter was built of handmade blocks with a flat roof of corrugated metal. Anatole explained that this was the home of the local *sorcier,* or wizard.

Anatole called out, then gestured for Danny to follow through the low doorway. Inside the hut, the walls were hung with evidence of the *sorcier*'s trade—odd bits of metal, small carvings, bundles of fur and feathers, mortars full of powders and herbs, clay urns for water and millet beer, smooth skins curing as they hung from the roof poles. And drums.

"Tambours!" Anatole said, spreading his hands wide.

Judging from the craftsman's tools around the hut, the *sorcier* made the village's drums as well as stored them. Danny saw several small gourd drums, larger log drums, and hollow cylinders of every size, all intricately carved with serpentine symbols, circles feeding into spirals, lines tangled into knots.

Danny reached out to touch one—then the *sorcier* himself stood up from the shadows near the far wall. Danny bit off a startled cry as the lithe old man glided forward. The *sorcier* was tall and rangy, but his skin was a battleground of wrinkles, as if someone had clumsily fashioned him out of papier mâché.

"Pardon," Danny said. The wrinkled man had been sitting on a low stool, putting the finishing touches to a new drum.

Fixing his eyes on his visitor, the *sorcier* withdrew a medium-size drum from a niche in the wall. Closing his eyes, he tapped on it. The mud walls of the hut reverberated with the hollow vibration, an earthy, primal beat that resonated in Danny's bones. Danny grinned with awe. Yes! The gaunt man's drum had not been a fluke. The drums of

Kabas had some special construction that caused this hypnotic tone.

Danny reached out tentatively. The wrinkled man gave him an appraising look, then extended the drum enough for Danny to strike it. He tapped a few tentative beats, and laughed out loud when the instrument rewarded him with the same rich sound.

The *sorcier* turned away, taking the drum with him and returning it to its niche in the wall. In two flowing strides, the wrinkled man went to his stool in the shadows, picking up the drum he had been fashioning, moving it into the crack of light that seeped through the windows. Pointing, he spoke in a staccato dialect, which Anatole translated into pidgin French.

The *sorcier* was finishing a new drum today, Anatole said. Perhaps they would play it this evening, an initiation. The chief's baby son would have enjoyed that. From the baby's body, the *sorcier* had been able to salvage only enough skin to make this one small drum.

"What?" Danny said, looking down at the deep brown skin covering the top of the drum.

Anatole explained, as if it were the most ordinary thing in the world, that whenever one of the chief's many sons died, the *sorcier* used his skin to make one of Kabas's special drums. It had always been done.

Danny wrestled with that idea for a moment. On his first trip to Africa five years earlier, he had learned the wrenching truth of how different these cultures were from his own.

"Why?" he finally asked. *"Pourquoi?"*

He had seen other drums made entirely of human skin taken from slain enemies, fashioned in the shape of stunted bodies with gaping mouths; when they were tapped, a hollow sound came from the effigies' mouths. He knew that he was wrong for trying to impose his Western moral framework on the inhabitants of an alien land. I'm sorry, sir, but you'll have to check your preconceptions at the door, he thought jokingly to himself.

"Magique." Anatole's eyes showed a flash of fear—fear

born of respect for great power, rather than paranoia or panic. With the magic drums of Kabas, the chief could conquer any man, steal his heartbeat. It was old magic, a technique the village wizards had discovered long before the French had come to Cameroon, and before them the Germans. Kabas had been isolated, and at peace for longer than the memories of the oldest people in the village. Because of the drums. Anatole smiled, proud of his story, and Danny restrained an urge to pat him on the head.

Trying not to let his disbelief show, Danny nodded deeply to the *sorcier*. "*Merci,*" he said. As Anatole led him back out to the courtyard, the *sorcier* returned to his work on the small drum.

Danny wondered if he should have tried to buy one of the drums. Did he believe the story about using human skins? Probably. Why would Anatole lie?

As they left the *sorcier*'s homestead to begin the trek back to the village, he looked westward across the jagged landscape of inselbergs. As always at sunset, the air was filled with hundreds of kites, their wings rigid, circling high on the last thermals. Like leaves before the wind, the birds came spiraling down to disappear into the trees, filling them with the invisible flapping of wings.

When they reached the main village again, Danny saw that the women had returned from their labor in the nearby fields. He was familiar with the African tradition of sending the women and children out for backbreaking labor while the men lounged in the shade and talked "business."

The numerous sons of the chief and various adults gathered inside the courtyard near the fire, which the old sinewy woman had stoked into a larger blaze. Other men emerged, and Danny wondered where they had been all afternoon. Out hunting? If so, they had nothing to show for their efforts. Anatole directed Danny to sit on a mat beside the chief, and everyone smiled vigorously at each other, the villagers exchanging the call-and-response litany of ritual greetings, which could go on for several minutes.

The old woman served the chief first, then the honored

guest. She placed a brown yam like a baked potato on the mat in front of him, miming that it was hot. Danny took a cautious bite; the yam was pungent and turned to paste in his mouth. Then the woman reappeared with the promised chicken in peanut sauce. They all ate quietly in a circle around the fire, ignoring each other, as red shadows flickered across their faces.

Listening to the sounds of eating and the simmering evening hush of the West African hills, Danny felt the emptiness like a peaceful vacuum, draining away stress and loud noises and hectic schedules. After too many head-pounding tours and adrenaline-crazed performances, Danny had been convinced he'd forgotten how to sit quietly, how to slow down. After one rough segment of the last Blitzkrieg tour, he had taken a few days to go camping in the mountains; he recalled pacing in vigorous circles around the picnic table, muttering to himself that he was relaxing as fast as he could! Calming down was an acquired skill, he felt, and there was no better teacher than Africa.

After the meal, heads turned in the firelight, and Danny looked up to see the *sorcier* entering the chief's compound. The wrinkled man cradled several of his mystical drums. He placed one of the drums in front of the chief, then set the others on an empty spot on the ground. He squatted behind one drum, thrusting his long, lean legs up and to the sides like the wings of a vulture.

Danny perked up. "A concert?" He turned to Anatole, who spoke rapidly to the *sorcier*. The wrinkled man looked skeptically at Danny, then shrugged. He picked up one of the extra drums and ceremoniously extended it to Danny.

Danny couldn't stop smiling. He took the drum and looked at it. The coffee-colored skin felt smooth and velvety as he touched it. A shiver went up his spine as he tapped the drumhead. Making music from human skin. He forced his instinctive revulsion back into the gray static of his mind, the place where he stored things "to think about later." For now, he had the drum in his hands.

Drumbeats

The chief thumped out a few beats, then stopped. The *sorcier* mimicked them, and glanced toward Danny. "Jam session!" he muttered under his breath, then repeated the sequence easily and cleanly, but added a quick, complicated flourish to the end.

The chief raised his eyebrows, followed suit with the beat, and made it more complicated still. The *sorcier* flowed into his part, and Danny joined in with another counterpoint. It reminded him of the "Dueling Banjos" sequence from *Deliverance*.

The echoing, rich tone of the drum made his fingers warm and tingly, but he allowed himself to be swallowed up in the mystic rhythms, the primal pounding out in the middle of the African wilderness. The other night noises vanished around him, the smoke from the fire rose straight up, and the light centered into a pinpoint of his concentration.

Using his bare fingers—sticks would only interrupt the magical contact between himself and the drum—Danny continued weaving into their rhythms, trading points and counterpoints. The beat touched a core of past lives deep within him, an atavistic, pagan intensity, as the three drummers reached into the Pulse of the World. The chief played on; the *sorcier* played on; and Danny let his eyes fade half-closed in a rhythmic trance as they explored the wordless language and hypnotic interplay of rhythm.

Danny became aware of the boys standing up and swaying, jabbering excitedly and laughing as they danced around him. He deciphered their words as "White Man drum! White Man drum!" It was a safe bet they'd never seen a white man play a drum before.

Suddenly the *sorcier* stopped, and within a beat the chief also quit playing. Danny felt wrenched out of the experience, but reluctantly played a concluding figure as well, ending with an emphatic flam. His arms burned from the exertion, sweat dripped down the stubble on his chin. His ears buzzed from the noise. Unable to restrain himself, Danny began laughing with delight.

The *sorcier* said something, which Anatole translated: *"Vous avez l'esprit de batteur."* You have the spirit of a drummer.

With a throbbing hand, Danny squeezed Anatole's bare shoulder and nodded. *"Oui."*

The chief also congratulated him, thanking him for sharing his white man's music with the village. Danny found that ironic, since he had come here to pick up a rich African flavor for *his* compositions. But Danny could record his impressions in new songs; the village of Kabas had no way of keeping what he had brought to them.

The withered *sorcier* picked up one of the drums at his side, and Danny recognized it as the small drum the old man had been finishing in the dim hut that afternoon. He fixed his deep gaze on Danny for a moment, then handed it to him.

Anatole sat up, alarmed, but bit off a comment he had intended to make. Danny nodded in reassurance and in delight as he took the new drum. He held it to his chest and inclined his head deeply to show his appreciation. *"Merci!"*

Anatole took Danny's hand to lead him away from the walled courtyard. The chief clapped his hands and barked something to the other boys, who looked at Anatole with glee before they got up and scurried to the huts, apparently to sleep. Anatole stared nervously at Danny, but Danny didn't understand what had just occurred.

He repeated his thanks, bowing again to the chief and the *sorcier*, but the two of them just stared at him. He was reminded of an East African scene: a pair of lions sizing up their prey. He shook his head to clear the morbid thought, and followed Anatole.

In the village proper, one of the round thatched huts had been swept for Danny to sleep in. Outside, his bicycle leaned against a tree, no doubt guarded during the day by the little man with the enormous cutlass. Anatole seemed uneasy, wanting to say something, but afraid.

Trying to comfort him, Danny opened his pack and withdrew a stick of chewing gum for the boy. Anatole spoke rapidly, gushing his thanks. Suddenly, other boys materialized from the shadows with childish murder in their eyes. They tried to take the gum from Anatole, but he popped it in his mouth and ran off. "Hey!" Danny shouted, but Anatole bolted into the night with the boys chasing after.

Wondering if Anatole was in any real danger, Danny removed the blanket and sleeping bag from his bike, then carried them inside the guest hut. He decided the boy could take care of himself, that he must have spent his life as the whipping boy for the other sons of the chief. The thought drained some of the exhilaration from the memory of the evening's performance.

His legs ached after the torturous ride upland from Garoua, and he fantasized briefly about sitting in the Jacuzzi in the capital suite of some five-star hotel. He considered how wonderful it would be to sip some cold champagne, or a scotch on the rocks.

Instead, he lifted the gift drum, inspecting it. He would find some way to use it on the next album, add a rich African tone to the music. Paul Simon and Peter Gabriel had done it, though the style of Blitzkrieg's music was a bit more . . . aggressive.

He would not tell anyone about the human skin, especially not the customs officials. He tried without success to decipher the mystical swirling patterns carved into the wood, the interwoven curves, circles, and knots. It made him dizzy.

Danny closed his eyes and began to play the drum, quietly so as not to disturb the other villagers. But as the sound reached his ears, he snapped his eyes open. The tone from the drum was flat and weak, like a cheap tourist tom-tom, plastic over a coffee can.

He frowned at the gift drum. Where was the rich reverberation, the primal pulse of the earth? He tapped again, but heard only an empty and hollow sound, soulless. Danny scowled, wondering if the *sorcier* had ruined the drum by accident, then decided to get rid of it by giving it to the unsuspecting White Man who wouldn't know the difference.

Angry and uneasy, Danny set the African drum next to him; he would try it again in the morning. He could play it for the chief, show him its flat tone. Perhaps they would exchange it. Maybe he would have to buy another one.

He hoped Anatole was all right.

Danny sat down to pull the thorns and prickers from his clothes. The village women had provided him with two plastic basins of water for bathing, one for soaping and scrubbing, the other for rinsing. The warm water felt refreshing on his face, his neck. After stripping off his pungent socks, he rinsed his toes and soles.

The night stillness was hypnotic, and as he spread his sleeping bag and stretched out on it, he felt as if he were seeping into the cloth, into the ground, swallowed up in sleep. . . .

Anatole woke him up only a few moments later, shaking him and whispering harshly in his ear. Dirt, blood, and bruises covered the boy's wiry body, and his clothes had been torn in a scuffle. He didn't seem to care. He kept shaking Danny.

But it was already too late.

Danny sat up, blinking his eyes. Sharp pains like the gash of a bear trap ripped through his chest. A giant hand seemed to have wrapped around his torso; it would *squeeze* until his ribs popped free of his spine.

He gasped, opening and closing his mouth, but could not give voice to his agony. He grabbed Anatole's withered arm, but the boy struggled away, searching for something. Black spots swam in Danny's eyes. He tried to breathe, but his chest wouldn't let him. He began slipping, sliding down an endless cliff into blackness.

Anatole finally found an object on the floor of the hut. He snatched it up with his good hand, tucked it firmly under his withered arm, and began to thump on it.

The drum!

As the boy rapped out a slow, steady beat, Danny felt the iron band loosen around his heart. Blood rushed into his head again, and he drew a deep breath. Dizziness continued

Drumbeats

to swim around him, but the impossible pain receded. He clutched his chest, rubbing his sternum. He uttered a breathy thanks to Anatole.

Had he just suffered a heart attack? Good God, all the fast living had decided to catch up to him while he was out in the middle of nowhere, far from any hope of medical attention!

Then he realized with a chill that the sounds from the gift drum were now rich and echoey, with the unearthly depth he remembered from the other drums. Anatole continued his slow rhythm, and suddenly Danny recognized it. *A heartbeat.*

What was it the boy had told him inside the *sorcier*'s hut—that the magical drums could steal a man's heartbeat? *"Ton coeur c'est dans ici,"* Anatole said, continuing his drumming. Your heartbeat lives in here now.

Danny remembered the gaunt, shambling man in the marketplace of Garoua, obsessively tapping the drum from Kabas as if his life depended on it, until his hide-wrapped fingers were bloodied. Had that man also escaped his fate in the village, and fled south?

"You had the spirit of a drummer," Anatole said in his pidgin French, "and now the drum has your spirit." As if to emphasize his statement, as if he knew a White Man would be skeptical of such magic, Anatole ceased his rhythm on the drum.

The claws returned to Danny's heart, and the vise in his chest clamped back down. His heart had stopped beating. Heartbeats, drumbeats—

The boy stopped only long enough to convince Danny, then started the beat again. Anatole looked at him with pleading eyes in the shadowy light of the hut. *"Je vais avec toi!"* I go with you. Let me be your heartbeat. From now on.

Leaving his sleeping bag behind, Danny staggered out of the guest hut to his bicycle resting against an acacia tree. The rest of the village was dark and silent, and the next morning they would expect to find him dead and cold on his blankets; and the new drum would have the same resonant quality, the same throbbing of a captured spirit, to add to their collection. The sound of White Man's music for Kabas.

"*Allez!*" Anatole whispered as Danny climbed aboard his bike. Go! What was he supposed to do now? The boy ran in front of him along the narrow track. Danny did not fear navigating the rugged trail by moonlight, with snakes and who-knew-what abroad in the grass, as much as he feared staying in Kabas and being there when the chief and the *sorcier* came to look at his body in the morning, and no doubt to appraise their pale new drum skin.

But how long could Anatole continue his drumming? If the beat stopped for only a moment, Danny would seize up. They would have to take turns sleeping. Would this nightmare continue after he had left the vicinity of the village? Distance had not helped the shambling man in the marketplace in Garoua.

Would this be the rest of his life?

Stricken with panic, Danny nodded to the boy, just wanting to be out of there and not knowing what else to do. *Yes, I'll take you with me. What other choice do I have?* He pedaled his bike away from Kabas, crunching on the rough dirt path. Anatole jogged in front of him, tapping on the drum.

And tapping.

And tapping.

THE CONTRIBUTORS

KEVIN J. ANDERSON
A Stoker award nominee for his first novel, Anderson credits the music of Rush as being instrumental to his writing. The Californian has written short fiction for *The Ultimate Werewolf, The Ultimate Zombie,* and other publications, as well as the science fiction novel *The Trinity Paradox,* and *Afterimage,* cowritten with Kristine Kathryn Rusch.

MIKE BARON
This well-known comic book writer lists *Nexus, Badger, Punisher,* and other titles among his credits. The Wisconsin writer is breaking new ground with his prose story in *Shock Rock II.*

GARY BRANDNER
Best known for his *Howling* books, which have been turned into a successful series of movies, Brandner has written more than twenty novels, eighty short stories, and several screenplays. He lives in California.

MAX ALLAN COLLINS
Iowa's Collins is the author of some thirty suspense novels, including the Shamus award-winners *True Detective* and *Stolen Away.* Writer of the *Dick Tracy* strip from 1977 to 1993, his comics work includes *Batman* and his own *Ms.*

Tree. Collins is also a rock musician with his longtime rock band, Crusin'.

DON D'AMMASSA
D'Ammassa, from Rhode Island, is the author of *Blood Beast* and a forthcoming book about horror fiction. The full-time writer has had short stories in the anthologies *Hotter Blood*, *Shock Rock*, *Chilled to the Bone*, and *Souls in Pawn*, as well as various horror magazines. He regularly reviews books for *Science Fiction Chronicles*.

PETER DAVID
David is the author of several *New York Times* best-seller *Star Trek* novels, plus the original novels *Howling Mad* and *Knight Life* and several novelizations. In the comics field, New York's David has written *Hulk*, *Aquaman*, *Spider-Man 2099*, *X-Factor*, and more.

LONN FRIEND
Friend, a Californian, was the coeditor of *Hot Blood*. He is currently the editor of *RIP* magazine, host of a nationally syndicated hard rock radio show, and a metal radio columnist for an industry publication.

MICHAEL GARRETT
Coeditor of the *Hot Blood* anthology series and author of the suspense thriller *Keeper*, Garrett's work has appeared in numerous periodicals and collections. He is also an instructor for the Writer's Digest School and teaches writing seminars at college campuses across the Southeast. Garrett, who lives in Alabama, once fronted a band called the Productions of Time.

JEFF GELB
Gelb is the coeditor of the *Hot Blood* anthology series and the editor of the forthcoming anthology *Fear Itself*. His horror novel *Specters* appeared in 1988. The Californian's

The Contributors

favorite musicians are Peter Gabriel, Kate Bush, Tori Amos, and Vangelis.

NAT GERTLER
A resident of New Jersey, Gertler is a comic-book writer with extensive credits. "Rockin' On Home" is his first published prose horror story.

RICK HAUTALA
Maine's Hautala is the author of ten novels, including *Ghost Light*, *Dark Silence*, *Cold Whisper*, and *Nightstone*. He's had more than thirty stories published in such anthologies as *Stalkers*, *Predators*, *Narrow Houses*, *The Ultimate Zombie*, and *Night Visions 9*.

TINA L. JENS
Jens, an Elvis fan since she was five, does her best writing to the music of Eric Clapton, Aretha Franklin, and the Rolling Stones. The Illinois resident has sold stories to several anthologies, including *Secret Prophecies of Nostradmus*. "Elvis Can't Dance" is her first published horror story.

TH. METZGER
Metzger, a New York resident, is the author of *Big Gurl*, *Shock Totem*, *This Is Your Final Warning*, and *Drowning in Fire*.

REX MILLER
Miller honed his rock chops as a popular Chicago disc jockey. The Missouri writer is the creator of the Chaingang character, and author of *Savant*, *Butcher*, *Slob*, *Profane Men*, and more. He also owns a company that specializes in selling memorabilia.

A. R. MORLAN
Morlan's short fiction has appeared in *Twilight Zone*, *Weird Tales*, *Night Cry*, *Cold Shocks*, *Obsessions*, *The Ultimate Zombie*, and more. Her novels include *The Amulet* and

The Contributors

Dark Journey. Morlan lives in Wisconsin and is also an instructor for the Writer's Digest School.

BILL MUMY
Californian Mumy has appeared in more than one hundred fifty TV episodes, including *Lost in Space* and *Twilight Zone,* plus more than a dozen movies. He is an Emmy nominee for his music scores and a member of a band called the Jenerators, and has written for such comic books as *Spider-Man, Hulk,* and *Iron Man.* His prose work appeared previously in *Shock Rock.*

NEIL PEART
Peart, an Ontario resident, is drummer and lyricist for Rush, a platinum-selling group with fourteen studio albums, several live recordings, and numerous worldwide tours to its credit. Peart is a devoted Afrophile whose bike trips to Cameroon and other exotic locales painted the background for "Drumbeats."

JESSE SUBLETT
Sublett's Martin Fender is the hero of several hard-boiled rhythm-and-blues detective novels, including *Rock Critic Murders, Tough Baby,* and *Boiled in Concrete.* Californian Sublett has written hundreds of songs, played bass for more than twenty-five years in various professional touring rock bands, and put out numerous singles, EPs, and albums.

JOHN F.D. TAFF
Missouri's Taff is a short-story writer with credits in *Eldritch Tales* and *Midnight Zoo.* He is currently working on his first horror novel.

TIA TRAVIS
Travis is a Stoker award nominee for her short horror fiction, and is completing her first novel, *Stripland.* A resident of Alberta, she plays bass in the rockabilly/cow

thrash bands the Jack Straws and the Bobby Fullerbrush Men. This is her fourth published story.

SCOTT H. URBAN
Urban is a new writer whose work is about to appear in comic books, including *Morbid Angel* and *Bloodkind*. He lives in North Carolina.

EDO VAN BELKOM
Canadian van Belkom's very first short horror story was chosen for *Year's Best Horror XX*. Since then, his short stories have appeared in *Deathport*, *Midnight Zoo*, *Haunts*, *Northern Frights*, and *Eldritch Tales*.

MARK VERHEIDEN
Verheiden, the creator/writer of the *American* comic series, has also written comics featuring *Aliens*, *Predators*, and more. The Californian's screenplay for *Timecop* is currently in production.

GRAHAM WATKINS
North Carolina's Watkins, who has extensive background playing tenor sax in rock bands, builds and repairs electronic and pipe organs. He is the author of *Kaleidoscope Eyes*, *The Fire Within*, *Dark Winds*, and several short stories, one of which appears in *Hottest Blood*.

BOB WEINBERG
A two-time World Fantasy award-winner, Illinois's Weinberg is the author of four nonfiction books and four novels, including the new *A Logical Magician;* he is also the editor of more than a hundred anthologies. A rock fan for most of his life, Weinberg's two favorite artists are Buddy Holly and Billy Idol.

Innocent People Caught In the Grip of TERROR!

These thrilling novels—where deranged minds create sinister schemes, placing victims in mortal danger and striking horror in their hearts—will keep you in white-knuckled suspense!

- ☐ BRETHREN by Shawn Ryan 79243-1/$4.99
- ☐ DEATHCHAIN by Ken Greengall 69407-3/$4.50
- ☐ GHOST STORY by Peter Straub 68563-5/$6.50
- ☐ FLESH AND BLOOD by D.A. Fowler 76045-9/$4.99
- ☐ NEVERLAND by Douglas Clegg 67279-7/$4.95
- ☐ GOAT DANCE by Douglas Clegg 66425-5/$5.99
- ☐ NIGHT THIRST by Patrick Whalen 70654-3/$4.95
- ☐ THE UPRISING by Brent Monahan 70429-X/$4.99
- ☐ THE VOICE IN THE BASEMENT 76012-2/$4.99
- ☐ THE DEVIL'S END by D.A. Fowler 72659-5/$4.99
- ☐ SCARECROW by Richie Tankersley Cusick 69020-5/$4.99
- ☐ BREEDER by Douglas Clegg 67277-0/$4.95
- ☐ UNDER THE FANG Edited by Robert R. McCammon 69573-8/$5.50
- ☐ SOULS by Katrina Alexis 67626-1/$4.99
- ☐ SHOCK ROCK Edited by Jeff Gelb 70150-9/$4.99
- ☐ SHOCK ROCK II Edited by Jeff Geld 87088-2/$5.50
- ☐ FREAK SHOW Edited by F. Paul Wilson 69574-6/$5.50
- ☐ PANIC by Chris Curry 74947-1/$4.99
- ☐ VIPER QUARRY by Dean Feldmeyer 76982-0/$4.99

All Available from Pocket Books

POCKET BOOKS

Simon & Schuster Mail Order
200 Old Tappan Rd., Old Tappan, N.J. 07675

Please send me the books I have checked above. I am enclosing $_____ (please add $0.75 to cover the postage and handling for each order. Please add appropriate sales tax). Send check or money order—no cash or C.O.D.'s please. Allow up to six weeks for delivery. For purchase over $10.00 you may use VISA: card number, expiration date and customer signature must be included.

Name _____

Address _____

City _____ State/Zip _____

VISA Card # _____ Exp.Date _____

Signature _____ 803-02